Dauntless

Blood on the Stars VI

Jay Allan

Also By Jay Allan

Dauntless

Dauntless is a work of fiction. All names, characters, incidents, and locations are fictitious. Any resemblance to actual persons, living or dead, events or places is entirely coincidental.

ISBN: 978-1-946451-06-4

Chapter One

Pamphlet Posted Outside Factory 17A3

Workers of Barroux, unite! Too long have you worked to exhaustion to support a corrupt and incompetent ruling class, to feed the insatiable appetite of an unjust war. Too long have you watched your families suffer. You have shivered in the dark as power and heat rations have shrunk. You have seen friends and neighbors taken in the night, never to be seen again, for no worse crimes than demanding basic human rights. Enough! We can endure no more. We will endure no more. Side with us. Support us. Barroux is ours, and we shall take it back. – Ligue d'Egalité.

Barroux City, Union Sector Capital
Barroux, Rhian III
Union Year 217 (313 AC)

"Did you send the dispatch?" Mathis Bonnaire stood in front of a large desk, dressed in his best uniform. He'd given no small amount of thought as to what to wear, and he'd almost grabbed the filthy field uniform he'd cast on the floor the night before for his servants to launder. It was a choice between showing respect to the man behind the desk, or trying to display his tireless work in quelling the disturbances sweeping across Barroux. It had been a close decision, but in the end, he'd relied

1

on the fact that Victor Aurien was a vain, pompous man. The spotless dress reds had won out.

There was a pointlessness to such considerations…in theory. The situation on Barroux was tense, to say the least, and it was worse on some of the province's other worlds. There should have been far more important things to consider than appealing to the petty vanities of the sector commissar, but that was the reality of life in the Union, at least as a mid-level official. He and Aurien had worked well together for years, but in times like these, caution was well advised. If things got any worse, Aurien would be looking for a scapegoat…and Bonnaire was one of the few likely candidates for that unappealing role.

"Not yet." Aurien sat at the desk. His demeanor was odd: an arrogant man, constrained now by the realization he was in trouble. And maybe big trouble. The war with the Confederation had been a disaster. Not so much militarily—that, at least, seemed to be somewhat of a stalemate—but economically. The Union economy was simply no match for the enemy's, and six years of trying to pretend it was had driven a hundred worlds to the brink of starvation and ruin.

Bonnaire hesitated. He'd been clear enough two days before, when he'd told Aurien in no uncertain terms, they needed additional resources, preferably Foudre Rouge units, to suppress the riots—and, truth be told, outright rebellions—breaking out across the sector. He understood his friend's resistance. Reporting what could only be viewed as failure was not a route to success in the Union. But if they did nothing now, things were only going to get worse. And video of rebels hoisting their flag up on the provincial capital's Government Complex was the kind of thing that could land both of them in one of those chairs in the sub-basement of Sector Nine headquarters.

"Sir…"

"I know, Mathis, I know." Aurien had been looking down at a large tablet sitting on his desk, but now his head popped up, eyes focused on Bonnaire. "And, for God's sake, sit. I appreciate the exaggerated display of respect, but I can assure you it won't do any good. If we don't get things under control, and I mean soon, we're both going down, and you'll have wasted all that effort greasing me."

Bonnaire was surprised at Aurien's directness, at the lack of his comrade's usual haughtiness. *He's really scared...*

He sat in the chair closest to where he stood, and he looked across the vast desk. Finally, he said, "I understand the concern about requesting aid." It was never good to go to superiors with problems in the Union. They were as likely to use you to absorb the blame as to send help. After all, dispatching aid added their names to the whole mess. "But, things have progressed too far. Our resources are grossly inadequate to handle all the fires that have broken out already, not even considering what else is brewing." He hesitated before adding the last comment. It was the kind of thing he'd have usually withheld, but Aurien seemed reasonable right now, so he decided to press on. "If we'd have requested aid months ago, when we first discussed it, we might have saved ourselves from this situation."

Aurien was silent for a few seconds, and Bonnaire felt a twinge in his stomach. He hadn't meant for his words to sound like he was blaming Aurien—though it *was* the Commissar's fault, at least the refusal to request aid—but he was worried it had come out that way. Superiors often scapegoated their subordinates to shift blame from themselves, but it was almost as common for officials to stab those above them in the back. Well done, it was an excellent way to advance, though Bonnaire knew this was not the time or place for that sort of thing.

"Yes, Mathis, you are correct. I had hoped we might manage to control things on our own, but clearly, that has not been the case." Bonnaire sat quietly, listening. That had been a shot at him, a subtle suggestion that he should have been able to cut the trouble off before it grew into the current problem. He disagreed, of course, but there was nothing to be gained by arguing the point now. "We must send for assistance now." Aurien continued. "There is no other option. Still, we must look to protect ourselves, to make it clear that the magnitude of the troubles in the province was beyond control, especially after so many of our resources were diverted to the front lines."

Bonnaire felt a bit of relief at Aurien's use of "we." Still, he was edgy. If Aurien intended to stab his friend in the back to try and divert blame from himself, he wouldn't say a word about it. The first Bonnaire would know was when the Sector Nine agents showed up at his door.

"I will send the dispatch today, Mathis. It could only be helpful if we are able to show *some* progress toward halting—or even slowing—the spread of dissension. Perhaps another crackdown is in order, right here, in Barroux City."

"Yes, sir." Barroux had been an enforcer his entire career, and he'd never had a problem with employing harsh sanctions to control the masses. He still didn't, but now he was worried about something else. The methods that had worked so well for so long had begun to lose their effectiveness. The people had slipped from a grim and bare existence to outright starvation and despair. They had little to lose by rebelling. He would do as Aurien commanded, of course, and, in truth, he had no other ideas of his own. He'd have to come down on the population even harder than he already had. He would have to show them that there were worse things to fear than a lack of food.

*   *   *

"Remy, please...no." Elisa Caron looked across the barren room at her husband. She was hunched forward, pulling an old, tattered blanket around her shoulders as she shivered. The heat ration was less restrictive than the one that reduced electrical service to four hours a day, but the bare walls of the tenement did little to keep out the cold the half of the day when the heaters were off.

"I have to, Elisa. There is no choice." Remy gestured toward the far side of the single room he shared with his wife and daughter. Zoe was asleep now—thank God—but she'd cried for two hours before exhaustion had won out. She was still quivering from the cold under the small mountain of clothes and blankets her parents had piled on her. Remy had given his daughter his own meager ration in addition to her own, but she'd still been hungry. And Remy had decided then and there he would take any risk before he would look into his little girl's eyes and see tears because he had no food to give her. "For her, if nothing else, Elisa. How can we live like this? Do you want to watch her starve? Freeze to death?"

"What if you are killed, Remy? They are too strong. Defiance never succeeds, my love. We have seen what happens to those who resist. Stay here with us. The war has to end one day."

"And then what? Return to our old lives? Is that the extent of your dreams?" Remy understood his wife's fear. Her brother Jacques had been a firebrand even before the economy collapsed, but after…

He'd hooked up with an underground resistance group, and he'd given a few speeches in the streets, urging the workers at the local factories to band together, demand better rations and safer working conditions. Then, one night, Sector Nine came for him. They took him away…and they made it clear to the rest of the family what would happen unless they forgot he'd ever existed.

"I know what happened to Jacques scared you, Elisa."

She flinched at the mere mention of his name. "No…don't. There was no Jacques." Then, a few seconds later: "Please… stay here with us."

Remy felt a pang of sadness. He loved Elisa, with all of his heart, as he did his daughter. It hurt him to refuse her pleas, to walk away when she begged him to stay. But he had to go to the meeting. Something *had* to change. He would not watch his daughter cry herself to sleep every night, stand by and do nothing as his wife withered away. Elisa had always been a slender woman, but now she was rail thin and weak. She'd been sick twice already this winter, and she'd never fully recovered the second time. His family was dying, and whatever the risk, he needed to do something. Now.

"I have to go." He stood still for a moment, struggling to hold his wife's gaze, even as tears began to well up in her eyes. "I'm sorry, Elisa…I love you with all my heart. But I can't watch you and Zoe live like this anymore, not without doing *something*. I will be careful, my love, I promise you." He stayed where he was for another few seconds, and then he turned and stepped through the door.

*   *   *

"The time is here, citizens of Barroux. Time to take your futures into your hands, to strike a blow…for liberty, for a tomorrow for our children."

Remy Caron stood and looked up at the speaker. There had been half a dozen already, and as he watched, his inspiration grew. Everyone at the meeting was in great danger if they were discovered, but the speakers were almost guaranteed the worst Sector Nine could offer. It was a terrifying prospect, but one they had all overcome. Remy felt ashamed for waiting so long, for cowering in fear when others were ready to actually *do* something. He felt energized, and a spark of hope began to form inside him. Perhaps the people could do something. Perhaps they truly could throw off the yoke of the Union.

"I call upon all of you here, factory workers, miners, servants in the houses of those who live above us…join us now, rise up." The speaker gestured to a line of people standing along the back of the room. "Now, Henri," he said, looking back over the crowd. "Those who would fight for a brighter future, stand with us now. We have weapons here. Take one with you. Defend your homes, if need be. And be ready to come when we call you, to stand with your brothers and sisters."

Remy turned and looked back, even as the row of resistance members began walking forward, each carrying an armful of guns. The weapons were of all types, and mostly old. He wasn't sure how they'd found any guns at all with the rigid controls in place in the Union. He hesitated for just an instant, his thoughts drifting back to Elisa. She had been terrified of his going to the meeting. He couldn't imagine how she would react if he brought home a gun. The consequences of being found with a weapon were severe. He decided against taking one…but then, as the woman moving closest to him came by and offered him an aged pistol, he reached out and grabbed it, along with a small bag of ammunition.

He couldn't watch Elisa go hungry anymore, both of them giving most of their food to Zoe. He understood her fear. He *felt* it, so much that he could barely keep himself from shaking with terror. But there was only so far a man could be pushed. There was a time for action, a point when the desperation was great enough to overcome fear.

Even as he steeled himself to join the resistance, he heard a noise outside. He turned and looked back toward the large bay doors of the warehouse, a burst of near-panic almost overtaking him. But then there was nothing. No sounds save for the nervous chatter of the crowd around him.

You're hearing things, you damned fool…

Just then the doors blasted in, shards of the thin sheet metal flying into the room. There were shouts from all sides, pain from those hit by the chunks of metal, and fear from the others. Remy froze, stunned, unsure what to do. The doors were the only way out, and even as he stood where he was, he saw a line of security troops advancing. They were armed, their rifles extended in front of them as they moved forward. It took an instant for him to hear the loud cracks, to realize they were firing into the crowd.

He didn't know what to do, and he could feel himself shaking, his head turning one way and then the next as he looked desperately for a way out. Then he heard the shouts from the small stage. "Fight! You are men and women, not sheep. They have guns, you have guns…fight now, for your families, for the future!"

Remy was lost in a frantic swirl of thoughts. It took a few seconds before he realized the crowd was firing at the soldiers… and an instant more before he was fully aware that he was, too. The security forces were better armed and trained, but they were massively outnumbered. Union forces were not used to armed populations fighting back, and the battle was a short one. Half a dozen soldiers dropped, and the others began to pull back.

Fifty or more of the citizens—rebels, now, Remy realized— were down, but the rest were firing their weapons as quickly as they could. Few of them could aim, and most fumbled when trying to reload, but numbers began to prevail. The soldiers were withdrawing, but even as they did, the crowd took on a persona of its own, acting now without encouragement, without leadership. They were a wild, elemental force, beyond control.

The throng of workers and citizens surged forward, chasing the soldiers into the street, firing steadily. More soldiers fell, and the crowd grabbed the wounded enforcers, literally tearing them apart in a blood-soaked frenzy. Two centuries of oppression poured out as unbridled fury, and the screaming rebels overtook the now-fleeing soldiers, beating them savagely, screaming with a wild abandon that would have scared Remy to death…if he hadn't been right there with them, shouting savagely himself.

The soldiers had been sent to wipe out the resistance, but it was they who were exterminated, save for a small handful who managed to escape into the darkness. All around the street, citizens held their weapons in the air and shouted wildly, even as they tossed around the horribly mangled bodies of those who would have killed them all.

"The time has come, Citizens!" It was the last speaker— Remy couldn't even remember his name. But that didn't mat- ter…he was ready to follow the man to hell itself. "To the Gov- ernment Plaza. Barroux City is ours, and it is time we took it back."

"Yes, Citizens," Remy shouted, looking around at those near him, "it *is* time. Let's go…it's time to make these bastards pay!"

Chapter Two

"*Dauntless*, you are authorized to conduct your final approach. Welcome back."

"Confirmed, Grimaldi Base…and thank you. It's good to be here. *Dauntless* out." Captain Atara Travis twitched a little in the command chair—Tyler's chair to her, *still*, despite almost six months as *Dauntless*'s captain.

She flashed a glance across the bridge, toward her old station. Commander Wolfe should rightfully have handled the exchange with Grimaldi, but Travis's adjustment to command was still a work in progress, and she found it difficult to give up some of the tasks she'd carried out in nearly seven years as *Dauntless*'s XO.

"Bring us in, Commander."

"Yes, Captain." Stefan Wolfe was a gifted officer, one she knew she was lucky to have as her second-in-command. But he had a single flaw, one that afflicted many of her officers. He was new to *Dauntless*.

Personnel transferred between ships all the time, of course. She, herself, had served on three vessels before she'd ended up with Barron and *Dauntless*. But the old ship had proven herself to be something special, and Travis knew much of that had been the extraordinary crew, one that had served together with a devotion to each other that had brought them through seemingly impossible situations.

Many of the spacers from those days were still onboard, mostly junior personnel, but after the return from Alliance space, *Dauntless* had lost many of her officers, along with her legendary captain. Tyler Barron hadn't had a choice, of course, not really. With Admiral Striker wounded, the fleet needed him elsewhere. Besides, she knew as much as it hurt him to leave his ship, he'd felt as though he'd been in her way, holding back her career and denying her the command position she deserved. She'd never found a way to tell him she was happy in the number two spot for as long as he cared to occupy the captain's chair. But staying on *Dauntless* would have held him back too, and worse, denied the Confederation of a flag officer it desperately needed.

Travis didn't doubt any of her crew. She'd hand-picked a number of them and approved all the rest. She just missed her family.

"Nearing designated docking portal, Captain."

"Very well, Commander. See to the final approach." *Dauntless* had been assigned a direct connection, at least, one that would save her people all the fussing around with shuttles and the like. Plus, it would get her aboard the base sooner. She hadn't seen Barron in months, and she was anxious to connect with her old commander. Her friend.

Hopefully, he'd have some kind of news about the war, more than her mission had produced. The work on the bases was coming along, ahead of schedule even, but the roundabout route into the Union was still long, and it passed through sparsely developed systems that weren't even close to industrialized enough to support an invasion fleet. The enemy's superweapon utterly controlled the Bottleneck, however, and a move directly through that powerfully-held system was out of the question. The war had become a stalemate of sorts, the Confederation and its Alliance allies too powerful for the Union forces to attack...and the alien weapon holding the only invasion route that didn't require at least two years of logistical development to attempt.

She had a strange feeling as she watched her crew manage the final docking. She'd always been comfortable around Barron, but now there was a nervousness that hadn't been there before. She'd done her best as *Dauntless*'s captain, but this time when she saw her old friend, he would be judging how she'd taken care of his ship.

And, Travis knew, regardless of rank and assignment and who sat in the captain's chair, *Dauntless* would *always* be Tyler Barron's ship.

*   *   *

"You look great, Admiral." Tyler Barron stood along the wall, watching as Van Striker pulled himself along a set of parallel bars, sweating profusely as he did it. It was Barron's standard greeting to Striker. He'd begun saying it to try to bolster the admiral's spirits, and somewhere along the line it had become a private joke between the two of them. This time, however, Striker wasn't in the mood.

"The last thing I need from you, Ty, is the usual patronizing banter. You can give it to me straight. I look like shit... but shit is a lot better than dead, so that's not so bad, I guess." Striker had been assigned four hours a day of intense physical therapy, a prescription he'd changed to ten hours with the stroke of the fleet admiral's pen. Not a pen, exactly, since he still didn't have those kinds of motor skills back, but the navy commander's howl was just about an irresistible force. His doctor—the fleet surgeon general—had given him a perfunctory warning that he was pushing himself too hard, along with pointed and colorful reminders of just how close he'd come to a permanent nap. Striker had listened patiently...and then utterly disregarded everything the doctor had said. There was a war on, he'd told anyone who came close enough to listen, and he needed to get back to his post, fully-functional and in one piece, as quickly as possible.

Tyler suppressed a laugh. "All right, sir, you look better than you did, how about that?"

"I can buy that, Ty." Striker was the only one who called Barron, "Ty." Even those who addressed him by his first name called him "Tyler." He'd never really thought about it, and to be honest, he didn't care at all, but he guessed it was his grandfather's shadow at work again, coaxing the slightly more respectful full version of his name, even from his friends. From Andi, too. Though she called him a few other things no one else did.

"Any updates on the base construction program?" Striker's voice wasn't a growl, not quite.

Barron smiled. "I'm not sure the surgeon-general would approve of me hitting you with work while you're in therapy. He'd say it distracts from your intensity."

"The surgeon-general can go…" Fortunately for all concerned, Striker stopped there. "What is the latest? I know the Senate is bombarding us with requests—or, probably more likely, demands—for a timetable. You think you deflect most of those from me, Ty, but the fleet admiral has more than one source of information."

"Yes, they are becoming impatient, sir. But I really don't have much news on the actual progress. The distance is slowing the construction program, and even our ability to monitor progress. Grimaldi was built here precisely because any invasion, into or from the Union, was expected to go through the Bottleneck and not through a dozen backwater systems."

"Well, Ty, the Senate can eat shit. If they don't like that, they can have these damned stars back, and one of the pompous windbags from that esteemed assembly can get his fat, pimply ass up here and lead the fleet into battle." It was an empty threat, one Striker made at least once a week. If there was one thing Barron was sure about, it was that Van Striker would have to be dragged away in chains before he'd let some unqualified hack lead his people into battle.

Striker had never been delicate with words, but the frustration of his long and slow recovery had made him downright ornery, at least when it came to creatures like Senators and their ilk.

"Well, sir, hopefully it won't come to that." He paused a few seconds, as Striker completed another trip across the bars. "*Dauntless* is docking now, Admiral, and I'm sure Captain Travis will be able to update us on the construction program as soon as she comes aboard." Another pause. "You'll recall, we instructed all vessels to cease transmissions of any militarily-sensitive information in the system since we caught the enemy spy ships. Otherwise, no doubt, she would have already sent a full report." Barron wasn't sure at all that Striker would remember that, mostly because he'd been about three days from being semi-frozen and unconscious when Gary Holsten had told Barron to institute the rule. Holsten had assigned Barron to look after Striker, a clever way to keep him on Grimaldi in a position to effectively oversee operations when he was far too junior in rank to be officially put in command of the fleet's main fortress and headquarters.

"Oh, yes…" Barron wasn't sure if Striker actually remembered or not. The admiral's poker face was legendary in the fleet, a match for Barron's own, more than one officer had told him, though the two had never put their skills to the test against each other. "We should meet with Captain Travis immediately."

"Sir, perhaps I should get the captain's report. You've been at therapy for a long time. I'm sure Doctor Javis would want you to get some rest."

"I'm sure Dr. Javis wants a lot of things he's not going to get, but he'll survive." Striker smiled, at least the closest thing he could manage while he struggled to move down the bars. "Why don't you just tell me the truth, Ty? You're dying for some time alone with Captain Travis to discuss all things *Dauntless*. I hope you don't think you hide those thoughts well…or at all. You'd think I beat you with a stick instead of promoting you to flag rank." A pause. "But I had a first command once too, my friend, so I understand far better than you think I do. I'll tell you what. You meet with Travis. I'll get cleaned up and join you in, say, an hour. I don't suppose that's enough time to ask her about every rivet on *Dauntless*'s hull, but we do have a war to deal with, so that's all you've got. Make the best of it."

"Thank you, sir." Barron nodded, an odd sort of grin slipping onto his face. He was anxious to see Atara Travis, there was no question about that. And *Dauntless* too. It was normal to have a soft spot for a first command, as Striker had suggested, but Barron felt lost without his ship. No one deserved her more than Travis, but Barron had a special connection with his vessel, and he still felt the loss keenly.

"Go, already. The last thing I need is a babysitter. Go down to the docking portals, snatch a glimpse at your ship."

Barron was a bit surprised at how closely Striker had read his thoughts. "Very well, sir." He turned and then stopped. "And, thank you, Admiral." Then he walked out of the room toward the bank of lifts at the end of the hall. His stride increased as he got closer, and he could feel the excitement building inside him.

He was going to see his best friend...*and* his ship.

*   *   *

It was an unmilitary display, one that would give the crew in the docking bay something to talk about over their post-shift drinks. But Barron didn't care if it was unseemly or not for a commodore to hug a captain as she debarked from her ship. He walked right up to Travis and, without a word to his old friend, threw his arms out and warmly embraced her.

"Commodore," she said, as she returned the hug, "it is good to see you, sir." Travis had always been formal with Barron in public, despite the closeness of their relationship and the informality they displayed toward each other in private. But this time, Barron was having none of it.

"That's the last time I want to hear a rank, Atara, at least until Admiral Striker joins us. For now, two friends have perhaps an hour together. Let's not waste it with 'sirs' and salutes."

Travis smiled, nodding as she did. "It's good to see you, Tyler. It's been too long."

"Yes, it has. *Far* too long." Barron turned and looked through the clear, dense hyper-plastic of the observation port.

About half of *Dauntless* was visible from where he stood, from about the midsection to the aft, offering a good look at the battleship's great engines. The dull gray smoothness of her hull was still marked in places where hurried patches covered battle wounds, but overall, the ship looked good...and to Barron, she seemed perfection itself. *Dauntless* wasn't the newest ship in the fleet—in fact, she was getting closer to a claim on being the oldest—but Barron would put her list of battle honors against any vessel the Confederation had put into space. Ever.

"I knew you'd be happy to see me...and I knew I couldn't compete with her." Travis turned and stood next to Barron, looking out over the rear half of the ship they had both commanded. "She did well, Tyler. You would have been proud of the old girl."

"I couldn't not be, Atara." A pause. "And I know she couldn't be in better hands. I don't think I could have left her, if I'd been giving her to anyone else." Barron stood where he was for a moment, and then, with a sigh and some visible effort, he pulled himself away. "Let's go down to my quarters. We don't have a lot of time, and we definitely have some catching up to do. It'll be like old times." Barron smiled, but it dropped quickly from his face.

He was glad to see Travis, but he knew things would never be the same as they had been. His crew on *Dauntless* had been something truly special, and he knew in his heart he would never see its like again.

Chapter Three

Dispatch from Victor Aurien, Senior Commissar, Jurain Province

I must urgently request additional aid to suppress unrest on multiple planets, and particularly on the sector capital. Barroux is in open rebellion, and traitors have seized control of much of the planet. It is essential that Foudre Rouge forces be dispatched to crush the rebellious forces and reestablish control over the planet.

Sector Nine Headquarters
Liberte City
Planet Montmirail, Ghassara IV,
Union Year 217 (313 AC)

"That damned fool, Aurien." Gaston Villieneuve slammed his fist down on his desk. It was an antique, a new acquisition, built from now-extinct Amerallian Blacktree. An attempt to cheer himself up, and one that had failed utterly. He'd hardly noticed the new desk since it had been delivered. He was besieged with problems. Economic collapse was certainly at the top of the list—and greatly exacerbated by the various frauds he'd used to fund his earlier projects, most of which had

16

failed to some degree or another. The Union was in a precarious situation, and the need to try to match the production of the Confederation's industrial worlds was pushing things to the brink. Villieneuve had been overwhelmed with reports from intelligence assets behind enemy lines, and it seemed like the Confeds were launching another battleship every fifteen minutes. Meanwhile, he'd had close to a dozen production managers shot, and yet unbuilt ships lingered in the yards, beset by one delay after another.

"I've never met him, Gaston, but from what little I've heard, he seems to be typical for a provincial commissar." Ricard Lille sat opposite his friend, sipping casually at the coffee Villieneuve's assistant had just brought in. From his tone, it was clear that "typical" was not a compliment.

Villieneuve looked back at his friend, suppressing a touch of irritation. Lille had long been his most reliable operative, but the assassin's efforts over the past few years had been no more successful than his own. He'd considered—briefly—holding Lille more…accountable…but he'd decided against it. Despite recent missteps, the operative was still his best. And Lille had one more attribute, a trait that was exceedingly rare among high level agents and officials in the Union. He didn't have a shred of political ambition. Lille was as ruthless as anyone Villieneuve had ever known, and a bit twisted to boot, but as long as he was personally secure, and was able to live the lifestyle he wanted, he never craved political power. Indeed, he showed an active disdain for it, as though he didn't want to be bothered. That made him trustworthy in a way none of his other senior subordinates, all the rest of whom wanted to take his place, could match.

There was something else, too. Villieneuve didn't doubt Lille had gone to great lengths to secure his own status, and he suspected the agent had made certain to ensure anyone who successfully moved against him tasted his posthumous revenge. That had been a factor in Villieneuve's decision to forgive his friend's mistakes. The last thing he needed now was to deal with whatever traps a murdered Lille might have left behind.

"He is not particularly inept, Ricard, or at least not uniquely so." Villieneuve waved his hand toward several tablets lying on the edge of his desk. "There are reports coming in from all across the Union. Dissent, riots, uprisings. I doubt there was much Aurien could have done." A pause. "Of course, that doesn't mean I don't have to hold him responsible. I can't really tell the Presidium that Barroux is in the hands of rebels because the funds expended on our past failed endeavors have helped push the Union even closer to the brink of disaster, can I?"

"No, I would think that an unwise course. Certainly, far better in the short term to serve up Aurien as a scapegoat. But that doesn't really solve any problems in the long run, does it? The pulsar has secured the Bottleneck without question. But it does nothing to force the war to an end. Worse, the enemy has another route of invasion. It is a longer path, of course, one that will compel them to build a series of bases to support their advance. But time is on their side in this regard, is it not?" Lille hesitated, shifting uncomfortably in his seat. "Especially now that they have Alliance forces supporting their own fleet." His tone was softer, more tentative than it had been a few seconds before.

Villieneuve gave his friend a hard gaze. *Yes, you should be uncomfortable. It's your fault the Confeds have the Alliance on their side instead of us.* The thought of the vast resources wasted on the effort to coopt the Alliance, expenditures that backfired badly, briefly reignited his anger. "The situation at the front is...difficult." His words here hard-edged, and he kept his eyes boring into Lille's own.

The room was silent for a moment. Finally, Villieneuve pushed aside his anger again, and he said, "I have every top scientist and engineer in the Union analyzing the pulsar. If we can build three more, we can cover every possible approach to our space. That would essentially eliminate any danger of invasion."

"Has there been any progress on that front?"

"I will know better soon. I have summoned the project heads back here to report. I felt some...encouragement...would be helpful in speeding their efforts. But, I suspect we're looking at a longer than ideal time frame on building new pulsars."

"Even if we *are* able to build copies of the weapon, and to do so quickly enough, does that solve our problem? Defending our borders is certainly useful, but can we sustain ourselves without a victory? A strong frontier is of little value if the Union collapses from within."

"You are right, Ricard, of course. Which is why I have prioritized work on a mobile solution, a way to move the pulsar from system to system. The weapon itself is not so large as to prevent moving it. It is the string of reactors required to replace the antimatter power system that are the problem. The system is fragile as it is. Moving it will require a large and very carefully-aligned system of engines, especially if we are to have the ability to put it into action as soon as it transits. We need massive batteries as well, enough energy storage to power a first shot, even as the reactors come back online."

Lille looked downcast. "That seems unlikely."

"Unlikely, perhaps, but not impossible. I will share a closely-held secret with you, one I have withheld even from the Presidium. The work is nearly done. In a brief time, perhaps a few months, we will be ready to move forward."

"That is amazing." Lille was rarely surprised, but even his rigid control couldn't hide his shock at his friend's words. "I had heard we were making *some* progress, but I had no idea we were close to completion."

"Virtually no one does. Even the crews working on various aspects are unaware of the progress made by their counterparts. There can be no mistakes here, Ricard, none of the miscalculations that have impacted our previous operations."

"You are right, Gaston. We are fortunate that your efforts appear to have borne fruit. The pulsar is powerful enough to destroy the entire Confederation fleet. If you are able to move it, we can go all the way to Megara, if need be. The conquest of the Confederation, or even a substantial part of it, would be of tremendous value in restoring our economy as well."

"My thinking, exactly. We have few options. We cannot outlast the enemy in a stalemate. The Union is far closer to collapse than I have allowed anyone to know. This is our last chance to salvage anything from this war but total ruin. The absorption of the Confederation, or even the conquest of a significant portion, will give us the productive capacity to restore stability."

The two men were quiet for a moment before Lille broke the silence. "Do we have months? Months to complete the infrastructure to move the pulsar…and more to move forward? Even if we drive the Confeds before us, it will still take considerable time to push into their vital areas, to force capitulation or even an advantageous peace. And, if their fleets fall back, rather than commit to a single fight, they could delay us further."

"That is another reason I called you here, Ricard…the primary reason, actually. I must go to the front. I must make sure everything moves as quickly as possible. But we also need time. This situation on Barroux is extremely troublesome. There is problematic unrest on many worlds now, but the loss of a provincial capital, the entire planet in the hands of traitors…it is intolerable. I have managed to keep the truth from the Presidium, but I cannot maintain that for long. We must crush the rebellion there, and we must do it in a way that sends a message to those who would rise up against their government."

"I agree…wholeheartedly. But, what does that have to do with me? It is a job for Foudre Rouge, and for fleet units."

"Normally, that would be true. But this matter is too sensitive to trust to any but my most reliable agents. I know you are not primarily a military officer, but you do carry a commission."

"That is just a formality, Gaston, you know that."

"Yes, but I cannot focus on Barroux. I *must* go to the front and ensure that the work on the pulsar is completed on time. I need someone I can trust to handle Barroux. I need you, Ricard. I don't have fleet units to spare, not many at least, but you can have all the Foudre Rouge you want…and any officers you select. I am confident in your ability to keep operations on Barroux quiet, and to handle anyone who threatens that discretion."

Lille sat for a moment, still and quiet. It was clear that he didn't like it. "How much flexibility do I have as far as…tactics I may employ?"

Villieneuve stared across the table. "Total. You may do whatever you feel it takes to recapture Barroux and restore order."

"Anything?"

"Anything. Put the fear of the night back into them. Just see that the rebellion there is crushed…before it spreads."

Lille nodded. "Very well, Gaston. I will go to Barroux."

Villieneuve smiled. Thank you, my friend. With you in charge there, I can focus on the pulsar, on ending this war."

He sat for a moment, his smile slowly fading. His plan to invade the Confederation, to move the pulsar forward…it was as well-conceived as he could make it. But it was far from foolproof. He'd given considerable thought to what he would do if it failed.

He looked again at his friend, trying to decide for a moment if he wanted to tell him, to trust him with his backup plan. He almost held his tongue, but he knew he'd need Lille to help carry it off if the time came.

"I have another plan, Ricard, in case we are unable to develop the movement system for the pulsar in time. It is not as appealing a solution as a military victory, but perhaps a way to survive if the worst happens." He paused, pushing back another wave of uncertainty. Then he told Lille everything he had in mind.

Chapter Four

"At least eighteen months, Admiral…and that assumes no unexpected problems." Travis paused. "And, based on what I saw, I wouldn't make that assumption."

Striker sat at the end of the conference table. He was supposed to be on bedrest between therapy sessions, but he'd demanded a mobile power chair, and he'd used it to terrorize the staff just about everywhere on Grimaldi he could reach in it. "What are the issues, Captain? If anyone out there is failing to do their duty…" His words trailed off, but Barron had no doubt what would have followed had they not.

"No, sir, it's not really that. No one I saw is impeding completion. It's just…well, Admiral, that's such a remote area. Everything has to be brought in from so far, and there is so little native industry. The Union hit us in several systems when they launched their initial invasion, but their forces all came through the Bottleneck before they split. In four wars with the Union, no major assault force has come through these outer systems. The Periphery is even less developed than the Rim, and it's no better across the border in Union space. Right now, we're just

22

dealing with our own systems, but if we invade there, we'll be right back in the same situation, stalled and trying to build support infrastructure on their backwater planets…which are even worse than our own."

"Your insights are spot on, Captain, save for one problem. We have no choice. The Bottleneck has long been considered the only practical invasion route into the Union, one featured in every plan developed by the general staff for a century. We always knew any advance would encounter significant resistance there. The Union fortifications are substantial. But this new weapon is something entirely different. We've analyzed it a hundred different ways, and we've come up with the same result. Any assault against it is suicide. The whole fleet would be destroyed before we got a ship in range."

"Of course, Admiral. I realize that." Travis hesitated, and Barron shot her a quick nod. "But I feel you need to consider exactly what an invasion along the peripheral route would entail. Can we sustain an effort that lasts another two years before we can even launch the operation? Then, perhaps another two years of delay midway through, as we built another series of bases on occupied systems? And, what of Grimaldi and the standard route between the Union and the Confederation? What is to stop the enemy from invading once our own fleet is bogged down out on the Periphery? It's not like we'll be able to quickly shift forces back and forth between fronts."

"Captain, I understand everything you are saying. I agree with every word. But, I'm afraid we are short on options. We can't invade through the Bottleneck, so we must find a way to make an advance work through the Periphery."

"Is it possible to negotiate a peace, Admiral?" Barron asked. "The Union fleet is certainly battered, and I have to believe their economy is in even worse shape. Normally, I wouldn't be for a resolution that practically guarantees yet another war, but perhaps now, there is no better alternative."

"From what Gary Holsten has told me, the Union is demanding unacceptable terms. Now that they have their superweapon, they feel they have the upper hand."

"What terms, sir?" This was the first Barron had heard of potential peace talks, or for that matter of communications directly between Holsten and Striker since the admiral emerged from his coma.

"They're demanding we cede half a dozen planets and pay them reparations...massive reparations. They want Grimaldi disassembled and the frontier disarmed...and they want to impose fleet tonnage limits."

"So, they failed to conquer us this time, but they want to make sure the next war is a walkover."

"Basically...yes."

"Perhaps we should just let the stalemate continue, Admiral." Barron glanced over at Travis and then back to Striker. "I don't like the idea any better than you, but we've got the Alliance on our side now, and our production is almost certainly greater than theirs. We might be able to outlast them. Indeed, we almost certainly can, if what little I've heard about their economic situation is true."

Striker shook his head. "Even assuming we could restrain the Senate, convince the population to accept a cold war, the problem is the same one stopping us from hitting the Bottleneck. That ancient weapon they found. How long do we give them to study it, to figure out how it works? The Union doesn't have our industrial capacity, but they've got scientists and engineers too. If we give them enough time, they'll figure out how it works. How to build more. Then, we're in a world of hurt."

Barron sighed softly. "I hadn't really thought that through, sir." He paused. "But that doesn't solve the problem of how to invade along the Periphery while also holding this border. Grimaldi is strong, but it can't hold back a real Union assault without fleet support...and, possibly worse, it's not our version of the Bottleneck, a system where all the transit points converge. The Krakus system is the likeliest invasion route in this sector, but not the only one. And none of the other frontier bases pack close to the punch Grimaldi does. Do we have enough ships to properly garrison this border, while simultaneously launching a full-scale invasion on the other?" His tone suggested he already knew the answer.

"We come to the heart of the matter, Ty. We have no good options. The Periphery invasion plan was begun while I was unconscious. Gary Holsten was the driving force behind it, not so much because he considered it viable, but because he needed something to control the Senate. Apparently, there had been considerable discussion about ordering a full-scale invasion through the Bottleneck, an attempt to rush the pulsar and destroy it."

"That would be suicide."

"Yes, it would. But convincing Senators of that is another matter. They see the vast expenditures, the steady flow of new ships coming to the front, the vastly increasing war debt. They hear constituents screaming for peace. Then, they figure the military is exaggerating, that a strong enough attack, especially with Alliance support, can end the war in one quick stroke."

"So, we're spending billions building supply bases we aren't going to use?" Travis had been silent for a few minutes, but now she jumped back in.

"I wouldn't say that, Captain. In the end, some kind of invasion through the Periphery may well be our only real choice. But the initial impetus was more to make it appear we had a well-developed plan in place to relieve the political pressure."

Striker was silent for a moment. Then he said softly, "I am going to tell you both something that is highly classified. What I say is not to leave this room. Understood?"

"Yes, sir."

"Of course, Admiral."

Striker nodded. "Holsten and his people have been monitoring the status of the pulsar and the Union forces at the Bottleneck."

"Monitoring? Does he have spies among the Union forces?"

"I couldn't say, Ty. Probably some, though I suspect the problem there is one of communication. I'm afraid Gary doesn't share that kind of information, even with me. But he has been sending scouts to the system."

"Scouts? How is that possible?" Grimaldi and the fleet

were a considerable distance from the Bottleneck, and Barron couldn't conceive how any kind of scoutships large enough to make the trip could reach the system and then escape.

"Do you remember when Commander Stockton flew a modified fighter through multiple systems to warn the fleet of the enemy's advance?"

Barron nodded. It had been years before, just after *Dauntless* had returned from Archellia. "Of course."

"I'm afraid that's why you lost Commander Stockton as your strike force leader, Captain Travis. Gary needed him more."

Barron blinked. "You mean Stockton…"

"Yes, he has trained a group of pilots to run long-range scouting missions."

"I could see a fighter slipping by once in a while, but the risk…"

"The casualty rates have been very high."

"Jake…"

"Commander Stockton is fine, Ty. In fact, he's right here on Grimaldi, though his presence is classified…which is why you didn't know."

Barron was taken aback. He'd thought he was privy to everything going on at Grimaldi, but now he realized the supposedly incapacitated Striker had been up to far more than he'd known. "This is a surprise, certainly, Admiral, but I'm not sure how it has a direct effect on our course of action."

"We have greater concerns, Ty, than the enemy building more pulsars. That, at least, would almost certainly take years. But the last scouting mission has returned with some disturbing intel."

Barron and Travis were silent, looking across at Striker.

"The fighters are able to obtain only long-range scans, and quick ones at that, but they got enough to cause considerable worry. There is an elaborate superstructure around the pulsar and the reactors that power it. The enemy is building something. More accurately, they are erecting a whole series of constructs."

"Constructs?"

"Yes, Ty. Gary's people have analyzed the intel. The data is sketchy, but they've come to an unsettling conclusion. It appears they are building a series of engines and support structures." He paused, his eyes moving from Barron to Travis and back again. "They are preparing to move the pulsar."

Barron was stunned. He'd been worried that the enemy might do just that very thing at first, but then he'd considered the specifics. The pulsar was massive, and no doubt designed to be powered by antimatter. The Union had managed to develop an alternative, but the power generation system was utterly massive, a series of several dozen large fusion reactors. Moving such a series of structures, and keeping the whole thing operational during transport, would be a monumental task.

Could they really manage it?

"They can move the pulsar?" Barron tried to disguise the horror in his voice, but he suspected he'd failed utterly.

"Not yet. At least we don't think so. But they are clearly working on it, and from the scale of the operation, *they* seem to believe they can do it."

"That's even more reason we can't move the fleet from Grimaldi, Admiral."

"Grimaldi is useless as a defense against a Union fleet armed with the pulsar. If we mass the fleet and try to hold the line near the transit point, they will just go through a different system. And if we spread our ships out, cover every possible approach, they will mass their fleet and drive us deeper into the system. Then, they will bring the pulsar through and wipe out the rest of our forces."

Barron wanted to argue, but Striker's logic was flawless. The fleet could outmatch any task force the Union could mass, but it couldn't do it in three or four spots at once. If the enemy was able to move the pulsar and bring it quickly into action after a transit, the Confederation was in big trouble.

"I have been meaning to bring you up to speed on all this, Ty." Striker looked across the table. "I'm glad you're here too, Captain Travis. You have served in the glare of Ty's bright sun for many years, but do not think your own skills have escaped my notice. Your promotion to flag rank is certain after you complete a seemly period as *Dauntless's* captain. For now, perhaps we can simply pretend you are already there. Your input would be greatly appreciated. We need all the help we can get. I'm afraid we have a significant problem, and I'll be honest, I have no idea what to do. I've ordered another scouting mission to confirm the findings of the last one, but assuming that checks, we're going to have to develop *some* kind of plan."

The room was silent for a long time, the three of them sitting, deep in thought. Barron was about to say something when Travis beat him to it.

"We have to attack them in the Bottleneck, Admiral. We have to destroy that…thing…before they can advance with it. We can't let that weapon get to Grimaldi, much less the Iron Belt or the Core. Whatever it takes…even if it costs us every ship in the fleet."

Striker leaned back. It was clear he was far from comfortable in the power chair, mostly, Barron suspected, because he was still in considerable pain. Striker had come as close to death as any living person could, and Barron had only heard a partial list of the repairs his dedicated medical staff had been forced to make. He was grateful the admiral had survived, but now that Striker had come clean with the amount of work he'd gotten done, more or less in secret, Barron's respect increased. It couldn't be easy to manage all that when every movement was its own small agony.

"You are correct, Captain, of course. But your words are far too prophetic. We have analyzed the tactical situation from every imaginable angle. Based on the power and firing rate of the pulsar, and its range, not to mention the presence of the Union fleet, we have projected a ninety-six percent chance that none of our capital ships would make it into firing range of the weapon itself. An assault would throw away the fleet for no gain, and it would leave us even more open to an enemy invasion."

"There must be a way, sir." But even as he spoke, Barron knew there wasn't. The Bottleneck was so named for a reason. Only one system in Confederation space led to it, and one in the Union behind it, and it was the only route to the enemy's heartland, save the extremely long route through the Periphery. There was no way to attack except a straight frontal assault… against a weapon that could destroy a battleship with a single shot.

"You see the problem. Our ship production has hit its stride, the Alliance is on our side, and every report suggests the Union economy is approaching total collapse…in every way, we should be on the verge of winning the war. And yet, we are desperate, staring inevitable defeat in the eye no matter what we do."

"What if we used the stealth projector to—" Barron bit off the end of his sentence, and turned to look at Travis. He wasn't even supposed to know about that, and he wasn't sure he should have blurted it out in front of his old exec.

"Why am I not surprised you know about the generator?" Striker flashed a brief smile. "I don't need to say again that everything we discuss in this room stays here, do I?"

"No, sir."

"Of course not, Admiral."

"Good." He paused. "Then to answer your question, Ty, I have considered the use of the stealth generator. The problem is a simple one. We only have the single unit. We've barely figured out how to make it work, *if* we've even really figured that out. There have only been two brief test runs, and neither of these was under anything remotely approaching combat conditions. We're no closer to replicating the thing than I hope the Union is to building more pulsars. And, even if we could be sure it would work reliably—which we most definitely are not—we could still sneak only a single ship into the system with it. Hardly enough to engage the pulsar, and deal with the Union fleet."

Barron felt something, a thought being born. Rough, partially formed…but definitely there. "Why couldn't one ship go in, Admiral?"

"Ty, come on…"

"No, hear me out, sir. I'm not talking about one vessel taking on everything the Union has. But what if the entire fleet transited in…with the stealth ship in the lead? All the rest of our ships advance slowly. From what I've read, we've got a solid estimate on the pulsar's range, don't we?"

Striker nodded.

"So, we make sure not to move into that range too quickly. We give the stealth ship time to advance."

"Advance where?"

"Into point blank range of the pulsar." Barron paused. He could feel the surprise from his companions. "We open up with primaries, as many secondaries as we can power, and every missile aboard in sprint mode. We pack her full of ordnance, as much as she can carry. Then, I take that thing down, its destruction will be guaranteed."

"*You* will take it down?" Striker sounded doubtful. "Ty, please tell me you're not thinking *you'll* take *Dauntless* into the Bottleneck, right past the entire Union fleet, and down the throat of the most dangerous superweapon we've ever seen? I know you miss your ship, but this is a bit of an extreme way to get back onboard, isn't it?"

"Do we have another choice, sir? *Dauntless* has come through some tough spots before. She's got one more in her." He looked over at Travis, concerned she might be upset he was conniving his way back into her command. But she was sitting there, nodding her head slowly, agreeing with him.

"Ty...even if you succeed, you'll be stuck behind the entire Union fleet."

"We'll still have the stealth generator, sir. Once the pulsar is destroyed, we can shut down all weapons and reactivate it."

"Assuming it's still operative. It feels like a long shot just keeping it working long enough to get you across the system. You're betting it will still be functional after the battle, and that you'll have the energy capacity left to power it." A pause. "It's a suicide mission, Ty."

"I don't do suicide missions, Admiral. Even if the stealth generator dies on us, that's when the fleet will hit the Union line. Those enemy battleships will have their hands full dealing with your task forces, and the Alliance's." He hesitated. "We'll find some way to slip out of there in the middle of all that chaos."

Striker stared back at Barron, and then at Travis. "Captain, I can see from your face you agree with this insane plan."

"I don't see a better alternative, sir. And Tyler is right... *Dauntless* has come back from other tough spots."

"Nothing like this. I'd hate to see what odds the main AI would give this of succeeding. My money's on low single digits."

"That's better than nothing, sir."

"And you don't mind giving up your command to Commodore Barron?"

"*Dauntless* will always be Tyler's ship, sir. I'm just warming his seat there." She looked over at Barron and smiled, a clear message, he knew, that she was truly okay with the plan.

"Ty, are you sure about this?"

"What other choices do we have, Admiral?"

Striker was silent for a moment. Barron knew there were none, and he knew the admiral would have to admit that. Would have to approve his plan.

Striker sighed hard. "All right, Ty...assuming I go along with this, and that is far from a certainty, what would you need?"

"I want my old crew back together, every one of them. I especially want Commander Stockton and Captain Fritz."

"Commander Stockton is running the last scouting mission, but if...when...he gets back, he's yours. Captain Fritz is at the Academy on Megara, terrorizing the engineering cadets."

"And hating every minute of it, sir. At least if her last comm to me is any indication."

"No doubt, she'll jump at the chance to run back to you. I have to confess, I've never seen an officer better at getting others to follow him into hopeless situations. You have some kind of gift, Ty...or a curse. I'm not sure which."

"Perhaps there should be a service commendation for that, Admiral."

"Perhaps." Striker hesitated again, for a long while this time. "Okay, Ty. Make me a list of anything you want. Repairs or upgrades to *Dauntless*, equipment, ordnance, personnel. Whatever you want, if I have it, it's yours."

"You mean you're going to approve the mission?"

"I don't like it. I don't like it one bit. But you're right...I don't have any choice. You get *Dauntless* ready, and I'll make sure the fleet is prepared to set out with you."

"Thank you, sir." Barron felt a smile pushing out onto his lips. *Why are you smiling, you fool? It will be a miracle if this works… and if it doesn't, you'll be leading all your people to their deaths.*

Even if it does work, you may be leading them to their deaths…

"I will put it all together. But for now, one thing. I'd like to get Fritzie here as soon as possible. She should have been working on that stealth generator all along, and I want to get her in the mix as soon as possible."

Chapter Five

The line of white-coated engineers and scientists stood utterly still, staring in horror at what they saw through the clear plastic of the observation deck's outer wall. Two bodies, frozen, their faces transfixed, holding the terror they had felt as they were thrown from the airlock. They were tethered to the station by small cables that prevented them from drifting off where they could no longer serve as examples for the others.

Gaston Villieneuve was not a sadist, not in the way most of his predecessors in Sector Nine's top chair had been. He was simply practical. He didn't enjoy inflicting pain or fear, but he didn't let anything so vague and immaterial as sympathy or pity keep him from doing whatever was necessary to see his goals met. The two fools floating in the frigid vacuum had let their own greed interfere with their duty to the state. That was common enough. Corruption was endemic in the Union. But only a fool would grasp greedily on a project so clearly vital, not only to the state itself, but to the head of Sector Nine.

Or, two fools in this case.

The way Villieneuve figured it, the two thieves he'd spaced owed him for their thefts, and for the delays they'd imposed on the project, and just about the only value he could squeeze from them was fear. Fear that would drive the others to work harder, and to put their own petty larcenies on hold. At least until the project was complete.

"These two criminals betrayed the Union. They betrayed all of us. And justice has come to them, at last." Villieneuve stood there, dressed head to toe in a fine black suit, looking in every way the head of a dreaded secret police organization, which, of course, he was. Everyone present knew there were great rewards to be had for success. He'd been abundantly clear about that. Now it was time to show them all the other side of that coin…the cost of failure.

"They stole from this project. They diverted needed supplies to the black market to line their pockets, actions which delayed the completion of our work here, placing the entire Union in danger." Villieneuve glared at the terrified group, wondering for a moment if he was laying it on a bit too thick. "They paid a terrible price, yet one too lenient for such traitors." He let the words sink in. He had every supervisor and manager on the project lined up there, and he wanted them leaving with a cloud of fear surrounding them. He wanted them worrying that they might be next to go out the airlock.

Or worse.

"There is no longer any time to lose. We must complete the work and ready the pulsar for movement." He held up a data chip. "This chip contains the latest timetables all of you submitted to me for project completion." He let the chip drop, and then he slammed his boot down, crushing it.

"Your proposed completion date is unacceptable. The maximum acceleration figures, the time to move through a transit point and reassemble, the parameters for system reliability…all unacceptable. That is why I am here. That is why I have left Montmirail, and the myriad responsibilities I have there. Because this project is the most important one in the Union right now, and you people have treated it like some kind of tea party." He paused, panning his angry gaze across the group again.

"That ends now. From this moment forward, all work on

this project will proceed at maximum possible speed. All work periods are extended, all safety regulations suspended. We are going to revise these timetables, and we are going to come up with completion dates that reflect the hard work and dedication I know I can expect from each of you. We are going to increase the operational capacity of the mobile system to levels that sustain the combat mission lying ahead."

He paused again, turning his head and glancing out at the two frozen corpses. "Do you all understand me? Are you with me, as any loyal citizen would be?"

There were nearly three dozen people in front of him but not one made a sound.

"No one is with me?" Villieneuve's tone was ominous.

"Yes, sir, of course." It was one nervous voice, a woman, clearly terrified.

"I am with you, Minister."

"Yes, we are all with you. Long live the Union!"

Villieneuve held back the smile that tried to slip out onto his lips. There wasn't a hint of real sincerity in any of the voices, but that didn't matter. Loyalty was fickle…fear lasted forever.

"Then back to your stations, all of you. Address your teams, advise them of the new priorities. You will all receive updated work schedules today. See that they are implemented at once." A pause. "We're going to finish this project, fellow Unionites, and we're going to do it faster than any of you imagined possible."

The group stood in place, all listening, waiting to see if Villieneuve was going to say anything else.

"I said, go! What are you waiting for? There is work to be done." He waved his hand, watching as the group moved, rushing toward the exit like the herd they were.

He stood silently, until the last of the engineers had gone, leaving him alone with his four guards.

"Shall we have the bodies untethered, sir?" The captain, the commander of his bodyguard stood in front of him at rigid attention.

Villieneuve looked back one more time, silent for a moment before he answered. "No, Captain, I don't think so. Just leave them where they are to serve as a…reminder."

"Yes, sir."

Villieneuve turned and walked toward the hatch, following the path his now-motivated crew had taken. He had a long day ahead of him, schedules to prepare, manifests to review, shipments to inspect.

People to scare.

*   *   *

"All right, we're going through in thirty seconds. That means complete radio silence, no matter what. Get in, get your scans, and get out. And once you're back here, you head home. Immediately. No waiting for the others. The return trip is every man for himself. The admiral needs these scans, so that means some of us—*one* of us, at least—has to make it back."

That's a pretty grim rallying cry.

Jake Stockton twisted his body, first to the left and then to the right, trying to work out the kinks. He'd flown a multi-system run before in a fighter, as far as he knew, the only pilot to have done it before these recent missions. It was no mystery why Gary Holsten and Admiral Striker had recruited him to make spying runs to the Bottleneck. He'd made three trips so far, making it back each time soaked in sweat and feeling as though he'd beaten the odds. The first two journeys had been solo runs, and the last one had been at the head of eight other pilots, only two of whom had made it back with him.

The first time he'd gone, he was pretty sure he'd slipped in undetected. The second time the enemy had sent a squadron after him, but his modified bird had more thrust than anything the Union possessed, and he zipped back through the transit point and managed to avoid everything sent after him. Fortunately, the systems between Grimaldi and the Bottleneck had become something of a no man's land, virtually abandoned as the opposing forces massed in their respective fortress systems.

He had two dozen fighters with him now. He'd argued with the admiral, practically begged to go alone, or with two or three others at most, but Striker had been blunt. The lives of two dozen pilots didn't matter, not really. Not when the fate of the entire Confederation was on the line. Stockton knew Striker was right. Defeat meant death for millions, and slavery for tens of billions. But those two dozen pilots were *his* responsibility, and that altered the math considerably, at least in his own mind.

He'd trained his small force relentlessly, not only in the cockpit, but in the classroom and the simulator as well. Flying a fighter through half a dozen systems was as much a psychological challenge as a physical one, and Stockton had brutally weeded out his recruits, tossing anyone who showed the slightest inability to endure extended periods in the small confines of a fighter. The trip to the Bottleneck was six days, and that meant maximum acceleration and deceleration, with robot tankers attached to a ship. That was a long time to live more or less in a chair, eating nothing but concentrated nutrition bars, with a bag for a bathroom and no way to stretch your legs. It was torture of a sort, and most pilots would lose their minds before they got back.

He angled his thrust, adjusting his vector slightly. The enemy was aware of his scouting missions now, and he had no doubt about what awaited his small, elite force. The Union ships were deployed well back from the transit point, formed up in front of the pulsar, ready to face a fleet assault. But, the last time, they'd had pickets close to the point, waiting for his scouts.

"Ten seconds to insertion." Stockton had never been a huge fan of his fighter's AI, but twelve days was a long time to be alone. Since most of the trip was conducted under strict radio silence, the electronic assistant had been his only conversation partner. He'd grown accustomed to the almost-human sounding voice.

His hand shifted to the top of the controls, an instinctive move he hadn't been able to shake. He would normally be ready to fire before he ventured into possible enemy space, but one of the costs of reworking a fighter for long-range use was ripping out every weapon. His bird didn't have a laser hot enough to light a candle, nor any missiles, bombs...not even a bag of rocks to throw. His sole weapon against enemy fighters was maneuver…otherwise known as running like hell.

He took a deep breath just as his ship slipped into the strange alternate space of the transit tube. Translight travel was a weird enough feeling in a large spaceship, but his fighter lacked the shielding a warship possessed. He could feel the strange alien sensation of the space, something he recognized but could never really describe. The trip took perhaps twenty seconds, but it seemed far longer. And then, he was through.

He felt his adrenaline surge. He turned his head, looking out through the clear hyper-plastic of his cockpit. It was a pointless effort, he knew. The odds of anything being in visual range were infinitesimal. But he had nothing else to do. It would take a while, perhaps a minute or more, for his systems to reconfigure and restart.

His heart was pounding hard, almost making a sound in his ears. He nodded to himself, acknowledged his intensity. That, at least, sounded better than fear.

He stared down at his display, but the screens were still scrambled. He'd come through at a strange angle, just one more tactic to try to evade defenders, at least until he reestablished control of his ship.

It was torturous, sitting there waiting, but then his systems snapped back on. He moved his hand instinctively, blasting his engines, changing his thrust vector. If any enemy was in range, they'd had plenty of time to target his course.

He looked down at the display, just as the scanners began feeding information.

Damn.

It was a Union battleship. Not a particularly large or modern one, but as far as his unarmed fighter was concerned, it might as well have been the god of war himself.

His eyes darted around looking for fighters. If there was a squadron on patrol, his people were in big trouble. There were small dots clustered around the big ship, squadrons launching, no doubt.

They must have been on alert to react that quickly…

He scanned the rest of the display. Nothing else.

But no ships out on patrol. Some Union officer's going to hear about that...

Stockton frowned. From what he knew of the Union service, an officer who allowed Confederation scouts to get into the system and escape would get worse than a talking to. Much worse.

Stockton put the thought out of his mind. It wasn't his problem...and getting some scanning data and getting the hell out most definitely was.

He brought his ship around, feeding power into the thrusters, trying to put as much distance between him and the now-pursuing enemy fighters. He flipped on the long-range scanners and directed them toward the pulsar's location.

Only it wasn't there.

He set the sensor suite to a wide scan, even as his gut tightened with the realization of what he'd just discovered. For an instant, he feared the great weapon was gone entirely, but then he saw it, about ten thousand kilometers from its former position. It was still covered in superstructure, and still surrounded by service craft. He could tell almost immediately that the Union hadn't completed their work.

But there was no question the thing had moved.

A test, probably. That means they're getting close.

Stockton sighed softly.

We don't have much time...

His head snapped back to the tactical display as he saw one of his fighters disappear. Then, almost immediately, another. His instinct, the result of years of combat leadership, was to bring his ship around, fly back and aid his pilots. But the priority for this mission was clear, and the admiral's words echoed in his mind.

Two dozen pilots don't matter, not when billions of lives are at stake...

Besides, there wasn't much he could do without weapons, even if he did respond.

His hand moved over the controls, realigning the scanners, getting as much as he could on the pulsar and its new location.

His eyes darted back and forth, watching the scans come in and keeping an eye on the approaching fighters. He didn't have long. If he didn't swing around and head back soon, he'd have half a dozen enemy birds on right on top of him, and a squadron at least between his ship and the transit point.

He'd always pushed things to the brink, but usually, there was a mothership nearby. An escape from a tough spot was typically a quick dash to a landing bay, not a six-day journey through empty space. Even minor damage could finish him out here, and as much as his reputation said he was crazy, the truth was, Jake Stockton didn't want to die.

He'd watched his best friend die, in the cockpit where so many he knew had met their ends. For a while after Kyle Jamison's death, Stockton truly *hadn't* cared if he survived. He fought with abandon, and he chased down the pilot who had killed Jamison...only to let her go in the end. Jovi Grachus was an Alliance ace—*the* Alliance ace—the best pilot the Palatians had. Perhaps had ever had.

She'd been a match for him, as well, though in the end, he'd had her, dead to rights. She was an ally now, and he knew she'd do the fleet some good in battle, probably even save a lot of Confed pilots. But though he hadn't killed her, he hadn't been able to accept her either, or to forgive her.

He looked down at the display again. He had good scans. Not as much, perhaps, as he might have liked, but enough. Now, he had to get them back to base.

Half his fighters were gone, and the rest were heading back toward the transit point, enemy fighters close on their heels. Stockton swung his throttle hard to the side, blasting his engines at full, adjusting his vector to take him back to the point. Toward home.

He'd waited just a bit too long, though. A pair of Union fighters was coming at him, firing as they did. He shifted the controls again, pulling his best evasive maneuvers. The scout fighter was fast, at least in terms of straight line acceleration, but it wasn't as maneuverable as an unmodified Lightning. That meant evading enemy attacks was...difficult.

But Stockton was one of the best. He angled his vector, back into the system, luring his pursuers after him. Then he swung around and blasted at full thrust, throwing off his safeties and burning the reactor at one hundred ten percent.

The move took the Union pilots by surprised, and he gained a jump on them. He blasted hard, his ship tearing toward the transit point and escape.

The enemy fighters were right behind him, still in firing range. Stockton zigzagged his ship, taking as irregular a course as he could without giving up too much of his advantage in velocity. He was almost there, just a few more seconds.

His ship shook hard, spinning end over end.

He'd been hit. It wasn't that bad, at least he didn't think it was, but the small explosion had altered his vector. He was gyrating wildly, and worse, he was going to miss the point.

His hands whipped to the throttle, angling the controls, trying to regain his ship's course. There was no time to recalculate, no time to think. It was blind instinct. If he missed the point, he'd never make it back around, not before he had a dozen enemy birds on him.

He saw the circle on his display, the transit point. It was growing, getting closer. His vector was moving back toward his earlier course...but he was still wide.

The enemy fighters were on his tail, firing even as his course correction consumed his attention and his evasive moves dropped off. But luck was with him, as it had been so many times before. The pursuing pilots should have hit him again, they should have taken his ship down. But they missed.

Stockton upped the power to one hundred fifteen, and he blasted every bit of it toward the point.

This is going to be close...

He counted down softly. "Three...two...one..."

He closed his eyes. For an instant, he wasn't sure. Had he made it? Then he felt the strange feeling, the mild nausea of alien space.

He'd never appreciated the usually unpleasant sensation before, but now he relished it.

He was in the tube. He'd made it.

Chapter Six

Public Address in Barroux City

Workers of Barroux, you have been liberated. No longer shall you suffer under the yoke of offworld masters who work you to death while your families starve. No longer shall your labor go to support a pointless and unjust war. No longer we will allow ourselves to be used as slaves, ruled by an oppressive and abusive government. Stand up now, with us. Stand up, and join the revolution. – Ligue d'Egalité

Barroux City, Union Sector Capital
Barroux, Rhian III
Union Year 217 (313 AC)

"If your soldiers had done their jobs, Bonnaire, none of this would have happened." Victor Aurien sat on a hard wooden bench, a half-eaten chunk of stale bread in his hand. The Planetary Commissar, so recently the effective master of all Barroux, was clad in a tattered suit, dried blood crusted on a gash down his cheek and hanks of greasy and disheveled hair hanging down on both sides of his face.

"With all due respect, Commissar, with the war requisitions, my forces were down to minimal strength, backed up by planetary levies, half of whom deserted to the rebels the first chance they got. If I'd had any real forces, even a battalion of Foudre Rouge, I would have crushed this uprising the first night."

"I'm not interested in excuses, Bonnaire. You and I are in this together. Fortunately, I was able to get off a call for aid before the rioters seized control of the comm stations." Aurien paused, and when he continued his voice was edgier, the fear in it apparent. "Whatever our opinions of each other, Major, I suggest we put our heads together, not only on a plan of action, but on our story when the relief forces arrive. Pointing our fingers at each other won't help either of us, and we'd damned well better have something more to say than that a botched pacification raid triggered a worldwide uprising."

Bonnaire nodded. He didn't much care for Aurien, but the Commissar was right about this. *That doesn't mean he won't shove a knife in my back though, if he thinks it will save his ass…*

"I agree, Commissar. Our first priority is finding a way to hold out until the relief gets here. We're safe for the moment. I have enough troops to defend this facility for the foreseeable future, at least against a disorganized rabble."

"That disorganized rabble drove us here, Major."

Bonnaire didn't answer. He wasn't sure if Aurien was trying to bait him, or if the comment had simply been an inarguably honest assessment of their predicament.

"You have what," Aurien asked, "three hundred troops here?"

"Two hundred ninety-four. Not including myself. Fortunately, they are all well-armed, and we have sufficient ammunition to hold the facility for the foreseeable future."

Aurien looked down at the bread in his hand with a scowl. "I wish our supply of other necessities was a bit better, Major. Your soldiers may be able to hold the compound, but they are likely to starve to death while doing it."

"We are low on fresh food, Commissar, but we have a reasonable stock of combat rations. They've been in the warehouses for quite some time, but I suspect they're edible, if less than appetizing."

"Let's get an inventory of that right away, so we know exactly where we stand. And I want guards on the food supplies at all times. We're probably going to have to put your troopers on some kind of restricted rations, and we don't need hungry soldiers ransacking what supplies we have."

Bonnaire nodded, surprised at the practicality the Commissar was displaying. He'd always considered Aurien somewhat of a fool, but now the deposed planetary governor was showing some common sense...and some strength too.

"Yes, of course. I will see to it immediately."

"And make sure you have enough guards posted at the perimeter walls. That rabble out there is after our blood. We should be able to hold out here, as you said, but if we let our guard down..." He paused. "I also need an inventory of military and security force supplies stored anywhere *but* here. Whatever is out there, that rabble will find it sooner or later. If they're going to come for us with our own heavy weapons, we need to be ready for it."

"Yes, Commissar, of course." The last two weeks had been brutal, difficult, but now Bonnaire felt something unexpected, the last thing he might have imagined he would. Respect for Aurien. It was a spark, a small one in the darkness, but it was there, and he found himself wondering if, against all odds, Aurien could be the leader they needed now.

Because, if he wasn't, they were all likely to die at the hands of an enraged mob.

                    *   *   *

Remy Caron stood along the side of the room, watching the others argue. The past few weeks seemed a blur to him. The attack on the League's meeting had backfired, and all across Barroux City, the people had risen up, surged into the streets. The soldiers on duty were overwhelmed and killed, many of them beaten to death by enraged mobs. Remy had his share of resentment for his sufferings, and those of his family, but the sheer brutality of the uprising had shaken him. His fellow rebels had been like a horde of wild animals unleashed, rampaging through the streets, chasing down anyone even remotely related to the apparatus of Union government, beating, raping, killing. Remy had thought himself angry for what had become of his life, but he found the intensity of the violence sickening, all the more because he suspected many of the victims had been other workers, guilty of nothing save being in the path of the mob's rage.

"Remy, come here. You must stand with us. We must assault the compound. We must destroy every vestige of the Union's foul hand here on Barroux."

"No, Remy…that is a fool's game. They are trapped, surrounded. Let us starve them out instead of losing hundreds in a bloody assault."

For all the past two weeks had shocked and stunned Remy Caron, nothing surprised him more than the inexplicable way he'd somehow ended up among the rebel leaders. He'd been there the night of the initial raid, of course, but not as an organizer. He'd only come to watch, and it had been his first meeting among Barroux's resistance. But now he was part of the leadership, and the various groups were urging him to support them.

He'd known his co-workers and neighbors had thought well of him, but he'd never expected them to look to him for inspiration and direction when they streamed out into the streets to join the uprising. In what seemed like a brief moment, he'd gone from scared and confused onlooker to rebel instigator. Still scared, though.

He'd done what he could to limit the brutality, but in the end, that hadn't been much. He understood the anger the workers felt, but he ached for the innocents killed, the children he'd seen dead on the streets.

"I believe we should be cautious," he said tentatively, still uncomfortable with the role that had seemed to find him from nowhere. "Many have been killed already, and we have much to do. We need to secure the food supplies, make sure vital services are restored. The hospitals have become a nightmare, virtually abandoned by their staffs, filled with the dead and dying."

"No, Remy, we must first eliminate any possible challenge to our authority. We need to form a governing body now, and we must organize our people. It is vital that we eliminate any who would threaten our control."

Remy shook his head. "The Unionists in the compound hardly threaten us, Matthieu. I agree we must keep them under siege, but it hardly seems necessary to risk assaulting the facility. At least not now."

"I disagree." Matthieu Vaucomme turned and looked around at the others. "Leaving the Unionists there only encourages other groups that would challenge us…and threaten the purity of the revolution."

"What other groups?" Remy was uncomfortable with the way the conversation was going. "Most of the Union officials have been murdered, butchered in their homes along with their families and children. Even the workers who did no more than routine jobs in Union offices have been massacred. A few hundred holdouts in a military compound do not threaten us. It is the response that will undoubtedly come from higher authority that is the real danger. Do you think losing hundreds of our best people in a pointless attack is going to help us deal with that? Do you think more mindless barbarity against Union officials and soldiers is going to lessen the intensity of the government forces when they get here?"

Remy wasn't sure where the words were coming from, or the energy with which he delivered them. "We must get ready to defend ourselves. We need to find any of our people with military experience, with technical expertise. We must gain control of the planetary defenses. We must get to the military storehouses and see what weapons and ammunition we have. It is not a time for pointless vengeance, nor for uncontrolled violence. When the Union comes, they will have real soldiers… Foudre Rouge. We must be ready."

The room had been more or less silent as he spoke, but now it was utterly so as Remy uttered his reference to the Union's dreaded clone soldiers. "Would you waste time and resources on foolishness now? We have risen up, taken our freedom, but if we are to hold it, we must be ready. Every citizen of Barroux must be organized, prepared to fight. Our greatest test lies ahead, not behind us. Either we stand, hold our world and win our futures…or we fall, into a darkness few could even imagine. What do you think the Union forces will do to Barroux? Everyone here, leaders of a rebellion, will almost certainly end up in the cellars of Sector Nine." He paused, allowing his last words to sink in. Every citizen of the Union grew up around tales of the fearsome intelligence agency.

"Do you think only you will suffer? Will the oppressors spare our families? What will they do to your wives and husbands? To your sons and daughters?" He tried to push back an image of Zoe brutally murdered, and Elisa…

"What example will they make of this world? How many thousands will die? Millions, even? We must forgo these petty arguments over vengeance and squabbles over power. We must stand together, as one…or else we shall all surely fall."

He stood in the room, suddenly aware that his colleagues were utterly silent, staring at him with strange expressions on their faces. They were still for what seemed like a long time. Then, one began clapping…and then another. Almost as a group they stood and joined in, and then they began shouting, "Remy!"

He stood where he was, uncertain, scared, unsure what to do, even as the chant became thunderous.

"Remy…Remy…Remy!"

Chapter Seven

Fleet Base Grimaldi
Orbiting Krakus II
Krakus System
Year 313 AC

"Fritzie!" It wasn't the way commodores were supposed to greet their subordinates, but Barron didn't care. He'd always had a close connection to his engineer, and Anya Fritz's near-wizardry had saved his ship and his people more times than he cared to count. For all the accolades he'd collected, all the honors and the claims that he was his grandfather's true successor, he knew just how much he owed to Fritz and her unbelievable ability to drive her people beyond what seemed possible.

"It's good to see you, sir." Fritz was a bit cold by nature, and she stood stiffly at first, uncomfortable for a moment before a rare bit of emotion took hold and she returned the embrace.

"I'm sorry I had to drag you back here, Fritzie. I hate to interrupt your new position." Though he rather suspected there were some cadets who would buy him a drink for relieving them of an instructor who, by all accounts, had become the terror of the Academy. He imagined they'd come up with a whole collection of names for Fritz, and probably none of them flattering.

"You rescued me, sir." Fritz had never wanted to teach at the Academy in the first place, but she'd fallen victim to her own

49

notoriety, as well as Barron's repeated statements that none of his victories would have been possible without her skills. She was too good to assign to just another ship, and as an engineer, there were limited opportunities in the high command. So, teaching the next generation of technicians seemed like the best use of her talents.

To everyone but her.

"I'm glad to be of service, Fritzie, but this one's going to be dangerous. It's strictly volunteer, and I can't state strongly enough, I'll have no ill thoughts of anyone who takes a pass on this one. That includes you."

"I'm in, sir."

"At least wait until I tell you what we're going to do. It's a long shot, Fritzie, maybe even on coming back."

"We've made it through everything else, sir."

Barron felt a little uncomfortable. He knew Fritz would walk into a fire behind him, but he was a little troubled by how his reputation had grown, and how it affected his people. Fritz seemed really confident that Barron would get his people through…anything. It was a confidence he didn't share.

"I mean it, Fritzie. I don't know if we can pull this one off. I just know I have to try."

"And if you have to try, so do I. It's that simple, sir."

"Thanks, Fritzie." He paused, still unsettled. If Fritzie was acting this way, none of his people would question a word out of his mouth. Even Atara had stepped aside without hesitation when he'd suggested resuming command of *Dauntless*. She'd even seemed relieved.

"Is it true we'll be back on *Dauntless*?" Barron could tell from her tone; the old ship's draw didn't only affect him.

"Yes, Fritzie. I'm afraid we'll be asking a lot of the old girl this time."

"She'll be there with whatever we need, sir. She always has been."

"Yes," Barron said, trying to keep the sadness he felt out of his voice, "she always has been." He paused for a few seconds. Then: "Before we discuss the mission itself, I have something else for you. You're aware of the stealth generator Andi and her people found."

"Yes, sir."

"I'd like you to take charge of the research team. The generator is a crucial part of our mission, and we're going to need it functioning as reliably as possible. I can't think of anyone better suited to handle that than you."

"Thank you, sir…but that device is very sophisticated. How much time do we have?"

"I don't know, Fritzie." That would depend on Jake Stockton's report…and his birds were a day overdue. "Probably not long. Two months, maybe three at most."

She exhaled slowly. "That's not a lot of time…but we'll manage, sir. I assume we're installing the generator in *Dauntless*?"

"You assume correctly, Fritzie. We'll want it operational for extended periods, but there will be one stretch, a few hours at least, when we'll need it at one hundred percent. Even a few seconds of failure could be disastrous."

"That's a heavy standard to meet, sir." She paused. "But, we'll manage it, somehow." She turned her head and glanced behind her at the small stack of duffels piled alongside the hatch. "If someone can take my bags to my quarters, sir, I'll get started right away." She looked at Barron and smiled. "Just point me in the right direction."

$$*\qquad\qquad *\qquad\qquad *$$

Stockton's hand was wrapped around the throttle, his fingers pale white from the pressure. He was almost out of fuel, his ship was shot up, and he was on the verge of a psychotic episode from all the stims he'd taken. It was a race to see which problem would kill him first, and against all the challenges threatening to finish him so close to base, he had nothing left to hold it all back but pure stubbornness…and he was working it for all it was worth.

Even his AI had cut out on him. The hit he'd taken hadn't been critical, at least it wouldn't have been if he'd landed on a mothership afterward, instead of flying through half a dozen systems, practically begging his equipment not to give up the ghost. Quite a bit of it had done just that, one circuit at a time, and it had almost gotten down to using his nose to find Grimaldi. Now he was less than ten thousand kilometers away…and he still wasn't sure he was going to make it.

He had Grimaldi control on his comm, but he couldn't answer. His transmitters had gone the way of half his other systems, shorted out and non-operative. He tapped his positioning jets, wobbling his ship—"waggling his wings"—his best guess on how to let Grimaldi ops know he was reading them. One way communication was limited, but with so much of his equipment gone, it would be a big help if they talked him in. Which they'd be more likely to do if they knew he was getting their messages.

He pushed forward on the throttle, pouring what thrust remained into a full deceleration. He'd been slowing since he entered the system, but he'd done it in stages, giving his engines a rest before firing them again for another burst of thrust. He just didn't like the pressure readings in the engines, and if they gave out on him it was over. He'd be out of life support before a rescue ship from Grimaldi could match vector and velocity and tow him into the bay. And he *had* to get back.

He wanted to get back because he ached to live, because for all his bravado, he was as scared of death as any rookie pilot. But he *had* to get back because of the intel he carried, the simple message that the enemy was close to moving the pulsar.

The message that his broken comm couldn't transmit.

He started to take a deep breath, but he stopped himself. His life support had been slipping for the last two systems, and it was close to critical now. He had enough air if he made it to base on the initial pass, but if something else went wrong, he was going to need all the oxygen he could get. His survival suit and the insulated blankets in the emergency pack could ward off the cold for a while, but once he ran out of air…that was it.

"Recon fighter one, this is Grimaldi base. Do you read?" It was the same message they'd been sending for fifteen minutes, but something was different this time. The voice.

The comm speakers were barely functioning, and the static and distortion made it hard to tell, but he was somehow sure. Stara!

"Jake, if you're hearing this…and from that thing you're doing with your ship, I'm betting you are, vector toward landing bay four. We've got the bay cleared and emergency equipment standing by."

He felt a rush of excitement. Stara was a lot of things to him, but most important right now, she was the best flight control officer in the fleet.

"I'm going to assume from the look of that ship, your nav-com is as shot as your comm. So, I'm going to take you in, okay? Just follow my instructions, and we'll get you back aboard."

He sighed softly and loosened his grip. Stara would give him a chance of making it, a good chance. He realized how much he'd been bullshitting himself before, how poor his odds of making a clean landing were without some kind of nav.

"Reverse thrust…I'm going to guess that bucket can't do anything we haven't watched it do as you made your approach. That doesn't leave much margin for error, so for once, shut up and do what I say. Tap another 2g on that backward thrust, and get ready to swing 234 to starboard."

He smiled. He could hear how worried she was through the banter.

"Okay, Stara," he said to himself. "Reverse thrust up 2g. Ready for starboard burst, course 234."

He followed her directions, and in another moment, he had a visual on the station. Grimaldi was a vast structure, visible from a hundred kilometers or more.

His eyes dropped to the thrust reading. He was moving a little faster than he'd like, but there was nothing he could do about it. *Stara knows what she is doing…*

Now, he could see the different sections of the station. *Bay four…*

It was on the far side. *That's why she has me going there. Another few kilometers to slow down.*

"Okay, Jake, your line is good. We just have to slow you down. I want you to hit your thrusters for all they have left… and don't worry if you're still coming in a little quick. We've got the bay filled with enough foam to catch that ship before it gets anywhere vital.

The vital parts I'm worried about are in *this ship…*

He could see the open hatch of the bay now, the flashing lights of the emergency crews visible beyond. *Stara wasn't kidding…it looks like a ten-alarm fire in there.*

He slammed his hand forward, squeezing out every bit of thrust his engines had left. He was almost to the bay, then he was inside. He could feel the fighter moving, still too fast. And then an abrupt halt.

His body lurched forward hard, his chest slamming into the harness. It hurt. It hurt like hell. But he was alive, and he was pretty sure he wasn't seriously injured. And his ship was at a stop.

He'd made it back. Somehow, he'd made it back.

*   *   *

"There is no doubt. Commander Stockton is correct. The pulsar *was* moved from its previous location." Admiral Striker was sitting on one of the chairs around the conference table. The fact that it had taken two aides to get him there from his power chair didn't diminish from the satisfaction he felt.

"That seems clear, Van. Normally, I would say a move of such a short distance was a repositioning, not a sign of a true movement system. But all the intel points to the same thing. They're building a system to move that thing, and when they finish it, they're going to invade." Gary Holsten sat across from Striker. The spymaster had docked at Grimaldi just a few hours before Stockton's rather tenser arrival, and now he sat grimfaced and somber. Striker had filled him in on the plan. Barron's plan. Holsten had agreed with Striker's initial assessment…it was pure lunacy. Then, a moment later, he'd reluctantly concurred with the admiral's second acknowledgement. There was no other choice.

"Commodore Barron, perhaps we should consider sending another ship, another crew, one more…"

Striker watched as Holsten fished around for a subtle was to say what he was thinking. Expendable.

"I believe if anyone can accomplish this mission, it is my people on *Dauntless*."

"I believe that too, Tyler." Holsten glanced across the table toward Striker, as if hoping the admiral would come to his aid somehow. But Striker just stared back, shaking his head ever so slightly. "It's just that…we can't spare you. You're the future of this fleet. One day you'll sit in Admiral Striker's chair. I know it, he knows it…and if you're honest with yourself, you know it too."

"I appreciate the confidence, Mr. Holsten, but what difference does it make who will lead the fleet in ten or twenty years if the Union conquers us now?"

Holsten was silent, and Striker too. The admiral had already gone through the process Holsten was now. This plan was the closest thing he could imagine to suicide, and as much as he hated sending anyone on such a mission, the idea of letting Barron go to his death cut at him deeply. But he also realized no one had a better chance, and at the core of it, that was all that mattered. If the Union could turn the pulsar into an offensive weapon, they could destroy the entire Confederation fleet. Their advance would be unstoppable.

"At least take one of the new ships, Tyler," Holsten said, tentatively beginning to accept the idea. "*Dauntless*, for all her unquestioned good service, is an old ship. A *Repulse*-class battleship will give you much more power. We can only use the stealth generator on one vessel, so it should be the strongest we have."

Striker knew what Barron was going to say before the commodore uttered a word. Holsten, for all his undeniable skill and talent, had never been a naval officer. He'd never commanded a ship, so he probably wouldn't understand. Not really.

Barron looked uncomfortable. "I know what you are saying, Mr. Holsten, and I appreciate the sentiment." He paused.

"But, there is more to a fight than guns and reactor capacity. It may not make sense, at least in hard terms, but if I'm going to do this, if my crew is going to, we *have* to do it on *Dauntless*. She may be an old ship, she may not have the quad primaries of a *Repulse*-class battleship or the modern armor of one of the new vessels…but there is more to her than steel and plastic and fusion cores. She's…she is *one of us*, sir. We can't go on a mission like this and leave *Dauntless* behind. We just can't."

Holsten didn't look entirely convinced, but he didn't argue. He looked over at Striker, as if waiting to see what the fleet admiral would say.

Striker just nodded. He understood how Barron felt. He'd been there once. His first command hadn't been a battleship, it had been a frigate, a ship called *Wolverine*. She'd carried a crew of eighty-three, and her armament had been nothing compared to *Dauntless*'s, but he still remembered every meter of her corridors, the sounds her engines made when he'd ordered her to full thrust, even the smell that used to waft into the main corridor from the main mess. He understood why Barron had to take *Dauntless* on this mission…but he still had to hold back his own impulse to send his protégé out with the strongest vessel he could. In the end, he told himself Barron needed *Dauntless*, that he wouldn't be able to give his best if he was forced into another ship. He wasn't sure that was true, but it was enough, at least, to forestall any argument with himself.

"Very well," Striker finally said. "*Dauntless* it is…but I want her refit from bow to stern, and I want that ship packed with every weapon and system we can cram in there."

Barron nodded. "Fritzie will make sure she's ready, sir. *Dauntless* couldn't be in better hands."

The other two men just nodded. No one was going to challenge Anya Fritz's status as the fleet's greatest engineer.

Chapter Eight

Fleet Base Grimaldi
Orbiting Krakus II
Krakus System
Year 313 AC

Andi Lafarge sat in her room. It was more than a room, it was a suite fit to house a visiting admiral. While she appreciated it, she also found it somehow…uncomfortable.

All her life she'd pursued wealth, indeed, she'd long had considerable resources, including a ship of her own. *Pegasus* was old, but Andi'd had more than a few improvements installed, and she owned it free and clear. But now she possessed *true* wealth, the kind she had sworn to obtain years before when she watched the local magnates of her homeworld living almost unimaginable lifestyles.

It was an old cliché, told in many versions, all testifying to the seemingly illogical and inexplicable superiority of wanting something to actually having it. It made no sense, none at all, and yet now she was beginning to understand the truth of it. Gary Holsten—spy, playboy, scion of one of the wealthiest families in the Confederation, whatever version of him one chose to see—had been a man of his word. He'd paid her and her people for the stealth generator, a sum of money so vast, she wondered now what she would do with it. She'd known he was rich, but the ease with which he transferred such a fortune gave her a hint of just how enormously wealthy the Holstens were.

She knew he'd make it all back, and then some. The stealth projector was an incredibly valuable piece of technology, and she couldn't begin to guess how many billions more would be added to the Holsten coffers once its secrets had been decoded and more had been produced.

She didn't care about that. She wished Holsten well. She had more money than she could spend in a hundred lifetimes, but now that she'd attained the goal that had driven her for so long, she felt unsettled, unsure of what to do next.

She'd searched the databases, glanced at the highest end properties available on the choicest worlds of the Confederation, but about all she'd decided was the one place she wasn't going was back to the shithole that had spawned her.

She'd been about as close to an outlaw as possible without, at least in her mind, crossing that line. She'd broken laws, of course. *Pegasus* had long carried weaponry she wasn't licensed to have, and certainly prospecting for old tech in the Badlands was illegal. But that was all nonsense as far as she was concerned, a level of villainy that rested solidly in the "gray area" of government overreach.

Still, she'd always seen the authorities, the navy included, as something to be avoided. She was loyal to the Confederation, though that hadn't stopped her from purchasing leads from scoundrels she knew were Sector Nine agents. She had avoided official contacts for so long, it was hard for her to realize that she had not only cooperated with the naval powers that be, but she had come to call some of them friends.

And one more than a friend.

Tyler Barron. He was a complication in her life, one she'd decided a dozen times to leave behind. But she'd never managed it. She liked him—in the brief moments when she acknowledged her own susceptibility to the weaknesses that affected people, she might say she loved him. They'd had fun together, more than that, even. She was different when he was around. She felt as she never had before. But Andi Lafarge was nothing if not a realist. Tyler Barron had been born onto a path as rigid as the one her own impoverished beginning had set before her. More so, even. She couldn't imagine Barron ever leaving the navy. Or the feelings that would haunt him if he did. She suspected he just *might* leave his career behind for her if she asked him, after the war ended, of course, but she couldn't do that to him. She didn't want to be the cause of the guilt that would follow him, of the shade of his famous grandfather haunting him for abandoning the legacy that went with being the Barron heir.

Barron bore the weight placed on him by his name and birth, and for all the privilege and advantages they conferred, they were also chains that bound him. He was tethered to his path, and she wasn't the kind to follow an illustrious mate around from posting to posting, a navy spouse ready to charm the higher ups and look dazzling at his side. Nor, she suspected, would a mate with as dubious a past as hers be an asset to an officer destined to rise to the top ranks of the navy.

Still, she found it hard to leave. The Confederation was at war, of course, but she played no role in that, not really. She had no duty, nothing to do but sit in her opulent quarters and pick up whatever bits of gossip she happened to hear. And she didn't like what she'd heard recently.

Something was happening, something big. She knew about the pulsar—perhaps not everything, but enough to understand what a problem it was. But now it seemed like the fleet was getting ready to leave. She knew there had been preparations for an invasion of the Union on the Periphery, but she understood the logistics of space travel well enough to realize there was no way the extensive preparations for such a long and circuitous attack could be in place this soon.

So what? What are they doing?

And what crazy part is Tyler playing in this?

It wasn't her problem. Neither she nor Barron had made each other any promises they couldn't keep. There was affection on both sides, but nothing more. She should just choose where she wanted to live and get on with the fabulous life for which her adventures had provided the means.

"You have visitors, Captain Lafarge." The AI's voice was soft, and very human sounding, so much so, it made her jump every time, thinking someone else was in the room.

Damn. The party. She'd been brooding so long, she'd lost all track of time. Her crew, each of them wealthy now too, were splitting up, heading to their individual destinations throughout the Confederation. But first, they were throwing her a party. It was their way of showing appreciation for the success she'd led them too…and also a way to say goodbye. She was appreciative, and deeply gratified they felt that way, but she'd have rather fought her way through a pack of pissed off Sector Nine agents. She hated parties…and she hated emotional goodbyes. Left to herself, she would just fade away, wishing the best for all of them. But there had been no way to say no.

"Open," she said to the AI. Then, a few seconds later, after she heard the door slip to the side, she added, "I'll be right there. Almost ready."

She ducked into the bedroom of the suite. She wasn't close to ready. But then she wasn't one to spend hours fussing with herself either. She tore off the pants and shirt she'd been wearing, reaching out and grabbing the dress—her only fancy bit of attire—from the closet. She turned and glanced quickly in the mirror as she slid it on. It dropped right into place. Her constant adventures had kept her in shape, at least, and she had to admit, she looked good.

She stared for a moment, running her hand through her hair quickly and then pausing, feeling a rush of irritation at the passing wish that Tyler could see her now.

"His loss," she said, feeling almost immediately sorry for the resentment she felt. Barron was somewhere on Grimaldi—they'd seen each other quite frequently over the past several months—but he'd almost disappeared the past few weeks. Now she realized with ever greater certainty that something was going on. Something big.

Something dangerous.

"C'mon, Andi…it's time to celebrate." Vig Merrick's voice, loud, excited, from the other room.

She sighed softly, even more worried about Barron, about all her navy friends, than she had been.

C'mon, Lafarge…it's time to have a good time. Or, at least, pretend to. They deserve that much.

She forced the frown from her face, an endeavor requiring even more effort than she'd expected it to. Then she smiled, hoping it didn't look as fake as it felt, and she walked out into the other room.

*   *   *

"It's good to see you both." Jake Stockton reached out and took Dirk Timmons's hand. The two had once been rivals, but whatever bad feeling had existed between them at one time, it was long gone. Timmons stood looking as steady as Stockton had ever seen him, despite the fact that *Dauntless*'s once and future fighter wing commander knew his friend walked around these days on two prosthetic limbs, courtesy of one of the desperate battles during the Alliance Civil War. Timmons was— had been—one of the best pilots in the fleet, but he'd run into an enemy who'd been better than him, at least on that day. He'd made it back to *Dauntless*, barely, courtesy of Stockton's frantic efforts. Still, despite his strong recovery, flight regs mandated his career in the cockpit was over.

"It's good to see you, too, Raptor." Timmons' voice was friendly, almost cheerful, but Stockton knew it was a façade. Timmons was a creature like himself, and barring him from a fighter was like caging an animal accustomed to the open steppe. He'd hesitated before sending the communique recalling Timmons, but then he'd decided that, despite the danger of the mission, it would be worse for the once-great pilot to feel unneeded.

"And you, Olya, what can I say?" He turned toward the other officer present, and he reached out and embraced her. He had served alongside Federov his entire stint on *Dauntless*, and for most of that time, she had commanded the Reds that would have been the ship's elite squadron…had it not been for his own Blues.

"I'm happy to see you, Jake." She used his name and not his call sign, as Timmons had done. "I mean that. Things haven't been the same without you."

She hugged him back with an intensity that lent credibility to her words. He'd been a little concerned about how she would react to his coming back. Federov had been *Dauntless*'s strike force commander under Captain Travis, and he'd been concerned how she'd feel about his return—in effect, her demotion. But there was no sign of resentment. Commodore Barron hadn't addressed the crew yet, but they all had varying degrees of information about the pending mission. Some knew more than others, of course, but all were aware that Barron was returning to command *Dauntless*, and he was reuniting as much of the old crew as possible. Even without details, they all knew the mission would be difficult and dangerous…and probably, damned near impossible. But they'd been there before, and not one of them would refuse to follow Barron wherever he led them.

Stockton stepped back after the hug and paused for a few seconds. He was happy to see his old comrades, but he was worried about the mission. He'd only had a brief meeting with the commodore, and for the first time ever, he'd gotten the impression Barron didn't expect to come back from this mission. That wouldn't affect Stockton's own actions, but it cast a pall on his efforts to recruit old comrades. Fighter pilots led dangerous lives, and they had a small enough chance of surviving to retirement. He didn't like the feeling of urging good men and women to join a suicidal expedition. Barron had mandated that all personnel recruited for the mission would be volunteers, but that was a distinction without meaning, at least for old *Dauntless* personnel. Stockton couldn't think of one crew member who wouldn't throw his hand up to join Barron if the mission had been to fly the ship into the heart of a sun. The fanatical loyalty of *Dauntless*'s crew went far beyond the already half-crazy members of the fighter wing, and Stockton was fairly sure even the spacers fourth class who cleaned out the reactors' cooling tubes would rush to answer the call.

"Jake!" It was a woman's voice, coming from the open hatch

behind him.

"Stara…" He turned and smiled. She raced over and threw her arms around him.

"I'm so glad you're back."

He felt a twinge of guilt. Stara had transferred from *Dauntless* to accept a post as second in command of fighter ops for Grimaldi…and, with Gary Holsten's help, he'd lied to her about his whereabouts. His scouting missions had been beyond top secret, and Holsten had insisted that no one but his own people be involved, or even know what was going on. He understood—though he found it rather disconcerting to see how worried about spies Holsten appeared to be right in the center of the Confederation's largest base—and he went along with it. Lying to Stara had been the hardest part of the whole thing, and though he felt the urge to tell her, Holsten had been insistent that the entire operation remain a secret, at least until *Dauntless* and the fleet were back from the Bottleneck.

"I'm glad to be back. It's been too long." He and Stara had never discussed the specifics of their relationship, but there wasn't any doubt in his mind they'd be together for as long as they lived. *Which might not be much longer…*

He hugged her back, letting his emotions escape for just a moment before clamping down his discipline again. It felt strange. Stockton had never been so controlled in his behavior. He'd long been the brilliant but unrestrained pilot, the bad boy of the fleet who was too good to cashier. But he'd changed… the instant he'd watched Kyle Jamison die. Jamison had been *Dauntless* strike force commander, the restraining force in his life…and his best friend. His youth had died in that moment, the uncontrolled cockiness replaced by an irresistible need to become what Jamison had always urged him to become, to take his friend's place.

"I'm so glad to see you all, but I'm afraid we've got work to do." He looked at his three companions. "We're going to be packing *Dauntless* full of fighters, and I mean *full*." Barron's ship had carried extra squadrons since the early days of the war, when she'd taken on survivors from some of the ships destroyed in the massive battle in the Arcturon system. But Stockton had something else in mind now, and he planned to take it even further. "So, that means we need more fighters. They have to volunteer, and I don't want a mass of disorganized individuals. I want whole squadrons, so that means every member has to be onboard. And we need the best we can get. It's going to take all we've got to pull this one off." He felt uncomfortable at gathering together the cream of the fleet's fighter corps and leading them all to their deaths, but he'd *seen* that thing in the Bottleneck, and, more importantly, he'd seen the work the enemy was completing. He'd come away with no doubt, none whatsoever, that they were on the verge of being able to move their superweapon. It was a major problem as a defensive obstacle…as an offensive resource it was a disaster.

"We're not going to have any trouble getting whole squadrons to follow Commodore Barron." Timmons's voice was edgy. Stockton could only imagine how much it would eat at his friend to watch the wings launch on such a desperate mission, and to stay behind to watch on the monitors and spit out advice to the pilots in space.

"No, I don't imagine we will. I've gone through fleet reports, and I've made a list of possible additions." The squadrons were deployed all around the fleet, and Stockton could only imagine the private invective of battleship captains relieved of their best wings by his efforts. But they could scream and shout all they wanted, Stockton had the absolute authority to transfer any squadron in the fleet, a power granted by no less authority than Fleet Admiral Striker himself.

"Jake…I've got another squadron to add to that list." Stara's tone was uncomfortable, and then she paused. "I talked to Jovi Grachus, and…"

"No." Stockton's voice was cold, hard.

"Jake…"

"I said no, Stara. I will not have that woman and her pilots in my command." He could feel his body tense, and his fists clenched. Commander Jovi Grachus was an ally now, the senior commander of the Alliance squadrons attached to the Confederation fleet, but she would always be an enemy to Stockton. Grachus had killed more of his pilots than he cared to remember, including Kyle Jamison. He'd spared her life in the final battle, reluctantly obeying Commodore Barron's order, but truth be told, he regretted not firing that last shot.

"Jake, I think you should at least listen to Stara. Commander Grachus is one of the best pilots out there—*I* know that—and she could bring the best Alliance aces with her."

"You of all people should be with me on this, Dirk. She gave you those artificial legs. She banished you from the cockpit." Grachus had defeated Timmons as well, though he'd survived at least, unlike Jamison.

"That was war, Jake. We all have our pain and loss, but Grachus is an honorable warrior. She…"

"She will never serve under my command. I had her in my sights…but I obeyed Commodore Barron. She's alive, but that is all she can expect from me." Stockton felt the anger and bitterness. On some level, he knew it was the pain of loss for his friend. If Kyle Jamison had been standing there, Stockton knew his friend would have told him to get past it. But Jamison *wasn't* there—that was the whole point—and Stockton couldn't change how he felt. "There are plenty of good pilots in Confederation service. We don't need some Red Alliance leftover to bolster us."

Stara looked like she was going to argue—and that wouldn't have surprised Stockton—but she held her tongue. They were all quiet for a moment, and then, mercifully, they started discussing specific squadrons to go after.

Chapter Nine

Tarkus Vennius sat in his chair at the large round table. His seat was bigger and plusher than the others, a token prerequisite to set him apart as the greater of those present. The whole thing seemed ridiculous to him, but he'd been compelled to endure some of the trappings of the office he despised.

He'd swept away every trace he could of Calavius, starting with that abominable throne the damned fool had built for himself. Vennius was Imperator, largely because he'd found no way to avoid it, but he'd be damned if he was going to playact like he was some kind of king. The Alliance didn't have monarchs. The Palatian people were warriors, first and foremost, and the office of Imperator was a rank, not a royal title.

A rank he hated. If he longed for anything through the fatigue that ruled his life now, it was to return to his old place as Commander Maximus…or better still, to retire to his estates and pass the torch to the next generation. But that wasn't a choice. The disease Calavius had spread had not been eradicated, and all around him, Vennius could see signs of decay, indications that the old Alliance, the Palatian warrior culture that had been his

66

life, was slipping away. Duty demanded that he stand where he was, that he do all he could to stop the deterioration. And duty came before desire.

The men and women serving him were still warriors, most of them at least. But much of the old selflessness was gone, the dedication to duty above all else that was the heart of the "way" slipping into the past. He saw Calavius's vanity repeated all around him, if in lesser degrees, and he chafed at how his people, especially those who'd fought at his side in the civil war, seemed to have lost something.

"Your Supremacy, I urge you to consider this commitment to the war between the Confederation and the Union. We have never aligned ourselves with outside powers, and now, to commit so much of the fleet to a distant front, and a conflict that cannot benefit us in any meaningful way, seems…" The officer paused. Vennius suspected he was looking for a more diplomatic word than "foolhardy." "…a matter of some concern."

Vennius inhaled, and then he quietly exhaled. It wasn't the disagreement with his policy that troubled him, it was the mealy-mouthed way his subordinate, Clevus Daggus, a Commander-Altum of high rank, had expressed it. Respect was one thing, but a failure to discuss military matters openly sapped the strength that had led to sixty years of continuous victory.

"It should be a…matter of concern, as you put it, Commander-Altum." Vennius spoke softly, suspecting his efforts to hide the crushing exhaustion inside him were less than totally successful. "The fleet was very badly damaged during Calavius's rebellion…" He refused to call it a "civil war." He felt that instilled some level of legitimacy in his old friend's actions, and what remained of his own determination knew he could never allow that. Not if he was going to have any chance of preserving the Alliance he'd served for so long. "…and the level of commitment to support the Confederation leaves us…thinly stretched…at home."

"Perhaps we should recall part of the fleet, Your Supremacy. At least until we are able to replace the losses from the recent conflict."

"That will be years, Commander. I appreciate the need to defend Palatia and the Alliance, but there is no one on our borders who would dare to attack us." Vennius winced slightly at the hubris in his own words. He imagined how he would have castigated one of his subordinates for that kind of overly confident statement. It was far from a complete truth to suggest that he, too, wasn't concerned about the state of the Alliance's home defenses, that he didn't worry that the Krillians or the Unaligned Systems might choose now to seek their vengeance. But that changed nothing. He didn't have a choice. He'd sent more than half the fleet to the front lines of the Confederation-Union war, and he'd do it again if he had to. Duty and honor were inseparable, at least as far as Tarkus Vennius was concerned, and his word was like granite.

"Perhaps we can accelerate production and pull back even a small part of the fleet, Your Supremacy." That was Commander-Altum Cilian Globus. Globus was an old stalwart, a man who followed the way with all the fervor Vennius always had. *Even Globus...*

Vennius slammed his hand down on the table, immediately regretful that he'd allowed his frustration to take control, even for an instant. "Let me make this profoundly clear to all of you. The Confederation sent ships to our aid, even as they faced their own war, a conflict that called for every vessel they had. They sent one of their greatest commanders as well, and brand new ships, fresh from the production lines—combat units they desperately needed for their own fight. We will do no less. To fail them now would bring shame upon us all. It is true, we have not sought out allies in the past, yet we took their aid when it was offered and when we needed it, and there can be no doubt that we would have fallen without it.

"We will do no less than they did. Having taken an ally when we needed help, we will not forsake one when they require our aid. To do so would be a dishonor that would stain Palatia and the Alliance for all time."

The room was silent for a moment. Finally, Globus dared to speak again. "I understand, your Supremacy, and I agree.

I regret my earlier weakness. We must aid the Confederation. But we cannot ignore reality. The most recent reports from the Unaligned Systems, and from the Krillian Holdfast are not encouraging. By all accounts, Union agents are active there, encouraging these disparate powers to join forces, to take the opportunity to invade the Alliance."

"Would they dare?" Vennius felt a wave of Palatian pride, but it quickly faded, leaving in his mind an answer other than the one he wanted. *Maybe.*

"Can we take the chance? Our own weakness aids the Union ambassadors. We do their work for them, allowing them to point in our direction, to show our neighbors just how much of our fleet was lost in the civil war, and how much is now twenty jumps away, on the Confederation-Union border."

"I understand, Cilian. The situation is not ideal. We must do all we can to defend ourselves against any neighbors encouraged to attack us. And yet, we must do so without abandoning who we are. I will not forsake my promise to the Confederation, nor to Tyler Barron, who was true to his word to me." Vennius saw the restlessness among his officers, and he held up his hand, stilling them instantly. "However, I will not ignore the threats we face. I shall prioritize all new construction with projected completion dates of one-half year or less, diverting resources from less complete projects. Further, I shall activate the remaining ships of the mothballed reserve and recall warriors from the retired list to help crew them."

Vennius felt a surge of energy. It always made him feel better to actually *do* something rather than just planning and talking. "I will also issue a decree accelerating Citizenship for all Probationary-Aspirants who serve in any pending conflicts… and Pleb families of good records will be allowed to advance to Probationary status by providing recruits to the service."

He could tell the other officers were surprised. The way was a model of duty and service, but it had always had somewhat of a dark side, a rigid caste system that relegated various residents of the Alliance to lesser statuses than the Palatian Citizens and Patricians. Vennius was devoted to the way, but he also recognized the ways in which it might change. *Had* to change, if the Alliance was to prosper.

"Are you sure about this, Your Supremacy?" No one seemed to have the stomach to challenge Vennius outright, and he knew that Globus spoke for them all with his question.

"We must decide, my fellow officers, who we will fight in the future. Outsiders? Enemies? Or our own people? The way has inspired us for sixty years, but even that must change. We must retain the best elements of the way…duty, courage, hard work, but we must also allow it to evolve, so that it may survive. So that we may survive. We have just endured a struggle against our own people, one begun not by rebelling Plebs or invading foreigners, but by our own Palatian brethren. If warriors like Calavius and those who followed him are capable of such treachery, what future unrest do we court by making the lowest levels of our society into enemies, by denying them any path to Citizenship?"

He looked out at his officers, at the stunned looks on their faces. He'd been thinking about this for some time, but he hadn't intended to go so far, not yet. "You are concerned, Commander Daggus, are you not, that the Unaligned Systems might join forces against us, that the Holdfast might choose this moment to invade? Perhaps you are correct. How, do you imagine, would the Plebs on our subject worlds react? Would they fight off the invaders, with farm implements and kitchen knives if need be, as no doubt, the residents of Palatia would? Or would they welcome these enemies with open arms, as liberators? If we deny any hope to those we rule, we make our own enemies. For sixty years, we have been warriors only, courageous, strong…but now the Alliance must move forward, it must become a true nation, one supported by its people—all its people. One with allies and interstellar relationships. One that honors its commitments."

Vennius could feel the shakiness in his gut, the uncertainty at the future he was laying out as he spoke. His words were his own, the thoughts ones he genuinely believed, but a lifetime of culture and indoctrination fought against each word.

"We must prepare to meet any enemy, to use what remains here to us to endure what challenges come, to defeat any adversary that dares to move against us. We must embrace the best of old Palatia, of the Alliance we have known, and take it boldly into the future."

Vennius sat where he was, still now, silent. He panned his gaze across the room, looking at the faces staring back at him. Some looked intrigued, others confused. His own mind was clearer than before. He knew what he had to do, though he didn't like much of it. But liking it was irrelevant, and he knew what he had to do.

*   *   *

"Great and Terrible Krillus, I thank you for this audience." Desiree Marieles stood below the large pedestal, looking up at the man seated on the golden throne. Krillus was a disappointment, visually at least, as she'd discovered on her first visit months before. He was small in stature, far from the image of the great conqueror his minions tried so hard to project. *Of course, that conqueror was his great-grandfather. The line has clearly withered since then.*

Even Krillus I had been overestimated, she suspected. The Holdfast was a middling power at best, a collection of systems that had enjoyed some martial success against weaker neighbors several generations back, before they ran into the larger and more capably-led Alliance. Marieles imagined it owed its continued existence more to the fact that the Palatians had enough other enemies to keep them busy over the past half-century or so, though no doubt Krillus had convinced himself it was fear of his fleets and armies.

"I am pleased to welcome you again into my presence, Ambassador Marieles. Your beauty graces my Court."

She held her gaze steady, not a trace of the disgust she felt showing through the impenetrable façade of her face. Sector Nine training covered many areas, but deception was near the top. The fool had a weakness for attractive women, that was almost certainly why she'd been selected for the mission. Desiree Marieles was a skilled agent, and an assassin of no slight accomplishment, but she was also a very attractive woman.

She stared at the pathetic excuse for a monarch and his grotesque smile. The fool must have had hundreds of women—most yanked from their homes in the middle of the night and dragged to his chambers—yet he fell into the weakness of wanting a foreign diplomat. *Perhaps even badly enough to start a war for me...*

She was repulsed by the pathetic fool, a juvenile caricature squandering the power of his grandfather's throne, but that wasn't important. She'd give him a tumble if that was all it took to bring the Krillians in against the Alliance. She'd always used any weapon at her disposal to get the job done, and she had no regrets. The key mission of her career to date, the one that advanced her to the top ranks of Sector Nine, and the wealth and power that came with it, had been the seduction and assassination of no less than a member of the Presidium. It had been a simple termination with no need to embellish or send any messages, so she'd let him finish first—there was never a time a target's defenses were so down—and then she'd done it quickly, almost effortlessly. She doubted he'd even seen it coming.

She didn't want to kill Krillus, at least not yet, but she knew success in bringing the Holdfast into the war against the Alliance would bring her to the very pinnacle of Sector Nine, within reach of the top job. Gaston Villieneuve wouldn't be such an easy target, and she suspected it would take far more than a spirited roll in the silk sheets to get his guard down, but if he was all that stood between her and that chair...

She forced her focus back to the matter at hand. *You have to get this done before you can worry about Villieneuve's job.*

"You are most kind, Great and Terrible Krillus. May I ask if you have considered my previous request?" She slid slightly to the side, giving Krillus a good view of her outfit. She'd felt a little foolish putting it on. No ambassador she'd ever seen had worn something this form-fitting, at least not outside a fantasy vid, but the way the Holdfast's monarch had stared at her the last time she was there, she was pretty confident it was the way to go. If he was going to undress her with his eyes, she might as well give him a head start.

"I have, Ambassador. I find your proposal intriguing indeed, and yet, I am uncertain. The Alliance is a dangerous enemy to face, even for forces as powerful as my own. I must be certain before I commit."

"Certain?" she said, trying hard not to sound condescending. "Great and Terrible Krillus, the Alliance forces are shattered from their civil war, and most of what remains to them is on the Union border, fighting alongside the Confederation. This opportunity is extraordinary, and it will likely never come again. I urge you once again to move as quickly as possible, to take this chance to outshine even the conquests of your illustrious great-grandfather." She stood there and watched as her words sliced into Krillus. If the Holdfast's ruler had one weakness besides women, it was being compared to his illustrious ancestor.

"What do you offer in support? For it is no secret that you seek such action on my part to aid your own war effort."

Marieles was surprised at the response. Perhaps Krillus wasn't quite as much of a fool as she'd thought. She'd considered him easily manipulated, but now she got the impression that he had already been considering action against the Alliance.

It was a weak point for her, one she'd dreaded. She had expected Villieneuve to send her to this wretched frontier with piles of currency, a treasure fit to entice a new ally. But she had almost nothing to offer. A few weapons shipments perhaps, mostly obsolete ordnance that had to travel so far from the Union, it wouldn't even arrive until after the Krillians had launched their attack. She had no significant sums of money. It had only been that moment, when Villieneuve had denied her the funds she'd requested, that she realized just how dire the situation was in the Union.

"I offer ongoing friendship, Great and Terrible Krillus, an alignment of the Union and the Holdfast that will strike terror in our enemies' hearts. And weapons, high tech ordnance to upgrade your military, to make you the great power in this sector." She paused for an instant and then added, "The *undisputed* great power." There was no sense in being careless with language and insulting her host. A lunatic like Krillus could have worked himself into believing nearly anything, including some sense of parity with the—normally—vastly stronger Alliance.

Krillus looked down at her, silent for a moment. I find your offer intriguing, Ambassador. I think we should discuss this further. Over dinner, perhaps?"

She didn't like the idea of being trapped alone with Krillus, not before she got something more definitive from him. She was willing to do whatever was necessary to see her mission to success, of course, but she wasn't about to give this pig anything for free.

She glanced quickly to each side. Krillus's guards lined the walls. She didn't think her host would risk war with the Union—or Sector Nine's retribution—by abducting an ambassador and forcing himself on her if she refused his invitation. The guards were armed, of course, but she suspected they were there mostly for show…and if they did come at her, they were in for quite a surprise. They'd overwhelm her, almost certainly—there were just too many of them—but not before more than one of them died.

She nodded her head slightly. "Of course, Great and Terrible Krillus. I would be honored." There was nothing to be gained by refusing the invitation. She was fairly certain he wouldn't force himself on her…and completely certain that if he did, in the privacy of his bed chamber and not the throne room full of guards, he would die.

"I shall send my chamberlain to bring you at the seventh hour, Ambassador. I look forward to a…most productive…conversation."

"As do I, Great and Terrible Krillus."

Chapter Ten

"I think I'll call it an early night, Andi. I've got a long day tomorrow. The admiral isn't up to full duty yet, and I'm afraid it's all falling on me."

Lafarge sat at the small table in her quarters, her eyes moving from the dinner Barron had hardly touched to his body, tense, standing next to the table looking as though he'd rather be anywhere else.

"If that's what you want, Tyler." Her words were carefully spoken, her tone intended to let no sign of any emotions she felt slip out. She and Barron had always had an odd relationship. They were both loners, at least in terms of romantic liaisons, and though she was fairly sure Barron felt the same way about her that she did about him, she had never fully adapted to the idea of an ongoing relationship. She doubted he had either. But still, the discomfort he clearly felt around her right now was upsetting, all the more so because of her own anger with herself for allowing it to bother her.

"It's not what I want..." He paused. He was looking in her general direction, but he was clearly avoiding her gaze. "I

75

wanted to ask you…are you planning to leave Grimaldi soon?" He hesitated again, clearly uncomfortable. "I just mean, I know Gary Holsten completed your contract…"

A nice way of saying "paid you off."

"Most of your crew seem to have made arrangements, or are getting ready to leave."

How would you know that unless you checked? Nice to see you prepped for this little…whatever this is.

"I know you've always wanted to retire to some pleasant world."

"Are you trying to get rid of me, Tyler?" Her tone was more pointed than she'd intended.

"No, of course not. It's just that I'm going to be very busy…and I'll probably be leaving Grimaldi for a while. Fleet exercises."

I hope you're a better liar than this with other people…

"So…"

"So, you want me to leave? If that's what this is, Tyler, all you have to do is say it." She was getting angry, even as she tried to hold it back. She hadn't been able to stop Barron from getting to her, from pulling strings no one else had ever been able to pull, but she'd be damned if she would show him that.

"No, I just thought…" Barron hesitated now. "Well, to be honest, I have wanted to discuss something. You've finished your work, but mine is still going on, and it will be as long as the war continues. I've enjoyed the time we've spent together, but…"

"Fine, Tyler. I agree. It was fun, but it's time to move on." She looked right at him. "And, you're right about tonight. I've got some business to attend to tomorrow myself, and I think it's time to get some sleep."

Barron stood where he was, looking troubled. "Andi…"

"No worries, Tyler. I hope your exercises go well. We're certainly all counting on you all to end this war as soon as possible." Then, a few seconds later, "Goodnight, Tyler."

Barron looked like he might say something else, but finally, he just nodded and said, "Goodnight, Andi." He turned and walked toward the door, opening it and slipping out into the corridor.

Lafarge sat where she was, not sure if the anger and frustration she felt were stronger than the hurt. She detested the weakness in her that made her care so much what Barron did or said, and also the foolishness that let his words cut at her even when she was so certain he was full of shit. He wanted her off Grimaldi, but she was pretty sure it had nothing to do with his being tired of her.

The war situation is worse than general knowledge suggests. He's worried about Grimaldi falling.

She pondered the image of Barron as he spoke to her, the tension she could see as though it was written across his face. *No, it's more than just that. There would be plenty of warning and time to try to chase me off Grimaldi if the enemy was coming.*

She sat for a few minutes longer, thinking. And then, suddenly, she knew.

He's going to do something crazy…and he doesn't think he's coming back.

*   *   *

"Commander…I mean, Captain, Fritz. It's good to see you."

"As it is to see you, *Commander* Billings." A brief silence. "But, perhaps we can dispense with the extended pleasantries and get right to the matter at hand."

Billings nodded, suppressing a grin. Fritz hadn't changed, and that realization suddenly told him he should have eaten before he'd come, because he was likely in for a fourteen-hour shift now, minimum.

Fritz extended her arm, gesturing toward a large cylindrical object, a little over three meters tall and about a meter in diameter. "This is the primary unit of this piece of old tech. It is…" She stopped abruptly. "Everything you see here is classified at the highest levels, Commander. Understood?"

"Yes, Captain. Of course." *Wow, this is serious.* Of course, he'd known something big was up when he'd gotten the recall, no, the *request to volunteer*, to serve once again aboard *Dauntless*.

"This device, and the several you see laid out around it, are all part of an old tech device, a stealth generator. It was found in the Badlands, and Grimaldi's research teams have spent the last six months trying to figure it out." She extended her arm, handing a medium-sized tablet to Billings. "These are their research notes." Her voice was dismissive, as if it was incumbent on her to display at least some disrespect for the base's engineering teams. Still, she followed it up with, "They have made some progress...a considerable amount, actually. But, now, we've got to finish it, and we've got to do it quickly. A week, two at most, and then we've got to get it installed in *Dauntless* and tested."

The recall began to make sense to Billings. Then, he realized... *Dauntless* was going out on a mission, mostly likely a very desperate mission, one where staying hidden was imperative. "Captain, I'm sure we can figure this thing out, but in a week? Even with the whole team back together, that seems almost an insane time frame...especially if *Dauntless*'s survival is going to depend on this thing functioning."

"It will, Commander. Very much so. Not only on its functioning, but at the critical stage, on its operating without any flaws or glitches of any kind."

Fritz's words hit him hard, and he realized immediately she wasn't exaggerating a bit. *Great, the mission depends on getting an ancient hunk of technology functioning in a week...and keeping it in perfect operation.*

Or we'll all die.

No, worse than that. The recall of the old crew, Barron's reassignment to lead his old ship, the ridiculous time schedules...the outcome of the war was on the line somehow. That was the only thing that made any sense.

"Well, Captain...I guess we'd better get started then, don't you think?"

He stared at the strange device in front of him, almost all his attention focused there. He had just one other thought, and though it consumed only the tiniest bit of his intellect, it was a persistent one nevertheless.

I really *should have eaten before I came here.*

*   *   *

"I think that's the plan. We get there ahead of the fleet, go through the gate alone and make a rapid course change as soon as we're through. Once we're in, and away from the gate, the fleet will follow. With any luck, the enemy's attention will be fixed on Admiral Striker and the main force. We're mostly counting on the stealth generator, but anything that takes enemy eyes off us is a good thing." Atara Travis was leaning forward over the map table, staring intently at the layout of the Formara System, more commonly known as the "Bottleneck."

"I think so. We've looked at it ten different ways, and I think that's it." Barron replied, the tension in his voice clear. It was obvious Barron was edgy about the mission, especially now that he'd studied it in detail. But there was something else bothering him.

"Atara, I was giving this some thought. Perhaps you should stay at Grimaldi. If this doesn't work, the fleet's going to fall back here, and Admiral Strik…"

"Forget about it, Tyler." Travis had never directly disobeyed one of his orders before, but this time she was adamant. "*Dauntless* is *my* ship now, and don't you forget it. I'm just loaning you your old chair."

"Atara, I was just thinking…"

"I know what you were thinking, and I love you for it, but if you're going on this insane mission, if the whole crew is going, I'll be damned if I'm staying behind. You're going to need every edge you can get, and I daresay we've been a good team for a long time. I think we have one more in us, old friend. Don't you?"

Barron hesitated for a moment, and then he nodded. "I'm sorry, Atara. Of course, you should be there."

"Then why don't we reinstate all our old habits, and you tell me what's really bothering you? I know you're worried about this mission. You'd have to be insane not to be. But that's not all that's on your mind…I'd bet my last credit on that."

Barron sighed hard, then he looked up at her. "It's Andi. I… broke it off with her. I told her I wanted her to leave Grimaldi."

Travis sighed softly. "You're a damned fool, Tyler Barron." She held up her hand just as he looked like he was going to reply. "First, you've got to get this, 'we're not coming back' nonsense out of your head. I'll grant you, the odds look long, but we've been there before, and we've come back every time. This is a dangerous operation, not a suicide mission."

She looked right at him, her stare almost withering. "Second, whatever kind of bizarre relationship you and Andi and your collective neuroses have created, it's pretty clear she has strong feelings for you. Have you met her, Tyler? She's not the type to go crawling off into the sunset because you hurt her feelings. And this, 'I'm Tyler Barron, and I'm tying up my loose ends before I go off to die' nonsense has to stop. If you don't think she can see through that as well as I can, you're really blind."

"I just want her to be safe, Atara. If we fail, the enemy's going to come to Grimaldi with the pulsar, and…"

"That's not your call, Tyler. Andromeda Lafarge has been calling her own shots since she was a child. You think she's going to go run and hide on some Core world and nurse her wounded feelings because Tyler Barron told her to? My God, you're like a brother to me, Tyler, but sometimes you can really be an ass."

Barron sat silently for a moment, and then he let out a small laugh. "I guess it's good to have someone who won't hesitate to tell you you're a fool. Everybody should have one of those."

"Well, everybody doesn't, so I guess you're just one of the lucky ones."

"I guess so."

She leaned back and stretched. "I'm not much of a drinker, and I know you're not either, but I heard there are nineteen officers' clubs on Grimaldi. What do you say we go find one and have a couple drinks? Just two old comrades, shooting the shit, so to speak?" She smiled. "It's on me, so there's no threat to the Barron fortune."

Barron returned the smile. "You're on. How can I say no to an old comrade?"

$$* \qquad * \qquad *$$

"This is the third…situation…we've encountered. Three Senators, all with significant financial troubles, all seeming suddenly to be quite flush. Senator Garabrant just purchased a massive estate on Megara, in the Nordlen District."

"*That* had to cost a nice chunk." Gary Holsten looked across the table at his agent. Shane Darvin was one of his most reliable people, and he was inclined to take the agent's concerns seriously. And he had a very clear idea of the cost of real estate in Nordlen. The Holsten family had a property there, one of more than a dozen in various locations throughout the Confederation. Holsten hadn't been there in—*what has it been, fifteen years?*—but he was keenly aware of its value.

"The transaction was complex. Garabrant made considerable effort to hide his involvement, but I was able to cut through it all. He paid fifteen million, five hundred thousand for it, and I haven't found any hint of partners or even debt financing. My best guess is, he bought it free and clear, sir."

"Where did Garabrant get that kind of cash? The reprobate squandered his grandfather's money years ago. He's been teetering on the edge of bankruptcy for at least five years." Holsten was well aware of Garabrant's situation. The only thing that had kept the fool from falling into a financial abyss was Holsten's own willingness to advance just enough cash to stave off disaster…and maintain an influence on the Senator. Holsten had IOUs and secret dossiers on many of the Senators who governed the Confederation, a resource he kept in reserve for desperate situations.

"I don't know, Mr. Holsten, but I knew you'd want a report immediately…and I didn't trust the normal comm channels, even the classified ones. I didn't want to leave Megara, but I figured it was the only choice."

"You did the right thing, Shane. If someone…" *And some-one can only mean Sector Nine.* "…is manipulating the Senate, it's wise to be cautious on communications as well. Who knows what other areas may have been infiltrated." Holsten was frus-trated. He was proud of his own agency, and he knew he had a lot of good people working for him. But Sector Nine was an amazing operation, one vastly larger than his own, with tentacles that reached…well, everywhere. The Union's spy agency had instigated an Alliance civil war, infiltrated the Badlands border in the hunt for old tech, and now it seemed Villieneuve's people were poking around the Confederation Senate.

What are they up to?

He knew politicians were corrupt, almost all of them. But he couldn't imagine many would be ready to completely sell out the Confederation. They had good lives, and most of them were smart enough, at least, to realize they would lose all that if the Union managed to win a complete victory.

Garabrant, Kellerman, Stilson…they're all doves.

He shook his head. The Senators the enemy was targeting were all highly skeptical of the war. Each of them had sup-ported peace talks at every turn, even if the cost of ending the war was ceding systems to the Union. *What is Villieneuve up to?*

"Shane, I need you to get back to Megara. Effective imme-diately, you are in charge of the entire operation."

"Operation?"

"Yes. We're going to expand our surveillance of the Sen-ate. I want every Senator followed. I want all communications monitored. Where there are three, I'm willing to bet there are more. I need to know what's happening."

"Monitoring Senate communications? That's illegal, sir."

"Yes, Shane, it is. But we're up against an organization that has virtually no limits. Sector Nine always gets the better of us, because we're restricted, and they can do whatever they need to do. But this time, there's too much at stake. We can't let them beat us again, not when they're operating this close to the top." Holsten paused. "I can't promise this won't end badly for you, Shane. It could take me down too. But I truly believe we have no choice. Are you in this with me?"

Darvin was silent for a moment—it was probably only a few seconds, but it seemed like an eternity to Holsten. Finally, the agent said, "I'm with you, sir. I understand what is at stake." Darvin took a deep breath. "And I'll be careful."

"You do that, Shane. Be careful." Holsten extended his hand toward the agent. "Be very careful."

Chapter Eleven

Formara System
"The Bottleneck"
Union Year 217 (313 AC)

"I am pleased, Admiral. Your engineers are to be commended. Can I assume we are still on the original schedule?" Villieneuve glared at the officer, even as he praised him. He didn't believe in slacking off on the pressure. Ever.

"Thank you, sir. Yes, we are...ah...close to the original schedule."

"Close?" Villieneuve amused himself at how skilled he'd become at projecting menace through a single word.

Admiral Velites was clearly intimidated, but he struggled to maintain his composure. No fewer than four senior Union admirals, commanders of the fleet, had been removed from command since the war began. Two of them—the lucky ones—had been shot. The other two had just disappeared, and Villieneuve was well aware most people imagined they vanished into some Sector Nine sub-basement. That was technically true, of course, but the two disgraced officers had been dispatched quickly and efficiently, double shots to the head for each of them after brief interrogations. They could have been terminated on their ships more easily, of course, but Villieneuve understood the benefits accrued by the fear Sector Nine projected. Watching a failed admiral executed on his bridge was certainly a powerful message to his successor, but images of torture at the hands of the dreaded intelligence agency, fictional or not, were even better.

"Yes…Minister Villieneuve…there have been several…problems. I have addressed them all, sir, as swiftly as possible…but, I'm afraid they have pushed us back…a week." The officer was sweating. Villieneuve watched a droplet slide from his hairline down the side of his face. "Perhaps two."

Villieneuve sighed. He knew all this, of course. He just wanted to squeeze everything he could from the admiral. The specter of Sector Nine might be enough to turn two weeks into ten days, and he would take anything he could get at this point. The Union was unraveling all around him, even as the massive operation to make the pulsar mobile crawled forward in Formara. The economy was in ruins, worlds were rebelling, the Presidium was restive. He'd hidden as much of it as he could from his comrades on that august body, but there was a limit to the level of disinformation even *he* could spread. There was no time to lose. He had to win the war, and he had to do it now.

"See that it is not two, Admiral." He softened his voice. He knew the power of fear, but he was also well aware it could go too far. Reducing Admiral Velites to a quivering lump wouldn't serve his purpose either.

"Yes, sir. I will do everything poss…I will get it done."

"That's what I wanted to hear, Admiral. Dismissed."

Villieneuve watched as Velites saluted and then scuttled away. The admiral's near-desperation to get out of Villieneuve's presence amused the spymaster. He wasn't sure Velites had the skill or the intelligence he'd have liked to see in his top commander, but he was sure the officer would do everything in his power to avoid failing him. Fear, properly executed, was as much a resource as any other, perhaps even the most useful of all.

He turned and looked through the clear hyper-plastic of the observation deck's hull. He liked this spot. He could only see a few of the fleet's ships from where he stood, and he had a thousand times more data at his fingertips in his office or the control center. But there was something about looking at the actual hardware that would fight the campaign that pleased him. He couldn't see the pulsar from where he stood, but he knew it was out there. Once the work was done on the engines that would drive the weapon forward, the crews would remove the massive superstructures that held it in place. Then, he would form up the fleet, every useful bit of might the Union had left. He'd have preferred to wait for the enemy to attack, but there simply wasn't time. If the war wasn't won—and soon—the enemy wouldn't even have to defeat the Union. It would fall to pieces from the inside.

He was frustrated, and surprised at how difficult it had been to defeat a power with a weaker military, but one with an economic capacity the Union couldn't hope to match. He'd been concerned at the outset, when the decision to invade had been finalized, but he had to admit to himself, he'd been surprised at just how hard the Confeds had fought and how many ships their many industrial worlds had produced.

Oddly, though the last chance to win the war lay firmly in his own hands, he hadn't been one of the Presidium members heavily in favor of launching the attack on the Confederation. He was as aware of anyone else of the disparity in the two economies, the growing problem it represented, and how the Union lost ground with each passing year. There had been strong arguments for war, but he'd been troubled by the failure of the last three conflicts to crush the enemy. None since the first had even been anything close to a victory, and the second had been an outright defeat no matter how much spin was applied to the retelling.

On one level, Villieneuve regretted his acquiescence then, his reluctant decision to support the war party. But even now, after all that had happened, he wasn't sure what else he could have done. If it hadn't been for the softness of the Confederation's population, and their voluntary disarmaments after each war, the enemy would have been out of reach already. There hadn't been any real choice. The Union *had* to expand. It needed resources from conquered planets to sustain its own stumbling economy, and the Confederation had the needed worlds. Villieneuve wasn't sure postponing the showdown would have accomplished anything but increasing the relative power of the Confeds.

But this was the *last* chance for a military victory. He had his operatives working on a peace initiative as a failsafe, but he wasn't sure that would be enough, especially if the Confeds discovered just how dire the situation was in the Union. Without an outright victory, the Union could split apart, as world after world rebelled against the central authority. Even the fear of Sector Nine had a limited effect when starvation was the alternative.

He'd sent agents to the far Rim, to stir up trouble for the Alliance, to attempt to draw away the Confeds' new ally, but that was only a stopgap. He had to make this campaign a success. He had to drive forward, crush the enemy fleets, and bring the superweapon to Megara itself, or at least as deep into the Confederation as he could. Then he could salvage the disaster the war had become.

*   *   *

"That was good, Commander, but there is still room for improvement. Advise all squadron commanders, I want thirty seconds shaved off their scramble times." Jean Turenne's voice was deep, his tone demanding. Turenne ran a tight ship, and he demanded the same effort from his crew that he always gave himself. That had been difficult at first, when his people were used to a more common Union standard of conduct, but they'd begun to adapt, and even to show some growing pride in themselves.

"Yes, sir." Michel Maramont was Turenne's exec. He'd been fairly typical of mid-level Union officers before Turenne arrived, but the demanding CO had pulled the best from within, and Maramont had grown into an effective and capable first officer.

Turenne sat in *Temeraire*'s command chair, staring across the bridge toward his second-in-command. He was bolt upright, looking almost as though he were at attention in his seat. He was aware how uncomfortable it seemed, but it had little to do with his rigid and demanding attitudes. It was the only way he could keep the pain in his back at bay. He'd been wounded in the first battle of the war, and he'd been two years recovering before he'd gotten back into the fight.

His family was a fairly highly placed one, which had aided in getting him the best care available. A first officer in the fleet, which was what he'd been at the time, had a fairly high medical priority rating even without family influence, but not enough to justify two years of specialists and surgeries. His father had pulled some strings, and against all odds—and the predictions of his original doctors—Turenne had returned to duty, along with a promotion to his own command.

His recovery had been miraculous, but it was far from complete. He had at least some pain virtually all the time, and if he slouched at all for any extended period, it was agonizing. But he'd always been tough, and he'd learned to endure, even to excel...his own kind of personal spite at the pain.

He'd made the most of his second chance, and the advance in rank that came with it. Turenne had chafed at the losses the navy had suffered, at the way the Confederation forces consistently outperformed the Union fleets. Confed tech *was* a bit better, and their ships were generally of higher quality, side effects of their economic advantage. But Turenne saw no reason Union spacers had to be inferior to their enemies, and he'd driven his own crew almost to exhaustion, until they operated like razors. *Temeraire* was the best ship in the fleet now, he was sure of that, and one of the few bright spots among Union arms in the war.   He'd put *Temeraire* against any ship the Confeds cared to throw his way, and he was confident his people would come out on top.

"Tighten those formations. Drop intervals to ten kilometers."

"Yes, Captain."

Turenne was watching his fighter squadrons conduct a training exercise. Union ships of the line had enough trouble facing their Confed counterparts, but the fighter battles had been an outright disgrace. The Union had gone into the war with almost double the enemy's squadrons, but the loss ratio had been better than five to one against. The trained pilots who'd been in place at the start of the war were mostly gone, replaced by a fourth or fifth wave of raw recruits. *Temeraire*'s squadrons had been no better when he'd first arrived but they were among the best in the fleet now, if still not a match for the veteran Confed wings.

Turenne thought about the way most Union captains managed their ships, and he felt disgust. They were far too ready to accept mediocre results, and they weren't willing to do the work or to set the example it took to coax excellence from their people. Still, for all his own dedication, he couldn't blame his comrades entirely. There were shortages of everything in the fleet…weapons, fuel, spare parts. Few captains had the luxury of conducting the kind of exercises he did. *Temeraire* wouldn't either, if Turenne hadn't been able to draw on family contacts to get extra shipments of fuel and ordnance.

His fighters looked good…but he knew they could be better. They'd be facing the Confeds again soon, and Turenne couldn't deny the fearsome reputation of the enemy's fighter corps was well-deserved. Confed squadrons had saved their fleets from defeat in more than one engagement in the war, and they'd usually done it despite being outnumbered. He knew *Temeraire*'s four squadrons weren't even close to enough to redress the imbalance, but he was determined that any Confed fighters that came his way would get a nasty surprise. Or, at least a heads up fight.

"Status on weapons system diagnostics?" Turenne had ordered the systems check mostly to keep his engineers busy. When *Temeraire* went into battle, they'd be on damage control duty, where a few minutes, even seconds, could be the difference between victory and death. He wanted them used to hard work and urgency. Driving them hard as they completed routine tests seemed like a reasonable way to keep them up to form.

"Engineering reports four minutes to completion, sir."

"They have three." Turenne held back a smile. Four minutes wouldn't be a bad time, but 'not bad' wasn't what he was after. He believed people could always do better when pressed, and he was determined never to let the pressure off. The men and women he commanded were going into battle, and they all had a better chance of coming back if they were as sharp as he could make them.

"Yes, Captain. Three minutes." A few seconds later. "Engineering confirms, sir. Three minutes to test completion."

"Very well." Turenne sat quietly, enjoying a self-satisfied moment. He knew his crew resented the way he drove them, the harshness of duty on *Temeraire* compared to that on most of the other ships of the fleet. But he didn't care whether they liked it or not. He was going to bring them into this next fight ready for whatever happened.

There was excitement in the fleet about the pulsar, a feeling that the ancient superweapon was going to win the war, almost by itself. Turenne knew the stats, the vast range of the deadly weapon, the incredible advantage it represented, but he was still concerned. The Confeds were *good*...and underestimating an enemy was about the dumbest thing an officer could do. The pulsar was a big advantage, huge perhaps. But the Confeds weren't about to roll over and die because the Union fleet advanced with its great gun in the lead. Sometimes he wondered if he was the only one in the fleet who realized that.

"I want all point defense stations ready, lasers set at one-half percent power. The squadrons are to launch a mock attack on their way back, and I want to see just how well our defensive array can perform."

"Yes, Captain."

Turenne didn't know what was going to happen, but he was sure of one thing. *Temeraire* would be ready.

Chapter Twelve

"Those bags over there, Spacer." Barron gestured toward the two duffels that contained everything he was bringing to *Dauntless*. He'd always been a bit spartan in his lifestyle, but he was traveling especially light this time. He wouldn't need much…whatever happened.

"Yes, sir." The steward reached down and grabbed the two bags, and then he slipped out into the corridor.

Barron had mostly taken Travis's advice to heart and tried to banish the shadow he felt looming over him. But he'd still left behind some correspondence, letters to his cousins, and to the executors who would manage the Barron holdings if he didn't come back.

Who already *manage it all.*

Barron had been in space most of the last twenty years, and in that time, he'd been back to the Barron family offices precisely three times. His cousins were far too typical of scions of wealthy families in the Confederation, and he'd long ago decided nothing good could come from giving any of them any real access to the businesses and investments that formed the basis

91

of the family's wealth. They got their annual allowances, far more than any of them were worth as far as he was concerned, and the professionals took care of the rest. Most of the respect accorded to past members of the Barron clan went to his grandfather, the war hero, but Tyler saved a certain amount of respect for his great-great grandfather, a man he'd never met, but one who'd built most of the family fortune, and who deserved better than to have his spoiled and lazy descendants squander it all.

He stared at the screen on the desk. He'd left a letter for Andi, too. Two letters, actually, and he was still deciding which one to leave and which to delete. The first had been an outpouring of heartfelt emotion, a true love letter in which he told her how he really felt, what she really meant to him. Or, at least what he thought she meant. He'd written that after his mini-binge with Travis, and he'd been just about as drunk as he ever got when he did it. He wasn't sure if the alcohol had been a truth serum or if it had driven him to exaggerate wildly, but when he'd awakened the next morning, he looked at what he'd written with a mix of sincerity and horror. Then he wrote the second letter, one full of polite and respectful apologies for being so hard on her the last time they'd spoken, and ending with a comradely wish that her life be a long and happy one.

He knew the second version was a cop out of sorts, but he wondered if the more emotional note wasn't, to some degree, an act of selfishness. She'd only get it if he didn't come back, and then, what could it do but hurt her more? And yet, didn't she deserve to know how truly important she'd been to him?

He sat quietly for a few minutes longer, and then he made his choice. He still wasn't sure, but he was out of time. He held his finger over the send button for a few seconds, and then he brought it down. *There, decision made.*

He stood up and reached down to his chair, grabbing the uniform jacket he'd hung over the back, just as his AI said, "You have a visitor, Commodore Barron. Commander Jovi Grachus, Palatian Alliance."

Barron was surprised. He hadn't expected anyone. Atara Travis was already aboard *Dauntless*, and Fritzie was busy supervising the final installation of the stealth generator. But Jovi Grachus? He knew she was in command of the fighter squadrons assigned to the Alliance expeditionary force, but he hadn't seen her in months.

"Open," he said, turning toward the door.

Grachus walked through. He could see from her motion, she was a bit tentative, as if she'd been unsure about coming to see him.

"Commodore Barron." She snapped to attention as she entered the room.

"Commander Grachus, welcome. What can I do for you? I'm afraid I'm a little short on time right now." An instant later, he added: "And please, at ease."

Grachus relaxed her posture, slightly. "Thank you for seeing me, sir. I have a request. I wasn't sure if I should approach you with this, but Commander Stockton wouldn't…" She paused.

"What did you need from Commander Stockton?" Barron knew his strike force commander held a grudge against Grachus for the pilots she'd defeated when she'd served on the Red Alliance side in the civil war. Not just any pilots—her kills included Kyle Jamison as well. Barron mourned for Jamison as he did for all those he'd lost in battle, but he knew Stockton and *Dauntless*'s old fighter commander had been like brothers.

"Sir, I don't know the full parameters of *Dauntless*'s mission, but…there are rumors. It seems clear you have some kind of plan to destroy the enemy pulsar, something other than simply launching the fleet toward it. I wanted to…volunteer, Commodore."

"Volunteer?" Barron was surprised. Whatever he'd expected, this wasn't it.

"Yes, sir. I know you've overloaded your fighter bays. I have assembled a picked squadron, the best aces from the Alliance fleet, and with your permission, we wish to join you aboard *Dauntless*."

Barron's first impulse was to politely decline. *Dauntless*'s crew was going to have enough to deal with without worrying about refitting Alliance fighters and managing two types of ammunition and spare parts. Besides, he didn't think getting Tarkus Vennius's top fighter commander killed was the best thing for the nascent Confederation-Alliance relationship. But there was something in her expression…

"Why, Commander? I don't doubt the skill of your pilots or the utility they would bring to our efforts, but the Alliance fleet is part of the operation, so you will be there anyway."

She looked uncomfortable for a moment. Then she said, "Again, with all due respect, I am convinced *Dauntless* will play a special part in the overall campaign. A vital one, if I am not mistaken." She paused. "I have tried to make amends with your officers, Commodore, to express my deep regret at the damage I did through my foolish allegiance to Calavius. It would… mean something…to help your people on whatever mission lies before them. I am certain you face terrible danger, and perhaps if I can help, if my people can save some lives among your crew…I could begin to make that amends."

"That isn't necessary, Commander. You served the Red Alliance because you were deceived, as thousands of others were, and when you discovered the truth, you made it right. Nothing more is required of you."

"I don't mean to disagree with you, sir, but we both know my motivations were affected by another factor, one for which I must accept responsibility. My lust for revenge against your ship, against you, was unjust. Katrine Rigellus was my closest friend, but you and your people did only as you had to do."

"As did you during the civil war." Barron could see the deep regret Grachus felt, and he understood. His own intervention into the Alliance civil war, the aid he'd led to support Vennius had served as much the same to him, salving the guilt he felt for killing Commander Rigellus. He knew Stockton would have a fit, and he still worried about the disruption the Alliance ships would cause. But he also knew he couldn't refuse. "Very well, Commander. But we're leaving in less than two hours, so you don't have much time to get your people over to *Dauntless*."

"Thank you, sir!" She looked like she wanted to give him a hug, but she snapped back to attention instead. "My people are

all on standby. We will be on *Dauntless* in an hour." She gave
him a crisp salute—a Confederation one, and not an Alliance
one, he noticed—and then she spun around on her heels and
marched back out into the hall.

Barron sighed softly. He wasn't sure how he was going to
tell Stockton. But first, he had to make some room in *Dauntless's*
packed bays.

He walked over to the comm unit and dialed up *Dauntless's*
command line. "Atara, Tyler here. I need you to reassign the
Red Wasps to one of the other battleships. We've got some…
guests…coming, and we've got to make room.

*   *   *

"I hope this works, Van." Gary Holsten was sitting next
to his friend, the two of them in an apparent competition for
the grimmest expression. "Tyler Barron is the best we have,
and there's no question of what that ship and crew of his have
managed to do…but the stakes have never been higher. We've
reviewed Stockton's scanning data from his last run, and there's
no question. They're building a mobile system for the pulsar,
and they're damned close to done with it. If Barron isn't able to
destroy that thing…" He let his words trail off.

"I know, Gary. I've tried to come up with another way—
any way—but there simply isn't one. The pulsar will obliterate
every ship in the fleet before we get into range. I hate the idea
of sending Tyler and his people right past the Union fleet and
into the maw of that monster, with nothing but some ancient
artifact to keep them from being obliterated. But what choice
do we have? If they manage to get that pulsar here, they'll blast
Grimaldi to scrap. We can try to hold them up at the transit
points, but you know as well as I do, that's a losing game."

"So, you command the entire fleet, and I have all the
resources of Confederation Intelligence at my fingertips, and all
we can do is hope Tyler Barron and his crew can pull a miracle
out of thin air."

"Yes, more or less." Striker was silent for a moment. "If

Dauntless fails…" He hesitated again, knowing full well Holsten was as aware as he was that would mean the old battleship had been destroyed. "…I'm still going in with the whole fleet."

"You don't stand a chance, Van. We just discussed the simulations. You'd need a hundred more battleships than you have just to get within range and have a chance of taking that thing out…and that doesn't even factor the Union fleet into it."

"The equation is the same here. The pulsar outranges Grimaldi's heaviest guns. Other than adding a few hundred fighters to the mix, the fortress does nothing for us. It's the same in either spot, and all things being equal, I'd prefer to make my final stand on the enemy's ground."

Holsten nodded. "I understand, Van. I was going to go with you, not that I'd add anything to the mix, but I just…wanted to be there." A pause. "But Sector Nine is up to something back on Megara. I don't know what, but I have to get to the bottom of it. You're leaving first thing in the morning anyway, so I ordered by ship prepped for departure within the hour."

The two men sat quietly for a few minutes. Then, Holsten got up, followed immediately by Striker. They stood facing each other for a moment, and then they shook hands, wordlessly. Holsten knew the odds were good he was saying goodbye to his friend. If the fleet didn't manage to destroy the pulsar, he was sure of one thing. Admiral Striker wouldn't be back. None of the fleet would. The future would be decided in the Bottleneck.

Gary Holsten's biggest regret was that he couldn't be there.

*   *   *

"What the hell are you doing here?" Stockton's voice was raw, his anger utterly apparent.

Jovi Grachus had been walking down the corridor, but now she stopped and turned to face her Confederation counterpart. "Commander Stockton…Commodore Barron approved the transfer of a handpicked Alliance squadron to aide you in the destruction of the pulsar." Her tone was soft. She was clearly trying to avoid any sort of provocation.

But Stockton didn't need to be provoked. The sight of her, especially wandering *Dauntless*'s hallways, was enough. *Dauntless* had been Jamison's ship, especially right there in fighter country. By God, she still was his ship, and there was no place aboard her for the enemy who killed him.

"No. No way. I know you've managed to work your way into the good graces of Commander Timmons and Commander Sinclair, but I want you to understand right now…that does *not* extend to me, and it never will." He turned and waved his hand through the air. "You see these corridors? Kyle Jamison used to walk through them all the time. You know Kyle…or at least the plasma cloud that you left of him."

"That is why I am here, Commander, why I assembled the squadron. I cannot undo what happened, I cannot bring back Commander Jamison, but I can help his comrades. I know we can help. Perhaps we can even save the lives of some of your pilots. From what I have heard of him, I believe he would have considered that a fitting testament."

"I don't need you telling me what Kyle Jamison would have thought." Stockton's rage surged to a new level. How dare this…*enemy*…tell him how Kyle would have felt about anything.

"I meant no offense, Commander…only that I wish to do what I can."

"If you want to do something, go. Get off this ship, and take your pilots with you."

"Commodore Barron approved our transfer. We are here under his orders."

"Yeah, well we'll see about that." Stockton walked to a comm unit on the wall, about two meters from where he'd been standing. "Get me the Commodore," he said brusquely. "This is Commander Stockton."

"I'm sorry, Commander, but Commodore Barron is currently in conference with Captain Travis."

"Tell him I need to see him right…as soon as possible."

"Yes, Commander."

He slammed his hand against the button next to the unit, shutting it off. He glared again at Grachus. "Don't get too comfortable, Commander." Then he turned and walked down the corridor, the sound of his footsteps echoing in the confined space.

Chapter Thirteen

The Krillian Hall
Planet Centara
Volgus System
Year of Krillus 71 (313 AC)

"You are very persuasive, Ambassador Marieles. Very persuasive indeed."

She *had* been persuasive, she was certain about that. Sector Nine training went well beyond weaponry and spying. As far as she was concerned, tradecraft was whatever got the job done, and if bedding the little creep was all it took, then so be it. Though she wasn't sure just what had done the trick. Krillus seemed to enjoy the empty praise she showered on him even more than her...other activities.

"Then you have decided to move against the Alliance?"

"I have. Though I would be more comfortable if your government provided more financial support. From what I have heard, the Red Alliance forces received considerable aid. You have been rather...vague...on this subject, Ambassador. I will need firmer assurances that our Union allies will assist us, both with funds and with supplies."

Yes, and sadly, that fiasco in the Alliance pretty much dried up the well...

"I have already sent an urgent communique back to Montmirail to request that the Presidium authorize greater funding. I can personally guarantee that you will receive all the aid you require." She knew she was full of shit on multiple levels. First, the Presidium had no idea she was dealing with the Krillians at all. And second, Villieneuve had been absolutely clear on one thing before she left. There was no money available, nothing except token amounts, personal gifts for key officials and the like. The kind of flood of cash that the Union had poured into the Alliance was a thing of the past, at least until the Union managed to conquer the Confederation or reorder its finances somehow.

But lying was part of her tradecraft, too.

"We have a tremendous stake in your victory, Great and Terrible Krillus. We are your partners in this endeavor."

"Your assurances are most appreciated, Ambassador. The Holdfast has long needed a partner to aid us in asserting our dominance."

If you were dominant, you wouldn't need aid…

Krillus seemed to enjoy addressing her by her title…her cover title, at that. She'd told him to call her Desiree…considering the direction her tradecraft had taken her, a bit of informality only seemed to make sense. But in public or private Krillus called her "Ambassador" every time he spoke to her.

"I urge you not to wait, Great and Terrible Krillus." That title was really getting old. It was stupid, juvenile…but there was no question the fool enjoyed being called that. "The Alliance forces are battered now, and much of what remains of their fleet is posted far from their space, along the Confederation-Alliance border. That situation will not last. When our war with the Confederation ends, their ships will return…and my intelligence confirms that they are building new vessels at a breakneck pace." That was a lie—sort of, at least. The Alliance *was* trying to build ships as quickly as possible, but their industry and supply chains were in an absolute shambles following the civil war, and from what she'd heard, Vennius was having fits trying to get things operating smoothly again. It would be some time before new Alliance battleships would see service. She doubted the ability of the Krillians to actually defeat even a weakened and distracted Alliance, but anything that occupied the Confederation's new ally was worthwhile.

"I have no intention of waiting, Ambassador. I am Krillus, the lord and master of all space. When I choose to strike, I do so with blinding speed and overwhelming force."

"So I have heard, Great and Terrible Krillus. Your reputation extends as far as Montmirail and the halls of the Presidium." Actually, just about all she'd heard of in the way of military exploits was Krillus sending his fleet to put down a rebellion on one of his farming worlds. By all accounts, the rebels were armed with agricultural tools and a few ancient guns, and yet they'd sent Krillus's soldiers fleeing back to their orbiting troopships. In the end, the great "conqueror" had ordered the rebel world nuked from orbit and declared the whole thing a glorious victory.

The Alliance warriors are going to tear his people to shreds when they concentrate. But they will need to deploy forces to do it, and those ships will have to come from the front.

If luring the Krillians into a war they couldn't win was a way to weaken the main Confederation defensive line, so be it.

*   *   *

"This is the third report of activity along the Krillian border, Your Supremacy. We can no longer ignore the threat. We must respond immediately." Cilian Globus was clearly concerned about the scouting report. Vennius had rarely seen the normally calm and meticulous Commander-Altum so agitated. But he understood, and, truth be told, he felt the same way.

The Alliance was weakly held. Its fleets had been ravaged in the desperate fighting between the Gray and Red factions, and even the reconciliation and re-amalgamation of the two sides left strength levels lower than they'd been in forty years. Then, Vennius had dispatched more than half the fleet—the better half in terms of ships and crews—to the Confederation, to honor his promise to Tyler Barron. That was fully in accordance with the 'way,' at least as that Palatian code of conduct was evolving as things moved into an era of cooperation with other nations.

"I, too, am concerned, Commander. I am reluctant, however, to divert significant forces from our other frontiers. We have many enemies. To overreact to a perceived threat from one is to expose ourselves to another." Vennius hated feeling so weak. Palatian culture was almost entirely based on maintaining strength. It had derived from the shame of a people who had been held as slaves by offworlders for a century, and Vennius still felt the calling deep inside him, despite his recognition of the need for change.

"It is true that we are surrounded by potential foes, Your Supremacy, yet I daresay many fear us far too much to risk our wrath." Vennius sighed softly, trying to keep it to himself. Instilling terror in its neighbors had been deliberate Alliance policy for fifty years, but now he saw the other side of that dynamic. Hatred was fear's companion, and he was less willing to ignore other threats than Globus.

"We need better information, Commander. We must know if the Krillians are truly preparing for war, or if they are just posturing." There were ways to uncover such information—supply manifests, internal ship movements, alert levels—but once again Vennius realized the folly in his people's disdain for espionage. The Alliance had an intelligence service, of course, but careers of that sort were considered mildly shameful, and the spy agencies always struggled to attract the best and most capable recruits.

"Agreed, Your Supremacy…yet, I still urge you to consider some level of strengthening of the border patrol forces. We have three systems on the Krillian frontier and, while all of them are at least moderately fortified, they lack significant fleet support."

Vennius knew his officer was right. He'd deployed most of the ships remaining in the Alliance to the garrison the more recently-acquired planets and to patrol the borders with the Unaligned Systems, with whom the last several wars had been fought. The Krillian border had been calm for thirty years or more. It *was* weak. But Vennius didn't know where he would get the ships to reinforce it.

"I agree with your assessment, Commander. Unfortunately, I do not see where we can find the forces for an increased deployment, not without creating another weak point elsewhere."

Globus hesitated for a few seconds. Then he said, "Perhaps we should recall ships from the expeditionary force." Another pause. "Not all, of course. Honor demands we stand by our new allies. But perhaps we could reduce our commitment by a moderate amount."

Vennius shook his head. "No, Commander. The Confederation was in far greater danger when we faced the rebellion of the Red faction, and yet they sent us their best commander and newest warships. I will do no less."

Globus looked uncomfortable. He seemed like he was going to respond, but he remained silent.

"You may speak freely, Commander. You are a courageous and honorable man, and should always feel free to say anything to me."

"Yes, Your Supremacy…it is just that…" He paused again. "Sir, I am concerned about the forces dispatched to support the Confederation. Honor indeed demands that we support them, and yet, I can't help but think…" His words trailed off into silence.

"Continue, Commander."

"Well, sir, we have had reports that the Confederation is about to launch an attack against the enemy pulsar…and other rumors that the Union is close to developing a system to move that weapon. Either way…can we leave our ships to be lost in a suicidal battle, one with no real hope of victory?"

Vennius understood Globus's discomfort. His concerns could be perceived as cowardice of a sort. But the Imperator had known the commander for decades, and the last thing he would call Cilian Globus was a coward.

The Imperator didn't reply, not right away. The way demanded honor, and to falter in support of the Confeds now would be a terrible blight. And yet, no tenet of the way was more sacred than the defense of the homeland. The words "never again" were sacred to the Palatian people, and he could imagine no worse failure, no greater crime, than for an Imperator to stand by and allow the Alliance to be endangered from outside.

"We are Palatians, Globus. I do not accept that we must choose between endangering the Alliance or failing in an honor debt. We will mobilize every vessel that can fly…damaged units awaiting repair, units from the mothballed reserves, even private ships of the great families, anything that can carry a weapon. And let the word go out…all Palatians are called to arms. The retirees are already reporting for duty. Let us find ships for them to fly. Let us create fleets as if from nowhere. The Alliance will stand, Cilian, not because we recall our newest and best ships, but because we are Palatians, all of us…and no enemy can overcome us, not as long as we remember who we are."

Globus looked encouraged, and Vennius knew his words had served their purpose. He believed them himself, to an extent. But the doubts and concerns were still there, and he knew, if he was pushed to the last recourse, he would have to reconsider pulling ships from the forces sent to aid the Confederation.

If fate forced him to choose between sources of shame, he would take disloyalty and failure to honor a debt to an ally, he supposed. What he would not, *could not*, do was become the Imperator who lost the Alliance, whose leadership brought his people back to bondage and misery.

*   *   *

"You see, Ambassador? I am a man of my word. The might of the Holdfast is with us, and the border lies just ahead. It is time…time to embark on our glorious conquest." Krillus and Marieles were alone, or as alone as anyone ever got with the moderately paranoid monarch. She'd gotten used to having sentries in the room during moments that would traditionally have been more private, and she'd come to realize, whatever she thought of Krillus, his elite guards were well-disciplined…and seemingly utterly loyal.

"It is impressive, Great and Terrible Krillus…" She was having a harder time suppressing her sighs as she addressed him by his title. It seemed particularly ridiculous when the two were… almost…alone, but the Holdfast's absolute monarch seemed to enjoy it, even when his regalia were set aside, and he was covered by no more than a white satin sheet. "…a far greater display of might than I had imagined." His forces were actually a bit disorganized to her eye, but the fleet *was* larger than she'd expected, both in numbers and tonnage. Krillus had always struck her as an utter fool, but now she realized he'd done fairly well at driving his economy to build warships.

"I am pleased you decided to come with the expedition."

"As am I." She hadn't decided, exactly. It had been clear Krillus wanted her to come, and she didn't dare risk upsetting the operation she'd worked so hard to set into motion.

"I feel much better having you close." A pause. "Have you received any update on our aid shipment from the Union? I have taken your word, my dear Ambassador, that it is coming… but I will feel much better when the first ships arrive." There was a hint of menace in his voice, or at least she thought she picked up on that.

"I have not…but that is of no consequence, Great and Terrible Krillus. You will receive all I have promised, and more."

"I am sure I will, Ambassador." Her internal warning system flared up. There was definitely *something* there. Not anger, not exactly…

"Great and Terrible Krillus, apologies for disturbing you…" The voice blared from the comm unit next to the bed.

"Speak, Admiral." Krillus was still staring at Marieles, and again, there was something…different…in his expression.

"We are in position. We can begin transiting at your command."

"Excellent. You may proceed, Admiral. Bring the fleet to battlestations, and begin transit at once."

"Yes, Great and Terrible Krillus."

Krillus smiled at her, but somehow it only made her feel edgier. He stood up, turning toward one of the guards. "My valet…now!"

The sentry nodded, and turned sharply toward the door. He slipped into the next room and returned a few seconds later with a woman carrying an elaborate uniform.

"I must go now, my dear Ambassador," he said, as he gestured to the valet to begin dressing him. "I must lead my forces to victory, as my illustrious great-grandfather did."

"I will come with you…"

"No." His voice had changed again. There was coldness in the single word, strength. "You shall remain here, where you are safe. There is no chamber on this ship better protected than these quarters."

"Great and Terr…"

"I shall send for you if I require your presence…and, of course, you will advise me at once if you receive any updates from Montmirail regarding the promised aid."

She stared at the half-dressed dictator, struggling to keep the surprise from her face. She'd taken him for a fool, the foppish descendant of a long-dead conqueror. But now she saw something different. The fool was gone, to an extent at least, and in its place she saw hints of strength, determination. And a darkness she hadn't noticed before.

"See that the Ambassador is safe, and that she receives any food or drink she requests."

She watched Krillus speaking to the guard, while the valet slipped the elaborately-decorated coat over his shoulders. As she listened, she realized she had underestimated her mark.

"The ambassador is to have access to me at any time of the day or night if she receives any communiques."

"Yes, Great and Terrible Krillus."

Suddenly, she realized Krillus would not be so easily bluffed. He'd been insistent about the aid shipment—the convoy she knew didn't exist—and now she realized just how serious he was about it. She was unsure, uncertain what to do. A wave of fear crept into her thoughts.

She'd come aboard as a foreign dignitary, a spy, perhaps even a courtesan of sorts…but now she realized she was none of those things.

She was a prisoner.

Chapter Fourteen

Priority One Communique

General Lisannes, please be advised that I am en route to your sector at maximum possible speed. We will discuss strategies for dealing with the disturbances on Barroux and the other worlds of the sector when I am there. Under no circumstances are you to undertake any operations prior to my arrival. – Ricard Lille, Special Governor, Barroux Sector

In Planetary Orbit
Barroux, Rhian III
Union Year 217 (313 AC)

"General, all ships report ready to commence assault." The aide stood at attention, his combat fatigues neatly pressed and spotless, despite being crammed under his body armor. Emil Lisannes was a stickler for detail, the kind of officer who would carry around a white glove to conduct spot inspections on unsuspecting subordinates. His officers knew that well, and they made sure they were the image of military perfection whenever they entered his premise. Even right before a combat drop.

To be fair, Lisannes's forces were sector security battalions, hardly real soldiers...and they certainly weren't Foudre Rouge. But the general, assigned to such a backwater post after even his well-connected family had been unable to extricate him from his third military debacle, was sure they were more than enough to handle a bunch of factory workers turned into jumped up rebels.

"Very good." Lisannes paused, his eyes darting down to the tablet in his hands. "One more thing, Captain." He took a deep breath, rereading the communique from Ricard Lille. Then he handed the tablet to the officer. "You didn't receive this until we had already landed." He stared at the captain. "Do you understand?"

The aide looked back, clearly nervous. "Yes, sir. Of course, sir."

Lisannes nodded. "Then let's get this started. I want the landings hitting ground at planetary dawn over Barroux City. By nightfall, I want these traitors in custody…or face down in ditches."

"Yes, sir," the aide responded, with rather more enthusiasm than he'd shown for hiding clearly important communications from a senior official.

Lisannes stood still for a moment, his hand resting on the pistol at his side. He'd read the communique half a dozen times. He'd never heard of this Ricard Lille…and he should be familiar, at least, with the name of someone placed highly enough to take sector command. The fact that he had no idea who Lille was suggested one thing. He was Sector Nine. And if Sector Nine was handling the situation in the Barroux Sector, he was in trouble.

Deep damned trouble.

The odds were 50/50 this Lille would have him shot within an hour of arriving. His family wasn't going to be able to save him again, certainly not from Sector Nine. He had only one choice. He had to land his forces and pacify Barroux…in direct violation of Lille's instructions. Maybe, just maybe, that fait accompli would be enough to pull him out of the fire.

"Let's go, Captain. It's time." He reached down and grabbed his helmet from the table. Then he walked across the room, toward the door.

*   *   *

"Bring those crates forward, Citizen." Remy Caron stood on the rocky plain, surrounded by wreckage and debris. He'd ordered every building within five kilometers of the compound destroyed, leaving the last remaining stronghold of Union power on Barroux standing alone, exposed, a shard of defiant stone and steel, stark against the faint predawn light.

"Yes, Remy." The rebel forces—he supposed they were all rebels now—had no real organization, no ranks or titles save for the term "Citizen" they used to address each other. But Remy was one of the movement's leaders now, through a sequence of events he still couldn't fully understand. He'd resisted the responsibility at first, but then he'd come to like it, even to crave it. He'd only wanted to secure a reasonable future for his family, but now he found himself consumed with rage at the Union officials, at the hell they had inflicted on the people of Barroux for almost two centuries.

"We're going in, and I want the teams to bring those crates with us." The boxes contained explosives, gleaned from one of the mines near the capital city. He'd taken charge of gathering supplies, and he'd dispatched teams throughout Barroux City and the surrounding area. They'd found weapons abandoned by panicked security forces, heavy industrial equipment with considerable military potential, vehicles, food. Vast quantities of food, stacked up in warehouses, set aside for the use of government officials or prepped for transport to the military. The sight of box after box of meat, vegetables, grains—all drawn from the farms south of the capital—enraged him. He thought of the meager rations assigned to his family, of his daughter looking up at him with tears in her eyes as she told him she was hungry. And every memory drove him harder, made it easier for him to accept the responsibility that had found him.

It wiped away the hesitancy, too, the guilt he'd felt at first for killing those who stood in the way. Now, the death cry of every Union security soldier was a balance for his daughter's tears, for the sobs of every worker mourning a husband, wife, brother, sister, mother, father, dragged away in the night by Sector Nine.

He'd launched two attacks against the compound, and both had been bloodily repulsed. The security forces inside knew they were fighting for their lives. They'd seen what had happened to their comrades, shot down in the streets, and sometimes torn apart while they were still alive, mangled by the enraged mobs. They would fight to the end. This time Remy would use the explosives. His people would bring down a great section of the wall...and when they got inside, it would be over. The bloodletting would be quick, if terrible, and then Barroux would be free of the Union.

Freedom. He wasn't even sure he knew what it meant. Right now, his ambitions didn't stretch so far. All he wanted was vengeance. Ideals like liberty had been absent for so long, they almost seemed unreal. But he knew one thing. He would die before he would let his family live as they had, little better than slaves.

"We're ready, Remy!" Ami Delacorte jogged up to where he was standing. Delacorte was a slender woman, who looked like just about anything other than a soldier of some kind, but she'd taken to it surprisingly well. Remy knew for certain she'd killed at least three Union security troopers.

He turned and looked out over the open plain toward the Union stronghold. There were bodies everywhere, almost all those of his own Citizen-soldiers lost in the first two assaults. He had twice as many lined up this time, with explosives, and weapons a damned sight more effective than the ones his people had taken into those initial charges.

"All right, Ami...get back to your team. We go in five minutes." He stared at her intently. "Once we start, there's no turning back, no pausing, no stopping to shoot back. We get up there, blow the walls, and get inside."

"Got it, Remy." She sounded enthusiastic, despite the fact that Remy knew she'd been part of at least one of the earlier attacks. She'd made it back, obviously, but half of those who'd started out hadn't. Remy's enthusiasm for the rebellion hadn't diminished, but he was envious of Ami's seemingly sincere urge to jump off. He was going to go this time too, and he was scared to death.

"Citizen Caron!"

Remy turned toward the voice. There was a man approaching, one of his people. He recognized the face, but he couldn't place the name.

"There are ships coming."

"There are what?"

"I was part of the group sent to the main control station at the spaceport. The scanners there…they're automatic. They're picking up ships heading down, dozens of them."

Remy felt his stomach tighten. "What kind of ships?"

"We don't know. Small ones we think, but none of us know how to use the equipment. I'm afraid the normal operators all fled or were…" The man let his voice trail off, but Remy knew very well what had happened to anyone with the slightest taint of being part of the Union governing class.

Small ships? Troop landers.

Remy had known all along the Union would send forces to put down the rebellion, but he'd hoped for a bit longer to prepare. Barroux was an industrialized world, a planet with the resources to defend itself, given enough time.

Time it didn't look like they were going to get.

"Ami," he shouted after his comrade. "Cancel that attack order. We've got other problems coming."

Big problems. I just hope to hell those ships aren't full of Foudre Rouge.

*   *   *

"Group A, keep firing. Group B, forward." Remy looked out from behind the shattered masonry wall toward the vast stretches of concrete surface in front of him, an expanse now pockmarked with craters and covered small gray landing craft. The government forces had elected to come down right onto the spaceport, and their landing areas were tight and cramped together. Perfect killing zones.

Remy hadn't known what a killing zone was a few weeks before, but taking the lives of those he'd decided were his enemies had come easy to him, and directing others to do it was even easier. He didn't know a thing about the stratagems of warfare or infantry tactics, but somehow it just came to him. It seemed to make sense, and he snapped out orders without even thinking about them. Order which seemed to be spot on as often as not.

He hadn't even considered how decisively he'd been commanding those around him, but then he realized they were all doing as he said, following his orders without question and looking to him for more direction. It had been a shock at first, and he'd felt a wave of uncertainty, but that had passed quickly. Somehow, the whole thing felt right, and he began to embrace his command role, however informal it might be in the ranks of the still disorganized rebellion.

He watched half of his people move forward as the other group covered them with their fire. It seemed like common sense to him, the way to advance into enemy fire…but he was the only one. All along the perimeter of the spaceport the former workers, now fancying themselves rebel soldiers, gathered in confused, disorganized masses. Until Remy got there.

He raced from group to group, choosing individuals based on no more than gut feel or the fact that they were close to him. He appointed them section commanders and put them in charge of fifty or sixty of their fellows, something he utterly lacked any real authority to do. But that didn't stop him…and it didn't stop the growing horde of rebels from following his commands.

He'd been stunned as he watched the ships come down, all converging on the single location of the spaceport. He'd never even seen a landing craft before, but somehow, he knew the strategy was…wrong. They should have spread out, forced the defenders to split up into groups, compounding their disorganization. But instead, they landed one next to the other, the troops inside pouring out in jumbled formations only slightly more organized than the rebel defenders firing at them as they formed up.

Remy knew immediately the troops coming out of those ships were not Foudre Rouge. They weren't even second line reserve troops. They had to be local security forces, basically glorified riot police. Foudre Rouge would have been a problem, one he doubted his amateur army could have handled. But the thugs struggling to shake down into battle formation were a different matter entirely.

"Group B, halt and open fire. Group A, forward."

He lunged ahead with the A group as the Bs opened fire. They were almost a hundred meters closer than they had been, and now, even his former factory workers were taking down enemies. Remy had ordered all his people to fire on full auto. It was wasteful of precious ammunition, but the hard truth was, not one in a hundred of them could have hit a building with a single shot, much less a moving soldier. Saving resources for the next fight was a priority well behind surviving this one, and Remy had only too good of an idea what awaited those who'd taken up arms if the Union reasserted control. The whole planet faced a nightmare, but he was one of the leaders…and Union doctrine was all about making examples. He would not only die horribly, but the bastards would go after his family too. The thought of Elisa and Zoe being brutalized, murdered…no, there was only one option.

Win.

Whatever it took.

"A group keep moving past the Bs." He was going to take his people right up to those landers. The troops there were invaders, but his people were defending their homes and families. He knew it would show in the fighting, and he was determined to see every one of the Union vermin wiped off the face of his homeworld.

"A Group, stop. Open fire. Bs, forward." He stood screaming the orders as loudly as he could. He knew the sounds didn't reach all his people, but he could hear others repeating his commands, extending the effective area of his control.

His Citizen-soldiers surged ahead, the firing groups standing firm, the advancing forces pressing on, even as the enemy fire began to rake their line. Dozens fell, but hundreds continued forward. Remy was stunned…and proud. They were scared, he knew, almost certainly terrified, but they were standing, fighting, moving forward. Some broke and ran, of course, ten percent, perhaps twenty…but the rest held, firing their weapons, gunning down the surrounded security forces in their hundreds. And as they killed, their bloodlust increased, a howling, enraged tempest of death, surging over those who'd come to Barroux to put them back in chains.

Remy understood the fear that made some run, but as he watched the rest of his people stay in the fight, his feelings hardened. Those who fled had left their friends and neighbors to fight. They weakened the whole force, and more good men and women would die as a result of their flight. Understanding and sympathy slipped away, replaced by disgust, and then anger.

Now wasn't the time, not until the Union invaders were defeated…but he swore to himself, those who had had fled, who had abandoned their fellows, would pay. They were traitors to the rebellion. They deserved no more pity than the Union thugs who'd come to enslave his people…and they would suffer the same fate.

He felt his feelings hardening, the soft, genial nature that had always been his personality giving way to a hardness, an unyielding force of will, and he quivered with rage.

"Forward, all of you. It's time to finish this. Death to the invaders!" He waved his rifle in the air and then he ran toward the landers.

"And death to the cowards who ran. Death to all traitors!"

Chapter Fifteen

"All stations report condition green, Captain." Travis sat at her old station, feeling somehow as though she was back home, despite the effective demotion it represented. Something also felt right about calling Barron, "captain" again, despite his true current rank. The officers had all met before the fleet set out and agreed they would address each other by the ranks they'd held when Barron had been *Dauntless*'s captain. It was a simple way to avoid having multiple captains floating around the ship, but she suspected some degree of nostalgia, even superstition, was also at play. *Dauntless* had made it back from more than one tight scrape with a Captain Barron at the helm, and the current team at their previous ranks.

"Very well, Commander." Barron's tone was more troubled. Travis knew it had nothing to do with being called "captain" instead of "commodore." It was more likely guilt at banishing her from the command chair, though she'd tried to convince him she was perfectly happy with the situation. Truth be told, though her earlier life had been a relentless climb toward her own command, she'd never been happier or more satisfied, personally and professionally, than she'd been in her years as Barron's exec. She knew she couldn't freeze time. Barron had a

116

great future in the navy's upper echelons—assuming they made it back from this mission—and she, too, had her ambitions. But she knew things would never quite be the same, and she would look back on those years as perhaps the best in her life...despite the danger and pain and hardship of war.

"Captain, Commander Fritz reports she is ready to conduct the final test at your command." The stealth generator had been tested, of course, both in the lab and after its installation in *Dauntless*. But this would be the real moment of truth. If *Dauntless* could change course and elude detection right under the scanners of the entire Confederation fleet, then just maybe the crazy plan had a chance of success.

"Advise Admiral Striker we will be activating the stealth generator in thirty seconds."

"Yes, sir." She leaned forward and sent the message to the flagship. She wasn't surprised Striker was going along with the fleet. He'd had to override regs, of course. His condition was far from one that would normally allow a return to full combat duty, and she suspected the sight of the fleet admiral strapped into his command chair was quite a sight. Striker could walk—a little—but she wouldn't want to bet on him making it more than a few meters without help.

But a fleet is led from the seated position.

Beyond his unquestioned tactical skills, Striker was setting the kind of example that would inspire his spacers. The fleet would do its part, she was sure of that. And if this ancient contraption worked, so would *Dauntless*.

"Activate stealth generator, Commander."

"Activating, sir." She passed the command down to Fritz in engineering.

A few seconds later, the response came back. "Generator on and functioning normally."

She turned toward Barron. "Commander Fritz reports stealth generator activated and fully operational." Travis looked around the bridge. She couldn't feel anything, not that she should have. Fritz's best guess had been the effects of the device would be undetectable to those onboard, and that had been the case in all the previous tests. But she still had a moment of tension, a fleeting worry the artifact wasn't working.

"Bring us up to twenty percent thrust, Commander. Course 320.240.040. Black out all comm."

"Yes, sir. Course 320.240.040, twenty percent thrust. Comm blackout." She relayed the command to the engine room, and a few seconds later, *Dauntless* lurched forward. The impact of 4g thrust hit her for a few seconds, before the dampeners adjusted and restored the feeling of normal gravity.

She stared at her screen, watching the rest of the fleet. *Dauntless* was restricted to passive scanners while cloaked. No one had any real idea whether the active units would give away the ship's location or simply allow other ships to know they were being scanned, but either option was a deal breaker on this mission. *Dauntless* had to slip in and slip out, giving the enemy the least possible indication anything was happening except for the direct frontal assault by the fleet.

Barron watched as his battleship moved slowly on the screen, a complete course change from its previous heading. He sat for perhaps two minutes, and then he turned toward Travis. "Increase thrust to eighty percent, Commander. Vector change to 210.200.180."

"Executing," Travis replied. Again, the increase in thrust manifested as a hard, jerking motion before the dampeners adjusted. This time, however, they only absorbed part of the thrust, and she could feel the equivalent of about 3g pressing down on her, even after the dampeners worked on full power. It was uncomfortable, but her training and experience had prepared her to function effectively in such situations, and she easily ignored the feeling.

Her eyes darted to the display, watching just as Barron was. The fleet would fire at *Dauntless* if they could find her, their lasers set on one percent power. Just enough to give the ship a little nudge…and tell them all the mission was a failure before it had even begun. But there was nothing, no shots, and certainly no hits.

"Full power, Commander. And charge up the forward

batteries."

"Yes, sir." That was about all *Dauntless*'s reactors could handle, even at full output. If the stealth generator still hid their location, they were good to go.

She leaned back in her cushioned seat. The effective pressure from the thrust was close to 4.5g now, and training or no, *that* was uncomfortable.

"No sign anyone is detecting us, Captain." She tried to keep her voice steady, but she knew she'd let some excitement slip in. "I think it's working."

She could see the readings, the energy spikes as the ships of the fleet pounded away with their active scanners, but there was still no indication Striker and the fleet had any idea where they were.

Finally, the comm crackled, a wide area broadcast from the flagship. "All right, *Dauntless*…we give up. Not one ship in this fleet has the slightest idea where you are."

Barron nodded to Travis, and she flipped the comm unit back to active. She turned and gestured to Barron, and he pulled his headset on. "Cut thrust," he said softly to her. Then, into the comm, "It's a pleasure to hear from you, Admiral. We're no more than thirty thousand kilometers from your command ship." He pulled his hand across his throat, a slashing signal.

Travis leaned forward and ordered Fritz to cut the generator. A few seconds later, the engineer confirmed the unit was shut down, the first indication that *Dauntless* was no longer cloaked.

"Well done, Tyler. My compliments to all of your people… and to that ship of yours. If *Dauntless* isn't somehow sentient, she's the damned closest thing to it I've ever seen in four million tons of steel and hyper-plastic."

"Thank you, sir. What are your orders?"

"Let's form up, Captain Barron. It's time to do something about this Union weapon…something besides sitting here in Grimaldi and complaining about it."

"Yes, sir!" Barron cut the line. Then he turned toward Travis. "Bring us back into position, Commander. Most direct course."

"Yes, sir."

Barron stood up slowly. "I'll be in my office, Commander."

"Yes, Captain." She paused. "Sir, Commander Stockton has sent another request to meet with you."

Barron stood where he was for a moment. Then: "Time until we reach the transit point?"

"Three hours, twenty minutes, sir."

"Okay, tell Commander Stockton to come to my office now."

"Yes, sir." She sighed. She knew what Stockton wanted to talk to Barron about, as did the captain, she suspected, and she didn't imagine it would be a pleasant conversation.

One reason to be glad she wasn't *Dauntless*'s captain at the moment.

*   *   *

"I need to talk to you, Gary."

Holsten was walking down the corridor toward the docking bay. "I'm sorry, Andi, but I'm in a bit of a rush. I'm afraid I don't have time right…"

"Make time." Lafarge slipped around him and stood directly in his way. He'd have to push her out of the way to continue— or, more likely, order the gargantuan guard standing behind him to do it—but Lafarge was betting he wouldn't do it.

And, if he did, well, she'd been through worse than getting knocked against the wall.

"Andi…"

"What's going on, Gary?" She'd become very friendly with Holsten. He'd kept every promise he'd made to her, paid her people for the stealth generator just as he'd said she would. Even more generously than she'd hoped. He'd even congratulated her, and thanked her for contributing to the war effort. Now, she was going to see how far she could push the proto-friendship.

"I am leaving for Megara. I'm afraid I have business that won't wait, so if you'll excuse me…"

"I don't need much of your time. Just answer my question, and I'll step aside."

"Andi, you know I admire your...aggressiveness, but I really am in a hurry, and I can't tell you anything." A pause. "I'm sorry. I really am."

She felt her insides tighten. It was worse even than she'd thought. Gary Holsten was nothing if not a stone-cold bluffer, but even he couldn't hide the tension he felt.

She stayed where she was. "I know Tyler's involved in something dangerous, Gary. Probably downright crazy, knowing him."

"He's with the fleet, Andi. That's really all I can tell you. I'm sorry." He moved forward, turning his body and sliding past her.

She turned and looked at him. "He doesn't expect to come back." She fancied herself possessing no less of a poker face than Holsten, but hers failed her too, and her voice cracked. She held back the tears that tried to escape, but the pain she felt was clear to see.

Holsten paused, a troubled look on his face. "Wait for me at the ship." He stared at his guard, and then a second later he gestured roughly toward the bay. The man hesitated for an instant, not looking happy about leaving Holsten unprotected, but then he obeyed the command.

Holsten waited until the trooper had passed through the hatch and the door had closed behind him. Then he turned toward Andi, a soft, sympathetic look in his eyes. "Andi... there's no point in pretending you don't know half the classified secrets on Grimaldi, so I'll just assume you know nearly as much about the Union's pulsar as I do."

She nodded. She might have guessed she knew more at one point, but she couldn't imagine the Confederation's intelligence chief hadn't passed her knowledge base by now.

"What you may not know is that they are close to developing a system to move it through transit points."

Andi felt as though she'd taken a punch to the gut. She *hadn't* known what Holsten had just told her, but the implications were immediately clear to her.

"I can see you didn't know. But no doubt you understand

the implications. We *have* to do something to stop them from invading Confederation space with that thing at the head of their fleet. Please understand, Andi, I can't give you actual operational details. You're going to have to take it on faith that Tyler and his people are doing what they have to do."

She felt a coldness inside. She didn't need Holsten to tell her. She knew exactly what Barron was doing.

The stealth generator.

The device she had found, the one that she'd sold to Holsten. "No…"

Holsten looked at her, a confused expression on his face.

"He's going to try to use the stealth generator to sneak past the whole Union fleet, right in the field of fire of that monstrous gun?"

Holsten didn't respond, but his uncomfortable look was enough to confirm her suspicions. "He's on *Dauntless*, isn't he? That's why so many of his old officers were back here." She reached out and put her hand on Holsten's arm. "He thinks it's a one-way mission. That's why he…" She replayed the last time she'd seen Barron in her head, his callousness, his clumsy attempt to drive her away. Suddenly, it all made sense.

"Andi…" Holsten paused and sighed. "Even if you're right, and I'm not saying you are, Tyler was under considerable stress. Whatever he said to you, I'm sure he meant…"

"He was trying to make it easier on me, to get me off Grimaldi in case his mission fails." The whole thing was starkly, unyieldingly clear to her now.

"Andi, I really think you should listen to what Tyler told you, at least about leaving Grimaldi. You can come to Megara with me if you like. You've never been there, have you?"

You think they're going to fail too…

"Thank you, Gary, but no…some of my people are still here, and I want to make sure they all get off to wherever they're going. A ship captain has to see things through to the end."

Holsten stood, silent, looking at her doubtfully. She could see his tension. She didn't really think he believed her, but it was very clear he had to get back to Megara.

"Are you sure?" was all he managed to say.

"Yes, Gary. I'll be okay. You go and do what you have to do."

She stood and smiled as he stared back at her. Finally, he nodded, and said, "Goodbye, Andi. Take care of yourself." And then he turned and followed his guard through the hatch.

Andi's smile dropped the instant Holsten left, replaced by a thoughtful gaze. The fleet *had* to be heading to the Bottleneck, so there was no mystery to their course...and *Pegasus* was still down in the lower docks. She hadn't been able to bring herself to part with her old ship, at least not yet. She was planning to fly herself wherever she decided to go...but now, she had another course in mind.

If you think you're going to leave me behind and go get yourself killed, Tyler Barron, you've got a lot to learn.

You pigheaded ass...

*   *   *

"Jake, I understand...believe me I do. But this mission is more important that any personal feelings or vendettas." Barron sat at his desk—Atara's now, really—looking at his strike force commander. Stockton had been flustered when he'd come into the room. Barron guessed that was what became of red hot rage when it hit the dousing effect of a superior officer's presence.

I understand, sir, but that doesn't mean we need *her*. Or any Alliance fighters. They're with the fleet. That's enough. Bringing that squadron aboard complicates resupply, repairs, even launch operations. For what?"

"Apart from cooperating with allies who are standing by us despite the seemingly suicidal nature of the operation, we get some of the best pilots in space. Commander Grachus handpicked them all. Every one of them is an ace, and most of them are several times over."

"We have good pilots too, sir."

"Yes, Jake, we do. And we've lost good pilots too. Lieuten-

ants Krill and Steele dead, Commander Timmons grounded."
Barron left out Kyle Jamison. He didn't think mentioning
Stockton's friend would help matters.

"We lost some of those pilots to Commander Grachus, sir.
She's the reason Dirk Timmons is hobbling around on artificial legs instead of manning his bird." Stockton didn't mention
Jamison either. He didn't have to. The spirit of *Dauntless*'s lost
fighter commander hung heavily in the very air.

"I killed her best friend, Jake." Barron's voice was somber.
"We all did. She blamed us, sought revenge, and that drove her
to serve the Red Alliance. What good did her rage do for anyone? Did anything come of it but harm? More hardship, more
suffering. Yet, in the end, she let it go. She understood, finally,
that when *Invictus* and *Dauntless* fought, it was war. I have felt
sorrow for killing Katrine Rigellus and her crew every moment
since that day six years ago. And yet, I would do the same thing
again. Because we are warriors. No one would have understood
that better than Kyle."

Stockton fidgeted uncomfortably in his chair. Barron suspected his pilot understood the truth of what he had just said, at
least on some level. But he also understood Stockton's rage. He,
too, had found it difficult to accept Grachus as an ally. But she'd
been an honorable warrior, and she'd been true to her word.

And she was an irreplaceable asset, especially for his depleted
fighter wings.

"Jake, you've got one hundred-six fighters crammed onto
this bird, and with Timmons relegated to flight control, without
Grachus, Federov's the only truly experienced squadron commander you've got. You're wearing two hats already, commanding Blue Squadron and the whole force. Timmons has accepted
her, most of the other officers have...I'm not saying you have
to forgive her, Jake. But you've got to find a way to work with
her. This mission is too important."

"But, sir..."

"That's an order, Commander."

Jake Stockton was somewhat of a maverick, with a tendency
to view orders as suggestions. But Barron's tone left no room

for doubt or argument, and even Stockton held his tongue. He sat for a moment, and then he said simply, "Yes, sir."

"Dismissed, Commander." Barron dropped some of the edge from his words, but not much. He understood how Stockton felt, and he sympathized with his officer. But this was the most important mission any of them had ever been on. There was no room for petty spite or vendettas. He needed all he could get from every man and woman onboard, including Jake Stockton and Jovi Grachus...and he intended to get just that, whatever it took.

Chapter Sixteen

Villieneuve sat alone in the conference room, staring at the system maps projected on the table. The pulsar was almost ready to go, the vast system of engines and tugs that would pull the great weapon and its vast power supply from system to system nearly operational. He'd seen to supplies—a much harder thing to do with the Union suffering rampant hyperinflation and with perhaps a quarter of its worlds exhibiting something between open unrest and outright rebellion. He could fix a lot of that with booty and reparations from an even partially defeated Confederation, he was sure of that. But he didn't have much time.

He wasn't a military man, at least not by trade, but he'd dealt with far too many incompetent generals and admirals squandering the Union's resources to trust anyone but himself to plan this final operation. He'd studied a fair amount of military science and theory—there wasn't much else to do on the long voyages from Montmirail to the front—and he felt he grasped the concept fairly well. The biggest challenge for his offensive would be forcing the transit points, gaining control of the space on the other side, so he could bring the pulsar through and get it set up. There were a lot of practical difficulties in mounting a defense close to one of the points, but it was clear enough it was the only thing the Confeds could try against the Union's super-weapon. Anywhere the pulsar got through and into the fight, a battle would be over.

He hoped for one huge battle, a fight to the death where his ancient superweapon could finish the war in a single stroke. But he doubted he'd get that. There had been rumors that Admiral Striker had been killed in the initial battle at the Bottleneck, but the latest intel reports confirmed what he feared. The Confederation's fighting admiral had only been wounded, and he was already recovering.

Striker was no fool, far from it. He would withdraw his fleet anywhere they were unable to hold at the transit point. He would force the Union to fight battle after running battle, slow the advance, drag the whole thing out well beyond the amount of time Villieneuve had before the Union collapsed behind him. He had dreamed of total conquest once, of standing on Megara as the conqueror of the entire Confederation, but he knew he didn't have the resources for that now, and he'd trimmed his goals. He would fill the Confeds with fear of the ancient super-weapon, and he would drive forward to spread that fear…and compel them to accept his peace terms. The reparations he demanded would allow him to salvage the Union's economy, while crippling the Confederation's for years to come. It would give him time, to crush the various dissenters and rebel groups within the Union, and to rebuild the fleet. Total victory would have to wait a few years, but it would be all but certain.

He'd hoped the Confeds would save him the trouble, that they would come to the Bottleneck and throw their fleet into the teeth of his deadly pulsar. Striker was aggressive, and he had no doubt the admiral *wanted* to do that…but his rival was also smart enough to realize there was little hope in that plan.

A defensive battle would have been preferable for many reasons, most importantly because it removed the largest likely source of failure in his own plans, technical issues with the drives and maneuver systems of the pulsar. Any mistake, a key bit of carelessness, could leave the pulsar exposed to a Confed attack. That was the one thing he couldn't allow, and in the end, it was the key factor in his decision to lead the attack personally.

He leaned back and put his hand to his face, rubbing his eyes. He was tired. He'd been doing the work of half a dozen, the inevitable result of his lack of trust in any of his subordinates. He took a deep breath, and then he returned his eyes to the screen, rereading the last communique from Megara. Not for the first time, he was grateful for the porous and poorly-protected nature of the Confederation's civilian communications net. Their military channels were secure enough, but he suspected any Confed spies on Montmirail had a much more difficult time transmitting reports through the tightly surveilled networks in the Union. Once again, the freedom the Confeds foolishly allowed to their masses had become a huge disadvantage in war.

His agents had been busy in the Confederation's capital. What had been his failsafe, a chance to survive, to avoid total defeat, had now morphed into a key part of his plan to bring partial victory within reach. The Confederation's Senators were as corrupt as the Union's politicians, and they had as many skeletons buried. His people had managed to influence a significant number of them. Not enough yet, but getting closer. A few victories—systems conquered, ships destroyed—would bring more to the table. The fear of the pulsar would push enough of them to join those he'd bought, to make the unpalatable acceptable. They would cripple their own vaunted economy to buy peace. Villieneuve's forces wouldn't have to push all the way to Megara, and risk having the Union fall to pieces behind them. They just needed a few victories.

The comm unit buzzed.

"Yes?" he snapped. He'd left instructions not to be disturbed.

"Minister Villieneuve, this is General Sebastien, in command of the control center. One of our scouting flotillas has returned. I believed you'd want to hear about it at once, sir." The general's voice was edgy. He was clearly nervous about disturbing Villieneuve.

Which means he was even more concerned about how I

would react if I didn't get this news...

"What is it, General?"

"It's the Confeds, sir. Their fleet." A short pause. "They're on the move, Minister."

"On the move? How many ships?"

"All of them, sir. It appears to be a massive fleet deployment, and it's en route to the border. The entire force appears to be heading here."

"I want to see the commander of those scouts. Get him here at once."

"Yes, sir."

Villieneuve looked up from the table and wondered. *Is it possible? Could Striker have blinked? Could he have decided he had no choice but to try to destroy the pulsar?*

He sighed, and sat, deep in thought. He'd been worried about moving the weapon, about malfunctions or other problems, more so than he'd even acknowledged to himself. Was Striker going to give him the defensive battle he wanted?

He moved his hands across the table, resetting the map to the area around the pulsar. If he could confirm the news, he would cancel the advance. He would stand and defend the Bottleneck.

His eyes moved across the table, darting from one part of the system to the next, plotting, planning. Striker was no fool. If he saw that his assault had no chance, he'd pull out before he lost everything. Villieneuve's original defensive strategy had been to hold the fleet back, close to the pulsar. But now, a different idea began to form. He would position half his battleships—no, two-thirds of them—behind the transit point, far from the pulsar but positioned to intercept retreating Confed ships. Striker's fleet would be battered attacking the pulsar, and then, when he retreated, the waiting force would engage. The Confederation ships would have to fight every kilometer of the way back. Whatever portion of Striker's fleet managed to escape, it would be small. The Confeds would be crippled. Villieneuve could dictate his peace terms without the risk of moving the pulsar farther than a system to two to demonstrate the capability.

He was exhausted, worn down. The last months had seen an unending series of crises, coming faster than he could resolve them. But now, he smiled, a sincere, wide grin for the first time in as long as he could easily recall. He would see Striker's fleet crushed, here, and the Confederation's Alliance allies with it.

He would have his victory.

*   *   *

Captain Turenne was perched on *Temeraire*'s bridge, his eyes moving quickly, from station to station, trying to think if there was anything else he could do to make his ship combat ready.

Turenne's family was an influential one, heavily involved in Union politics. His siblings were all government officials, schemers whose thoughts rarely strayed from the acquisition of political power. But he'd been different his whole life, and the games the political classes played left him cold. It was just as well, because he was the youngest of four, and if politics had been his vocation, he'd have been relegated to the scraps his two brothers and his sister had left behind.

Turenne had wanted to be in the military since childhood. He'd studied every book he could get about war, both those involving the Union, and also what he could obtain from the classified files of pre-Cataclysmic history. His first interest had been ground warfare, but the Union's infantry battles were mostly left to the Foudre Rouge, clones spawned solely to serve as soldiers, leaving little room for the scion of a powerful family to build a career. So, he'd chosen the navy instead.

He had started as an officer, and he'd come up through the ranks, surprisingly to some, as much on his own talent as the upward draft his family connections provided. Now he found himself in command of a battleship. *Temeraire* would serve well in the upcoming campaign, he would make sure of that.

He'd guessed the fleet would be attacking the Confeds, that the classified work so clearly underway was dedicated to making the pulsar mobile. The ancient weapon changed the nature of battle completely, and he knew it was capable of wiping out the Confederation fleet without any help at all from battleships like *Temeraire*. But there was more to an invasion than that, and Turenne knew the transits into each system would be difficult, and would leave plenty of fighting for warships like his own.

He'd done all he could to prepare his crew, to bring them up to the standards he demanded. He'd driven them hard, and he'd pulled a few strings too, even using his own resources to secure better rations. He'd won them over by looking out for their needs in a way few Union officers could be bothered to do, despite the tough standards and exhausting exercises. Some resisted of course, but, perhaps surprisingly, many did not, and a fair percentage even excelled under the relentless drive of their new captain.

Turenne had gotten rid of as many of the slackers as he could, resorting again to family influence to transfer them off *Temeraire*. There were plenty of Union captains who shirked their duties. Turenne had decided they could take his castoffs.

"Captain Turenne, we're getting a level one communique, Captain's ears only."

Turenne felt his body tighten. Was this it? Were the orders to move out about to come?

"I'll take it in my office, Commander." He turned and walked across the bridge, toward the set of double hatches that sealed his private room from the main bridge. "Open," he said crisply, not even pausing as the AI slid the doors to the side, closing them immediately after he entered. The light snapped on as he slipped through the doorway, and he walked around the large desk and sat down.

"Level one comm protocols," he said, again to the AI.

"Level one protocols active, Captain."

He reached out and hit the comm button. "Send in the communique, Commander."

"Yes, sir."

There was a pause, perhaps a second or two as the system decrypted the order. Then he heard a voice in his headset. For an instant, he wasn't sure, but then the speaker identified himself.

"This is Minister Gaston Villieneuve, Third of the Presidium, now in direct command of the fleet. This communique is for the ears of all personnel, ship commanders and above. Many of you have been expecting orders to set out from this system, to begin the final invasion of the Confederation. I can tell you now that those orders will not be coming."

Turenne was confused. He wasn't an expert on politics, but he was connected enough to have some idea that the Union didn't have time to waste. *Why would Villieneuve postpone the invasion? Is there a problem with the maneuver system?*

The answer was immediately forthcoming.

"Our enemies have relieved us of the need to take such a dangerous step. They are en route to this system even now, their entire fleet and their Alliance allies. They are coming to attack the pulsar, but they advance to their own destruction. We could stay as we are…but we will do more than simply shoot them down as they advance. You are all receiving navigational instructions. Several task forces will be deployed to the far side of the transit point, positioned in the dust clouds between planets two and three. You will be there, waiting for the enemy to retreat, and then you will attack, and destroy whatever vessels escape from the pulsar."

Villieneuve's voice paused for a moment.

"Victory is at hand, and all who distinguish themselves in this glorious fight will be rewarded…"

The tone coming through the comm changed, darkened.

"And any who fail to give all they can will suffer."

Chapter Seventeen

Fleet Base Grimaldi
Orbiting Krakus II
Krakus System
Year 313 AC

Andi Lafarge walked down the almost-deserted corridor. Grimaldi was the main Confederation military base, and as such, it ran around the clock. Now, it was on somewhat of a skeleton staff, and the secondary docking bays were a bit of a backwater with the fleet gone.

On their way to the Bottleneck…

Lafarge had passed two others since she'd gotten off the lift. One had been a guard, who'd given her access pass the quickest of cursory glances. The other had been a technician of some kind, looking tired and as though he was headed for his quarters. She wasn't even sure *he* had noticed her as they passed each other.

Pegasus had been granted special access to occupy its berth, by none other than the fleet admiral himself. That had been quite an exemption to normal procedure, especially when berths were at a premium. When the entire fleet had been formed up at Grimaldi, there were nearly two hundred warships in the system, not only the battleships that formed the core of the Confederation's might, but cruisers, destroyers, and frigates too, the support ships that protected the flanks of the battle line.

Lafarge knew more about naval combat than most people suspected—herself included sometimes. She'd learned most of it the hard way, finding ways to pull her tiny ship and its crew from one tight spot after another. The rest had come more recently, from talking to Barron, and even more, from studying everything she could on his various battles.

She'd never let him know, but she'd been fascinated by the natural skill he possessed. He'd run *Dauntless* like that massive ship was an extension of his own body. She still couldn't figure out just how he'd managed to save the day in that encounter out in the Badlands, when he'd somehow managed to defeat an entire Union fleet *and* destroy an ancient superbattleship before the enemy could salvage it. He'd saved her people there and, despite some initial friction between the two, it had been the start of the most important relationship of her life.

The *only* relationship that lasted much past sunrise. Lafarge didn't let people get close to her, save for her crew—or, at least she never had before. That policy had certainly failed where Barron was concerned, but even as she thought about him, she realized she had genuine feelings of friendship for Striker and Holsten…and she was just about positive she and Atara Travis would be the best of friends if they ever got to spend some real time together. Not to mention the Tyler Barron stories the two of them could trade.

Her life had gone in unexpected directions over the past few years, and as she thought about the insane thing she was about to do, she realized just how much *she*, too, had changed. Barron and those around him had become almost like a family to her. The thought of losing them all in some hopeless battle while she searched the Confederation's most exclusive worlds for a new home, was sickening.

She continued down the corridor, still surprised at the lack of activity. With the whole fleet gone, the lower docking bays were mostly superfluous, and the few ships left behind were either freighters berthed closer to the storage holds or damaged ships under repair in the shipyard.

She turned the corner and walked toward a door, pulling the tag from around her neck and pressing it to the small sensor panel next to the hatch. It pinged softly, and the door slid open, revealing the transparent walls of the bay, and beyond, her ship. *Pegasus* was right next to the station, a small umbilical connecting to the ship's main hatch.

She paused and looked out at the vessel. *Pegasus* was just a free trader, and an old one at that, but Lafarge had poured most of her early profits into her ship. There was more to *Pegasus* than met the eye, and that was just how she liked it.

She'd decided what she was going to do almost immediately after she realized where Barron had gone. She wasn't sure it made any sense. *Pegasus* was armed, much more powerfully than the other free traders in its class, but the strength of her guns was mathematically indistinguishable from zero next to the might of the entire fleet. She wasn't going to come to the rescue, tip a close battle to a victory. She didn't know what she could do that would make any difference. She just knew she had to be there.

Flying *Pegasus* alone would be a handful. She could manage it, as long as nothing malfunctioned seriously. She'd had to repair systems on the ship herself in the past, especially before she'd pulled Lex Righter from a drunken binge and added the brilliant but troubled engineer to her team.

Still, she knew it would be difficult. She could fly the ship, but she'd have a hard time manning the weapons at the same time. And if she had to make any repairs, she wouldn't be able to fight *or* pilot the ship until they were done. There were countless ways that could lead to disaster.

She'd been too distracted to be scared, though, first angry at Barron, and then determined to rush to his aid. But now, fear crept in. She might make her way to the Bottleneck, but *Pegasus* wasn't going to make any kind of difference in what happened there. For an instant, she felt the urge to turn around, to walk back to her quarters and forget the whole thing. But she didn't move. She *had* to do this, even if it was a waste of time.

Even if it was suicide.

She turned toward the hatch and reached out for the controls.

"Hey…"

She spun around, startled at the voice from the far doorway. Her first thought was some guard was going to ask for her ID, but then her eyes settled on the shadowy figure standing there. Vig Merrick.

"Vig?" She was confused. "I thought you were on your way to Olysar?"

"I was, but then I realized you hadn't made any arrangements at all, and I got suspicious. So, I pushed my reservation to the next scheduled ship. I thought you might need someone to talk to." He stepped into the room and looked out at *Pegasus*. "At first, I figured you didn't sell the old girl because you couldn't bear the thought. And, after all, it's not like you need the money now. But then, I got the alert that her bay had been activated. I figured maybe you'd decided where to go, and you were taking *Pegasus* there, but then I saw there was no destination in the file. I asked myself, why would she try to keep a secret of where she was going…"

"Vig…"

"The next time you decide to sneak away and do something foolish by yourself, remember to wipe everybody else off the alert list."

"Vig, I appreciate you coming down here, but this is something I have to do, and I can't ask you—I won't—to come with me."

"Who said anything about asking? Unless you're planning to keep me on this dock at gunpoint, we can just cut this whole exchange short."

"You don't understand. This is dangerous." A pause. "It's even stupid. It's just something I have to do."

"Andi, you led us for years, got us out of one tight spot after another. You made us richer than any of us ever dreamed possible. Did you think we'd leave you to face anything alone?"

"We?"

"Yes, we. Lex is already aboard, giving her a full systems check. I managed to catch Rina and Dolph before they boarded their ships. They should be here any minute. The rest of the crew would have been here too, I'm sure, if they hadn't shipped out already."

Lafarge looked at her first officer, a stunned expression on her face. She didn't know what to do, or even say. She couldn't let them come, she just *couldn't*. If she felt some compulsion to throw her life away, that was her affair, but she wouldn't allow her crew, her friends, to follow her.

"Vig, I can't tell you how much this means to me, but I can't…"

"You can, and you will." The voice came from the hall, and even before the figure emerged from the shadows, Lafarge knew it was Rina Strand.

"Rina, I don't know what to say."

"You don't have to say anything. We're following the fleet, I assume?"

"We? No, I was just…"

"You were just nothing. We're going with you, and that's final. Don't make us waste a big chunk of our hard-earned cash buying some tub to chase after you."

"Rina…" Her voice tailed off. Rina Strand was even more stubborn than Vig. She was never going to get her to change her mind.

"I don't have any plan. I was just going to follow the fleet. It will be pointless danger, with nothing to gain. You both know *Pegasus* can't make a difference in a battle like the one that's going to take place out there."

"And yet, you're going."

"I have to…but you don't."

"If you think that, Andi, you don't know us as well as I thought you did." It was Vig this time, staring at her as intently as Stand had been.

She felt helpless. She wanted them to come, as much as she'd ever wanted anything, but the guilt she felt over the thought of taking them with her, into pointless danger…

"We're coming with you, or we're following you…it's that simple." Rina took a step forward, standing no more than a meter from Lafarge. "If you let us come with you, at least we'll be able to maneuver, shoot, and fix a blown circuit at the same time."

She hesitated, wondering if they would really find a way to follow her, or if that was an empty threat. *Yes*, she thought, *they just might.*

"Just say 'yes,' Andi. We're wasting time out here. Dolph will be down in a few minutes, and then we can get going. You think it's important enough to go, then let's go. There's no point wasting time."

"Rina…" Lafarge felt her resistance crumbling. She knew they wouldn't give up, and she loved them for it. "Okay, you can come." She sighed, and then she looked at each of them in turn. "You guys are a pain in the ass, do you know that?"

Then she smiled, fighting to hold back a tear. "And you're the best, too. All of you."

Chapter Eighteen

Approaching Transit Point Omega
Confederation-Union Border
Portas System
Year 313 AC

The room was quiet, dark, just the faint light from the desk lamp faintly illuminating the large space. Atara Travis had insisted he take the captain's suite of rooms, and she hadn't taken no for an answer. He wasn't sure how much of that was respect and friendship, and how much was a superstitious need to return as much as possible to the way it had been. Barron had felt bad about kicking her out of her rooms but, truth be told, he was just as happy to recapture as much of the past magic as he could.

His old quarters were familiar, of course, but strange and foreign in a way now, too. Travis hadn't changed anything, and the suite looked almost as it had for the nearly seven years it had been his home. But it felt different anyway, as did the command chair on the bridge, and everywhere else he'd been on the ship.

He still loved *Dauntless*, and he knew she'd always be his first ship, but he'd been surprised at the difference in how he felt. He'd conceived the desperate mission because there was no other way to save the Confederation from defeat before the enemy's superweapon, but part of him had also ached to return, to recapture the way he'd felt those years as *Dauntless*'s captain. But, try as he might, that feeling was proving elusive.

He stared at the small window, out into the blackness of space. How many times had he traveled from system to system, without so much as a passing notice of the beauty of that great, black ocean? He looked out at the pinpricks of stars, most of them out of reach, man's effective grasp stretching no farther than the network of transit points his ancestors had constructed centuries before.

He was going to die. All his people were going to die. He'd tried to shake that feeling, to grasp for the confidence that had always been there for him, but there was nothing. Only the gnawing thought that his people's loyalty would be their death sentence.

"How did you do it, Grandfather?" His voice was soft, sad. Some of his most cherished memories were of his childhood, time spent with his famous grandfather. They'd hiked and fished and spent days out in the far reaches of the Barron estate, and he knew the elder Barron had given him much, helped make him the man he'd become. But he'd lost his grandfather far too soon, to the crucible of the third war with the Union. The older man had died before he could teach Barron about war, about leading men and women. Before he could truly prepare him to carry the weight of the family's legacy.

"How did you deal with the guilt?" It was one thing to lead people into battle knowing many would die, and quite another to know they were going *because* of you.

Barron had sometimes felt he could hear his grandfather's voice in his head, most likely his mind's way of communicating what he thought the old man would have said. But now, there was nothing but silence.

The fleet was approaching the final transit. In a matter of hours, it would be time. *Dauntless* would engage the stealth generator and move into the Bottleneck. If the ancient device worked perfectly, if he made no mistakes, if luck was with them...*Dauntless* might just get close enough to destroy the deadly weapon and save the Confederation. But he didn't see any way his ship could get out afterward, past the entire Union fleet, and back to the relative safety of the Admiral Striker's armada. He'd tried to convince himself he would find a way, told himself his people were the best, that they would manage somehow. That had worked for him in the past, but now all he felt was coldness.

There was something else, too, another regret, beyond those he felt for the people he was leading into deadly danger. He knew he'd been harsh with Andi, that he'd hurt her. He had done it to protect her…but he still regretted that his last words to her had been hurtful.

Barron could feel the anger inside. He'd always fought the enemy, but now he truly felt hatred for those he faced. The Union had caused generations of pain to his family, to the entire Confederation. They were an evil that had to be eradicated, whatever the cost. He knew he might not live to see it, but if his people could destroy the pulsar, he imagined the fleet surging forward, crushing the Union defenses and driving all the way to Montmirail.

He imagined nuclear fires, total destruction. He wasn't proud, and he knew it wasn't the Confederation's way to exterminate enemies, but he couldn't help himself. It was what he wanted.

I guess I am whatever that makes me…

*   *   *

"He won't even speak to me." Jovi Grachus's voice was somber. She spoke softly. "Perhaps he's right. I did terrible damage to all of you." She turned and looked at Dirk Timmons, finding it difficult to maintain her gaze on the man she'd crippled.

"No," Timmons said, firmly. "No one has more cause for anger than I do, but war is war. Jake is indulging his own pain, yet how many people's loved ones has he killed in battle? When we're in space, facing each other, we fight. When we met, you won, and I lost. Had it gone the other way, I would have done the same to you."

"Jake understands that, Dirk." Stara Sinclair sat across the small table from the other two. "It's not that…it's that it was Kyle."

Timmons nodded. "They were close. Even when I first got here, when Jake and I were still…rivals…I could see they were almost like brothers." He looked across at Sinclair.

"Closer than brothers. Kyle told me what Jake was like when he first got to *Dauntless*. I wasn't on *Dauntless* yet, but Kyle was. Jake was wild then…I mean really wild, beyond what you've all seen. He was undisciplined. He'd have gotten himself killed for sure. You knew him, back then, Dirk."

Timmons nodded. "I never knew much about where he'd come from… But you're right, something was…driving him, back then."

"Kyle got through to him, reached him somehow. Jake didn't become disciplined, exactly, but he learned to think when he flew. A lot of his wild antics were deliberate, ways to build his reputation, but Kyle Jamison taught him how to think in the cockpit. Jake's distraught at losing Kyle, but he also blames himself for not getting there in time." She turned toward Grachus. "It's not about you, Jovi, not really. I've tried to reach him, to get him to let go. Not only to accept you, but to forgive himself too. But he's not ready."

Grachus nodded. "I understand, Stara. I felt the same way about Kat. I blamed Commodore Barron and *Dauntless*. I would have done anything to destroy this ship. It took me a long time to realize what a dangerous and wrongful road I was on, and to change my course. I understand Commander Stockton's anger, I truly do. But we're about to go into battle…" She paused. "Perhaps I shouldn't have come. My people will be a disruption."

"No," Timmons said. "It's good you're here. The pilots you brought are all top aces. If we're forced to fight our way to the pulsar, the squadrons are going to be vital. *Dauntless* can't use her weapons, not while she's in stealth mode. So, the fighters are her only offensive weapon until she gets to the pulsar.

"I just hope Commander Stockton is able to put aside his

anger during the battle. He is our leader, after all."

"He will. At least when it's most vital." Timmon's voice was firm.

"How can you be so sure, Dirk?" Sinclair looked at him with a quizzical face.

"Kyle will make sure he is."

Sinclair and Grachus looked at him in confusion.

"The part of Kyle that's still with Jake. The recollection of his friend, his mentor. The one thing Jake could never do is disappoint Kyle Jamison. Kyle would have put aside his own rage and anguish for the good of the mission, and Jake will know that when the time comes."

"I hope you're right." Grachus didn't sound doubtful, exactly, but it was clear she was far from convinced. Sinclair's expression suggested the same. But Timmons's stare transmitted nothing but absolute confidence.

*   *   *

"I want that power feed escalated slowly…and I do mean *slowly*. This thing's old, and we have no way of knowing how fragile some of these circuits are." Anya Fritz spoke smoothly, deliberately, but Walt Billings could see through it. The two had worked together during desperate battles, when *Dauntless*'s survival depended on them restoring systems in minutes, sometimes seconds, but he wasn't sure he'd ever seen her *this* tense.

It made sense, in a way. They weren't in the desperate fight yet, but they were about to be…and if this ancient hunk of only partially-deciphered tech failed, even briefly, it wouldn't matter how quickly they restored the ship's other systems. They were all done for.

"Increasing one percent every two seconds, Commander." Fritz was actually a captain now, and he a commander, but the whole crew had agreed to use the ranks they'd possessed in their days as members of *Dauntless*'s crew. He wasn't sure if it had more to do with the stated reason of not having three or four captains floating around or with pure spacers' superstition. He tended toward the latter, and though he was an accomplished engineer and a man of science and mathematics, he had to admit, he felt better for it himself.

"Very well, Lieutenant. Maintain that level." Fritz's eyes were locked on the row of scanning devices she'd connected to the generator. They'd come up with everything they could think of to track, to try to head off problems, but even Fritz understood only half of how the thing worked. There was a level of guesswork and faith in everything they did with the device, and as much as Fritz had cautiously nursed the thing every time she activated it, he knew once they were in the Bottleneck, she would have the rest of *Dauntless* to worry about as well.

"We're up to forty percent, Commander. That should be enough in our current position." The artifact was still a mystery in many ways, but Fritz and Billings had managed to get a handle on what it could do at various power levels. As far as they could tell, with the engines shut down as they were now, forty percent should prevent any scans from detecting *Dauntless*, or any signs of the big ship.

"Captain, Fritz here." She was speaking into the direct comm to the bridge.

"Where are we at, Fritzie?"

"Request fleet check. We should be off their scans."

"Hold for a second." The line went quiet, for perhaps a minute. The fleet was spread out, and transmissions were restricted to lightspeed. Barron's "second" had been overly optimistic.

"Confirmed, Fritzie. All ships report negative on scans."

Billings thought he could see a little relief on her face. *He* certainly felt better. But the tests would only become progressively more difficult.

"Thank you, Captain. Estimate two minutes to next check."

Forty percent was enough to hide the ship with minimal power output. Now, they would see just how far they could push the engines, without giving away their position. They'd done some testing already, but the whole mission had been such a rush, they were still going at least half on gut feel. Billings knew they weren't going to eliminate that entirely, but he was hoping to get down to a quarter raw instinct and the rest hard data.

"Power at forty-six percent and increasing, Commander."

He was hoping, but he just didn't know if they'd get there.

*   *   *

"There are trails everywhere, Andi. Across at least ten light minutes, and thick. I've never seen anything quite like it." Merrick seemed genuinely surprised, but Lafarge wasn't. She'd never witnessed such a dense level of ion trails either, but then she'd never followed almost the entire Confederation fleet before, not to mention a good chunk of the Alliance navy as well. The astounding readings Merrick was passing on to her were nothing more than she'd expected. It confirmed they were on the right course, but the sheer magnitude also validated her dread that Admiral Striker was leading the fleet on a desperate assault against the enemy pulsar.

"Have a guess on how old these trails are?" She was chasing the fleet, but she wasn't ready to catch it, not yet. Striker would just send her back if his scouts picked up *Pegasus* trailing the fleet, assuming some cruiser didn't just blast her tiny vessel to plasma before Striker even knew she was there. Those spacers *had* to be edgy, and it would only take one hair-trigger to finish off her ship.

"No way to be sure, Andi. It depends on how hard they burned their engines in this system, whether they executed any formation changes, and the like. Judging by the insertion and exit angles, and the distance between ingress and egress points, I'd guess they used a moderate amount of thrust." A pause. "Three days? Maybe four."

She leaned back and sighed softly, rubbing her head with her hand. She had to catch up, of course, but not too quickly. She looked over at the display, at the next system. It was about thirty-six hours from one point to the next, assuming standard burns and maneuver. Even if the fleet had slowed to reform, they'd be in the following system by now.

Probably.

"All right, Vig, let's head to that transit point. We don't want to fall any farther behind."

"Okay, Andi." She could tell her friend had done the same calculations she had, and come to an identical conclusion. The next system was clear.

Probably.

Chapter Nineteen

KCV Krillus
Krillian Flagship
Divanus System
Year of Krillus 71 (313 AC)

Marieles stood and watched the final stages of the battle. The Krillians had won, and now they were pursuing the remnants of the Alliance force. Krillus sat on his platform, looking insufferably pleased with himself. She wondered why. His forces had outnumbered, outmatched, and outgunned the Alliance border patrol by a factor of at least ten. Indeed, she saw reason for considerable concern in the amount of time it took the Krillians to push back their enemies, especially since the battle had been a surprise attack, one executed without a formal declaration of war.

She'd heard the Alliance warriors were good, but now she realized she hadn't truly understood how good. The Krillians would still have numbers, even after the Alliance rallied its available forces, but now she wondered if that would be enough. It didn't matter, she decided. In fact, the best possible scenario was for the powers to weaken each other in an inconclusive struggle. She just needed the Alliance to feel threatened enough to pull back its expeditionary force, or at least some of it. Then, her mission would be a success.

She was relieved, at least, to have been allowed out of the plush quarters that had served as her prison. She'd underestimated Krillus, deemed him a fool who would believe anything she told him. But he clearly doubted her promise that aid was on the way, which was disturbingly insightful considering there was, in fact, no assistance coming. The Union was out of resources, and she was there, beyond the Rim, effectively trying to make something out of nothing. She had succeeded, at least, in urging Krillus to take advantage of Alliance weakness and invade, but now she was becoming concerned she wouldn't live to make it back to the Union, to gather the rewards a grateful Gaston Villieneuve was certain to offer.

She was distracted from her thoughts by Krillus's voice, as shrill and annoying as ever, but now more sinister than she'd noticed earlier. "Do you see, Ambassador? The first engagement is ours. Alliance space has fallen to us, and even now, my troopships approach. Divanus III is not much of a world, I will admit that, but it will be a welcome addition to my holdings."

"Your forces are to be praised, Great and Terrible Krillus. A magnificent victory, by any measure." She was sick to death of humoring the fool with his ridiculous title, but now wasn't the time to pique his anger.

"Your praise is appreciated, Ambassador. We have defeated no more than a border patrol, of course, but it is a start. Only half of my forces have arrived, and when the entire fleet is here, we will cut right through Alliance space. They will expect us to seize their outer worlds, and the great industrial planets they have conquered in recent years, where we could hope to find support from the inhabitants. But we will not do as they imagine. This will not be a war over scraps. This is a unique opportunity, and we will not waste it. We will go right past their subjugated worlds…straight to Palatia itself." He paused, staring at Marieles as if they were on the best of terms, as if he hadn't held her captive for days.

"We will destroy the Alliance homeworld with nuclear fire, Ambassador. We will break the back of these arrogant warriors once and for all. And when that is done, we will conquer the

Alliance whole, and add its industry to that of the Holdfast. We will be the largest nation in the Rim, a match, even, for the inner domains."

Marieles smiled and nodded. She wondered if Krillus could pull it off, if he could actually conquer the Confederation. *And if he does, am I creating the next monster to slay? What would the Holdfast be with all the resources of the Alliance added to their own?*

But that was tomorrow's problem.

*   *   *

"All forces remaining in home space are to mobilize, Commander Globus." Vennius's voice was deep, hoarse. The Imperator of the Alliance was feeling every moment of his seventy-eight years. "All vessels are to be fully supplied and equipped for combat operations."

"Yes, Your Supremacy." Vennius could hear the anger in Globus's tone, a virtual copy of his own. The Krillians were no match for the Alliance, at least not in normal times. They were taking advantage of the fact that the Palatian forces had been badly damaged in the civil war, and the survivors had been divided, with the better half thirty systems distant, on the Confederation-Union line. Worse, Vennius knew it just might work.

Against any other power, it almost certainly would work. The Krillians would be well positioned to demand a favorable peace once they had conquered several planets. But the Alliance didn't yield. Never. The way was clear on this. Not only would Vennius never agree to offer the enemy a cubic meter of Alliance space, he would make that inbred piece of garbage sitting on his great-grandfather's throne, styling himself a god-king, rue the day he was born.

"You will take command and assemble the fleet…" *What remains of it in Alliance space, at least.* "…and move toward the Krillian border. I will join you there."

"Your Supremacy…I strongly urge you to remain on Palatia. This is your place."

"I will lead the fleet, Commander. We are weak because

of my actions, because I allowed Calavius to deceive me and bring civil war down on us. Because I was compelled to seek aid from the Confederation, creating an honor debt that drains our strength. I will take responsibility, Commander. It is my place to lead our warriors into this fight."

"Sir...we will likely be outnumbered. You will be safer here."

"That is of no consequence, Cilian, though I challenge that view in any event. There is no safe place. We must defeat the Krillians. We have become arrogant. We think Palatia is unconquerable. Yet, the defenses we built over a lifetime are gone, destroyed by us, and by our allies as we fought our own brothers and sisters. The capital is in grave danger if the enemy penetrates this far into our space. Certainly, no Krillian army could conquer Palatia, but with the orbital defenses gone, even a modest fleet could gain control and launch a nuclear strike."

He could see Globus's expression change as the realization set in that the Krillian invasion, happening just when it was, was a deadly threat. "Your Supremacy..."

"No, Cilian. Your loyalty and protectiveness speak well of you, and I am appreciative. But I am too old a warrior to stand down now. The Alliance needs me. It needs every warrior, young and old, raw and veteran. It is time to face this enemy... and to remind them who we are."

A wave of anger and determination swept through him. He'd felt weak, old and worn by all that had happened. But this was a threat from outside, clear and unquestionable, a surprise attack made without even declaration of war. He would not only see the Krillian forces defeated, sent back across the border in wholesale flight, but he would make certain that Krillus himself was held accountable for what he had done. He would see that the foreign monarch, a man without honor or integrity, paid the only price that would atone for what he had done.

He would see Krillus dead.

*   *   *

"You are both very dear to me, Lucius, Ariane, as children

of one I thought of—still think of—as a daughter." Vennius looked across the room at the two Rigellus heirs, trying to hold back tears.

"You are dear to us as well, Uncle Tarkus." Lucius stood facing the Imperator, at almost rigid attention. He was every centimeter the young warrior, the elder heir of the great Regullii, and in his noble bearing, all his mother Katrine would have wished for. All Vennius could have hoped to see as well, or at least what he would have wanted most of his life. Now, as he prepared for war yet again, he dared to let him think what other lives Kat's children could have ahead of them, if the Alliance were a different place than it was. They could be scientists, musicians, artists, inventors. These vocations were admired in other cultures. They led to wealth, admiration, honor…but in the Alliance such things were performed by subjugated people, little above slaves, and the only true calling for a Palatian was that of war. Certainly for Patricians as highly ranked as the Regullii.

He smiled at Lucius. The boy was taller now than his mother had been, and he was starting to fill out. He was less than a year from the Ordeal, and his sister just two years behind him. *Another generation to be fed into the fires.*

His eyes caught Ariane. In the fading afternoon light, she was the image of her mother at that age. Vennius allowed himself a memory, and for a moment, he was looking at Kat, and not her daughter. She was just one more part of his life gone now, as most things he valued were. He had wondered more than once if he hadn't lived longer than a warrior should, if each passing year brought nothing more than a clearer image of all that was no longer there; comrades, loved ones, even easy devotion to the way and the ideals of the Alliance that he now found increasingly difficult to sustain.

"Lucius, you are the head of the Regullii, one of the greatest Palatian houses. Never forget that."

"I won't, Uncle Tarkus." Vennius could hear the strength in the boy's voice, and he knew it had been forged by loss and pain. His father had not long survived his mother, leaving a boy barely ten years of age to stand alone. Vennius had tried to be there, though civil war and the demands of the Imperator's chair had made it difficult to give the children the time he wished he could.

"Ariane, I see much of your mother in you. She will be with you, always. Remember who you are, and from whom you come, as you move into womanhood and, as your brother before you, endure the true weight of your position and lineage. You are Patricians, and you will both be warriors. The great name you carry will bring you both great benefits and crushing burdens. The nobility and strength that course through your veins will sustain you, and lead you both to greatness. Remember that, always…both of you."

"I will, Uncle Tarkus." Ariane stood next to her brother, her posture no less that of the warrior, despite the fact that she was at least ten centimeters shorter than Lucius.

"I will as well, Uncle." Lucius had much of his grandfather and namesake in him, the same long, light brown hair, the same angular jaw. The elder Lucius had been Vennius's best friend since childhood, and now it struck him how long it had been since he'd lost the man he'd considered a brother. He *had* lived too long for a warrior, endured too much loss, and he felt it eating away at him like no enemy had managed in a half century of war.

"I must go now, children, but you will be well cared for in my absence."

Tarkus Vennius, the Imperator of the Alliance, turned and walked slowly toward the door. He didn't want to leave the children, but there was no choice.

Once more, Vennius was heading off to war.

Chapter Twenty

Transmission from Assault Force Alpha

We are under attack from all sides. The rebels are heavily armed and well-organized. We need reinforcements immediately. We cannot hold. Repeat, we cannot... – transmission terminated

Barroux Spaceport
Barroux, Rhian III
Union Year 217 (313 AC)

"Forward! No one escapes!" Remy Caron stood in the center of the maelstrom, thousands of citizens, rebel soldiers now, in name if not yet in training and discipline, screaming and racing forward, gunning down the fleeing Union security troops. There were hundreds dead in the fields around the spaceport and on its tarmacs, more than half of them his own. But the Union forces—the enemy—were surrounded. Some units had tried to surrender, but Remy had been clear to his sub-commanders. No pity for the oppressors. No mercy for those who had come to return his people to near slavery.

The field was soaked with blood, covered with the dead and the dying. Remy had never imagined himself in such a place. He'd been a meek man, quiet, always trying to stay out of trouble. But watching his family suffer, his wife and his daughter hungry, scared…it had awakened something in him, a rage he hadn't known existed. Now, he stood in the middle of a nightmare, a storm of death and carnage, and yet he felt invigorated.

He looked forward, toward the center of the landing area. The surviving Union troops were trying to get back to their ships. "They're trying to escape. To the ships…take the ships!" He ran forward, toward the closest landing craft, firing as he did. His aim was poor, but he managed to take out one trooper climbing up the side of the lander. A few second later, his soldiers, still more like a raging mob than anything else, reached the ship. The last Union soldiers trying to climb into the vessel suffered a fate worse than being shot. Dozens of hands grabbed each of them, pulling them down under a wild tumult of fists and feet and rifle butts.

The ships…

"Take the ships," he screamed as loudly as he could. "Take the ships intact!"

He'd rallied as many citizens to the colors as he could, armed them with weapons taken from Union stores, but the greatest weakness had been the fact that his people were stuck on the ground. They couldn't do anything except wait, and fight like hell to repel any Union invasions. And, even if they repelled every pacification effort, there was no way to stop a frustrated central government from finally blasting the victorious rebels from space. Even a successful rebellion would die in the fires of thermonuclear obliteration.

But if we can take the orbital defenses…

Barroux was a sector capital, one fairly close to the border. Remy knew very little about planetary defenses, but he suspected they were substantial. It seemed almost impossible, but if there was some way his forces could take those platforms, man the weapons systems…

No, there's no way. Even if we take those ships, we can't fly them. And how complex are those weapons systems?

He shook his head, but then he realized he had to try.

"Take the ships…but spare the pilots and crews." He turned

his head, screaming loudly to the shouting mob. "Pass the word. Take the ships, but leave the crews alive. We need those pilots!"

He rushed forward himself, racing toward the closest ship. "The pilots…don't kill the pilots!"

*   *   *

"That damned fool! He'd better hope he gets killed down on Barroux, because nothing that happens to him there will match what I'm going to do to him." Ricard Lille was absolutely enraged. He was usually a man who held his emotions in check, who controlled himself with great discipline. But he knew how important this mission was, and it had just gotten significantly more difficult. The cause was the usual one. Some idiot's screwup.

His orders to General Lisannes had been explicit, and crystal clear. Do nothing. Await his arrival.

Instead, the damned fool had launched a full-scale ground invasion…and, worse, botched it completely. The reports coming in were sketchy at best, but it was apparent the attack had been a total disaster. Resources were scarce enough already, and Lisannes had thrown away dozens of landing craft, not to mention weapons, ammunition, fuel…and hundreds, perhaps thousands of troops.

The soldiers were expendable, at least. Lille had eight battalions of Foudre Rouge with him. He had no need of sector security forces. But he did need landing craft and other support resources, and what he most definitely *didn't* need was an enemy resupplied with captured ordnance and encouraged by a victory against Union forces.

Lille was frustrated by the whole situation, and especially by Lisannes's stupidity, but he knew none of that was the true cause of his edginess. He'd failed in his mission in the Alliance, and failed badly. He'd not only lost the Palatians as potential allies, he'd driven them into the Confederation's camp. Villieneuve had taken it fairly well, which had been somewhat of a surprise. Lille had even considered assassinating his friend when he'd gotten back from Alliance space…before Villieneuve did the same to him.

It had been necessity rather than friendship, Lille was sure, that had instead driven the head of Sector Nine to forego retribution and entrust him with another important mission. Villieneuve himself was focused on the pulsar, and on the final push to defeat the Confederation. He was depending on Lille to crush the rebellion on Barroux, before it spread throughout the Union. *That* would finally be the end, and Lille knew his purpose was to prevent that disaster from bringing everything down, just as victory was at hand.

And now this damned fool does this…

Lille knew Lisannes was to blame for his own idiocy, for ignoring his orders…but he was also well aware that didn't matter a bit. Villieneuve would not allow a second failure to pass, and that meant Lille had to succeed here or…

Or what?

That was the problem. Villieneuve would almost certainly have him killed if he failed on Barroux. He didn't relish the thought of assassinating Villieneuve first, but he would do it if he had to. Still, that brought its own trouble, beyond regret at killing a friend. Villieneuve's death would almost certainly ensure the Union's defeat, and probably its total collapse. And killing his own sponsor and greatest advocate would jeopardize his own position.

Lille had his contingency plans, of course, escape routes in the event of disaster at home. Still, it would be a fight to survive, and certainly to live in the manner to which he'd become accustomed, if the Union fell.

No, failure wasn't an option. He'd been the deadliest assassin in Sector Nine for many years, his operations—until recently—crowned with almost automatic success. He could do this. He had the resources, and he would use them well.

There is no room for mistakes.

His Foudre Rouge would land, and they would cut down these rebels. He had no doubt about that. There was unrest throughout the Union, but Barroux was by far the worst. Now, they would be the example. When he was finished with these traitors, no one else would dare to challenge the government's authority.

What he would do to Barroux would become the stuff of nightmares, a grim warning to all.

*   *   *

"To the control center." Remy was leading his people through the corridors of the orbital station. It all seemed surreal. He'd never been more than ten kilometers from the hovel where he'd been born, and his life, until a couple months before, had been one of grim twelve-hour workdays, and fleeting moments spent with his family before exhaustion took him each evening.

Now, he was a soldier. No, more than a soldier. He was a rebel leader.

The events of the past two months had unleashed something he'd never known had been inside him, a strength he could never have imagined. He had no training, no experience with military operations...yet he seemed to have a gut feel for what had to be done. And every time he shouted out an unexpected command, led the rebel forces to another victory they hadn't imagined possible, his stature grew.

"Take prisoners," he yelled. "We need them to run this thing for us." He jogged down the tight corridor, his rifle out in front of him, as his forces surged through the innards of the fortress. The assault had been far easier than he'd expected. His forces had taken most of the landing craft pilots prisoner—they'd been only too ready to give up after they saw what happened to the security forces...and watched Remy's demonstration.

He'd had two of the captive pilots shot before the others agreed en masse to follow his commands. Again, he'd surprised himself. It was one thing to become an animal, part of the raging mob, taken by uncontrolled fury, and quite another to stand calmly and order a helpless man to be killed. He'd never have imagined himself capable of such a thing, and yet he'd had no hesitation...and no remorse.

He'd been scared to death of the stations, about how they would respond to the approaching troopships, but then he realized they'd been built to repel invasions from space. Their weapons were not positioned to fire at craft coming up from the surface. Three of his ships had strayed too far, been destroyed as they slipped into the fields of fire, but the rest made it to their targets. The landings had been difficult ones, of course, and some of the pilots tried to claim it was impossible to force a docking. Remy had found the cold feel of a gun pressed to the head worked wonders at improving their attitudes.

He suspected the tactic would work on the station crews as well, assuming his people could gain control without killing them all. He'd struggled to form his mob of factory workers into something more closely resembling a real army. He'd made some progress, but enforcing restraint was an area where he'd seen limited success. The rebellion was still running mostly on rage, and the flood of anger pouring out of his abused and oppressed comrades tended to manifest in brutality and violence.

"To the control center...and remember, we need the crews alive!"

At least some of them...

Chapter Twenty-One

Barron sat in his command chair, eyes focused on the still-blank display. His ship's systems were scrambled, all of them, the standard result of a journey through the strange, poorly understood, alternate space that made faster-than-light travel possible. Every system but the stealth generator.

Anya Fritz had suspected that the ancient technology was shielded against the effects of alien space. The mysterious device was a product of the same society that had conceived and built the transit points themselves, and sitting exposed to enemy scanners right in front of the point would have rendered much of the utility of a stealth generator useless. Still, he hadn't quite believed the thing would keep his ship hidden immediately after a transit, not until they'd tested it. Twice.

It had worked both times, and now, it seemed, a third. *Dauntless* was in the Formara system. The Bottleneck. The enemy stronghold.

Her scanners were still down, and the low power passive units would only pick up a small portion of what was out there. Anything firing thrusters or running the reactors at a reasonable level would be visible, but ships operating on low power might not. Still, none of that mattered. *Dauntless* had come for one enemy construct and one alone, and *that* would surely show up.

"As soon as we have power…" He'd been speaking to Commander Travis, but just then the display began to reboot, the blackness of the dead screen replaced with solid white, and then an interference pattern for a few seconds, as scanning data slowly began to pour in. He stared, watching, waiting, and then he saw it. It was back from the point, deep into the system. Just where it was supposed to be, where Stockton's last scouting report had placed it.

The pulsar.

There were other contacts, dozens of them, well over a hundred, more. Battleships, positioned in front of the pulsar, surrounded by their escorts. It looked like the entire Union fleet, formed up and ready for battle.

Barron felt a cold feeling between his shoulders. He had to drive right through that battle line, right past the battleships, every one of which was as well-armed as *Dauntless*, or at least close.

He sat and stared at the screen, looking for any indication *Dauntless* had been detected. Then, he realized he had been holding his breath, and he inhaled deeply. Nothing. No reaction. As far as his people had been able to tell, the stealth generator actually shielded even the energy spike that normally preceded a ship's emergence from the transit point.

The bridge was quiet, his officers practically whispering to each other. He realized he'd been doing the same, a natural instinct, he supposed, when sneaking past such an imposing force. An unnecessary one, too. His people could have screamed at the top of their lungs, played music loudly enough to shatter their eardrums, and it wouldn't have made a difference, not across millions of kilometers of vacuum. But *Dauntless*'s crew was focused, every one of them fully aware of how vital a mission they were on…and of the odds standing against them.

"Fritzie, how's the generator look?" Barron leaned down over his comm. He had it set on a direct line to Fritz. He'd always kept in close touch with his chief engineer in battle, but this time she held the mission's success almost totally in her hands.

"It looks perfect, sir. We had a little wobble in the energy levels back in the previous system, but it seems to have cleared up completely. All tests check. Generator operating normally. *Dauntless* appears to be undetectable." A slight hesitation in her voice told him she was as skeptical as always. To Anya Fritz there were only two statuses…active problems, and problems waiting to happen.

"Well, I can confirm that those Union ships don't seem to be reacting. So far, so good. Let's get some thrust going, Fritzie… slow at first. Give me ten percent, course directly toward the pulsar." Barron and his people had tested the stealth generator every way they could on the trip to the Bottleneck, but this was the only one that counted.

He'd conceived the plan, convinced Striker to authorize it, worked tirelessly to prepare for it, but now he looked out at the might of the Union forces, and he felt uncertain. Had he been crazy? Was this really possible? Or had he just re-formed his crew to lead them on a mission almost guaranteed to kill them all?

*   *   *

Villieneuve stood on *Chevalier*'s bridge, just outside the admiral's office. He'd planned to watch the battle from one of the planetary fortresses, but in the end, he'd decided to command from the fleet flagship itself. It was more dangerous, closer to the action, but Villieneuve was no coward…and he understood just how crucial this fight would be. His forces would hold the Bottleneck, he was confident of that much. The pulsar would ravage the Confederation fleet, gutting its great battleships like a chef cracking eggs. If any of the enemy line got into range of his own ships, it would be a vastly reduced and heavily battered shadow of the force that had arrived at the Bottleneck, one his fleet could easily dispatch. His concern wasn't winning the battle, it was the magnitude of that victory. Was Admiral Striker truly desperate enough to send his fleet into such a reckless attack?

For all the tactical advantages he enjoyed, Villieneuve knew time wasn't his ally. Reports had flooded in, even as he'd worked to prepare the mobile system for the pulsar. Worlds slipping into rebellion, work stoppages, supply shortages. He'd pushed things hard during the war, probably farther than anyone else could have, but now the price was coming due. The collapse was coming, faster than he'd expected. Indeed, it was already happening. He had to crush the Confeds, here, now. He had to send the shattered remains of their fleet reeling in retreat. Then, he would follow them to Grimaldi…and the pulsar would destroy the Confederation's great base. After that, his agents on Megara could force through a favorable peace, one that provided sufficient reparations to salvage the Union's economy, to avert total collapse. One that would cripple the Confederation economically, and set the stage for the next war to be the last.

"Minister Villieneuve, we have received a scouting report. The enemy fleet is massed on the other side of the transit point."

"Very well, Admiral Bourbonne." Villieneuve had been through four commanding admirals in the preceding months, but he hadn't found one he truly trusted to get the job done. Velites had come through with the mobile system, and he'd been duly rewarded, but he was more of a logistics specialist than a combat commander. Bourbonne was the best of the fighting admirals, but Villieneuve had decided to take charge himself, relegating the admiral to second-in-command. "All fleet units are to come to alert status two, Admiral." Status two was the Union equivalent of the Confederation's yellow alert. It initiated a heightened level of preparedness and crew deployment without the full-scale commitment of battle stations.

"Status two orders sent to all ships, Minister. Acknowledgements coming in now."

Villieneuve knew the responses would take time. The flanks of the fleet were light minutes from his position in the center, and each communication had to reach the target ship before a response could begin the journey back. But that didn't matter. He was less than thrilled about the quality of his officer corps, but he didn't doubt they could handle an expected alert well enough.

"Activate the pulsar's reactor chain." The fusion reactors that powered the ancient weapon were constantly operating at a modest level. But it took a few moments to bring them to full energy production, and to feed the almost incalculable amount of power the massive gun required.

"Yes, sir." A few moments later. "Minister, all task forces acknowledge status two alert, and the pulsar reactors report three minutes to full readiness."

Villieneuve just nodded, his eyes fixed on the main display. He'd been expecting to see enemy ships start coming through at any time, but there was still nothing.

Why are they waiting? They must know we've detected them, that we know they're coming.

He'd have thought the aggressive Striker would come through the instant his fleet arrived at the transit point. Striker knew what he faced. Sitting, thinking about it...it could only drain his people's morale.

But the image of the point was still, no activity at all.

Where are you, Striker? What are you up to?

*   *   *

"All systems check, Captain. The generator is functioning normally. Engines at sixty percent thrust. No problems."

"That's good, Fritzie, but don't take anything for granted." Barron felt like a fool the instant the words came out of his mouth. "I want constant checks on all systems." He finished the thought, foolish or not. Anya Fritz was the most meticulous engineer he'd ever known, and she'd forgotten ways to obsess that he'd never known. But it wouldn't take more than a minor malfunction to doom them all.

Not just them. If they failed, the fleet would be devastated by the pulsar, and the enemy would advance behind their superweapon, first to Grimaldi…and then to the heart of the Confederation.

"I'm running diagnostics every ten minutes, sir. Engines, reactors, transmission lines…all check out one hundred percent."

"Stay on top of it, Fritzie. We're getting close to the enemy's main force. We'll be passing right between a task force of battleships, so do whatever you can to keep that thing running."

"I'm here, sir, right next to it. I won't be leaving until we're back through the gate."

"Anything you need, Fritzie, just let me know. There's nobody in this fleet more vital now than you and your people."

"We'll get it done, sir."

Barron wasn't sure if she sounded confident or full of shit. Then he decided he didn't want to know. The truth either way would have no effect on what he did.

He cut the line, and turned to look over at Travis. Things looked like they always had, but he knew they were different now. He'd planned the mission because there had been no choice, because the future of the Confederation was on the line. But there had been a selfish side to it too, an urge to recapture what he'd felt as *Dauntless*'s captain, to go back in time, just for one last mission.

Things *weren't* the same, though, as much as they looked that way. He wasn't sure if it was the gravity of the mission, the enormous danger they all faced…or just some immovable reality that pushed relentlessly forward, defying all attempts to turn back the clock. Commanding *Dauntless* had been the greatest thing in his life, but he knew now, even if his people survived and returned to Confederation space, that was all over. He would always remember it fondly, ache to relive those years, but he could never go back.

"Primaries check out, Captain. Green and green. Initiating diagnostics on secondaries now."

"Very well, Commander." He'd ordered the test on the primaries a few minutes earlier, but from the brief length of time that had passed, he suspected Travis had begun it earlier, on her own initiative.

The weapons were the one variable still remaining, the last decision he had to make. The primaries were *Dauntless*'s most powerful batteries, but they required almost all the ship's power. Barron would have to drop the stealth field to fire them. The secondaries could engage while the generator was still active, at least a partial broadside, but he had nothing but guesses on how many hits it would take to destroy the pulsar with the lower-powered laser cannon.

We'll only have seconds to take it out, either way. Once the guns open up, we'll give away our position, regardless of the generator's status.

He'd been thinking for days, and he still wasn't sure what he would do. He wasn't sure he'd know until the orders left his lips.

*   *   *

Van Striker sat stone still, silent, almost like a statue in the center of *Vanguard*'s flag bridge. The new flagship was a modified *Repulse*-class battleship, the first enhanced and upgraded version of the massive new warships. She'd barely completed her shakedown cruise before Striker had enlisted her as the fleet's new command ship. There had been no choice, not really. One of *Vanguard*'s upgrades was its main AI, a quantum-computing marvel that had five times the processing power of the fleet's other units. A more sophisticated computer was useful for any ship, of course, but it was invaluable for a flagship commanding the largest force the Confederation had ever sent into battle.

Striker was in pain, though he was certain he was hiding that pretty well. The last thing he needed was everyone fussing over him. He shouldn't be back on duty, he realized that, but war was rarely accommodating of individual schedules, and he was going to lead this fleet into the Bottleneck if he had to do it from a bed in sickbay. He'd violated a dozen regulations in taking command before the surgeon-general certified him fit for duty...violated or suspended outright. The fleet admiral's prerogative in such matters had turned out to be a gray area in the regs.

Once again, the "book" proves to be overrated. If things go badly, they can put the blame on me, cashier me, do whatever they want. I'll be dead, anyway, and even if I wasn't, I wouldn't give a shit.

None of that fuss made any sense anyway. He had his faculties, and he could sit and give orders well enough. If he was a general in command of ground forces, he might understand. But he would direct this fight from a chair, and if his insides throbbed and his back ached, that was his problem and no one else's. Such sufferings were nothing next to what he was about to ask of thousands of his spacers.

"It has been four hours, Admiral."

Striker just nodded. The aide had given a time update every fifteen minutes since *Dauntless* had transited. *Does he think I managed to forget? That ten seconds has passed without me counting it?*

He knew the officer was just doing his duty, but he was edgy, and he felt as though the tension was closing in from all sides.

"Commander Garson…bring the fleet to red alert. All ships are to prepare for immediate transit."

The plan had been to wait six hours, to give *Dauntless* a chance to move deeper into the system…and to buy time so the fleet could appear to be there to engage the pulsar without actually advancing into range. But Striker had waited as long as he could.

"Yes, Admiral." He could tell from the tone that the aide agreed completely with his decision. His people were afraid—anybody who wasn't scared out of their wits was clinically insane—but they all knew what had to be done, and they'd come to do it. And the sooner the better.

Nothing is worse than sitting here staring at that transit point and thinking about what is waiting on the other side.

At least he felt that way now. He wondered how sitting and waiting would look in a few hours, when his ships were moving toward the pulsar…when his people started dying.

Chapter Twenty-Two

Formara System
"The Bottleneck"
Union Year 217 (313 AC)

"Captain, engineering reports the malfunction in cooling tube four has been fully repaired."

Captain Jean Turenne was staring at the display, his gaze intent, his mind completely occupied with his thoughts.

"Captain..." Commander Maramont spoke tentatively. The Union was a rank-based society, and it was generally unwise to irritate a ship's captain.

"What?" Turenne turned toward his first officer. "Repeat," he said, his voice now alert.

"Repairs to the cooling tube have been completed, Captain. Both reactors are fully operational and capable of one hundred percent energy production at your command."

"Very well, Commander," he said, his eyes already returning to the display. A few seconds later, he said, "Commander, I want a spread of probes launched to sector 2103."

"Yes, sir." Maramont sounded confused. The fleet was waiting for the Confeds to come through the transit point. The sector Turenne had identified was considerably deeper in-system, not at all where the enemy would emerge. A moment later: "Probes away, Captain."

Turenne leaned back in his chair, putting a hand to his face, rubbing his chin gently. He was probably seeing things, almost certainly so. The scans showed no contact of any kind, but he'd noticed something else, subtle changes in the light dust clouds floating through the sector. It wasn't anything significant, in fact, he'd told himself half a dozen times he was seeing things, but he still couldn't put it out of his mind.

He turned and look at the small screen on his workstation. "Feed probe input directly to my station, Commander."

"Yes, sir."

Turenne stared at the screen as data began to scroll down. It was preliminary—the probes were still some distance from the target area—and they showed nothing abnormal. Not yet, at least.

He looked back at the bridge's main display, still focused on the spot he'd specified. There was something…wrong. It was still more gut feel than hard data, but somehow, he was sure he was right.

His eyes moved back to the small screen, waiting as the probe moved closer toward the target area.

*   *   *

"Scanners coming back online, Andi. We've got trails everywhere. The fleet definitely…" Merrick spun around and looked at Lafarge. "Multiple contacts, the far side of the system. The fleet's still here, Andi, or it was an hour ago."

"Cut all power." Lafarge felt her stomach tense. Van Striker was a cautious man, and she wouldn't put it past him to have scouts all across the system. *Pegasus* had just transited, and the fleet was almost a light hour away. Even if they picked her up, it would take some time. But if there was a scoutship nearby…

Time to act like a hole in space.

The ships of the fleet weren't enemies, but they were bound to be edgy right about now. Even if her people managed to avoid a deadly encounter with a trigger-happy ship's captain, no good could come of being detected. If his people found her,

Striker would send her back to Grimaldi, she was sure enough about that. He wouldn't be wrong either. *Pegasus* had no place in a massive fleet battle. The small ship was armed, well-armed for her class, but against military vessels she had no chance. She could handle a fighter or two—probably—but even the smallest escorts in the Union fleet could blow her to atoms.

For about the hundredth time, she wondered what she was doing there. Her concern for Barron was no mystery to her, but exactly what did she think she was going to do? It seemed inconceivable that *Pegasus* could make any difference in what was going to happen in the next system, and for an instant she thought about ordering Vig to bring the ship about, to head back home.

But she couldn't. She might not be able to do anything, but she couldn't give up. Whatever was going to happen, she *had* to be there.

Right now, there was nothing to do but sit and wait. She'd expected Striker to have transited already, but the fleet was still there, formed up at the transit point leading to the Bottleneck. If she was lucky, their focus would be on the battle ahead and not on the tiny ship hiding a billion kilometers behind them. But she couldn't blast her engines and move across the system. That would be begging to be found.

She wondered if *Dauntless* was up there with the fleet, if Barron's ship was hidden by the stealth device. It was all supposition on her part, of course. She had no confirmation that the stealth generator was being used at all, or that *Dauntless* was the ship carrying it…but she had no real doubt either. She'd wager she knew Tyler Barron as well as anyone ever head, except, perhaps, for Atara Travis. But Travis would be a co-conspirator in this escapade, an officer just as crazy as Barron.

"What do we do, Andi?"

She glanced over at Merrick. The plan had been to get across the system as quickly as possible. She'd expected the fleet to have transited already. Now, there was only one thing to do.

"We sit here, Vig, as quiet as a mouse. And we hope they aren't that interested in anything behind them.

*   *   *

"Captain…we're picking up a spread of probes. They're moving up, about two light minutes behind us." Travis turned and looked at Barron, her expression betraying her concern. "Their vector is very close to crossing ours."

Barron felt his stomach tighten. If the enemy was somehow able to detect *Dauntless*…

"On the display, Commander." He looked up just as Travis fed the data to the big 3D hologram. There was a pale blue line displaying the course *Dauntless* had followed, and a small cluster of white dots, the group of probes. They weren't close to approaching *Dauntless*'s path. They were right on top of it.

"Calculate projected future course for probes."

"Yes, sir." A few seconds later, a white line extended forward from the center of the probe spread. It passed within ninety kilometers of *Dauntless*'s path. In space, that was close. *Damned close.*

"That can't be a coincidence." The enemy hadn't launched any other probes, or executed any abnormal scans, at least as far as his cloaked ship had been able to detect.

"Fritzie, what's the status on the stealth generator?" He leaned over the comm as he spoke.

"Green, Captain. All systems check. No irregularities."

"Check it again, Fritzie. I want a full diagnostic, or whatever you're able to do on that thing, but I want it checked from top to bottom."

"Yes, sir."

"Atara, track those probes back. What ship launched them?"

"Yes, Captain." Travis leaned over her workstation for a few seconds. Then, one of the nine triangles in the display—the closest group of enemy battleships—got larger. "No ship ID available, sir, not with passive scans from this position, but mass readings suggest a Union battleship of moderate size and age. Best guess, 3.4 to 3.8 million tons. If pressed, I'd say, *Leval*-class or *Confiance*-class.

Barron nodded. "Very well." *Not one of their best...nothing special.* "Any abnormal activity from the other ships?"

"Negative, sir. No scans, no additional probes. All other Union vessels appear to be inactive, standing on station."

Barron's comm crackled to life. "Captain, Fritz here."

"Report, Fritzie."

"The generator checks out, sir. It's working perfectly. I also ran tests on the reactors and engines. All output well within expected parameters. If anything, we're running quieter than normal."

"Thanks, Fritzie." He paused. "Keep a close eye on everything." He hesitated again, and then he added, "I mean a closer eye than normal."

"Yes, Captain."

Barron leaned back in his chair and took a deep breath.

He stared at the large triangle. *Who are you?*

"Atara...I want a course change. Bring us around, ten degrees to starboard and ten up in the z coordinate."

"Sir, that will increase our time to target by..." A brief pause, no more than a couple seconds. "...twenty-six minutes, forty seconds."

"I understand, Commander. But I don't like those probes. I have no idea what's going on back there, or how we could have been detected, but we've been on a straight-line course too long. Execute vector change immediately."

"Yes, sir. Executing now."

Barron's eyes were fixed on the display, on the ship that launched the probes. He was waiting...waiting to see what it did next, how it reacted to *Dauntless's* new course.

＊   ＊   ＊

"Incoming fire, Commodore." *Repulse* shook hard a few seconds later, as if to emphasize the tactical officer's point.

"Damage control...report." Sara Eaton was on the comm to engineering before the ship stopped shaking. That had been no potshot from a frigate or other escort.

"It's not bad, Commodore. The armor plating absorbed most of it."

"Very well." Eaton turned toward the tactical station. "Do we have inter-ship comm yet?" *Repulse* and her three sister-ships had just emerged from the transit point. Some of her flagship's systems were back online, but not all of them.

"Yes, Commodore. Just."

"Give me a force-wide channel."

"On your comm."

"All ships, we are under attack. Identify targets and open fire on your own as your systems recover." She glanced back to the tactical officer. "Gunnery?"

The officer shook his head. "Not, yet, Commodore."

Eaton saw that the display had rebooted, and the AI was updating it with the latest scanner feed. There was a normal screen of smaller ships, mostly frigates, but the forward line was backed up with half a dozen battleships. That was unexpected. Admiral Striker had anticipated the Union forces would concentrate to the rear, under the protection of the pulsar.

Which is just what they did. But they gave us something to think about up here too.

"Commodore, Captain Jergens reports *Illustrious*'s guns are online. He is opening fire."

"Very well, Commander." Eaton was about to jump on the comm and demand to know why *Repulse*'s batteries were still down, when the lights dimmed, and she heard the familiar whine of the primaries firing. *Illustrious* had beaten her flagship to the first shot, but not by long.

Her eyes darted to the display, and she felt a letdown as the shot went wide. But *Illustrious*'s hadn't. Jergens's vessel had scored a direct hit on the closest enemy battleship.

She was briefly annoyed that her ship had missed and Jergens's hadn't, but then she realized how foolish that was. They were *all* her ships. Eaton commanded the entire advance guard, four battleships and a dozen escorts. But *Repulse* was *hers*...just as *Intrepid* had been.

It had taken her a long time to get over the loss of her first command. Truth be told, she'd never really gotten past it, not entirely. *Intrepid* had been a good ship, one of many lost in the seemingly endless carnage of this war. *And a lot of good people with her…*

You'd better cut that kind of shit…if we're going to win this battle, we need the best from every ship, not a lot of melancholy mooning about the past.

"All ships are firing now, Commodore."

Eaton watched on the display as her task force, the spearpoint of Striker's fleet, poured fire onto the Union pickets. Two of the enemy battleships were already in trouble, clearly older, smaller ships that struggled to stand in the modern battle line. The enemy escorts outnumbered her own, but the Confederation ships were giving better than they got.

Eaton knew she had reinforcements on the way, that the rest of the fleet would be transiting any moment. Her job was to clear the space right around the point, to keep the enemy from taking potshots at the rest of the fleet as they came through.

She tapped her hand down on the comm unit, reopening the intership line. "All right, all of you, listen up. We're here to do a job, and we're running out of time. All ships, fifty percent thrust, directly toward the enemy. It's time to clear out this reception committee…before the rest of the fleet gets here." She paused, giving her captains enough time—barely—to get their nav orders in place. Then she said, "Execute. Straight for these bastards, and remember, any who get away from us now will just be waiting when we move forward against the pulsar."

*   *   *

"All ships, form up. I want to see tighter formations that that, and I mean now!" Vian Tulus sat in the center of *Argentum*'s main control center. Tulus had reached a height he'd never expected to attain, the exalted office of Commander Maximus, the highest military officer in the Alliance save for the Imperator himself. His family was fairly well placed, but not of the very highest order, and knew he owed his advancement to the tragedy of the civil war more than anything else. That conflict had seen many of those who might have risen to the top rank killed or disgraced, opening the way for someone of Tulus's background to claim the platinum star cluster. But it had been loyalty that had truly put those stars on his uniform...the loyalty he'd shown Tarkus Vennius during the darkest days of the civil war, and that which Vennius had ultimately returned. Vennius had pardoned Tulus of his secret crime, washing away his shame as he advanced the stunned officer in rank above all others.

Tulus had long kept a secret family. A liaison with a Pleb woman would have been accepted in the Alliance, as long as she was simply a concubine. But he'd had three children with his lover, and that was forbidden conduct for someone of his rank. A shame that could have cost him his career, even his freedom.

He'd kept it secret for years, aware it would have destroyed his career if he'd been discovered. Now, that worry was gone. With one decree, Imperator Vennius had pardoned Tulus of any wrongdoing, and he'd elevated the commander's family to Citizen status. The social stigma remained, perhaps, in scattered whispers, but it was highly unlikely anyone would risk the disfavor of the Commander-Maximus by shunning his now-recognized sons...and even less likely they would risk being seen to challenge the Imperator's command.

Tulus's secret would not have been an issue in the Confederation, of course, or even in the Union, but for an Alliance Patrician it had been more than a disgrace. It had been a crime. He'd sworn his service to Vennius because he considered the former Commander-Maximus to be the rightful successor to the deceased Imperatrix, but now his loyalty went far beyond such considerations. Vian Tulus would follow Tarkus Vennius to the ends of space, to hell itself, if need be.

He stared at the display. His ships were following his orders, but not to his satisfaction. The Alliance fleet had been ripped apart by the civil war, and it was still showing the disruptions from that tragic event. There hadn't been time to do more than simply throw the formations together, and remove the worst of the Red Alliance hotheads from the crews. News of the pulsar had only increased the urgency of sending aid to the Confederation. Barron and his people had come to the aid of the Gray Alliance forces, saving them from almost certain defeat. Tulus agreed completely with Imperator Vennius. The Alliance owed a sacred honor debt to its allies, one that had to be repaid.

"All ships, increase thrust to sixty percent." He could see Eaton's advance guard, about one light minute forward, still engaged with the enemy pickets. It looked like her people had the situation at least somewhat in hand, but Tulus didn't let allies fight alone.

"All ships at sixty percent, Commander-Maximus. Weapons armed and ready."

Tulus looked at the display again, but this time he wasn't seeing Eaton's ships. His thoughts were with *Dauntless*, with Commodore Barron and his people.

Tulus had been resentful of the Confeds when they'd first intervened in the civil war, a perspective he'd extended in his disrespect for their famous commander. But he'd come to know Barron well, and to view his earlier hostility with shame. He placed Barron among his closest friends now, and a comrade he'd sworn to fight alongside whenever called.

But now his friend and his crew were out there, alone, likely surrounded by enemy ships. He inhaled deeply. There was nothing he could do to help Barron, nothing save fight alongside the rest of the Confederation fleet.

"All ships…open fire."

Chapter Twenty-Three

KCV Krillus
Krillian Flagship
Divanus System
Year of Krillus 71 (313 AC)

Marieles sat at the base of Krillus's massive seat. It was an honor to be offered a chair in the presence of the Great and Terrible Krillus, or so she'd been told at least a dozen times.

She'd found the last few weeks to be terribly confusing, and her usual confidence was shaken. One instant, Krillus seemed on the verge of uncontrollable rage, as though he'd have her tossed out the airlock if the aid she'd promised him didn't arrive. Then, there were times, like now, when he treated her with the utmost respect—or at least as much as he ever showed anyone— and seemed almost seemed like he was trying to impress her.

She was trained to evaluate every situation, to identify danger, opportunity, escape routes. The last was the simplest here. There weren't any. She was on Krillus's flagship, surrounded by his most loyal guards and spacers. She'd fight, of course, if they tried to move against her, but she didn't kid herself that she had any real chance of escaping. Losing control of the situation, allowing Krillus to turn against her, would be a death sentence.

The opportunities were just as clear. As strangely as Krillus sometimes behaved, it seemed she had managed to succeed in her mission, at least in a fashion. The Krillians had invaded the Alliance, and they'd even won the first battle. It hadn't been the kind of victory about which songs were written, but it would sting the Palatians, as would the realization that their neighbors were not as terrified of them as they thought. With any luck, some of the Unaligned Systems would join the Krillians in the fight. The Alliance had annexed half their worlds over the past twenty years, and they had every incentive to seek revenge, and even to liberate their old allies.

The danger was more difficult to evaluate. Certainly, there were hazards in facing the Alliance, weakened as it was or not. She hadn't initially cared whether the Krillians defeated the Palatian forces or not, as long as they created enough of a distraction to pull forces from the Confed front, but then, she hadn't imagined being on Krillus's flagship when he attacked. If the Alliance forces managed to defeat the Krillians, if they destroyed his ship, she would die too.

She'd put that out of her mind, at least for the moment. There was nothing to be done about it, no practical way to get off the ship. She had to rely on the Krillian fleet to hold its own against their weakened enemies. That didn't fill her with confidence, but she was disciplined enough to acknowledge she had no control over any of it.

She struggled with the other danger, that presented by Krillus himself. The monarch seemed almost to be several different people, one moment wild and uncontrollable, the next deliberative and thoughtful. At first, she'd thought he might be playing some sort of game with her, but then she watched how his courtiers and sycophants reacted to his mood swings. Finally, she decided he was insane.

Sector Nine training covered the manipulation of various personality types, but didn't include much on managing a monarch whose slightest whim could carry a death sentence, and who was also just flat out crazy.

"Great and Terrible Krillus, I beg your indulgence to report on ground operations."

The officer didn't seem overly nervous, at least no more than anyone seemed to be when addressing Krillus.

"You may report, Colonel." Krillus's tone was calm. Almost friendly. It was the sane Krillus in charge at the moment… though Marieles had seen that change in an instant.

"We have taken control of all major population centers."

Marieles suppressed a grin. Union data on this far out into the Rim was inarguably sparse, but it was complete enough that she knew the single inhabited planet in the Divanus system didn't have any "major population centers."

"Very good, Colonel. Casualties?"

The officer paused now. "I am afraid they were heavy, Great and Terrible Krillus." The officer didn't offer specifics, and Krillus didn't press. She got the distinct impression he didn't care.

"Prisoners?"

The officer seemed edgy again. "The Alliance legionaries fought to the death. We captured approximately two dozen, mostly those wounded and incapacitated. We also captured just over two hundred Palatian civilians, administrators and the like, out of perhaps one thousand on the planet. The others fought to the end, alongside the legionaries. The natives, however, have welcomed us enthusiastically."

"Yes, I imagine they have. I suspect the Palatians were difficult taskmasters."

Marieles thought she detected something in Krillus's tone, a malevolence behind the seemingly rational discourse. She suspected that in a year, the natives of Divanus III would be longing for their Alliance masters.

"We should make the most of their display of gratitude while it lasts, Colonel. Requisition all you can from the Alliance stores and the residences of the Palatians, but let's leave the natives alone. For now. In fact, let us distribute a small portion of the goods taken from the Palatians…say, five percent."

"Yes, Great and Terrible Krillus." A pause. "And the prisoners?"

"Perhaps they, too, can be of some use in expressing our friendship to our new subjects. Execute them, Colonel. All of them. And see that it is broadcast planetwide."

"Yes, sir."

Marieles listened quietly, impressed with Krillus's display of rationality. Maintaining favor among millions of inhabitants who, for the moment, at least, viewed the Krillians as liberators, seemed the wisest way to proceed now. Still, she suspected the residents of the planet would come to rue this day, whether they were subjected to Krillus's tender mercies over the long term... or the Alliance returned and took their vengeance for the disloyalty they had displayed.

"Success, Ambassador. You have this opportunity to witness firsthand the success of our arms. A world enslaved by the Alliance for two decades, now liberated by my forces."

"It is indeed an honor to be here, Great and Terrible Krillus." *Though I might quibble with the word "liberated."*

"We will continue forth, into the heart of the Alliance. Even now, the rest of my fleet arrives. In hours, we will be underway toward the transit point."

"That is wonderful news."

"We have received no word from your people on the shipment of the promised aid." His tone changed, and she could feel the darker persona emerging.

She would have lied to buy time, but she had no access to outside comm, at least none he knew about. "The Union is quite distant, Great and Terrible Krillus, especially when ships must transit around the Confederation. You will receive everything I promised, I assure you. It will just take some time." A moment later: "You saw the aid we sent to Calavius during the Alliance civil war. Though in his case, our support was ill-used. Do you believe we would provide less to an ally with the courage to invade the Alliance itself?"

It all sounded good, and one look at Krillus's satisfied expression told her it had done its job, at least for now. But she knew she was only making her situation worse. Krillus's patience would wear out eventually, and then...

She might be better off if his attack scared the Alliance into recalling its ships, and then they killed him for her...at least assuming she could find a way off his damned flagship before the Palatians blew it to scrap.

*   *   *

"Divanus III has fallen, Your Supremacy."

Vennius looked up from his desk. The words hit him hard. Not because Divanus III was a particularly valuable world. It wasn't. It was a resource-poor backwater barely worth the cost of occupying. Its primary purpose was the one it had just served, as a buffer between the Alliance and the Holdfast. Still, it awoke Vennius's pride, now wounded by the first loss of a world to an enemy in Alliance history.

For sixty years, the Palatians had been the attackers, the conquerors. Haunted by their enslaved ancestors, they'd blazed a trail through the Rim, and built an empire greater than all save the Union and the Confederation. Now, for the first time, an enemy had dared to invade, an Alliance system had been conquered.

"Status of the Krillian forces?"

"Only a few reports got through, Your Supremacy. Their fleet seems to be of considerable size...larger than the forces we have available in home space by a significant margin."

Vennius was fairly certain the aide thought he should have recalled the expeditionary force. Most of his officers probably did, though only a few had exhibited the courage to look him in the eye and tell him he was wrong. He'd been resolute in his decision, at least for public consumption, but in his private moments, doubts plagued him.

Honor demanded he do as he had done, but he was fully aware now that he'd placed the entire Alliance in grave danger. He was accustomed to considering the central worlds, and especially Palatia, untouchable, but he knew that was no longer the case, not with half the fleet destroyed and sixth-tenths of the remaining ships—and the best ones—six months' travel away. Even Palatia itself, once considered virtually impregnable, had seen its massive defenses completely destroyed in the final battle against Calavius and the Reds. If the Krillians got past the ragtag fleet Vennius would be able to assemble, the consequences could be disastrous.

Honor was important to Vennius, but now he contemplated being the Imperator who led the Alliance to its destruction.

No…I will not allow that to happen. Whatever I must do.

"Commander, the fleet will increase to full acceleration. Course, the Vendulum system." Vendulum was two jumps from Divanus. That would give Vennius's forces enough time to get there before the enemy arrived. He would meet Krillus in Vendulum…and there they would fight.

Only one fleet would leave Vendulum.

Chapter Twenty-Four

"Course change, Commander. Thrust at thirty percent, vector twelve degrees starboard and twenty down in the Z plane." Barron had been sitting, silently brooding for the last hour. He'd changed course twice already, modifications in vector that were subtle, but nevertheless added time until *Dauntless* would be in firing range of its target. He knew he didn't have that time to waste. Every extra hour put the fleet in greater jeopardy, and added to the chance the stealth generator might fail. Still, he didn't like the movement of that enemy ship. He didn't like it at all.

"Yes, Captain."

He suspected Travis might think he was overreacting. Or maybe not. She was as suspicious as he was most of the time, maybe even more so. Her tone let nothing on about what she was thinking.

Dauntless lurched once as the new thrust kicked in and the dampeners adjusted. Barron watched on his screen as the ship's vector began to change. It was a slow process, altering an existing vector, especially with low thrust levels. Barron hadn't wanted to risk heavy engine output from the beginning, and

182

now the specter of the enemy vessel looking for *Dauntless* really ate at him. He'd have to order higher thrust levels eventually, or his course changes would send his ship flying right past the pulsar. When that happened, it could only increase the chance of this enemy finding *Dauntless*, if he hadn't already.

The Union ship had launched more probes, which was disconcerting, but the ship itself had only repositioned slightly. None of the other vessels in the Union line had moved at all, but the location shift of the one vessel, combined with the probe launches, had Barron on edge.

"Course change executed, Captain." Listening to Travis's tone, he decided she definitely *did not* think he was overreacting.

"I want that ship's course changes tracked, Commander, and I want the AI to analyze and compare to our own. If they're responding in any way to our maneuver, I want to know immediately." He'd been trying to make that connection himself for over an hour, but as raw as his nerves were, he hadn't been able to connect the dots into a clear cause and effect.

"Yes, Captain." A moment later: "Feeding the track into the AI."

"Go back and add past data as well. I want every possible analysis, not only of whether they're following or looking for us now, but also when they started. If there's some way for the enemy to detect us, we have to know about it. Now." Barron knew the generator was working, not only because he'd checked with Fritz at least half a dozen times, but also because none of the rest of the Union fleet seemed to be responding at all to *Dauntless*'s presence. If the Union forces, and their commander, knew there was a Confederation battleship blasting toward their superweapon, every ship on that line would be after *Dauntless*.

"All information entered, Captain. The AI is chewing on it."

Barron nodded, and then he turned back to look at the display, at the symbol that represented the enemy ship, one out of over a hundred in the system, and the only one that seemed to suspect anything. Not many Union captains were as skilled as his gut told him this one was.

Who are you?

*   *   *

Tulus sat and listened to the high-pitched whine of *Argen-tum*'s laser cannons firing a full broadside. His ships had arrived in time to help Commodore Eaton's force finish off the enemy pickets, and the survivors had fled back to the Union line and the protective cover of the pulsar.

Tulus and his Alliance ships, along with Eaton's survivors, were several light minutes in-system now, well ahead of the main fleet, which was still transiting. Without any reliable data, Tulus could only guess at the pulsar's effective range, but he suspected his ships were close.

"Commander, I have Commodore Eaton on your line."

"Commodore."

"Welcome to the Bottleneck, Commander Tulus…and thanks for the assist." Eaton sounded tired. The enemy forces defending the transit point had been stronger than expected. Tulus didn't doubt Eaton's people could have prevailed alone, but they almost certainly would have taken heavier losses had his forces not been there.

"My honor and pleasure to aid an ally, Commodore. What should we do now?" The words expressed his feelings well enough, but for all his sincerity, it still felt strange to be speaking of allies and combined operations. For the more than sixty years it had existed, the Alliance had fought alone, never reaching out, never seeking aid from any of its neighbors. Its first ally had been Tyler Barron and his Confederation forces, and, despite his initial reservations, Tulus was enough of a realist to acknowledge that without the outside assistance, Imperator Vennius and the Grays would have lost the civil war. Vennius would be dead now, as would Tulus himself and thousands of other warriors. The Alliance would have become something quite different than the noble warrior nation he'd served his whole life, to the everlasting shame of the Palatian people.

"We hold here and wait for the fleet to form up and reach us." *Translation…we're looking for any excuse to give Dauntless more time before we move against the pulsar and the Union fleet.* It felt strange to delay battle—his Alliance training and experience usually pushed him to prefer bold moves—but he understood the strategy here. The chances of reaching the pulsar, of destroying it before it gutted both the Confederation fleet and his own expeditionary force, were nil. They were here more or less as a diversion, to fix the enemy's eyes, to do everything possible to help *Dauntless* slip through undetected. And to do that, they had to buy time. Time for Tyler Barron and his people to do the impossible.

"Understood, Commodore. Our velocity is zero. We are in place, and awaiting further orders."

Tulus looked out at the main display, staring at the blackness between the Union line of battleships and the pulsar positioned behind them.

Are you there, my friend? Are you somewhere in that open space, approaching the moment of your attack?

*   *   *

"Fleet command, this is *Temeraire*, requesting permission to leave assigned position. Our scanners have picked up an... anomaly...and I'd like to investigate more closely. I have sent my data for your review." Turenne had moved his ship as far as he dared without express permission from the admiral. The data the probes had sent back was alarming, to him at least, but it was also inconclusive. There *might* be something out there, but the density of the dust clouds, though far heavier in this system than most, were still sparse. The effect Turenne had noticed was tiny. There were a hundred things that might have caused it.

But how many would have affected just that one spot? No, more than one spot...a trajectory.

"Please hold for Admiral Bourbonne, Captain Turenne."

He sat, waiting, his hand moving slowly to his headset. He sighed softly, catching it before anyone else noticed. Showing disrespect for superior officers was dangerous—even when they were self-important fops like Bourbonne. It was always wise to remain silent, non-committal. As much as he'd worked to turn his crew into something special, he knew damned well Sector Nine could easily have spies among his people.

Probably had spies there.

"Yes, Turenne, what do you need?" The admiral's voice was loud, his massive ego obvious in every word.

"I am requesting permission to temporarily break formation to investigate an intermittent scanner…contact." He wasn't sure noticing minor density fluctuations in dust clouds qualified as a scanner contact, but he didn't have any better way to put it.

"Break formation? Are you aware, Captain, that the fleet is in line of battle, and that Confederation battleships are even now still transiting into the system?"

"Yes, sir, I understand the fleet is in combat formation, and I know I don't have much to go on…but I want to break out of the line and do a quick scanning run. Maybe I'm paranoid, maybe my instincts are running wild, but I feel there *is* something out there. If I'm wrong, no harm. The pulsar will obliterate the enemy advance, and *Temeraire* will be back in plenty of time to engage any survivors that make it into range. But if my hunch turns out to be something, some kind of Confed weapon or trick…isn't it better to be safe on this, Admiral?"

There was a long silence, part of it from the distance to and from the flagship, but as it stretched on, Turenne realized that wasn't the only delay at work. His stomach knotted. He'd gone to great lengths to state that he wasn't trying to escape the battle, that he just wanted to do a sweep and make sure there was nothing going on in the rear of the fleet. But senior officers were tricky beasts, and if Bourbonne took it the wrong way, Turenne could be in for a world of trouble.

Finally, the comm crackled to life. "Very well, Captain, but you are to move no farther than one light minute from your current position without further authorization…and don't even think about asking for that unless you have more to show me than a pile of meaningless scans and a feeling in your gut that's as likely last night's dinner as some Confed scheme."

"Yes, sir. Thank you. Turenne out." He cut the line. One

thing his experiences had taught him was to take yes for an answer and stop talking. Especially when dealing with flag officers.

He turned toward Maramont. "Lay in that course, Commander." He'd plotted everything already. There was something about the patterns in those dust clouds…they looked as though something physical had passed through. It was a slight effect—one no one else noticed, and the AI even discounted as unexplained but incidental, but that was far from conclusive.

He'd likely have ignored it himself, except for one thing: the approaching Confed fleet. From all he'd heard, and certainly what he'd seen in the war to date, Van Striker was a gifted commander, a highly skilled tactician…yet he was sending his fleet directly into the pulsar's kill zone. The Confeds didn't have the kind of operational details on the ancient weapon the Union did, but even a basic analysis suggested the kind of frontal assault apparently underway was almost doomed to failure. Why would Striker send his ships to nearly certain death? It made no sense. And that inflamed Turenne's suspicions. Something else *had* to be going on, and that made the minute disturbance in the particulate matter worthy of a second look, at least.

"Course change executed, sir."

"All scanners on full. We don't know what we're looking for, not exactly, so I want reports on anything out of the ordinary." He stared across the bridge toward Maramont. "Everything, Commander. I don't care how insignificant or unimportant it seems."

"Yes, Captain. Active scanners now on full power."

Turenne sat calmly, quietly, his eyes moving between the main display and his own workstation, watching the scanning data slowly start to come in.

We'll see if there's something out there…or if I'm just paranoid and crazy.

*   *   *

"That ship is definitely looking for something, and they're

too damned close to us for comfort. It could be a coincidence, but I think that's a fool's bet. Are you sure the stealth device has been operating at one hundred percent? A glitch maybe? Even a fraction of a second could be picked up if someone was scanning in the right spot at the right time. They might have detected something, some energy leakage perhaps. Maybe not sufficient to give them a positive ID, but enough to send them searching."

Fritz was shaking her head even as Barron was still talking. "No, sir, not a chance. At least on the energy leak. I've got half a dozen monitoring devices attached to that generator. If it flickered, even for a nanosecond, I'd know."

Barron exhaled hard. "If you say so, Fritzie, I believe you… but I need a good answer on what that ship is up to. And I mean a *good* answer, because barring another reasonable theory, I have to assume they're looking for us. Every other Union ship is sitting in that battle line, at a full stop, waiting for the fleet. Why is this one hunting around behind the main formation? There's no doubt the Union battleship *is* looking for something. Their active scanners are blasting away at full power and they keep launching probes."

Fritz was silent for a moment, but then she said, "Captain, we didn't have time to properly test the generator, you know that. Perhaps it has a malfunction of some kind, one we can't even detect, something we don't know to look for. Or a weakness of some kind. We have no idea what that ship saw, or more likely, thinks it saw. That search pattern is pretty generic, sir, and with only one ship looking, it's pretty definite they don't *know* we're out here. I agree, they must have picked up *something*, but it doesn't look like they know what, and definitely not where."

"Suggestions?" Barron looked around the table at his officers. "A course directly toward the pulsar, which, despite the vector changes we've made, is more or less what we are on, is as obvious as it gets. If they *do* decide there's something out here, you can be damned sure that, absent any other contact data, they will focus on that line. Then we'll be looking at intensive scans, overlapping fields, and waves of probes so thick we could hop from one to the other all the way to the pulsar."

Barron paused, letting his words sink in before he continued. "Or, do we make a significant course change, add time to our mission? If we go wide, something well outside the direct line, we'll need multiple course changes. That means burning the engines a lot more, and it damned sure means tacking time onto our projected H-hour. The fleet is expecting us to hit that thing at a certain time, and we're already behind schedule. We can only hold back so long before they'll be forced to advance into range. Increasing the time before our attack only makes that worse." He looked over toward Fritz and added, "And, notwithstanding Commander Fritz's opinion on the generator, upping our thrust can only make us easier for them to detect."

"I agree, Captain," Travis said. "There's no other explanation for that ship's behavior. Their initial maneuvers might have been written off to something else, but I don't think we can doubt they at least suspect *something* is happening here. At the very least, the captain and crew of that one ship are suspicious. If they discover anything else, even enough to increase their concern level, they're going to put the pulsar on full alert. Worse, they may send a whole task force of battleships back to protect it. If they do that…"

"We're dead." Barron shook his head. "That pretty much kills taking a wider route. That would just give them more time to pull back part of the fleet. We're just going to have to go straight in…we can hit the pulsar before they get any other ships back here, at least if we take a straight route. We'll just have to hope Fritzie's right that the generator can cover increased thrust."

"We still don't know what got their attention, sir. Maybe…" Travis hesitated. She jumped up and walked across the room, to the small workstation against the wall. Her fingers moved across the touchscreen, bringing up a map of *Dauntless's* course for the past six hours.

Barron stared at the screen, a confused look on his face. "What do you see there, Atara?"

"Here," she said, extending her arm and pointing toward a

section of hazy white light. "And here." She pointed to another one. She looked back toward the table. "This system's full of dust clouds, ten or twenty times the concentration of the average system. And the particulate matter in the clouds is much heavier than normal. My best guess is two bodies collided in this system long ago, perhaps even two planets."

"Dust? I'm not following you." Barron was looking intently at the display, shaking his head.

"Don't you see, sir? The generator cloaks emissions and screens the physical material of the ship. Traveling through a vacuum leaves no other traces."

"The dust clouds!" Barron finally understood.

"Yes, sir. *Dauntless* is still in physical space, even though the generator is hiding its presence. It still affects other physical bodies. If we slammed into a moon, for example, the stealth generator wouldn't stop us from being obliterated."

"And it doesn't stop us from disturbing dust clouds as we pass through them."

Barron had looked convinced, but now doubt crept back into his expression. But we're talking about minute changes, Atara. Even a dense dust cloud is pretty empty over a distance the size of *Dauntless*. I can't believe any kind of normal scan would pick that up."

"I agree, sir. I wouldn't think most scans would pick it up. Certainly, our AI algorithms wouldn't flag something like this as a likely contact…but what else could it be? Unless Commander Fritz is wrong about the generator…and I'm inclined to accept her certainty that the unit hasn't failed at all since we've been in system."

Barron nodded grudgingly. "Since that's our only theory, it's what we'll go on." He looked back at the display, at the location of the Union battleship. Its course wasn't directly toward *Dauntless*, but it was a lot closer than Barron liked.

He got up and walked toward the large screen, on the opposite side from Travis. "We're going to change course. I hate adding time to the approach, but I want some extra room between us and that line of battleships. If they do detect us, we're going to have enough trouble with the damned pulsar…we don't need a dozen battleships and all their fighters after us too. If we come around this way…" He moved his arm in an arc around the pulsar. "…we can come around from behind, putting maximum distance between us and that battle line. That's fewer ships that can search for us, and fewer that can engage before we launch our own attack."

Travis was nodding. "I agree, Captain…but I think we should increase thrust levels, up the acceleration and deceleration periods by an extra 3g. That will save us about half the time we're losing. We won't hit the pulsar on schedule, but with any luck, we'll get there before the admiral has to move the fleet forward."

Barron stared at the display, considering Travis's suggestion. He was still nervous about blasting the engines too hard. He didn't like trusting the lives of his people, not to mention the potential outcome of the war, to some ancient device they barely understood. But Travis was right. They had to make up time somewhere. If Striker had to order the final advance with the pulsar still operational, battleships would start dying. "Very well, Commander. See to it, at once."

"Yes, sir." Travis turned back toward the workstation, her hands moving over the controls, almost in a blur. Then she leaned over the comm and issued the orders to the engine room. "Course change executing in two minutes, Captain."

Barron stared at the display, his eyes on the enemy contact, silent for a moment. "I don't trust this ship," he finally said.

"Sir?"

"This ship. Its captain. If we're right, someone on that ship managed to pick up the trail we left through those dust clouds. Anyone who did that, who perceived it as a threat, is dangerous." Barron's mind wandered back, almost seven years, to the desperate battle against Katrine Rigellus and *Invictus*. *Dauntless* had won that fight, but by the slimmest of possible margins, and Barron never deceived himself into thinking luck hadn't played a huge part in the victory. He'd become accustomed to assuming Union captains would be mediocre tacticians at best, but he knew every service had its standouts. Was he facing the Union's version of Rigellus?

"I want all squadrons placed on full alert. Pilots to the ready rooms. All fighters armed and ready to launch." He turned and looked back at the display. "I just don't trust whoever's commanding that ship. I want to be ready…whatever happens."

Chapter Twenty-Five

Fortress A-074
Geosynchronous Orbit
Barroux, Rhian III
Union Year 217 (313 AC)

"Barroux Fortress Control, this is Union vessel *Flamant*, requesting status report."

Remy Caron stood in the orbital platform's control center. The room looked like a wreck, but miraculously, none of the vital equipment had been destroyed. The bodies of the security troopers, and his own people who had fallen, had all been removed, but the walls and floor were still marked by bullet holes and stained with blood.

He looked across at one of his soldiers—he'd decided they'd all had enough of a baptism of fire to be called soldiers now—and nodded. The man moved the rifle toward the man seated at one of the workstations.

"You're going to answer that communique, Lieutenant Cezare, and you are going to use normal protocol. Give no indication that anything is awry aboard this platform or any of the others." In fact, the entirety of Barroux's orbital defense network was firmly in the hands of Caron and his rebels, though it remained an open question if they'd managed to spare enough specialist crew to man the weapons systems.

The technician glanced hesitantly in Caron's direction. He was clearly terrified.

"If you give any warning, or say anything I think might be the slightest bit abnormal, Pierre is going to blow your head right off your shoulders. Do you understand?"

The quivering man managed a shaky nod.

"I want you to remember, even if you're able to give some kind of warning we don't catch, if they don't approach normally, we're going to assume you tipped them off…and Pierre will blow your brains out. We'll have plenty of time to kill you, no matter what they do. So, keep all that in mind." He gestured toward the wall. "And remember what happened to the security forces, and to many of your own comrades. There is only one way off this station for you still breathing, and that's with us. Understood?"

"Yes," the technician croaked weakly.

"Barroux Fortress Control, this is Captain Givan, commanding Union vessel *Flamant*. Please respond."

Caron nodded. "Go ahead. Answer them."

The man extended his arm, his hand shaking as he struggled to work the controls. "*Flamant*, this is Barroux Fortress Control. Lieutenant Alian Cezare on duty."

"What was the cause of your delay in responding, Lieutenant?"

"Nothing…I mean, we've been monitoring the surface activity, Captain."

"Report on status."

"Status green here, sir. The surface of Barroux is completely in the hands of the rebels, however."

"We had received a report that General Lisannes landed ground forces to pacify the rebellion."

Cezare turned and looked toward Caron.

"Tell him the landing failed. That Lisannes is dead."

Cezare turned back toward the comm unit. "Yes, sir. General Lisannes landed his forces, but they were overwhelmed and defeated. I'm afraid the general is dead, Captain."

"That damned fool." It was a different voice on the comm.

"Lieutenant, did you provide ground fire support to the General's operation? It was still unsuccessful?"

"Negative, sir. Our installations are not set up for ground bombardment, only to defend against approaching ships."

"Well, we've got a landing force with us, Lieutenant. Not glorified thugs like Lisannes's people, but *real* soldiers. Foudre Rouge."

Caron felt his insides clench when the voice on the comm mentioned Foudre Rouge. The Union's clone soldiers were dreaded by every enemy, and by the downtrodden masses of its own worlds too. Genetically engineered, conditioned from birth to be merciless, the Foudre Rouge were the stuff of nightmares.

"Very well, *Flamant*. You are cleared to approach."

"Acknowledged, Fortress Control."

Caron stood and watched. Then he reached down and grabbed a portable comm unit. "They're coming in, Henri…get your people ready."

"Yes, Remy. We're all set here."

Caron wasn't entirely confident his people and the captives they had with them would be able to operate the defensive grid. He *hoped* so, and he wanted to believe that was enough.

Because if they couldn't, there would be Foudre Rouge storming the stations in an hour…and he'd be dead a few minutes later, along with all his people.

But that wouldn't be the worst of it. After they reclaimed the stations, the Foudre Rouge would land on Barroux. They would crush his disorganized and terrified soldiers, and then they would exact their revenge on the people of the planet.

On Elisa and Zoe…

*   *   *

"Did anything sound strange about that exchange to you, Captain?" Ricard Lille was standing next to the comm station, looking across *Flamant*'s small bridge.

"No sir, not especially. The lieutenant sounded nervous, but he did just watch an entire planet overrun by rebels and then a landing force sent to reclaim it destroyed."

"Perhaps." Lille still wasn't comfortable. Something felt…
wrong.

He didn't know what it could be, what he expected. The
officer on the station *had* sounded nervous, but Givan was right.
The man had witnessed a planetary uprising, and then, a few
weeks later, he'd watched an entire landing force annihilated.
That would be upsetting to anyone.

*The stations can't fire at the planet. What genius thought of that?
It might have shaved two percent off the budget…two percent the project
manager probably stole anyway.*

The orbital stations would have been useful, especially since
Lille had full authorization to use whatever force he deemed
necessary. He was more than willing to bombard the surface,
prepared to accept any level of collateral damage to swiftly put
down the rising. But that option seemed off the table without
the fortresses. His fleet consisted almost entirely of troopships
and transports, armed, but not with sufficient weaponry for a
planetary bombardment. The Union didn't have warships to
spare quelling internal revolts, not now, not with the climac-
tic battle of the war imminent a dozen transits away, in the
Bottleneck.

"Bring us in, Captain. The stations may not be able to provide fire support, but they'll still be useful for managing the
landings."

"Yes, sir."

Lille turned and glanced back at the seat he'd been using on
the bridge. He was planning to sit, but he was tense, and he
decided to stay on his feet. He despised this mission. He was an
assassin, a manipulator behind the scenes. Leading more than
twenty thousand Foudre Rouge, crammed into every margin-
ally spaceworthy hulk he'd been able to scrape up, was about
as far as it got from his area of expertise. But he understood
the importance of sending a message across the Union. There
was unrest everywhere, but nowhere had it progressed as far as
it had here. Whatever happened in the next few weeks in this
system would reverberate throughout the Union.

It was time to drown all of this, the demonstrations, the strikes, the brewing rebellions—drown them in the blood of Barroux.

"Sir, we're picking up increased energy readings from the lead platform, sir."

Lille's head snapped around, toward the display. But before he would respond, Givan spoke again. "Energy spikes on all stations on this side of the planet, sir."

"Pull us out of here!" Lille's response was faster than his analysis. He'd already been concerned, worried something was wrong. Now he *knew*. The rebels controlled those stations.

He didn't know how. The whole thing seemed impossible to him. But Ricard Lille was nothing if not a realist.

"Get us out of here, Captain."

"Full thrust, reverse course," the captain snapped.

Lille reached out and grabbed onto the back of the closest chair, bracing for the thrust that came an instant later. It was hard, better than 10g for few seconds, and he fell to his knees, his legs slamming hard into the deck. Then, the dampeners activated and cut the effective pressure on the bridge to something closer to 3g.

The initial burst had pushed Lille to the ground, but now he reached out and grabbed hold of the chair, pulling himself up into the seat. His legs hurt, but he realized immediately it was just bruising, no real injury. His training and experience had given him an extraordinary sense of his own body.

"Status, Captain?"

"We're decelerating at maximum thrust, sir. Thirty-five seconds to dead stop."

Lille shook his head. That was too long. He despised space travel. On a planet's surface, if you decided to change directions, you could do it rapidly. In space, it took minutes, even hours, to reverse course. He'd given the order half a minute before, but the ships were still moving toward the stations.

Toward...

He didn't get a chance to finish the thought.

Flamant shook hard, and Lille reached out, barely stabilizing himself in the seat. Damn. He'd been fairly certain the platforms were rebel-controlled, ever since Givan reported the power spike. But there had been at least some doubt…

Flamant shuddered again.

No doubt now…

"Can we return fire, Captain?"

"Not with the engines at full thrust, sir. We don't have enough power." A pause. "Our armament isn't strong enough to engage the stations anyway, sir. It wouldn't make much difference, even if we could power the batteries."

"Okay…just get us out of here." It was perhaps the stupidest order Lille had ever given. *Flamant*—and the rest of the ships in his fleet—were already blasting at full, directly away from the attacking platforms. There was nothing more Givan, or any captain, could do…except maybe get out and push.

"We're getting reports from the other ships, sir." The captain turned and looked across the bridge toward Lille. "The platforms have opened fire."

Lille didn't respond. It wasn't fear…he'd faced death before. But now he struggled with his greatest weakness. He despised being helpless, and right now there was nothing he could do but sit where he was and hope *Flamant* was able to reverse course and pull out of range quickly enough.

"*Glycine* reports two hits. Her thrust is down to thirty percent." The communications officer was reciting incoming communiques.

"Very well," Givan acknowledged. "All vessels, maintain thrust and course." There was nothing else to do.

"*Thetis* reports severe damage, Captain." Before Givan could respond, the comm officer turned and looked toward him, his face pale. "*Thetis* has been destroyed, sir."

Lille sat silently. He had nothing to add, no way to improve *Flamant*'s chances…or those of any of his ships. His nearly eidetic memory flashed needless details into his mind—five hundred three Foudre Rouge soldiers on *Thetis*, along with nine hundred eleven assault rifles, three thousand six hundred four grenades, and assorted other ordnance he'd cataloged. All lost now.

Flamant lurched hard. For a moment, Lille wasn't sure the ship had been hit, but then he saw Givan on the comm, requesting a damage report. He listened, and from what he could hear, and the relative calm on the captain's face, he deduced that it hadn't been bad.

This time…

His eyes darted toward the display, fixing on the vector angles and velocity. *Flamant* was heading away from the fortress now, at least, though the ship was still closer than it had been when he'd issued the order to pull back.

He wasn't a naval officer, but his mind worked the numbers, the acceleration, in kilometers per second per second, comparing the results to the range he recalled for standard planetary defense grids. Six minutes, more or less.

Six minutes to safety.

At least temporary safety. He had no idea how he was going to get into orbit to land his army. But that wasn't the worst problem he faced.

The greatest danger was going back to Montmirail empty-handed…going back and telling Gaston Villieneuve that he had failed again.

Chapter Twenty-Six

Damn.

Barron had been watching the Union battleship, noting every vector change it executed. And every one of them brought it closer to an intercept course with *Dauntless*.

Barron's ship had moved through more dust clouds—there had been no way to avoid them, at least not without course changes that would have added hours to *Dauntless*'s trip. Barron was now certain that was how the enemy ship was tracking him. That was upsetting on more than one level. Not only was his ship's invisibility at least partially compromised, but whoever was in command of that vessel knew what he was doing in a way few Union commanders did. Barron had wondered if *he* would have picked up the subtle trail through the dust. There was no way to know, of course, but he'd admitted to himself, there was a good chance he'd have missed it entirely.

His problems were growing, and he was going to have to make a decision. If he did nothing, that ship would keep coming…and if it found a way to get a sensor lock, it might engage *Dauntless* just when she was closing on the pulsar. But if he attacked his pursuer, he would be sending up a flare to every

Union battleship in the system. He could only imagine how the enemy would react to the sudden realization that a Confederation battleship had slipped around their formation and was now closing on the pulsar.

He looked at the display, at the small line designating *Dauntless*'s current vector. He'd brought his ship deeper into the system, as far as he could from the enemy battle line. Even if the pursuing ship sent out the alarm, it would be difficult for any of the other ships to reach *Dauntless* before she got into firing range of the pulsar.

Just this one on our tail…

Of course, running into a dozen enemy warships after destroying the pulsar would make getting home a difficult proposition, even if the mission was a success. Barron thought about that for a few seconds, and then he put it out of his mind. He'd always known the odds on coming back from this mission were long.

"Enemy vessel adjusting course again, sir."

Barron had just noticed the modification when Travis reported it. He watched as the ship angled a bit, zeroing in even more directly on *Dauntless*. Barron didn't think his pursuer had an exact location for his ship, but even a general area was problematic. If the enemy came at him when he was ready to fire at the pulsar, the whole attack—the whole mission—could be endangered.

And he didn't even want to think about what would happen if that ship chasing him got a real scanner lock. Then he wouldn't have to worry about fighting an enemy battleship. One quick transmission of the coordinates, and *Dauntless* would be dodging shots from the pulsar itself. Barron had no illusions about the danger that would represent.

"Launch all fighters, Commander," he said abruptly, surprising even himself with the suddenness of the command. "They are to attack and destroy the pursuing enemy vessel."

"Yes, sir." He wasn't sure if he though Travis sounded surprised, a little perhaps, but not as much as he'd expected.

"As soon as launch operations are complete, execute course

change Gamma-2."

"Yes, sir."

Gamma-2, another vector change, a sharper one this time. It would add almost half an hour to *Dauntless*'s arrival into attack range of the pulsar, but Barron knew he didn't have a choice. Launching fighters would give away more than *Dauntless*'s presence in the system, it would place a pin in the map with its exact location. The course modification would address that, at least, and take the ship even farther from the enemy line, far enough, Barron hoped, to get his ship into firing range before Union battleships could intercept. He'd done the calculations in his head, and he'd had the AI crunch them. It wasn't an exact science…there were too many variables for absolute certainty. But every projection told the same story.

Dauntless would make it with time to take a shot, at least… unless the one battleship on her tail managed to track her new vector.

*   *   *

"Admiral, I am certain we have a contact. The pattern has been repeated in each successive dust cloud. Look at the data I sent. I don't know if it's a ship or some kind of weapon, or what it is. But it's on a line toward the pulsar!" Turenne was leaning forward in his seat. He didn't understand what he was following, but he didn't doubt any longer that he was tailing *something*. Still, he was having a hard time convincing the admiral to take it seriously. Granted, the fleet commander had other things on his mind, not the least of which was the entire Confederation fleet bearing down on him. But *this* was important.

He waited for the signal to travel to the flagship and back. He'd been moving away from the main fleet, and *Temeraire* was getting close to the one light minute limit Bourbonne had placed on him.

He glanced around the bridge. His people had come to trust him, he was sure of that. But he wondered how many of them were thinking their captain was crazy. The patterns in the dust clouds were slight…but they were consistent. He might have written off his earlier suspicions if he hadn't confirmed them again and again, at least minimally…and right on a course toward the pulsar.

"Captain Turenne, we are about to fight the largest and most significant battle of the war. I indulged your suspicions, but you have found nothing but more displaced dust. I repeat now what I said earlier. There are many potential causes for that, all far likelier than some invisible Confederation warship."

Turenne sighed softly. Bourbonne's tone left little room for argument. Still, he had to try.

"Admiral, if you will not dispatch additional ships now, at least allow *Temeraire* to close and try to obtain better scanning data."

He turned toward Maramont's station, putting his hand over the comm as he waited for his signal to reach the flagship and return with Bourbonne's answer. "Plot an intercept course based on our most recent readings and projections, Commander."

He could see Maramont hesitating. Executing that course would be a violation of Bourbonne's orders…unless Turenne could somehow convince the skeptical admiral to change his mind. "Yes, sir," the officer finally replied nervously.

"Negative, Captain." Bourbonne's voice blared through the bridge speakers. Turenne was regretting that he hadn't taken the comm privately, on his headset. "You are to return to your position in the battle line, at once. Understood?"

Turenne sat utterly still for a moment. Then, he turned his head and looked around the bridge. His people were definitely loyal to him, but he was far from certain they would go along with what he'd decided to do. The penalties for insubordination in the Union were severe, and a crew that followed a rogue captain would be punished almost as severely as their rogue leader.

He paused, the words he planned to utter stuck for an instant on his lips. Then: "I'm sorry, Admiral. Your transmission was garbled. Please retransmit. Pending further instruction, we are proceeding on an intercept course toward contact A-0."

He cut the line.

The bridge was silent, not a sound save for the distant hum of the engines. He could feel the eyes of the crew boring into him, hear each of their nearly silent breaths. He'd spoken impulsively to the admiral, and now, for a moment, he almost regretted it. But he *knew* there was something out there. Something dangerous. He was doing his duty, even though his disobedience to orders. It was the right thing to do, he decided...though none of that would matter if the crew didn't stand with him.

There was only one way to find out. "Is that intercept course ready, Commander?" He spoke calmly, as evenly as he could manage through the turmoil in his head.

There was a pause, long, torturous. Turenne sat in his chair, waiting for his first officer to order the guards to arrest him. But nothing happened. Finally, Maramont said, "Course laid in, Captain." He turned and looked toward the command chair, and he gave Turenne one sharp nod.

"Very well, Commander," Turenne said, trying not to let the relief he felt show in his tone. "Execute."

"Yes, sir. Intercept course...executing."

Turenne sat in his chair, wincing slightly as the blast of acceleration hit, and then exhaling as the dampeners absorbed most of the force. The bridge was still quiet, none of the normal chatter between officers. But then, gradually, Turenne could almost feel them all turning back to their workstations, the near silence slowly giving way to the normal sounds of fingers on keyboards and the like.

"Captain, we're receiving a transmission from the flagship, sir."

Turenne felt his insides freeze. It was hardly unexpected, but he still didn't know what he was going to say. And then, he didn't have to.

"I'm afraid it's garbled, sir. Must be some radioactives in these dust clouds interfering with the comm. I'll instruct them to retransmit."

"Very well, Commander." Turenne turned toward his first officer and nodded, a silent acknowledgement of his loyalty... and a sincere thanks.

He turned back toward the small screen at his station. *Temeraire* was blasting at nearly full thrust, on a vector that was his best guess at in intercept for…whatever it was he was tracking. Time wasn't on his side, especially not now. Bourbonne had to be livid…and Gaston Villieneuve was with the fleet as well.

Bourbonne wouldn't take insubordination lightly. Turenne knew the admiral was likely to lock him away for twenty years. Union prisons were not pleasant places, and the chance of surviving a hitch that long was something like one in three. But Gaston Villieneuve wouldn't waste time with court martials and prison terms. As likely or not, if he got involved, he'd just have Turenne thrown out the airlock with no ceremony at all.

*   *   *

"Squadron leaders, you've all got your assignments. Screening forces are to tie up their birds, keep them off the asses of the bombing groups. Blue squadron, Scarlet Eagles, you're with me. We're going right in with the bombers, and we're going to keep any strays from interfering with the attack run." Stockton had his hands on his fighter's controls as his eyes panned over his screens, checking the large formation behind him. He had one hundred-six fighters, including his own, a number that still didn't quite compute. *Dauntless* had been built to carry up to sixty, and she'd managed as many as seventy-six when she'd taken aboard strays after the Battle of Arcturon, but he still didn't know how Chief Evans and Commander Fritz had crammed so many birds into *Dauntless*'s crowded bays.

Not only fit, but launched. The whole operation had taken somewhat longer than usual, and there had been some confusion among the squadrons, but all things considered, things had gone surprisingly well, and he was at the head of the largest strike force ever launched by a single Confederation battleship.

More than enough to take out one middling Union ship…

He listened as the squadron commanders acknowledged, frowning as Grachus's voice joined the others. He still wasn't happy to have her in his command, but he'd done all he could to get rid of her, without success, so now there was no choice but to make the best of it. And, he had to admit, as irksome as he found having her part of his wing, she was *good*...and he suspected her hand-picked squadron was a force to be reckoned with.

"We all know what we've got to do, so let's get it done." His eyes were fixed on the symbol on his scanner, the only enemy ship even remotely in range. There were clusters of small dots, scattered around the target vessel now. The Union ship was launching its fighter squadrons in response to the appearance of *Dauntless*'s birds, and as Stockton stared and counted, he realized his guess on numbers had been spot on. Forty-eight fighters.

He was still too far out for intensive scanning results, but he was going on the assumption they were all outfitted as intercep-tors. *Dauntless* was still hidden, and almost outside of attack range, and the captain of that ship had to be alarmed at the size of the strike force heading his way.

Stockton had fought countless battles in his years of service to Barron and *Dauntless*, and most of those had been against long odds, much like this desperate mission to destroy the pul-sar. But, for once, his people had the numbers. If he couldn't take out one Union battleship with over a hundred fighters...

"Commander Stockton, this is flight control." It was Stara's voice, and he knew immediately, something was wrong. The mere fact that she was breaking radio silence would have told him that much, but her tone pushed it over the edge.

"*Dauntless* strike force leader here."

"Jake, we're picking up readings from around the pulsar. Fighter launches." She paused. "They must have some kind of fighter bases nearby."

Damn. Stockton cursed himself for his momentary opti-mism about numbers. And for carelessness. They'd had shit for intel on this mission. Why hadn't he anticipated the enemy would have some kind of fighter force positioned around the pulsar?

"How many?" It was the first question that popped into his mind.

"Too many, Raptor." A different voice this time. Timmons. "We've got five squadrons confirmed, and it looks like more coming."

Every curse word he'd ever heard in all the dive bars in every frontier base in the Confederation flooded into his mind. "We can intercept on the way back from the strike." *Without missiles and low on fuel...*

"Negative, Raptor. They'll get to you just as you're engaging. And, we can't take the chance that they can track *Dauntless*. You have to split your forces."

There goes the advantage in numbers...

"Roger that, Control." Stockton slammed his fist against the arm of his seat. He was angry, frustrated, but he knew what he had to do.

The signal from *Dauntless* was gone, radio silence clearly resumed. He suspected the ship would make another course change, an attempt to undo any damage the transmission had done to its stealth, and to further confuse any fighter squadrons heading her way. That meant he wouldn't know where to find her. No doubt, *Dauntless* would contact him when his people were on the way back, but there was no telling how much extra fuel his squadrons would burn with no reliable return route to base.

He flipped his comm to the main channel. "Listen up, we've got a change of plans. *Dauntless* picked up enemy fighters near the pulsar." *We were damned fools for not expecting that...the pulsar can protect itself from capital ships, but if fighters got through the outer defense grid...*

"We're splitting up..." His mind was racing, trying to decide what to do with his squadrons. He knew what he *should* do, but he just wasn't sure he could bring himself to give the order.

Jovi Grachus was the best pilot in the force after him—or *maybe, just the best*—and her oversized squadron had the cream of the Alliance fighter corps. *Anybody but her...*

Olya Federov was the only other choice—but her Reds were outfitted as bombers, and she was leading the strike against the enemy battleship. *Damn.*

"Commander Grachus," he said, using every bit of discipline he possessed to keep the emotion from his voice. "You will take your squadron—and Yellow and Green squadrons—and you will move toward the pulsar and intercept the enemy fighters deployed there."

"Yes, sir." There was a touch of surprise evident in her tone, but clearly, she too was trying to keep her emotions under control.

"Your first priority is to protect *Dauntless*, Commander. Covering our flank here is number two. If it comes to a choice..."

"Understood, sir."

"Go. Yellow and Green leaders, you're under Commander Grachus's command." Each word cut at him like a knife.

Stockton cut the comm and leaned back in his chair, letting out a long exhale. He felt guilt, the pressure of the loss and anger he felt over Kyle Jamison's death. But he also knew, without a doubt, that Jamison himself would have told him to do exactly what he'd just done.

That should have made him feel better, but it didn't.

Chapter Twenty-Seven

Formara System
"The Bottleneck"
Union Year 217 (313 AC)

"Yes, Minister Villieneuve, we're tracking over one hundred Confederation fighters." Turenne felt like he was going to throw up. He'd spent the past several minutes listening to Gaston Villieneuve, a man who carried a title no less terrifying that the Director of Sector Nine, castigate him for ignoring Bourbonne's commands. Turenne had stood by his "garbled message" story, but, unsurprisingly, Villieneuve had been having none of it.

Until the scanners picked up the Confederation fighters. They'd come from nowhere, seemingly. One moment, there were no scanner contacts, nothing save the minor disturbances in the dust concentrations. Then fighters began appearing, one squadron after another, heading right for *Temeraire*.

Turenne had waved to Maramont, even as he stood on the comm, Villieneuve's enraged yells replaced by silence. The first officer understood the silent command, and *Temeraire's* scanners were focused on that one area of space, with every watt of power the battleship could put behind them.

"Scanner data, Captain?" Villieneuve's anger was gone, replaced by a hard urgency.

"Scanning now, sir." Turenne looked across the bridge, but

Maramont shook his head. "Nothing yet, Minister Villieneuve."
Turenne looked down at his workstation's screen. "Bases
Rouge and Vert appear to have picked up the Confederation
force was well, sir. They are launching fighters now." The two
bases orbited the planet closest to the pulsar's location. They'd
been intended as a last-ditch defense against any remnants of
a desperate enemy fighter assault that penetrated the battle
line. But now they were reacting to an unexpected—and far
closer—threat.

Turenne tried to ignore the sweat pouring down his back
in rivulets as he waited for his message to reach the flagship
and for Villieneuve's response to return. The tension had faded
slightly, at least the direct fear of Villieneuve. He'd been about
thirty seconds, he suspected, from seeing whether Maramont
would have obeyed an order to shoot him and take command,
but the appearance of Confed fighters not only validated his
earlier concerns, they represented a far greater urgency than dis-
ciplining a single officer.

"The fighter bases are under your command from this
moment forward, Captain Turenne. I am sending additional
battleships to your location, but until they arrive you are responsible for the defense of the pulsar. Whatever the Confeds have
out there, you are to find and destroy it. Now."

"Yes, sir." Turenne didn't know what else to say. He'd been
trying to find the Confeds for hours, and the sudden appearance of the fighter squadrons was the first real verification he'd
had that he wasn't chasing his own imagination. "I will…" He
almost said, 'do my best,' but he caught himself, and he said, "…
find whatever is out here, sir."

He stared out at the display. His own fighters were finishing
their launch operations. He'd felt a burst of near-panic when he
saw how many enemy ships were coming at *Temeraire*, but then
he saw the Confed forces split into two groups. *The fighters from
the stations. Of course.* The squadrons Vert and Rouge launched
would reach *Temeraire* about the same time as the enemy strike
force.

He leaned back in his chair, taking a deep breath and trying to focus. *Temeraire* had a better chance of surviving the incoming assault now that half the enemy's strength had been diverted. Still, it would be a nasty fight. He had no idea who these fighters were or how they'd gotten there, but his gut told him they were the Confederation's best…and that meant even the reduced force coming in was a grave threat.

"Alert Status One, Commander. Battle stations.

*   *   *

"All right, Blues…Eagles, with me. We're going to open up the way for the bombers to get through." Stockton felt at home in the cockpit, going into battle once again. But there was still something there, bothering him. He hated Jovi Grachus, and yet he couldn't get her out of his mind. For all he blamed her for Kyle Jamison's death, he couldn't help but see how much like his lost friend she was. And, to the extent he could allow himself to see it, how similar she was to *him* in some ways as well.

He struggled to bring his focus back to his own cockpit. His strike force had a much tougher fight on its hands now that he'd detached half his numbers…and two-thirds of his interceptors. Blue and Scarlet Eagle squadrons were *Dauntless*'s best, the top outfits in the whole fleet—and he'd have words with anyone who challenged him on that—but he knew neither one was what it once had been. Among the Blues lost in *Dauntless*'s many battles were Corinne "Talon" Steele and Rick "Typhoon" Turner, two of the best pilots he'd ever known, and comrades he'd been proud to call friends. The Eagles had suffered no less than their Blue counterparts, and the loss of "Warrior" Timmons to a desk job in launch control had cut the head and the heart out of the squadron.

"The bombers are right behind us, so you know what that means. Any interceptors that get past us are going to slam right into them. We need that strike force to get through unscathed. We've got to take down this enemy battleship." His people knew everything he was telling them, but he did it anyway. Then, he turned away from the comm and gripped his ship's controls.

The lead wave of enemy interceptors was just entering range. They were too far for lasers still, but a well-placed missile could score a hit. Still, he held back. He only had two of the heavy weapons, and he was determined to take down an enemy fighter with each...and that meant closing.

He could see some of the Union fighters had already launched their long-range ordnance. The Union fighter corps was vastly inferior to its Confederation counterpart, but something didn't look quite right. The ships heading toward him were in a tight formation. They looked almost like Confederation squadrons. They maneuvered sharply, and they were coming on at full acceleration. He knew just what they planned to do. They'd do one pass with his interceptors, and then they would streak past, right into the bomber squadrons.

"They're looking to whip past us," he said into the comm. It was a bold maneuver, one that would leave the Union fighters at a disadvantage...but only for a short time. The whole thing was something Stockton might have done in their situation, but not at all the kind of daring move he expected from Union squadrons. "Decelerate hard...we're going to take them at as close to a dead stop as we can, and then we're going to spin around and blast at full after them." The Union ships would have a big momentum advantage once they cleared the killing zone Stockton's fighters would set up for them, but the Blues and Eagles would be coming from behind, picking up some extra time to fire into the dead zones of the Union ships.

"Launch missiles at will...but wait until you've got a good shot. We can't waste any ordnance, not now."

He trusted most of his people to make good decisions. He had a few new recruits in each squadron, replacing pilots lost in the last battles of the Alliance Civil War. He'd almost transferred them out before *Dauntless* had left Grimaldi, but he'd decided it made more sense to leave the formations together.

His eyes were focused on the screen. Half a dozen Union birds were heading right at him. His hand was tense on the throttle, his finger over the firing stud. He squeezed once, letting his first missile loose. Then his other hand extended forward, hitting the controls, arming the second. He launched that one just a few seconds later, and then he swung his arm hard to the right, bringing his ship around, and out of the path of the approaching fighters.

He watched as his missiles closed, and the target ships launched into frantic evasive maneuvers. Watching his chosen victims struggle to escape the doom he'd sent their way only confirmed what he'd feared. The formations he was facing were far from the Union's standard squadrons. These pilots were clearly some kind of elite force, and while he couldn't bring himself to imagine they were the equals of his own veterans, any hope of total domination and easy victory slipped quickly away.

He felt a rush of excitement as the first enemy ship vanished from his screen, falling to the missile it had almost escaped. His satisfaction was short-lived, however, as he watched his second target evade the warhead on its tail…until the weapon ran out of fuel and continued on in a straight line, well wide of the Union ship.

Damn.

Stockton hadn't been in battle for more than six months, and he wondered if his service on the long-range spy missions had left his targeting a bit rusty. The stat books said it took fourteen missiles to take out one enemy fighter, but Stockton had never paid any mind to such factoids. He wouldn't expect to take out Alliance fighters with every missile, but he'd done it against Union forces many times.

"Watch yourselves out there," he said into the comm, wincing as he saw one of his Blues disappear from the screen, even as he was issuing his warning. "These aren't ordinary Union pilots, they're some kind of veterans."

He angled his ship hard, firing his lasers. His shot went wide of his target, just, and he fired again. And again. Finally, he hit. It was a glancing blow, a shot that cut the enemy's thrust and maneuverability, but didn't score a kill. He tried to fire again, but he was already past the fighter. He searched around, his eyes darting all around his screen, looking for another target. The enemy ships were moving too quickly, and they were already getting past his screen. His people were scoring hits, cutting down their enemies, but not enough of them. The ships getting through would wreak havoc on Federov's bombers. He *had* to get more of them. If he didn't, the shattered remnants of the bombing strike wouldn't have a chance of taking out the Union battleship.

He swung around. "Blues, with me...full thrust, follow those bastards who got through. Eagles stay in position and engage squadrons still approaching." He didn't like splitting his force yet again, but there was no choice. He brought his ship around, matching vectors with the enemy fighters heading for the bombing group. The Union ships had a high velocity, and they were getting farther from his Blues every second. But they were still in range, and Stockton intended to make them pay while he could.

He fired...a clean miss. Then another, much closer. He stared at the small dot on his screen, the fighter he was targeting. The pilot he was after had seen the threat, and he was angling his ship back and forth, doing anything he could to throw off Stockton's aim. He fired again, and then again, missing each time.

He stared at the screen. Every second brought his target farther away, despite the fact that his own fighter was accelerating at full power. His eyes darted to the side every few seconds, checking to make sure no enemy was making a move on him. Otherwise, his concentration was fixed. In that moment, there was nothing but his ship...and the one he was pursuing. His enemy would be out of range soon, and each shot became more difficult than the last. He'd been relying on the targeting computer, but now, his old instincts began to fire up. He relaxed his arm slightly, let his instincts direct him. His arm moved, firing again...then again. Finally, the dot on his screen vanished. He'd taken out his target.

But over a dozen ships had made it through...and they'd be hitting the bombers any second. He swore under his breath, and then he leaned back, trying to ignore the discomfort of the intense g forces. He wouldn't get back quickly enough, at least not in time to prevent the bombers from enduring an enemy attack run. But the Union forces would pay a price for their high speed. They would blast right through the bomber formation, their attacks hamstrung by the limited window when they'd be in range. Stockton didn't kid himself. It was going to be bad. But, just maybe, not as bad as it might have been.

And he and his Blues would be there when the enemy slowed to come around and return toward the bombers. There would be no second run…he promised himself that much.

✳   ✳   ✳

"Prepare for evasive maneuvers." Olya Federov's face was grim. She'd watched the battle up ahead, and she knew the interceptors had done all they could to engage the attacking enemy fighters. But the Union pilots were far more skilled than usual, and their ships were coming in at high speed. Despite Stockton's best efforts, and the skill and heroism of *Dauntless*'s elite squadrons, the bombers were going to get hit.

She took hold of her own ship's controls, preparing to do what she could to make herself a difficult target. It was something she did well, at least when her normally-sleek Lightning was configured as an interceptor. But loaded up with the full bombing kit and attachments, the thing handled like a pig, something immediately noticeable to the touch of a skilled dogfighter like herself.

Sarcastic remarks she'd uttered many times floated around in her head, thoughts along the lines of "a bomber couldn't evade a rock thrown by hand." It wasn't that she disagreed with the essence of such statements…but they served no purpose now. Her Reds, usually deployed as interceptors, were carrying heavy plasma torpedoes in their bomb bays, and her only concern was to get as many of them as possible through what was coming, and to the enemy battleship.

She angled her controls again, still finding herself surprised at how sluggishly the ship responded. The incoming fighters all appeared to have expended their missiles fighting the Blues

and the Eagles. That, at least, was a small mercy. A missile barrage would gut her formation, taking down more of her ships
than she wanted to imagine. The fighters coming in now would
open up with their lasers, but they wouldn't be in range for long
before their velocity took them right past the bombers.

She changed her vector again, another slow and cumbersome adjustment, but it took her out of the direct path of an
incoming fighter. She was still taking fire, but the angle, and
the now-growing distance between her ship and her attacker's,
severely reduced the likelihood of a hit.

Federov hated dodging enemies—she was a fighter at
heart—but she had no choice now. Her bomber was fitted out
to engage the enemy battleship, not the sleek interceptors blasting through right now. The cumbersome ship didn't even have
laser batteries. The dual cannons she had used to take down so
many enemies were sitting in *Dauntless*'s landing bays, removed
to make room for the bombing kit.

Her ship lurched forward, again, out of the direct path of
one of the Union interceptors. She felt an instant of satisfaction, and then she winced as another of her bombers vanished
from the screen. The attackers were almost through her formation, but they'd exacted a toll. She'd lost seven of thirty-six
bombers. Four of those pilots had managed to eject, but she
knew *Dauntless* was committed to its run at the pulsar…and that
made any rescue attempt almost an impossibility. Those crews
would have been better off if they'd been killed instantly like
the others, rather than left to watch their life support dwindle to
nothing, gasping for breath in their frigid escape pods.

She'd lost another three ships to battle damage. Bombers
were more susceptible to system failures than the sleeker interceptors, and even a light hit was often enough to disable the
bomb bay launch system, rendering the ship useless, and sending it back to base.

But in this case, home base was hidden, cloaked by the
stealth generator and on its way to an all or nothing attack on
the enemy pulsar. There wasn't another friendly battleship anywhere in range. Every pilot that had launched was well aware

of the uncertainty of having a place to land. She'd sent her cripples back toward *Dauntless*'s location when they'd launched, for no practical reason other than to get the unmaneuverable ships away from the enemy.

"Okay, bomber squadrons," she said into the comm. "We made it through." *At least some of us did.* "Now, we're going in against that battleship in three waves. Eighty percent thrust, directly toward the target. That should let us finish our attack run before those interceptors can come about and hit us again." *If any come back.* The Blues and the Eagles were on their tails, and Federov suspected Stockton and his pilots would hit those squadrons hard…and exact a price for the damage they'd inflicted on the bomber wings.

She'd known Stockton a long time, and she almost pitied those Union pilots.

Almost.

*   *   *

"A definite fighter launch, sir. We're at extreme range, but it looks like *Dauntless* has launched all her fighters."

Striker sat in his seat in the middle of *Vanguard*'s control center. The new fleet flagship was a modified *Repulse*, the newest, largest, and most powerful class of warships in the Confederation navy. But *Vanguard* was something more, and she outweighed her sister-ships by better than 200,000 tons. The fleet control center, replacing what used to be called a flag bridge, had been specifically designed for the command of fleets larger than those of any previous war. The force Striker had led to the Bottleneck was the most massive the Confederation had ever put into space. Its battle line was a fearsome sight, and against any enemy force, he would have led it forward with the utmost confidence in victory.

Any force save the pulsar.

That bit of ancient technology had altered the balance of power, and it threatened to pull victory out of the Confederation's grasp. Striker was well aware of the awesome power of his fleet...and he also knew, if and when he gave the order to advance on the pulsar, he was likely leading his people to defeat and death.

He'd moved the main fleet slowly forward, toward the advance guard. He'd stopped several times, feigning disorder, and moved his ships around in the line, all in an effort to slow things down. He'd transited into the Bottleneck to fix the enemy's attention on his fleet, to take as much heat as possible off Tyler Barron and *Dauntless*. But now, an enemy battleship appeared to be moving toward Barron's vessel...and *Dauntless* had launched her fighters.

Striker's first concern was that the stealth generator had failed, but if it had, his scanners should be able to pick up *Dauntless*, even at extreme range. As far as he could tell, Barron's ship was still hidden. *But that battleship was tracking something.* Had the Union vessel found a weakness in the stealth generator, a way to scan *Dauntless*?

Something had forced Barron's hand, compelled him to launch his fighters to intercept the Union ship. Even if *Dauntless*'s exact location was still cloaked, the enemy knew she was there now. That forced Striker's hand.

"Commander..." His words died down as his eyes moved across the main display. A large group of Union battleships was moving off their line. It was too soon to discern an exact course, but Striker didn't think it was much of a stretch to assume they were after *Dauntless*.

"Commander, execute fleet operation Alpha-1. The battle line will advance."

"Yes, sir." Striker could hear the nervousness in the officer's voice...he could feel it all across the control center, and hear it in the silence of the forty officers at their stations.

They all knew the odds...and they all knew what they had to do.

They had to draw as much attention away from *Dauntless*... whatever the cost.

Chapter Twenty-Eight

Confederation Intelligence
Troyus City
Planet Megara, Olyus III
313 AC

"I told you never to come here." Lars Garabrant was a Confederation Senator, and his demeanor was as pompous as any other politician's. Garabrant represented Halkon, a backwater world out on the Periphery, and one of the most unimportant in the Confederation. But Garabrant had been its sole Senator for more than thirty years, and that seniority in the Confederation's governing body translated into political power. He'd never have the influence the representatives from Megara or one of the other Core worlds possessed, but he'd made the best of what he had.

"I took precautions, Senator. No one saw me arrive. I have an important message for you." The man had walked into the office and sat across from Garabrant, without invitation. The presumption infuriated Garabrant, but he controlled his temper. His visitor looked like some type of political operative, or even a prosperous constituent come to visit Halkon's representative, but he knew the truth. The man sitting on the other side of the desk, Banister was the only name Garabrant had for him, was from Sector Nine, and his very presence was threatening in more ways than the Senator could easily count.

He'd taken money from Sector Nine—from the Union, while that power was at war with the Confederation—and that alone would likely be viewed as treason, even though he'd done nothing in return for it. Yet.

Then, of course, there was Sector Nine's reputation. The fact that he was in the Confederation, on the capital planet of Megara pretty much eliminated some of the dire prospects that might have threatened if he'd been in the Union, but he didn't doubt the feared spy agency could manage an assassination if he crossed them sufficiently. They'd given him the funds to clear up all his debts, and enough beyond that to live the way he believed a Senator should, and he'd known full well that one day that bill would come due.

"I remind you, Mr. Banister, that I am a Confederation Senator, and our respective nations are currently at war."

"As we were when you accepted the funds we transferred to your accounts. Those monies came from well-constructed shell companies, but I assure you, if we wished, we could trace it right back to the Union treasury. That would be an...uncomfortable...revelation for you, would it not, if it were to be disclosed in open Senate session?"

Garabrant just sat still. He'd almost refused the money, too fearful of where the whole thing might lead. But, in the end, his finances had simply been in too desperate a condition, and he'd had no choice. His father had left the family's affairs in a lesser state than he might have hoped, and he'd been quite undisciplined in his youth. His political machine back home virtually guaranteed his continued reelection to his seat under normal circumstances, but Halkon was a conservative planet, and a scandal like a bankruptcy could have destroyed his career.

"I will not betray the Confederation, Mr. Banister." He tried to sound firm, but he wasn't sure it came out that way through his fear. The truth was, he'd do just about anything he had to in order to keep himself out of trouble. But plotting with a foreign agent was dangerous.

"I am not here to ask you to betray your people, Senator

Garabrant. Indeed, I wish you to help them, and my people as well. This war is pointless and destructive. It must end."

"I couldn't agree more, as I have said multiple times on the Senate floor." He paused. "You wish a ceasefire?"

Banister stared back. "Something of the sort, Senator. Peace is in all interests, but the Union has endured enormous costs in this war."

"As have we."

"Yes…but we have the pulsar. If the war continues, I strongly believe the Union will prevail. Even now, we are on the verge of putting new pulsar units into production. The Confederation has no path to victory, not against such power, but your economic strength allows the warmongers in your government to sustain hostilities, when the Presidium would almost certainly grant a peace…if the terms were reasonable."

"Reasonable?"

"That is where your aid comes in, Senator. You will lead a move to overcome the pointless pride and nationalism that has so dominated your Senate. You will propose a peace initiative." Banister leaned forward and slid a small tablet he'd been holding across the table.

Garabrant picked it up and read it. "Are you mad? You want us to cede ten systems? And this indemnity is…insane."

"And when our forces advance—when your fleet is destroyed by the pulsar—the terms will be far worse. Or, you can wait until we reach Megara itself…in which case the Confederation will be utterly destroyed."

"Even if I agreed to this, there's no way I can gather enough support, certainly not alone. The hawks are too strong."

"You will not be alone, Senator. Your colleagues, Senator Kellerman and Senator Stilson, are also…indebted…to us. We have some level of influence on at least twelve Senators. While far short of the number that will be required, it should be an ample start for a man of your legislative experience, Senator. Your successful efforts will erase your debt to us. In fact, I can promise that a significant additional payment will be forthcoming from the indemnity. You will be doing a true service for your people as well. The Confederation will suffer some economic damage from these terms, certainly, but your industry will recover quickly…and what value can equal the lives that will be saved? If you fight to the end and lose, if you end up facing multiple incarnations of the pulsar, you will be completely destroyed. I'm afraid the Presidium would not be so…reasonable…in such circumstances."

Garabrant looked across the desk at his visitor. He'd always been a dove, and he considered buying off an enemy like the Union far preferable to war. But the terms Banister had proposed were extreme. The Confederation's economy would be crippled for a generation.

If he didn't help, Banister and Sector Nine would destroy him. And there was a good chance the Confederacy *would* face an even harsher peace if the Union was able to deploy their new weapons and gain the upper hand along the front.

"I'll try," he said, feeling uncertain even as he did.

"You will succeed, Senator. I am confident. The stakes are high…for all of us."

Banister didn't articulate the threat again, but Garabrant understood perfectly. Get it done, and preserve his power, and enough wealth to last his entire life. Or fail…and face disgrace, arrest, imprisonment. Even death.

"I'll find a way, Mr. Banister." He had no idea how, but he knew he had to get it done.

"You have my every confidence, Senator."

*   *   *

Gary Holsten stepped out of the shuttle onto the hard metal of the deck. His legs were sore, his back was sore…every centimeter of him was sore. It was a long trip from Grimaldi to Megara, at least it was when the head of Confederation Intelligence wasn't aboard, demanding maximum acceleration/deceleration and anything else that would cut a few hours off the trip. Even with the dampeners, more than two weeks of carrying around the equivalent of three or four times his bodyweight left him feeling like he'd been run over by a heavy transport.

"I got your signal, sir, but I didn't really believe it. Your passage from Grimaldi must be a record." Shane Darvin stood a few meters from the shuttle in the otherwise empty bay. There were no technicians, no stewards, no one else. It was an abnormal sight in almost every circumstance, save perhaps, when the head of Confederation Intelligence wanted to get back to the capital without anyone knowing.

"All I want to do is go to bed, Shane. Have you ever tried to sleep at 4g acceleration?"

The bay was almost silent, save for the soft hiss of the shuttle's engines. Even the pilot and crew remained in the small ship, ready to take off again as soon as Holsten cleared the bay. Officially, they weren't there at all.

They were his own people, with top clearances, but it was still safer having them off Megara and on their way back out of the system, where they wouldn't be reachable or subject to calls to attend Senate hearings or to cooperate with enforcement agencies outside Holsten's control. *Something* was going on in the capital, and Holsten intended to find out what it was, and do something about it. He was prepared to cross certain lines, something best done with the knowledge of as few people as possible.

"I have additional information, sir. I believe we should discuss it at once."

Holsten forced a smile to his lips. "Of course, Shane. I was just joking about going to bed." *Well, not exactly joking*, he thought, struggling to suppress a yawn. "I assume this bay is secure?"

"It is, sir. But I think perhaps we should get back to headquarters before we say too much." The agent looked around, more an instinctive impulse, Holsten figured, than an actual belief the secure bay had been somehow infiltrated. "The Sector Nine presence on Megara is far larger than we thought, sir." Darvin lowered his voice and leaned toward Holsten. "And I'm afraid its tentacles reach into the Senate itself, far more deeply than we had thought at first."

"I'm not surprised." Holsten walked toward the main hatch leading out of the bay, extending his arm behind the agent and nudging him forward as well. "I'm sure the bay is clear of surveillance devices, but there is no harm in going back to my office before we get in any deeper. Did you arrange discrete transport?"

"Yes, sir. There is a car waiting in the secure sub-level. We can avoid any chance of your being seen."

Holsten nodded. His position as the head of Confederation Intelligence was far from general knowledge to most of the Confederation's people, who saw him only as a staggeringly wealth heir and dissolute playboy…but Sector Nine knew *exactly* who he was, and keeping his presence on Megara a secret might just give him an edge.

The hatch opened as the two men approached, and Holsten led the way through, toward a single elevator. He stepped in, and as soon as Darvin had followed, he said, "Sub-level three."

"That location is restricted. Please provide code for access."

"Code alpha-two-three-sigma-nine-four-three."

"Access code recognized. Retinal scan confirmed. Welcome back to Megara, Director Holsten."

Holsten just nodded. The AI didn't need any acknowledgement, and it wouldn't take offense at being ignored. Though he wondered for an instant if he shouldn't have let Darvin provide the code. The AI should be impenetrable, but excess caution wasn't the worst thing he could have working for him right now.

The car began to drop, accelerating sharply for a few seconds before it came to an abrupt halt, and the doors opened again.

The two men walked out into the underground garage, right up to a large transport. It was black and non-descript—to all external views, the type of conveyance that could be carrying any well-off executive or government official. And, if anyone traced the car's ID beacon, they would find it registered to a moderately-sizing mining firm, one specializing in squeezing a few extra years of productivity from nearly-spent mines abandoned by the large combines. It was as boring an entity as Holsten had been able to invent, and wherever a deep analysis of it might lead, it wouldn't be to him, nor to Confederation Intelligence.

Which was good…since as far as anyone else on Megara knew, he was still on Grimaldi, sending out regular communiques from his office on the station. He'd written enough of them to last a month, which should be enough time to find out what was going on…what Sector Nine was up to on Megara. And to do something about it.

Chapter Twenty-Nine

"We have lost three systems, Your Supremacy. By all accounts, our border forces have fought well—and, in most cases, to the death—but they have been massively outnumbered in every engagement. Many of them were old reserve units, their weapons and systems quite outdated."

"Yes, Commander…I have read the reports." Vennius was grim. He had been sitting in his office in near-darkness, contemplating or brooding, depending on how one chose to define it, when Globus had come in.

"Sir…I understand how you feel about your—our—debt to the Confederation, but there is too much at stake here, perhaps even the very survival of the Alliance. The defense of Palatia is sacred, Your Supremacy. It supersedes all other considerations, even obligations of honor. We *must* recall at least some of the forces sent to aid the Confederation."

Vennius felt a burst of anger at being pressed on the issue again, but he pushed it back. Globus had been far less insistent than some, and, if he was being honest with himself, voices in his own mind were pushing him to do exactly the same thing. A

226

dark pit had opened in his inner thoughts, a chasm of despair… images of Palatia fallen, of Krillian soldiers setting foot on the home world's sacred ground.

No, the Krillians could never conquer Palatia. Every school child would take up arms to defend the homeland…but with the defenses in their current state, the Krillians could just bomb it to oblivion.

The loss of Palatia would be the end of the Alliance, of his people. Many Palatians would survive offworld, of course, but they would be scattered, lost. And Tarkus Vennius would be remembered as the Imperator who had led his people to doom. If he was remembered at all.

"Sit, Cilian." Vennius gestured toward one of the chairs in the room. "Please."

Globus walked toward the Imperator and sat next to him, wordlessly.

"We face a great challenge, my friend, and it is my shame to acknowledge that I did not see it coming. My arrogance led me astray. I thought our neighbors feared us too much to seek to take advantage of momentary weakness…and I underestimated the strength of the Krillians." He looked up at Globus, a man he called his friend as well as his comrade. "I received a communique from Commander Tulus this morning. The fleet has set out with the Confeds. They are launching an attack on the Bottleneck, even as we sit here."

Globus stared back for a second before he responded. "They have already set out?"

"Yes. Calling back a portion of the force now would compel the commander to withdraw from the combined force just before battle, when our Confederation allies were counting on their presence. It would be twice the dishonor, a rank betrayal of those who stood by us."

Globus sat silently, taking a deep breath. It was clear he didn't know what to say.

"And, Cilian…with the fleet on its way to Union space, the distance back here is that much longer. The Krillians would reach Palatia before Commander Tulus could get any units here.

It is too late. Even if we chose the path of dishonor, we would do so to no avail." He paused and looked into his friend's eyes, sure his weakness was obvious in his own. "We must stop the Krillians, Cilian, and we must do it with what we have here. Normally, I would say, let them advance, let them throw themselves into Palatia's unbeatable defenses."

"But those defenses are gone."

"Yes…Commodore Barron and his forces obliterated the fortresses, and we have not had time to rebuild them. Palatia is wide open, Cilian. We are all that stands between the home world, and those who would come to destroy it."

"Then, we must defeat the Krillians, Your Supremacy…with what we have here. And the sooner, the better. I would see us set out to meet the enemy, not hang back waiting for them to reach the home world."

"My thought exactly, Commander." There was a rush of energy in his voice. He leaned to the side, his hand tapping the small comm unit. "Commander Severus. The fleet will be advancing within the hour. All ships are to be ready to transit to Intarus."

"Yes, Your Supremacy."

Vennius closed the line and looked back at Cilian. "We will follow the way. We will fight as Palatians." He tried to push away the weakness he felt, embrace the small wave of strength that came from making a firm decision, but age and fatigue bore down on him from all sides. "I need your help, Cilian, my friend. I am old, weak. I have one last battle in me, but I fear the warrior I was in my younger days is no more."

"Nonsense, Your Sup…Tarkus. There is no warrior I would choose to follow into this fight, save for the man sitting at my side right now."

Vennius appreciated the words. He wasn't sure he believed them, but he worked to banish the doubt, and they helped. There were moments where a bit of well-placed delusion was helpful.

*   *   *

Marieles watched Krillus as he sat at the head of the conference table, his chair raised above all the others—*of course*. The council of war had been going on for more than an hour. The scout ships had confirmed the initial reports. An Alliance fleet was heading toward the system.

That surprised exactly no one. The Alliance culture was a clear and simple one in many ways, and there was no doubt what their response would be to an invasion. Some nations might wait, they might fall back, seek to exhaust an enemy, stretch out his supply lines. They might even put out peace feelers, see if a wider war could be prevented. But the Alliance had only one way. Counterattack. Claim vengeance against those who invaded.

Krillus hadn't been any more surprised than his officers appeared to be, but Marieles thought she saw a tension that hadn't been there before, a fear even his bluster couldn't completely hide. He'd massed a great fleet, and she had to give him credit for the numbers of ships he'd managed to build over the years, apparently in secret. The Krillian fleet was more powerful than she'd dared to expect…and considerably larger and heavier than the Alliance force en route. But the Palatians were a warrior culture, and the Krillians, though descended from conquerors, had become decadent and soft over the past several generations. They wielded power, but Marieles wasn't sure it was enough to defeat even an outnumbered Alliance force.

"Great and Terrible Krillus, perhaps we should withdraw back across the border, take up position in one of our fortified systems? We can test the Alliance, see if they will follow us into Krillian space…and we can engage them supported by our own fortresses."

Marieles felt a burst of tension. The suggestion made sense, at least as far as her tactical knowledge extended, but it didn't serve her purposes. She needed the pressure kept on the Alliance. She was about to say something to poke at Krillus's pride, when he relieved her of the need to do so.

"Do you think we cannot face the Palatians, Tectus, though we outnumber them and outgun them? Do you believe they are better than us, that we lack the skill, the courage, the *leadership*, to prevail?" He emphasized the last word, practically daring any of his officers to respond.

Marieles almost joined the discussion. The words were on her lips, but she remained silent. Her presence at the meeting suggested a certain amount of favor at the moment, but she decided discretion was the wiser course, and she remained silent. Until Krillus pulled her into it.

"Ambassador, what are your thoughts?"

She froze for a moment, wondering if he was about to go into one of his abrupt mood swings. She wanted to him to stand, of course, to face the Alliance, but she wasn't sure how best to reach that goal. If she urged aggressive action, he was as likely to see it for what it was: action beneficial to the Union, whether or not the Krillians prevailed.

"It is not for me to decide, Great and Terrible Krillus. There can be little doubt I would wish to see you face the Alliance, our shared enemy, nor can there be any question of my confidence in your abilities. But it is for you to decide and no other. You are from a line of conquerors; the blood of heroes flows in your veins. If you think it wise to pull back, to allow the Alliance to undo all that has been done in your grand invasion, then so be it." She went a little farther than she'd intended. But she knew Krillus was sensitive about comparisons to his predecessors, and she'd wanted to insert that dynamic into his mind.

"Do you hear that?" Krillus glared at the men and women around the table. "Our esteemed ambassador has her own interests to pursue, no doubt, but still, hers is the council of a lion and not a sheep. Would my great-grandfather have crawled back to the cover of his fortresses, leaving behind all he had conquered? Think you, I am lesser than he? That I cannot lead my fleet to victory over the Alliance forces?"

The room was silent. No one dared to challenge Krillus, whatever their true thoughts.

"We will fight. We will destroy that tiny Alliance fleet. We will crush the Palatians, and then we will advance to their home world…and reduce it to radioactive ash."

He paused a moment, looking across the room, seemingly at something only he could see. *And my legacy shall surpass yours for all time, grandfather…*

*   *   *

"We are heavily outnumbered, Your Supremacy." Globus's words were a statement of fact, and nothing more. The Imperator had committed the fleet to battle, and that was the only consideration to a Palatian warrior. The time for debate, for analysis of the enemy's strength had passed. Still, for all his experience and training, the fleet's second-in-command couldn't help but realize the importance of the struggle about to begin. For sixty years, the Alliance had been on the offensive, their fleets pushing into enemy space, conquering worlds, while behind them, the sacred home planet lay safe behind an array of massive fortresses.

Those forts were gone now, blasted to scrap by the superior range of the Confederation primary batteries, and Palatia now stood open, almost undefended against an attack from space. If the fleet failed to stop the Krillians here, the Alliance—at least as Globus had known it his whole life—would be gone. The main fleet, if it survived the battle in Union space, would return to ruins, and a shame that would last to the end of the universe.

"We have been outnumbered before, Commander. We have never allowed numbers to concern us." Globus was impressed at the calmness in Vennius's voice. His dedication to the Imperator was total. He would fight at Vennius's side, he would die there if need be, but even the confidence he felt in the man was insufficient to overcome his doubts. The Krillian fleet was not only larger, but the Alliance force was far from the elite of the Palatian service. Many of the ships Vennius had managed to assemble were old, hastily returned to service, and manned by retirees, brought back to the colors to face the crisis.

They were warriors all, and committed to the fight, but Globus knew many would struggle. Age wore better on the top ranks, those who waged war sitting in chairs, issuing orders. But many of the vessels formed up around the flagship had aged warriors racing through corridors and crawling down access tubes. He didn't doubt their courage, but he questioned whether they could match the standards they'd shown in their youth.

"Of course, Your Supremacy. Every warrior in this fleet will stand against the enemy…and fall, if need be." It was an empty statement. Sacrifices could be made in defeat as well as victory.

"It is time, Commander." Vennius was looking up at the display. "We will be in range in moments. All ships are to prepare for battle."

"Yes, sir." Globus turned and relayed the command. "Will you address the fleet, Your Supremacy?"

Vennius looked hesitant for a moment, the fatigue Globus knew the Imperator felt inside showing for just an instant. "Yes, Commander."

Globus turned and snapped off an order to the communications officer. Then he turned back toward the command station. "On your line, Your Supremacy."

Vennius didn't speak immediately. He stared down at the deck, seeming uncertain. Then, Globus could see his strength rallying. Vennius looked up and put his hand to the microphone on his headset.

"Warriors of the fleet, this is your Imperator. We are about to go into battle, as we have so many times. This fight is different than those that have come before. We stand now without many of our comrades at our sides, men and women who are with the expeditionary force, fulfilling our honor debt to our Confederation allies. For this reason, and because of the losses we endured during the civil war, we face a more difficult struggle here. But we are Palatians, and such things mean exactly nothing. We will fight here, and we will prevail, whatever the cost or sacrifice necessary. I am your Imperator, warriors, and I am here with you. I shall lead you into the battle and fight at your sides…until the enemy is defeated. Until they are destroyed."

Vennius cut the line, and then he looked across toward Globus. The commander could see the intensity in the Imperator's eyes. For all his rank and his true understanding of the situation, he found himself as rallied by Vennius's words as a first-year spacer.

"Commander Globus, go to the shuttle bay. I want you to transfer to *Patentia* at once."

"Sir?" Globus was surprised at the order.

"This will be a hard fight, Commander. It is foolish to have both of us on one vessel."

Globus was going to protest, but the logic of Vennius's statement was obvious. Still, he felt something else. There was more to it than just rational precaution and good tactics. There was something in Vennius's tone…

"Yes, sir," he finally said. He was still uncomfortable, but he knew his duty…and Vennius's order was militarily correct. He saluted, and then he turned and moved toward the bank of lifts, taking one last look at Tarkus Vennius before he slipped inside one of the cars.

Chapter Thirty

"There's something, Commander. I can't quite figure it out, but the rhythm of the thing is somehow…off." Walt Billings was lying on the deck, his arms extended over his head and under the bulk of the stealth generator. He was checking connections. It was just about all he could do. For all of Fritz's and his own engineering skill and experience, they were still mostly uncertain about exactly how the thing functioned.

"I don't like it." Anya Fritz was standing off to the side, her eyes moving back and forth between Billings and the panel of gauges she had set up next to the ancient device. She had been monitoring everything she could think to check since the instant the device had been installed on *Dauntless*, and none of her readouts had deviated from dead normal. But she agreed with Billings. Something wasn't right. The generator was vibrating more intensely than it had. It could be something loose inside…or a hundred other things, half of which she doubted would ever occur to her.

"Everything looks normal down here, Commander…at least as much as I can tell."

Fritz shook her head and sighed. She wanted to tell herself

234

she was being paranoid, that there was nothing wrong with the ancient machine that was keeping them all alive. But her gut, which had served her well for so many years, was screaming otherwise.

"I want to rerun every diagnostic we've got for this thing, Lieutenant. The power conduits and reactors too. If anything is affecting the flow of power to the generator, we're going to find it."

"Yes, Commander."

Billings slid out from under the generator, and climbed up to his feet. He tapped the small comm unit clipped to his collar. "Treiger, we need the full scanning suite in here, and I mean right now."

"Roger that, sir. On the way."

Billings slapped the comm unit again, closing the line. Then he looked over at Fritz. "Don't you think we'd better report this to the captain, Commander?"

"Report what? A couple engineers with the willies? We don't *know* anything." Fritz shook her head, but even as she did, she realized Billings was right. She activated her own comm unit. Unlike most ship's engineers, she had a direct line to the captain.

"Sir, Fritz here."

"Yes, Fritzie…what is it?"

"Sir, Lieutenant Billings and I are concerned about the stealth generator…."

*   *   *

"Engage!" Jovi Grachus stared at her bank of screens, watching as the Union fighters closed. They outnumbered her force, but she didn't let that bother her. She'd heard enough about Union pilots to have a pretty good idea her squadron, and the Confed veterans flanking it, could handle their enemies.

She brought her ship around, eyes fixed on her chosen target. The Union pilot's response was more sluggish even than she'd expected. She had become accustomed to fighting Confeds, to dealing with the technical superiority of their Lightning-class fighters. But the Union ship was less maneuverable and, for once, she had the technical edge. She blasted her engines hard, and then she launched her first missile. She'd closed to point blank range, and the weapon homed in on its target in a matter of seconds. The Union ship jerked around wildly in an attempt to evade the deadly attack, but it was too little, too late. She watched as the image disappeared from her screen. Then she scanned for another victim.

She felt much of her old strength invigorating her in combat. Sitting in her quarters on *Dauntless*, and earlier on Grimaldi and with the Alliance fleet, she'd had too much time to think. She felt like a fool for the hatred she'd nursed toward those she now called allies, and for all the intensity of Stockton's dislike for her, the guilt plaguing her was just as strong. She'd killed many Confed pilots, men and women who weren't here for this fight because of her. Noble warriors who should never have been her enemies, who'd died because she'd sought to indulge her own pain in mindless vengeance.

Now, she felt the cleansing nature of battle. The Union had manipulated Alliance affairs, incited and funded a civil war that had not only brought shame on her, but also had wreaked havoc on the fleet. Thousands of good warriors had died fighting each other in a pointless struggle, one based almost entirely on lies. The whole thing was a lesson in futility and waste…but it told her one more thing. The Union was definitely her enemy. There was no doubt, no hesitation, no misplaced rage…and she smiled as she took down her second target, making her tally two for two with her missiles.

She dove in with lasers, swinging her ship around and firing at a third Union ship. She was still far out, and her enemy took off, trying to escape her attack. Her eyes narrowed, her hand tightening on the controls. The thoughts that had plagued her were gone, even the worry about the desperation hanging above the overall battle. There was nothing now but the predator… and the prey she had chosen.

She stayed on her enemy's tail, matching every maneuver he made, closing steadily. She fired again, closer this time, and her shots came within meters of hitting the target. This Union pilot was better than most, she suspected, certainly more skilled than the two she'd taken down with missiles. But he wasn't good enough. She fired, again and again, as her hand moved back and forth, adjusting her thrust and vector, hunting her victim.

Suddenly, the enemy ship vanished. She felt the rush of adrenaline, the feeling of the kill that had always driven her. She'd taken down three of the enemy so far, and as she looked at the screens, she saw that her people—Alliance and Confederation alike—were slicing through the enemy formation. They were taking losses, of course—they were too outnumbered to simply sweep away their foes, no matter the skill differential—but she was sure they would prevail. Whatever else happened in the Bottleneck, these fighters would not attack *Dauntless*, nor the other Confed squadrons engaging the enemy battleship.

And that was all she could do, at least right now. That, and wish the best to her comrades elsewhere in the system.

*   *   *

"Lex, can you coax a little more thrust from the engines?"

Vig Merrick looked across *Pegasus*'s cramped bridge toward Lafarge, his pained expression leaving little doubt how he felt about upping the already uncomfortable g forces pressing down on them all. *Pegasus*'s dampeners weren't a match for those on a modern vessel or a warship, and Lafarge had compounded that over the years by investing heavily in her ship's engines. *Pegasus* was the fastest free trader she'd ever seen, a fact that had not only been a source of pride, but had probably saved their asses more than once too.

"I'll give it a try, Andi." There was a hint of doubt in the reply. "I'm hesitant to push them too hard considering where we're going. You don't want to be in the middle of the biggest space battle in three hundred years and have the abused engines give up the ghost, do you?"

"No, of course not. But I know you won't let that happen." She turned her head and looked toward the display. She'd had to wait until the entire Confederation fleet had transited, and then *Pegasus* had to travel across the entire system to the transit point leading to the Bottleneck. It was killing her not know what was going on there. Was the fleet engaged? Were they winning? Losing?

And where was *Dauntless*? She'd tried to stay focused, but her mind kept drifting off toward Barron, imagining him on *Dauntless*'s bridge, creeping through dozens of enemy battleships, right in the pulsar's deadly field of fire, with only the ancient artifact she'd brought back from the Badlands between him and total destruction.

Could it possibly work? Could *Dauntless* truly sneak up close enough to the Union's superweapon to blast it to bits with those deadly primary batteries? And, even if Barron managed that, how would he escape? *Dauntless* would be trapped behind the entire enemy fleet. She knew Striker would do everything he could to break through in time, but she didn't see how it was possible.

"I'm upping the power to the engines by eight percent, Andi...but don't ask me for more. Not if you want to be sure we've got full power once we transit."

"You're the best, Lex." She felt a flash of gratitude, for Lex Righter, and the rest of her people. She hated the fact that she was putting them in danger, but she was also glad she wasn't alone. For all she felt driven to follow Barron to the Bottleneck, she was enough of a realist to know there probably wasn't much she could do when she got there. She'd likely arrive just in time to watch him die...and if that happened, she would truly be grateful for her people. She would need them then, and she knew they'd be there for her.

*   *   *

"Task forces Beta and Delta, full deceleration. Come about and prepare to engage the enemy forces behind the point." Van Striker was sitting in the center of *Vanguard*'s massive control center, in more pain than he'd admit to anyone. He knew he owed his life to his doctors, to the amazing care that had put him on the road to recovery. *Albeit, a long road.* His entire medical team, from the surgeon general to the technicians who'd changed his dressings and supervised his therapy sessions, had told him the same thing. He wasn't ready to lead the fleet into battle.

And he'd told them all the same thing too…but now he wished he'd been a little more diplomatic in his phrasing, especially since they'd been right.

He was uncomfortable, pretty much all the time, and the pain was relentless, especially when he didn't take his painkillers, which he hadn't touched since before the final transit. If there was one thing Van Striker knew without a doubt, it was that he would need every bit of mental clarity he could get. He might have ignored his doctors' orders to take the command of the fleet, and paid the price in pain and fatigue, but he never let his mind wander from just what was at stake…and the terrible risk Barron and his people were taking. *Dauntless* and her crew needed everything the fleet could give them, and that included Striker himself sucking up and enduring whatever pain he had to.

He hadn't expected any tactical wizardry from the Union fleet commander, and he'd almost been careless. But there had been fewer Union ships waiting under the guns of the pulsar than he'd expected. At first, he'd worried that the enemy had lured him forward, so they could lash out somewhere else, while the entire Confederation fleet was in the Bottleneck. But any force of that size was unlikely to have been able to advance around his fleet…and the only other route of attack was through the Periphery, fraught with all the same problems that had made it an untenable option for his own, better supplied, forces.

He'd launched the probes on an impulse, one he could easily have failed to indulge. And, the probes found the "missing" Union ships, massed together in the heavy dust clouds behind the transit point, systems powered down, waiting to attack his forces if they retreated.

It was a clever plan, one he fancied he might have devised in his enemy's place. And one he hardly expected from the latest in a string of mediocre Union admirals.

"Beta and Delta task forces confirm, sir. They project twenty-three minutes to a full stop."

The fleet had been moving in-system, away from the hidden enemy forces, if at a moderate acceleration.

He'd been about to give the order to increase acceleration and advance when the probe reports came in. He hated dividing his forces, but if he didn't, his fleet would be caught between two enemies and surrounded. And, he couldn't turn the entire force and engage the ships behind. Barron needed him to divert the enemy's attention. *Dauntless* already had one enemy battleship on its tail, and if Striker didn't move the main body into range, the Union commander would be free to detach as many ships as he wanted to hunt down Barron and his people.

"Very well, Commander." He paused, his eyes on the display, counting the enemy battleships behind the fleet…and calculating how outnumbered the two task forces he'd sent to intercept them would be.

At least they'll be moving away *from the pulsar…unlike the rest of us.*

He took a deep breath, almost wincing at the pain it caused. Just about everything he did hurt. He knew what he had to do, what he was going to say…but it still took him a few seconds to actually get the words out.

"Commander…all other fleet units are to advance. Full acceleration, directly toward the pulsar."

*   *   *

"Captain, the stealth generator is down!"

Barron sat in his chair, frozen for just an instant as Fritz's words echoed in his mind. It was the one thought that had occupied his thoughts since the fleet left Grimaldi, the one thing that could doom his ship and mission. And it had finally happened.

"Evasive maneuvers, Commander," he snapped toward Travis. "Random pattern at your discretion."

"Yes, sir." He could hear the emotion in Travis's voice, not fear—at least, not only fear. Frustration too. They were close, so close to completing their seemingly impossible mission. To fail this close…it was unimaginable.

He felt *Dauntless* lurch hard to starboard, then, almost immediately, back to port. He knew Travis would manage the evasion pattern every bit as well as he could…and he knew it wouldn't save them, not in the long run. It might buy a few seconds, perhaps a minute or two, but *Dauntless* was over ten minutes from even the extreme range of its primaries. He'd seen enough of the recordings of the fleet's last encounter with the pulsar to fully understand the power, not only of the weapon itself, but of the sophisticated targeting system the ancients had built into it. *Dauntless* might evade one shot, maybe two…but there was no way she was going to make it into her own firing range.

"Fritzie, we need that generator back online. Now."

"We're working on it, sir."

Barron felt a coldness inside as he recognized something in Fritz's voice he'd never heard from his engineer before. Uncertainty. She was lost, overwhelmed by the ancient technology she didn't understand. And if his engineer couldn't pull off her usual wizardry, *Dauntless* and her crew were finished.

And the war may be lost.

"Picking up a power spike from the pulsar, Captain." Travis was scared, that was obvious, and hearing the fear in his resolute first officer's tone unnerved Barron more than any combat crisis alone ever could.

He was staring at the display when it flashed. The enemy weapon had fired…and missed. It took a few seconds for him to realize the shot had come within four hundred meters of *Dauntless*, too far away to cause damage beyond a few surface system blowouts, but the nearest of misses by the standards of space combat.

The ship shook again as Travis wildly changed thrust vectors, angling the ship's position and firing the engines in a different direction every few seconds. Barron was a hardened veteran of space combat, but even he was feeling the wild gyrations in his stomach. He gritted his teeth and tried to focus his eyes on a single point, trying to steady his gut. He could face danger, battle to the end against the enemy, but he didn't want to vomit in front of his crew. He was a Barron after all, and if he was going to die, he was going to die like one.

"Gunnery...I'm going to want those primaries ready the instant we're in range."

"Yes, sir. We're updating firing solutions every thirty seconds. Project first shot in nine minutes forty seconds, subject to variation from evasive maneuvers."

"Very well." It was all academic. He didn't know the odds of surviving for nearly ten more minutes, but he didn't think they were very high. If pressed to make a guess, he'd have said two percent.

The display flashed again, another shot from the pulsar. This one was even closer than the last, less than two hundred meters. Barron's board lit up with damage control reports, a whole series of external scanners and antennae on the starboard side of the ship.

Barron turned toward Travis, but he didn't say anything. She was as capable as any officer in the fleet of conducting evasive maneuvers. Nothing he could do, nothing he could say, would help *Dauntless* now. He felt helpless, and frustrated that his people had gotten so close...all for nothing.

He felt the ship jerk hard again, then a second or two later, he heard a loud crash...and *Dauntless* started spinning wildly out of control.

The lights on the bridge went out, the space lit only by showers of sparks flying from two dozen places, workstations and equipment overloading. The display was out, and his own workstation screen was dark. He could hear distant rumbles, explosions deep inside the ship. He wondered for an instant how many of his people had just died, but then he put it out of his mind. Without a miracle, he and the rest of the crew would all be dead too in a minute.

He knew immediately...the pulsar had scored with its last shot. He didn't have any hard data, not with so many systems down, but he realized immediately, it couldn't have been a direct hit. If it had, he'd never have known it. He and *Dauntless* and everyone aboard would be gone already.

Still it was clearly bad…bad enough. *Dauntless* was crippled, out in the open and sitting helpless, right in the deadly weapon's field of fire.

Chapter Thirty-One

"It is done, First Citizen. Vaucomme and his inner circle were the last of them." Ami Delacorte's tone was so calm, anyone not privy to the events of the past several days would have thought she was talking about supply convoys, building projects, job appointments...anything but a series of more than three dozen political murders, all carried out over a period of less than thirty standard hours.

"That is good, Citizen. You and your people are to be commended." Remy Caron sat in his office, which had been previously occupied by Victor Aurien, the former Commissar and senior Union official on Barroux. Aurien and his surviving cohorts were prisoners now, enjoying a level of hospitality far below that they were used to. Caron had almost executed the survivors after his forces had finally taken the compound where they had held out for weeks, but he'd hesitated. His mercy hadn't been spawned out of pity. The two failed Union attempts to reassert control over Barroux had made it clear to him, the struggle for independence was not over. He didn't know if hostages of high rank would be useful at some point, but it didn't hurt to keep them alive until he was sure.

That logic hadn't applied to his political rivals like Matthew

Vaucomme. Caron may have been swept unexpectedly into the frenzy of the revolution, but he'd quickly adapted to his role, learning to use—and enjoy—power. His victories, against the landing force and again in repelling the invasion fleet, had won him the admiration and loyalty of the people, and they had given him an edge over other ambitious revolutionaries. He'd tried to work with Vaucomme and the others, but they resented his newfound power...and they threatened the new order he was creating. He'd finally decided he couldn't risk their scheming, that to ensure Barroux's survival and independence, he had to take total control.

So began a day of terror that was already being called the Putsch. Most of those targeted had been killed in the night, shot in their beds without warning. A few had gone out with more exciting finishes, including Vaucomme, who'd managed to barricade himself in an old warehouse with half a dozen stalwarts. He had only held his murderers at bay for a few moments.

Caron leaned back in the chair, savoring the plushness and comfort Aurien had enjoyed for so long as he practically starved the workers of Barroux. The massive food stores destined to be shipped off world had been confiscated by Caron's people and a portion of them had been distributed to the population, enough to double the food rations. That was more than enough to buy the loyalty he needed to secure his position, and he didn't see any need to waste more.

Caron had held back some of the supplies to feed his soldiers, as well. He needed their loyalty more than anyone's, and their readiness to face any threats to the new order, external from the Union forces he knew would be back...and internal ones as well. He didn't doubt there were others out there who would challenge the revolution, besides those he'd eliminated. No one could be allowed to interfere with the new Barroux, and Caron would do whatever was necessary to ensure the revolution survived and prospered.

"Thank you, First Citizen. I will pass on your words to my people."

"I would have you do more than that, Citizen Delacorte. We

all despised Sector Nine, yet we can also see how the agency was integral to the Union's ability to maintain control. Our former masters did so for their own selfish purposes, to the great suffering of the masses. We seek something better, higher, a world where workers can live their lives, where all share in the bounty of their labor. But to attain that lofty goal, we must defend it. Against outside attack, certainly, but we must also face enemies within, those who would seek to derail the revolution." Caron was blissfully unaware how similar his words sounded to standard Union dogma.

"Like Vaucomme?"

"Yes, Citizen Delacorte, exactly like Vaucomme. He was not unique, nor, I am afraid, is there any shortage of his ilk out there. We must defend the revolution. I would have you keep your team together, form them into a special unit. We will call them the Protectors of the Revolution, and you will be their leader...and report directly to me."

Delacorte smiled and nodded, obviously in complete agreement with everything Caron was saying. "I am honored, First Citizen, and proud to serve the revolution every way I can."

"Thank you, Ami. It's a great relief to have a comrade like yourself whom I can trust. Whom I can call my friend." He paused. "I would have you do more than assemble your existing people. We must know what's happening all across Barroux. I will authorize you to draw from the supplies—food, medicines, luxuries. I want you to assemble a network of watchers, loyal citizens who can inform on those who would seek to destroy the revolution. There is no place for traitors in the future before us, Citizen, and we must root them out and destroy them."

Delacorte nodded. "I agree completely, First Citizen." She stood up. "With your permission, I will get to it at once. We have much to do before Barroux is the worker's paradise we will make it into."

Caron looked up at his comrade. "Go then, First Protector. I will work to build the new order...to lead Barroux into the future."

*   *   *

Ricard Lille sat in his office, brooding. He hadn't wanted to take the Barroux mission. He was no admiral, no general, and he'd said so. He'd only accepted it because he'd seen no way out. It had been clear Villieneuve was desperate, that his old friend needed him

And now, my old friend will kill me for failing him again. Unless I kill him first.

Lille didn't like the idea of assassinating Villieneuve. The first negative, and the one he tried to tell himself was the only one of consequence, was simply that it would be difficult and dangerous. It had been quite some time since Villieneuve had last conducted an active field operation, but Lille wasn't foolish enough to underestimate Sector Nine's chief. Villieneuve knew *him* as well, how good he was, which meant there would be no notice of displeasure, no warning at all. When Villieneuve decided to terminate him, he would see it done as quickly as possible. *Unless he's already decided…*

Lille felt an uncharacteristic edginess, and he looked around the office, suddenly suspicious of everything. It was really just a cabin he'd appropriated. The water on the table might be poisoned, every closed drawer might hide a bomb. *For that matter, every spacer on this tub could be an assassin waiting for a chance to strike. I wouldn't put it past Gaston to have sent his killer out here with me, disguised among the spacers or Foudre Rouge.*

Lille had always been cynical and cautious, but never paranoid. Until now. He tried to push the panicky thoughts from his mind, but they clung stubbornly. He had to get off the ship. He had to get back, and kill Villieneuve as quickly as possible.

That brought him to the second problem. He didn't want to eliminate his…patron. Part of his mind had struggled to put the word "friend" in that place, but he'd resisted. The death of his longtime ally would be a blow to him and, depending on who won the power struggle to take Villieneuve's place, perhaps a grave danger. He'd kept as low a profile as he could, but there were others in Sector Nine who knew just how dangerous he was. He might kill Villieneuve only to face a new assassination plot by the successor to Sector Nine's top spot. He was just too dangerous to be allowed to survive.

The friendship issue was there, too, still plaguing him. One part of his mind was sure Villieneuve would kill him for his failure on Barroux. The problem on that world was worse than his friend had imagined, and he hadn't managed to do anything about it except lose fifteen ships and over two thousand Foudre Rouge, without even reaching orbit. But the other side argued that Villieneuve couldn't afford to lose one of his closest allies, and that even Sector Nine's legendary commander was affected by normal human emotions like friendship. The truth was, he didn't know the answer, but trusting to Villieneuve's mercy seemed like a shaky wager with his own life on the line.

Villieneuve was in trouble, too. Lille knew that, perhaps more than anyone else. His friend had lied to the Presidium, manipulated them, and ransacked the Union economy to fund his schemes. When his colleagues on the ruling council found out all he had done, he was as good as dead.

Unless…

He had an idea, one that sounded crazy. No, more than crazy…outright insane. But if he could pull it off, he might save Villieneuve, and restore his place in his friend's good graces.

It would be difficult, something no other operative would even imagine possible. But Lille was a master at what he did, a virtuoso unmatched by any of his peers. And what he did was kill.

His mind raced, considering potential strategies. It would be his masterpiece, the crowning achievement of his already impressive career. If he could manage it, Villieneuve would be in his debt, and in a position to show appropriate gratitude. Lille's recent failures would be washed away in one brilliant moment.

Yes, he knew exactly what he was going to do. He had to get back to Montmirail immediately…and he'd work out the details on the trip.

Chapter Thirty-Two

Formara System
"The Bottleneck"
313 AC

"Fritzie, we've got a minute, maybe ninety seconds. Then that thing's going to blast us to plasma." Barron was hunched over the comm unit, telling his engineer what she already knew. He was speaking loudly, slowly, clearly. The connection was staticky, full of interference. He could barely hear Fritz, and he didn't suspect she was doing any better with his own transmissions. But he was grateful to have *any* comm at all. Thirty seconds before, that had seemed an impossibility.

"I know, Captain." There was an edge to her tone. In seven years of riding his chief engineer, of expecting—no, demanding—the impossible from her, he'd never heard her sound as stressed as she did now.

He didn't say anything else. Distracting her could only lessen whatever chance they had that she could get the ancient device operational again.

"Atara, what's the engine status?"

"I think we can manage thirty percent, sir. Forty is possible, but we'd be risking a total blowout if we push that hard."

"Get ready. If Fritzie gets that thing back on, I need you to get us the hell out of here. Random course change…somewhere that thing can't calculate."

"I'm ready, Captain."

Barron took a deep breath. He was scared, of course, but mostly he was focused. The situation seemed pretty close to hopeless, but less so than it had half a minute before. When the pulsar had first hit *Dauntless*, he'd thought his ship was finished. Sitting in the near-darkness of the stricken bridge, his vessel seemed crippled, almost dead. But then, the backup systems came online, and the automated damage control sprang into action. Emergency power restored lighting, core scanning, and workstation capacity to the bridge, as well as intraship comm. And as his people tallied the damage to the ship, they discovered that while one of the reactors was useless scrap, the other was still operational.

He'd felt a flash of gratitude to his ship, which he'd always personified. She'd come through for him again. But then he realized none of it mattered. Not unless Fritz could restore their stealth capability.

He knew he expected the impossible from her, but it wasn't the first time…and she'd come through before. He had long attributed a massive credit for the success he'd enjoyed in his career to his astonishingly talented engineer and her team, and through the darkness and despair clouding his mind right then, a spark of hope endured. Some part of him actually expected Anya Fritz to save the day again.

It made no sense. His rational mind told him it was impossible, that they were all doomed. And then the comm crackled, and he heard Fritz's barely audible voice. "I think we got it back, sir."

"Atara," he said, almost shouting her name across the bridge. But she was ahead of him. He felt the ship lurch as the engines blasted back to life…and a few seconds later, his restored screen lit up as the pulsar's deadly beam ripped through the space *Dauntless* had occupied seconds before, no more than a kilometer from where the engine thrust had moved the ship.

He could feel his heart pounding in his chest, the wetness of his shirt, soaked with sweat and plastered to his back. They weren't out of the woods yet, not even close. But the list of *Dauntless*'s seeming miracles was one longer than it had been a moment before…and his crew was still alive, still in the fight.

*   *   *

"There's another wave coming, Commander. At least fifty, maybe more."

Jovi Grachus sat in her cockpit, shaking her head as the message came through her comm. She'd led half of *Dauntless*'s strike force, her own squadron and two of the Confed ones, against more than twice their number. They'd won, sliced through the enemy formation and blasted almost every ship to dust. The enemy had been no match for her people one on one, but with better than a two to one edge, it had been somewhat of a fight. Still, she'd had reason to feel good about what they'd done and the light casualties they'd taken.

Until the second wave came. Another hundred Union fighters, launched again from the bases around the pulsar. This time her people had to endure the enemy's missile barrage without firing one of their own. Then, the fresh birds came in on her people with a fury she hadn't expected from Union pilots. She'd told herself she shouldn't be surprised, that the enemy would assign their best squadrons to protect their superweapon. But that didn't help, not when her people started to take losses. She'd seen more than one of her own Alliance aces fall, and a number of the Confeds too.

She'd been subject at one time to the same pride that affected Alliance warriors, an unwavering belief that she and her comrades were the best, the bravest. But she'd seen the Confed pilots in the battles during the civil war and again here, and she was hard pressed to detect any inferiority in them. They fought as hard as her people, and they died as bravely.

"We've got a third wave coming in," she said into the comm. I know you're all tired, and some of you are getting low on fuel, but we're warriors, all of us, and we do what we must. I've never led a group of pilots that filled me with more pride than all of you. Let's finish this…now."

She pulled back hard on the throttle and blasted her engines, changing her vector toward the incoming ships. Her people would have to face another missile attack, and as she looked at the display, she realized there were a lot more than fifty ships coming at her. It looked like another full wave…a hundred more fighters coming for her exhausted, depleted squadrons.

*   *   *

"Break off!" Stockton shouted the order into his comm unit. The first wave of bombers had gone in against the Union battleship. They'd scored two hits, done some damage, enough to set things up for the second line. But now, Stockton was calling them off, just as they were about to make their final approach.

"Commander, we're almost in range. We can finish this thing." Federov's normally cold voice betrayed her surprise.

"Break off," Stockton repeated, louder this time. "That's an order. Bring your ships around, one eighty degrees, full thrust."

Stockton knew his pilots were frustrated, that they didn't understand. That was fine—they didn't have to, only he did. He'd been as anxious to finish off the Union battleship as anyone under his command. But he'd also been watching what was going on around *Dauntless*.

The battleship had popped onto his scanners, and that had immediately diverted his attention to the mother ship. He'd realized immediately that the stealth generator had failed. That was the only thing it could be…and without that bit of ancient tech, *Dauntless* was doomed.

He'd watched the crazy evasive maneuvers, the two misses from the giant enemy weapon. And then, the hit. *Dauntless* had taken a glancing blow, one that tore off a big chunk of the starboard hull. The ship had been badly damaged—but Stockton couldn't tell if those wounds were mortal. Not from his fighter.

For a minute or two, he was sure the fight was over. The crippled *Dauntless* was a sitting duck. As soon as the pulsar recharged, it would fire again, and without any evasive maneuvers, it would hit. Tyler Barron would be dead, and Commander Travis, "Warrior" Timmons.

Stara...

Stockton was frustrated, angry. He knew there was nothing he could do.

He felt a spark of hope as he saw the big ship move. *Dauntless* had some engine power left, at least, some chance of evading the death blow. Then, she vanished.

For an instant, Stockton thought the ship had been destroyed, that he'd missed the killing shot. But then, the pulsar fired, its massive blast ripping through open space where *Dauntless* had been a few seconds before.

He knew immediately. Commander Fritz had pulled off her incredible wizardry one more time. Somehow, despite whatever malfunction had dropped the cloak, despite the damage the ship had suffered, she'd managed to get the generator functioning. *Dauntless* was cloaked again.

His relief had lasted for six minutes before the ship reappeared on his scanners, less than twenty thousand kilometers from her previous location. She sat there for almost a minute, as Stockton again steeled himself to watch the destruction of the vessel, of everyone he cared about in the universe. But once again, he was spared the agony. *Dauntless* again slipped into nothingness, just before the pulsar was able to get a target lock and fire.

He could imagine the desperate scene on *Dauntless*, Fritz and her team frantically trying to keep the ancient device functioning, knowing failure meant death within minutes. Their evasive maneuvers had taken them off their direct course, adding thousands of kilometers to their trip to firing range...and now, every enemy in the system knew they were there.

The ship appeared again, for only a few seconds this time before vanishing. He held his breath for a few seconds after the pulsar's next blast ripped by where *Dauntless* had been...but there were no signs the ship had been hit.

As he watched, it was all suddenly clear to him. *They're never going to make it.*

He was no engineer, but he had enough experience with complex systems to guess that Fritz and her crew, as brilliant as they were, didn't have much chance of keeping the generator working long enough for *Dauntless* to get into range and fire.

Assuming Dauntless *is still functional enough to attack.* Which he doubted.

His eyes dropped to his long-range scanner. The fleet was moving forward. Clearly, Admiral Striker had decided to do all he could to pull attention away from Barron's wounded ship.

Stockton's face was twisted into a frustrated grimace. He had to do *something*. And then, suddenly, he knew what.

His fighters could never attack the pulsar…but maybe they could hit enough of the line of reactors that powered the thing. If they could knock out the power supply, even temporarily, they could buy time for *Dauntless*, for the fleet.

His eyes darted from one screen to another. His fighters were scattered all around, each with a different vector and velocity. There was almost no time to get them into battle formation. If they were going to do anything, it had to be now.

"All fighters…we're going to attack the power stations behind the pulsar. *Dauntless* needs us. The fleet needs us. I know you want to finish off this Union battleship—and I do too—but, we've got to get the pulsar out of action, at least for a while, and we can do that by cutting off its power." He was far from sure they *could* do it, but he knew they had to try.

"Come around, follow me in. Whatever it takes, we've got to knock out enough of those reactors to cut that thing off." He reached down, as he had more than once, and pulled the cover off his safety override switches. His fingers moved over the series of levers, flipping each of them to the 'off' position, ignoring the series of warnings from his AI as he did. Then he turned his reactor power level to one hundred fifteen percent.

"Cut your safeties, all of you. Everybody at one fifteen on their reactors. Time is one thing we don't have." He'd never ordered his pilots to follow his lead in this way before, to engage in the recklessness of abusing their ships' reactors. But everything was on the line this time. Failure meant death, for all of them.

He could hear the acknowledgements flooding in, not a single complaint among them, despite the extreme danger of the orders he'd just given. He'd lose ships to reactor overloads, he had no doubt about that. But there was no other way.

Not if we're going to save Dauntless. *And Stara…*

Or the fleet.

He grabbed his throttle and slammed it back full, feeling the massive force of thrust slam into his body. He'd been in desperate situations before, but none worse than this one. He didn't know how he'd get to those reactors in time.

He just knew he *had* to do it.

*   *   *

"Fleet units three, four, and five are to proceed immediately to the designated coordinates. Somehow, a Confederation battleship got past our lines. I want that ship found, and I want it destroyed!" Gaston Villieneuve had always prided himself on his cool demeanor, on his ability to hold his temper, or hide it at least. But that was shot to hell now.

The enemy fighters had come as a shock when they'd suddenly appeared, and rationally, he'd known the instant he saw them that they'd come from somewhere. But staring at the small oval on his screen, the designation for a Confederation battleship, his control had snapped. The fighters were dangerous, but they couldn't threaten the pulsar, not seriously. The ancient weapon was defended by a dense point defense network, and almost three hundred fighters in the bases that surrounded it. Its armor was thick enough to thwart the small laser cannons of the tiny ships. Not even the legendary Confederation squadrons could endure long enough to close and take down the pulsar one laser hit at a time.

But a Confederation battleship was a different story. Its primaries were powerful enough to blast the great weapon to atoms and, if it was able to hide from all his scanners—and the pulsar's targeting systems—it just might get close enough to do just that.

For a moment, he'd watched as the pulsar opened fire, even scoring a hit. But then, his nascent hopes were dashed. The enemy ship vanished again, and the massive weapon's finishing shot ripped through empty space instead of slamming into its target.

Wherever that ship was, it had to be found. Now.

"Units three, four, and five all acknowledge, Minister."

Villieneuve watched as the dozen battleships pulled out of the main formation. Combined with the ships he had detached as the flanking force, it left the main line weak. But, as long as he could keep the pulsar in operation, he was confident he could destroy the approaching enemy fleet. Striker had discovered the ships waiting behind the transit point, and he'd dispatched part of his own force to engage. That was inconvenient, but at least the Confed line moving toward the pulsar had also been weakened. The battle was shaping up well…except for the Confederation incursion to the rear.

"I want to know how that ship got back there," he roared. "Review every scan. They slipped past us, and I want to know how. And who is responsible." There was a darkness in his tone for the last sentence. Villieneuve wasn't a sadist, not normally. He was just a man who used whatever tactics were necessary. But when he found out who had let a Confed battleship sneak around the fleet and get that close to the pulsar…he was going to make an exception. Whoever screwed up was going to wish they had never been born. They would beg him for death, and his only response would be laughter.

*   *   *

"The fighters are breaking off, sir. It's a miracle." Maramont was stunned, and it showed in his voice. *Temeraire* had already taken a pair of hits from the enemy's first wave, and the second group of bombers was even larger, its approach ominous in the extreme.

"Set a course toward the last sighting of that battleship,

Commander. Every bit of thrust engineering can give us."
Which will be a lot less than one hundred percent.

Temeraire was damaged, but so was the Confed ship out there...and Turenne knew his enemy was in worse shape. The pulsar had scored a glancing blow, but it had been enough to practically tear open the ship's starboard side. Turenne had been studying the incoming scans, trying to do a damage assessment, when the Confed battleship disappeared again.

He'd thought for a moment his adversary was crippled, that the pulsar would finish it off before he could intervene. But then the vessel vanished, and obviously moved from where it had been. That indicated some level of remaining functionality. Still, Turenne had seen that hit, and he knew the Confed was badly hurt. He was confident *Temeraire* would have the edge in any fight, even without the pulsar.

If he could find his target.

"Engineering reports forty percent thrust, sir. Fifty-five percent possible in approximately ten minutes."

"Very well, Commander. All weapons crews are to be ready for action on a moment's notice."

"Yes, sir."

Turenne looked at his screen, at the enemy fighters pulling away. Maramont was right...it was a miracle of sorts. He continued watching the tiny dots on the display changing their vectors.

No, not a miracle...

He felt a coldness inside as realization dawned.

They're heading for the pulsar.

The enemy's other fighter wing—and he was still not sure how there were so many Confed squadrons out there—had blasted through the first waves of fighters, forcing the bases defending the pulsar to launch more and more of their ships. With all their squadrons deployed, there was no defense remaining against a fighter attack.

Still, the fighters would never get through the point defense around the pulsar, he was sure of that. Even the bombers still armed with their torpedoes would never get in range to be a serious danger.

The power plants…

Suddenly, he saw the vulnerability. The reactors were mostly outside the heaviest zone of point defense, and they were vital to the weapon's operation. An attack on the power stations wouldn't destroy the pulsar, but it would disable it…with the entire Confederation fleet coming on.

He had to stop those fighters…but there was nothing he could do. His own wings had been savaged, barely a third of his ships making it back, and none of those were refueled or rearmed.

He shook his head. The fighters were somebody else's problem. All he could do was finish off the battleship, the one he'd tracked, the one no one else had taken seriously.

"Tell engineering I want that fifty-five percent, Commander. Now."

Chapter Thirty-Three

Formara System
"The Bottleneck"
313 AC

"Maximum evasive maneuvers. We're going in." Sara Eaton sat on *Repulse*'s bridge, staring at the display showing the entire advance guard, every ship in her command, moving forward. There were light red ovals just next to the crisp white icons of her task force, each representing one of Commander Tulus's Alliance battleships. Farther down the line, there were symbols in half a dozen colors, depicting the locations of all the ships of the combined Confederation-Alliance fleet, save for those detached to engage the enemy flanking force. All the might the Confederation and its new ally could muster, and it was moving forward, into the maw of the enemy's great weapon.

There was a shaded area in the 3D display, a bit ahead of her force's current location, the best projected guess of the pulsar's effective range.

The ancient weapon was deadly, capable of crippling or destroying even a massive battleship like *Repulse* with a single direct hit. That much, everyone in the fleet knew. But the actual effective range was an educated guess, and the fact that her force was still one hundred twenty thousand kilometers outside the designated space was cold comfort.

She could feel the tension even now, the fear that any instant, even before *Repulse* crossed into the shaded space of the presumed death zone, a great lance of concentrated energy might cut through her ship. Despite her efforts to set aside the doubts and fear, she couldn't banish thoughts about how she would live her last seconds, watching as she lost her second ship, as *Repulse* disintegrated all around her. She'd known for weeks now what the mission would entail, but she hadn't felt the true coldness of her fear until the order came through to begin the final advance.

She'd been watching the chronometer. Enough time had passed for *Dauntless* to reach the pulsar, but, of course, much depended on the exact course Commodore Barron had taken and, now, on what damage the ship had sustained. *Dauntless*'s problems with the stealth generator, and the hit she'd taken from the pulsar, did nothing to sustain Eaton's hopes that Barron and his people could succeed.

She'd been waiting before *Dauntless* was hit, counting each second, hoping to see the pulsar blasted to atoms before her ships had to move into its range. When she'd first seen *Dauntless* suddenly appear on her long-range scanners, she'd felt a burst of excitement, a fleeting thought that the moment had come, that Barron's people had done it, and in a second, perhaps two or three, the battleship's primaries would open up and tear the deadly Union superweapon into harmless chunks of semi-molten metal. But it didn't take more than a few seconds for her to realize *Dauntless* was still too far away from its target. She wasn't picking up Barron's location because he'd decloaked while preparing to fire, the ship was on her scanners because the stealth generator had failed before *Dauntless* had gotten into range.

An instant later, the pulsar fired, its shot just missing, courtesy of *Dauntless*'s wild evasive maneuvers. Eaton had clung to hope since the fleet left Grimaldi, a belief she hadn't even consciously realized, that Barron's crazy plan could work, that *Dauntless* would save them all. Now she felt that hope draining away, like air from a punctured balloon. She watched, her stomach twisted into knots, her eyes watery, knowing *Dauntless* was doomed, that Barron and his people were finished, that she was about to watch them die.

She saw the shot that hit the wildly evading ship. For a few seconds, she feared it was over…but then she saw that *Dauntless* still had power readings. The pulsar's shot had only clipped the side of the great ship, and while it appeared the battleship was badly hurt, she was still there. Then, a few seconds later, Barron's vessel vanished again. Eaton gasped, panicked for an instant, but then she realized she hadn't seen another shot from the pulsar. *Dauntless* had not been hit…she was cloaked again. Somehow.

Anya Fritz…

Barron's amazing ship had survived the hit, and it was clear now that she was still producing enough energy to power the apparently restored stealth generator. An instant later, Eaton realized *Dauntless* still had engine capacity too, when the pulsar's next shot ripped right through the space Barron's ship had occupied…hitting nothing.

She could feel her heart pounding in her chest, and she realized she was breathing heavily. The bridge was virtually silent, and she knew every pair of eyes was fixed on the display, on the empty space where *Dauntless* had been. And every heart was with Tyler Barron and his crew.

*   *   *

"All ships, fire at will." Commodore Ambrose Duncan stood on *Guardian*'s bridge, gripping the back of his chair and wincing at the pressure of 3g bearing down on him. Duncan was a veteran, one who bore the scars of his service. He'd been wounded at Arcturon, so badly hurt that his surgeon had given him a ten percent chance of survival. Stanford Emory was a gifted medical professional—at least he had been before he died aboard *Pathfinder*, when that ship was destroyed at Grimaldi—but he'd underestimated Duncan's ornery stubbornness. As far as the medical professionals around him had been able to diagnose, Duncan had simply refused to die.

The wounds were still with him, or at least the pain was.

There wasn't a moment he didn't endure some level of discomfort, and he felt a kinship of sorts to the fleet admiral, a sympathy for Striker's pains that went beyond that of the other flag officers. Still, if the fleet made it out of the Bottleneck, Striker's agonies would diminish as he continued to heal. Duncan had already recovered as much as possible. The pain he felt was there for the rest of his life.

He found sitting to be the most uncomfortable, and it was compounded by the g forces of acceleration and deceleration. He'd been offered retirement, desk jobs, even command of Grimaldi base, but he'd turned them all down, more than once with a level of colorful admonishment that left no question he intended to see the war through from the front lines...to its end or to his own.

"All ships engaging primaries, sir." Sonya Eaton was Duncan's tactical officer. Eaton was a decorated officer, and one who had climbed quickly in rank, even if she tended to be overshadowed by her older sister. Sara Eaton had won her own glory in the aftermath of the terrible defeat at Arcturon, and the aura that surrounded her had only brightened when chance caused her to wander into Tyler Barron's orbit. Duncan respected Sara Eaton enormously, but he also recognized the quality of her younger sister, and he considered himself fortunate to have her with him. He wouldn't have her for long, though. He intended to make sure she got her own command, as soon as the fleet got back to Grimaldi. Assuming any of them got back.

Duncan watched on the display as his ships opened fire. The Confederation primaries were the longest ranged weapons possessed by any of the powers—at least until the Union found the pulsar. They'd been a tremendous tactical advantage during the war, both against Union forces and out on the Rim during the Alliance civil war. Duncan knew his force had the advantage, at least for a short time...that they could shoot at an enemy that couldn't return fire yet.

He clenched his fist tightly as he saw a series of hits. The distance to the targets was still long, and he recognized that the fifteen percent hit rate his ships had achieved so far was actually quite good. But the math in his head told him a somewhat different story.

Admiral Striker had detached two task groups to face the Union forces that had been hiding behind the fleet's entry point, but as Duncan's ships approached, they discovered more enemy vessels, sitting idle in the dust clouds and hiding behind asteroids. He known he'd be outnumbered from the moment Striker had placed him in command of the intercept force, but now he realized just how many enemy ships he faced.

"All ships, increase deceleration to 10g." He almost winced out loud as he gave the order. The dampeners would do all they could, but the 3g bearing down on him would increase to 4g, perhaps a bit more. That was tolerable, if uncomfortable, in the specially-designed acceleration chairs scattered across the bridge…at least for the rest of his officers. Standing as he was, his partially-mended bones and ligaments pressed to the brink, it would push Duncan to the limit of his own endurance. But he needed to bring his ships to a halt…he needed to make the enemy come to him. That would extend the amount of time his ships had an effective monopoly on deadly force. If they could take out enough Union battleships before the enemy could return fire, maybe they could lessen the odds.

"Increasing deceleration, Commodore." He could hear the concern in Eaton's voice, and respect as well. His exec knew perfectly well how painful the execution of his order would be for him.

Duncan closed his eyes as the pressure increased, struggling to keep himself from crying out. His knees shook, but they held, and his hands gripped the back of his chair tightly, the muscles all the way up his arm tense, rigid.

"All ships decelerating at 10g, Commodore."

Duncan managed a jerky nod. "Very well." He struggled to turn his head, to look at the display, just as the first enemy battleship disappeared. It wasn't enough to make a real difference, not yet, but it was a start.

"Enemy ships increasing acceleration, sir."

He'd have known that was coming even without Eaton's

report. The war hadn't left him with much respect for Union leadership, but he didn't anticipate the enemy would just sit there, out of their own range, while his ships picked them apart with primaries.

"Maintain maximum fire until the enemy enters secondary range." In some ways, the slow rate of fire of the deadly primaries made the huge broadsides of his battleships the more effective weapon once they were in range. The laser cannons weren't nearly as powerful as the big particle accelerators, but there were as many as a dozen on each side of his larger ships, and they could fire every fifteen to twenty seconds instead of once every two or three minutes.

"All ships report primaries active at maximum fire rate, secondaries on standby."

Duncan watched as the enemy ships advanced toward his force. He glanced down at the AI's projection, the time estimate until the Union vessels entered their own firing range. Eleven minutes, twenty seconds. Not long, especially when it took two and a half minutes to recharge one of his ships' primaries. He did a series of calculations, really no more than wild guesses about how many hits his people could score, and how many enemy ships they could knock out. Even with his most optimistic assumptions, his force was going to have one hell of a fight on its hands.

But none of that mattered. His ships were here to hold back the enemy, to prevent them from striking the main fleet from the rear, or blocking the escape route if Admiral Striker gave the withdrawal order.

Duncan intended to do just that. He wasn't going to let them pass, no matter what it took.

No matter what the cost.

*   *   *

Stockton was staring straight ahead, through the clear portal of his cockpit, as if he could see his targets, still almost fifty thousand kilometers in front of his ship. His fighter was ripping through space at close to one percent of light speed, but the pain of acceleration was gone, at least. There was no point in getting there sooner if he would just blast by so quickly, he couldn't even target a shot. His people would have to take out more than one of the power plants, he was sure of that, but he had no idea how many. That meant they had to decelerate on the way in, and it was just about time to hit the engines again and start braking.

His eyes moved across his screens and scanners, doing his best to keep track of what was going on around him. His squadrons had broken off from the Union battleship. That had been the right call…he was more certain of that now than he'd been when he gave the order, despite the frustration at letting that ship go when they could have destroyed it.

The way was almost clear of enemy fighters. Grachus's struggle had pulled away more and more of the squadrons the enemy had deployed to defend the pulsar. Maybe, just maybe, that left enough of an opening to get to the reactors, to take out enough of them to knock the pulsar out of action…at least for a while. Stockton had no idea how badly *Dauntless* had been damaged, but it was obvious the stealth generator was barely functioning. If it went down again long enough for the pulsar to get a target lock—and that was only a minute, perhaps two, at most—the ship was finished.

He knew his desperate plan was a long shot…but he didn't have any other ideas.

He realized one other thing, and it was uncomfortable for him to accept. The only reason his attack had any chance at all was the incredible skill and bravery exhibited by Jovi Grachus and her mixed group of Alliance and Confederation pilots. They had engaged wave after wave of enemy fighters, and they'd grimly fought on, outnumbered and outgunned. Stockton's rage toward the Alliance ace was still there, but now confusion and doubt ate away at his resolve. She'd placed herself in the forefront of the attack, and as he'd watched the great dogfight, he'd seen her take terrible risks to aid her pilots who were in trouble…and she'd shown no differentiation between Alliance and

Confederation fighters. She was exhibiting faithfulness, courage…every attribute of an honorable ally. But the image of Kyle Jamison was still there, the ghost of his friend haunting him, though he suspected Jamison would have been the first to tell him to get over it.

"We've got enemy squadrons coming in, Commander." The voice crackled in over the comm, just as Stockton noticed the launches himself. For an instant, his heart sank. If the enemy had a significant number of fighters left in those bases, his strike for the reactors was a lost cause. His squadrons were battered, and many of his ships were outfitted as bombers. Enough Union fighters would overwhelm them, and stop the assault in its tracks.

Then he saw the formations coming toward his ships. They were ragged, partial squadrons, poorly organized. He felt a burst of renewed hope. There were a good number of Union birds coming his way, but from the looks of them, they were the last. There was no way to be sure, but it certainly looked like the enemy had scraped up every fighter they could, a last-ditch attempt to intercept his strike force.

His eyes were fixed on the screen. The situation wasn't as bad as he'd feared for those first few seconds, but the wings coming in still outnumbered his people. He'd have one hell of a fight to break through, especially since he had to protect the bombers at all costs. But he had Blue and Scarlet Eagle squadrons with him. The two elite formations had taken grievous losses over the war, but they were still the best in space, he was sure of that. And they could get the job done…they *would* get it done.

"Bombers…maintain your headings. You've got to take out those power plants…I don't care how you do it." He paused, taking a deep breath and squeezing his hand around the throttle. "Blues and Eagles, you're with me. We're going to take on these incoming squadrons, and we're going to make damned sure none of them get to the bombers. Whatever it takes."

Because there's no choice.

Chapter Thirty-Four

Damn!

Tyler Barron slammed his fist down on the arm of his chair, his frustration pouring out despite his greatest efforts to hold it back. The stealth generator had failed again.

He was scared, of course, but the urgency to save his ship was central in his mind, and it drove the fear back into the recesses. "Evasive maneuvers, Commander Travis," he said, almost automatically.

"Already engaged, Captain," came the reply, as sturdy and stalwart as ever.

Travis would do everything possible, but this time a wounded *Dauntless* could only give her thirty percent thrust. The ship's damaged engines most likely didn't have enough in them to prevent the pulsar's advanced targeting from scoring a hit, one that would almost certainly finish *Dauntless*. But Travis was still doing her job effectively, projecting confidence to the other bridge officers as she used every skill and trick she had to keep them all alive, even for a few minutes.

A few minutes for Fritzie to get that thing working again...

Barron knew Fritz didn't understand what was wrong with

267

the stealth generator, why it had begun to fail. Nothing serious seemed to be wrong with the device, at least nothing she'd been able to detect. Her last report had been a guess that it was something minor, akin to a blown circuit. But, it didn't matter why the thing was down. If Fritz didn't get it working again, and soon, they were all dead.

"Throw in the positioning jets, Atara. They'll give us a little extra push."

"Yes, sir…setting that up now."

Barron wasn't surprised that she was already doing what he suggested. He'd always thought Travis as at least his equal—and truth be told, better than him in many ways—and he'd never been hesitant to give credit to her and the rest of his crew. It always bothered him that people didn't seem to care, that all they wanted was to make him into a hero, the second coming of his grandfather, and damned all the other men and women who fought, sweat, and bled to win those victories. He'd loved the older Barron dearly as a boy, but now, as much as he'd fought the feeling, he'd come to resent the family's great hero, not for anything the man had done, but for the weight of the legacy he'd carried since his days in the Academy.

He glanced down at the comm unit alongside his chair. He wanted to talk to Fritz, to get a status report, but he held back. He would only waste her time…time none of them had. Fritz knew what was at stake, what she had to do.

Tyler Barron hated feeling helpless…he hated it above all things. But that was what he was. There was nothing else he could do to save his people. All he could do was wait…and hope Anya Fritz managed to do the impossible one more time.

*   *   *

"Shit!"

Jake Stockton had his hands full. The enemy fighters outnumbered his small force, but that wasn't the biggest problem. His veteran aces could handle a larger force, but they were hampered now by the enemy's failure to engage them. The Union pilots understood the situation, too. They had to get to the bombers and stop them before the attack had a chance to knock the pulsar offline. Stockton had suspected the Union had stationed its best pilots to protect the pulsar and now, as he watched them whip past his fighters, almost ignoring their deadly fire, he was sure of it.

That was bad enough…but now, *Dauntless* was back on his scanner. That meant the stealth generator was down again.

"Blues, Eagles…come about. We can't let those birds get through." Stockton was angling his own controls hard, bring his ship around, trying to alter his vector to a pursuit course. He fired his lasers half a dozen times, taking out one more enemy ship as the Union squadrons blasted toward the edge of his range.

He squeezed every bit of thrust he could get from his ship, knowing he was burning his fuel at a rapid rate. He'd flipped the safeties back on, giving his abused reactors a rest, but now he switched them off again, feeling the massive g forces as his engines blasted once again with more thrust than they were designed to endure.

Confederation Lightnings were a bit faster than their Union counterparts, especially when they were pushed as recklessly as Stockton was driving his. But the enemy had the advantage of momentum, and Stockton and his pilots had to offset their own velocity and match the course of their targets. That took time… time Stockton wasn't sure he had. If those Union interceptors got to the bombers…

He'd been hesitant to order his pilots to cut their safeties again, as he had. He'd lost three ships on the original approach, and he knew things would be worse now, with the power plants pushed so hard, their seals and cooling systems already pushed to the limits. But there was no choice. His hand moved to activate the comm when his eyes locked on the small display. Every interceptor with him had matched his acceleration. His pilots had already driven their ships to overload levels without his order.

He took a deep breath, at least as deep as he could manage

with the forces pushing against his chest. His Blues had always been veterans, and they'd always done what had to be done, whatever the risk. But he still felt the emotional toll of driving so many to their deaths. They deserved better…but they would do what they had to do.

He stared at the screen, at the distance between his fighters and the Union survivors who'd burst through his formation… and to the bombers, blasting at full directly toward the line of power plants. It was going to be close…

Then he saw a flash as the pulsar fired. For an instant, he had a feeling that *Dauntless* had been destroyed. But the icon was still there, the small blue oval representing a ship that had been his only real home, and that carried inside her every person in the universe that meant anything to him.

There was nothing he could do to help, just continue his attack, try against the odds to take out those power plants… and hope to hell Anya Fritz and her band of engineer-magicians managed to pull another miracle out of their hats. One that lasted long enough for the bombers to cut the pulsar's power.

He moved his hand, hesitating for an instant over his override circuits. Then, he nudged his reactor output to one hundred twenty percent. He'd never risked going that high—he wasn't sure if anyone ever had. But the danger wasn't important to him, only the mission. And chances were, he wasn't going to have anyplace to land anyway, even if, through some miracle, his own reactor didn't kill him first.

*   *   *

"We have the enemy battleship on our scanners again, Captain." Maramont reported the instant he'd seen the symbol return to the display, but he hadn't been quick enough to beat Turenne. The Union captain had seen the Confed ship, and he was already calculating an intercept course.

The Confed vessel hadn't gotten as far as he'd feared it might, almost certainly because the pulsar's partial hit had damaged its engines or reactors. Or both.

He didn't care about specifics, not now. Anything that slowed that ship gave his own wounded vessel a chance to catch up, to get into weapons range and engage. *Temeraire* was limping, in no proper shape for combat…but so was her prey.

"Maximum thrust, Commander, vector 019.345.132." Maximum sounded great, but Turenne knew thirty-five percent was the best his ship could give now. The two enemy plasma torpedoes had badly damaged *Temeraire*, and Turenne knew his ship would almost certainly be gone by now, had the enemy assault force not veered off at the last minute.

But *Temeraire* was still there, and even with reduced power and blasted systems, she packed a punch.

"Projected time to firing range, eight minutes, sir." Maramont turned and looked over at Turenne as he made the report.

"Very well." Turenne was on the hunt, craving the kill he'd pursued—that he'd risked the wrath of Sector Nine to chase—but he knew his ship wouldn't get there in time. The pulsar would finish off the enemy ship before *Temeraire* got into range. That would be a slight disappointment, but nothing he couldn't live with. As long as…

Turenne was watching as the enemy vessel vanished again. Once again, he'd had the brief hope that the pulsar had scored a hit, that the Confederation ship had been destroyed. But he realized almost immediately that the enemy had restored whatever cloaking capability they seemed to have.

"I want a full analysis on possible locations of the enemy," he roared. We've got their last location, time, vector, velocity. Assuming they were at maximum thrust, I want a complete breakdown of where they can get, by time."

"Yes, sir."

He might not have the enemy on his scanners anymore, but he knew where they'd been a few seconds before…and he knew where they were going.

And *Temeraire* was going there too.

*   *   *

"It's back online, sir…"

Barron felt a jab in his gut at Fritz's hesitation. He'd already known the stealth unit was functioning again, mostly because the pulsar had fired, and *Dauntless* was still there. His ship was still outside its own firing range, but it was well within the deadliest perimeter of the Union's weapon, and Barron suspected even a repeat of the earlier glancing blow would have finished them all. Still, despite the satisfaction at having escaped yet again, his insides were twisted into knots. He couldn't remember the last time Fritz had been slow to report anything, and the concern in his engineer's voice chilled him to the bone.

"But?" It was all he could think of to say.

"Weapons control is down, Captain."

Barron paused. The implications of Fritz's report slammed into him like a train. He'd known the fragile primaries were offline, courtesy of the pulsar's deadly blast. That meant *Dauntless* would have to get closer, that its secondaries would have to bombard the pulsar for a longer time, giving the deadly artifact a chance to fire back. The loss of his main weapons had decreased the chances of success, perhaps markedly, but there still had been a *chance*…the loss of weapons control reduced that percentage to dead zero.

"What happened, Fritzie?"

"It was that hit, sir." She paused again. "I should have seen it sooner, Captain. It's my fault. I've been so focused on the stealth generator, I missed some of the damage." Another hesitation. "I've got so many of my people working on this artifact that…no, no excuses, sir. I'm sorry. It was my fault."

"The hell it was, Fritzie. You didn't fire that pulsar at us, and you've gotten that device working multiple times now. You saved our asses each time." He was silent now, staring at the comm unit, uncertain what else to say. It wasn't Fritz's fault, but it was devastating news nevertheless. "Estimate on getting at least the secondaries back online?" He was grasping at straws. The answer to his question had been there already, in the grimness of Fritz's tone.

"I have no idea, sir. I've detached a crew to check out the

damage. It's serious. We've got multiple ruptures in both power feeds and control lines. I don't think there's any hope of getting the whole system up and running any time soon, but we're going to try to get a few batteries up. I can't guarantee anything, sir."

Barron held back the sigh that was trying to push its way out. "Do what you can, Fritzie."

"Captain…if I leave the artifact…"

Barron had been thinking the same thing. Yet again, his ship had escaped destruction by the slimmest of margins. Had Fritz been anywhere but standing next to the stealth generator, *Dauntless* would have been destroyed several times over. If he sent her away to deal with the weapons control system…

"Go, Fritzie. We need those weapons." *And if we don't have them, it doesn't much matter if the stealth system holds…we're dead anyway. The whole fleet is.*

"Yes, Captain. I'll keep you posted."

Barron sat and panned his head from left to right, looking around the bridge. His people were at their stations, working as diligently as ever, but he could feel the demoralization. The news about the weapons had hit them all hard. It was too much…the close calls, the desperate, deadly journey. It was one thing to take a terrible risk, even to make the ultimate sacrifice to save friends, loved ones, country…but the realization that it all may have been for naught, that *Dauntless* and her people had come this far, only to fail, was more than even Barron's devoted veterans could endure.

More, even, that he could take. He couldn't destroy the pulsar without *Dauntless*'s batteries…and the Union battleship was closer than ever, having gotten a solid lock while the generator was down.

Barron had always believed in his ship, his people. But now, he saw failure looming ahead, and he couldn't look away. Even if Fritz and her team got a couple batteries online in time, there was no real hope of destroying the pulsar with so little firepower, not quickly enough, at least. The massive weapon would blast *Dauntless* to oblivion long before her guns could do enough damage to prevent it.

Barron sat rigidly in his chair, trying to maintain appearances for his people. He owed them at least that much. But behind the façade, he was as close to giving up as he'd ever been.

Chapter Thirty-Five

Formara System
"The Bottleneck"
313 AC

Stockton brought his fighter around, altering his vector slightly, just enough to bring another enemy ship into his targeting range while preserving most of his momentum. His mind was racing, keeping a keen watch on his velocity and resources as his instincts took control of his flying. He'd caught up with the enemy fighters, though he'd only done so by taking wild risks. He knew he could lose his engines at any moment—or worse. Three of his pilots were drifting through space now with fried reactors...and two more were dead, the victims of more catastrophic malfunctions.

But the rest were engaged now, and every Union bird they took down was one less that could hit the bombers. The enemy bases had remained inactive, no more launches showing on his scanners. With any luck, his assessment had been correct. The ships his people were chasing were the last ones the enemy had to send out.

He fired again, taking down yet another enemy fighter. His aim had been uncanny. As well regarded a pilot as he'd always been, he'd never flown like he was now. His fighter moved at his will, as if he was operating it by pure thought. His instincts had been dead on. He knew what was at stake, not just his own life or those of his pilots, but perhaps the fate of the entire Confederation. If *Dauntless* couldn't destroy the pulsar, the ancient weapon might very well obliterate the fleet, leaving Grimaldi exposed to attack…and then an open road to the heart of the Confederation. If that happened, everyone important to Stockton would already be dead, but now he realized there was a true patriot lurking under his cocky and restless demeanor.

There was one other thing. He knew Kyle Jamison would have driven his people to the end of their abilities, that *Dauntless*'s old strike force commander would have stopped at nothing to see the mission completed…and Stockton intended to see his friend's will be done.

He fired again, his eyes darting back and forth, between the target and the ships at his side, the survivors of *Dauntless*'s two famous squadrons. Olvirez was gone now, one of the few original Blues, a victim of three enemy ships that had turned suddenly and hit him from multiple sides. Two of Timmons's Eagles had been hit in the last few minutes, as well, one gone, the other floating helplessly, his bird's engines melted to useless scrap.

He swung the throttle again, and he pulled back hard, squeezing out every bit of acceleration his tortured ship could give him. He didn't know what was keeping the abused fighter functioning. It felt almost as though his own stubbornness had somehow extended to the physical equipment of his ship. Whatever it was, the fighter continued to obey his every command, and as it did, more Union fighters were blasted to hell.

He tried not to think of the cost his people had paid, of how few of the veterans who'd launched with him were still in the formation. The space all around was littered with the debris of destroyed ships and life pods holding surviving pilots, men and women who knew perfectly well how unlikely it was they'd be rescued.

The two squadrons fielded less than half the numbers that had launched hours before, but there was no sign of disorder, no letup in intensity. The Blues and Eagles were hot on the tails of the enemy force, cutting them down one fighter at a time.

Stockton was impressed with the Union pilots, as well. He'd come to expect a certain level of mediocrity in the enemy, but these squadrons were exhibiting skill and elan far in advance of the average Union wings. They continued to chase the bombers, most of them ignoring the Confeds on their tails as the running fight continued.

Now, the lead elements opened fire on Federov's assault force, and Stockton saw the first bomber taken out. The strike craft were cumbersome and sluggish, and even the veterans in those cockpits were vulnerable to interceptors coming up from behind. The Blues and the Eagles had done all they could, gutted the enemy squadrons, but some ships got through, and now Stockton watched helplessly as bombers started to fall. He fired his lasers, even before he was in range of any new targets. The pilots in those bombers were his people, his friends and comrades. But it went far beyond that. They were also the best hope to disable the pulsar, to save *Dauntless*, the fleet...and maybe the Confederation.

*   *   *

Guardian shook hard, showers of sparks flying around the bridge as an electrical conduit split down the middle, its remains falling in two different directions and hitting the deck with a loud crash. Ambrose Duncan was still behind his chair, holding on, shouting orders to his officers. Not only to *Guardian*'s crew, but to the rest of the forces under his command.

His people had made good use of their range advantage, but even with half a dozen enemy battleships destroyed or knocked out of commission, they were still outnumbered...and now the Union vessels were firing back.

The fight was a nasty one, with little finesse. Duncan had been concerned the enemy would attempt to blow past his ships, to close on the rear of the main fleet. It was what he would have done in their position, and he wasn't surprised when it became apparent that was just what the Union forces were trying to do.

The rest of the fleet wasn't engaged yet, save for the sharp battle Eaton's advance guard and Tulus's Alliance ships had fought against the enemy picket line at the transit point. But if he let these ships get around him, they'd likely hit Striker's force just as it was entering range of the pulsar—and engaging the main Union fleet.

"Task group seven is to come around. I want to bracket the enemy left. If we can hit that flank from two sides, we can gain temporary superiority."

"Yes, sir." Commander Eaton nodded as she answered, and Duncan could tell from her tone she agreed with his decision. "Task force seven acknowledges, sir."

Guardian shook again, not as hard this time. Duncan's flagship was facing two enemy battleships, and the multiple angles of fire were complicating evasive maneuvers. The ship was jerking around wildly, random spurts of thrust in all directions. Duncan's fingers were clenched, the flesh around his knuckles pale white as he steadied himself. He'd almost fallen twice, but he'd managed to stay on his feet. Now, exhaustion was taking its toll, and he edged around his chair, wincing in pain as he sat down. *Guardian*'s thrust levels were lower now, but Duncan's old wounds ached from the abuse they'd suffered during the approach, and pain radiated out from his back in every direction as he bent into the seated position.

"Bring us around…course 310-211-009." His eyes were fixed on the display as he gave the order. It was difficult to keep track of the relative movements of multiple ships all in the three dimensions of space, but he was trying to get around the flank of one of the enemy battleships *Guardian* faced, to block or at least obscure the line of fire from the other one. His ship and his people were more than a match for any Union counterpart, he was sure of that. But two to one was a different story, and even if his people pulled out a victory against both enemies, *Guardian* would be badly damaged. He had to protect his ship, keep it combat ready. The fight in the Bottleneck was just beginning, and there was a massive struggle ahead before victory—or defeat—would be determined.

"Executing course change now, sir."

He watched as Eaton worked at her board. A vector change in the middle of battle was far more involved than simply angling the ship and firing the engines. Any ship that ceased evasive maneuvers would find itself easily targeted, and blasted to wreckage in minutes, if not seconds. Duncan's orders were for a net course, the angle and speed where *Guardian* would end up. Now, Eaton had to layer on random vector mods and bursts of thrust. Anything to thwart enemy targeting systems, sophisticated AIs that were constantly trying to estimate where a target would be, where to place the next shot.

Guardian jerked hard again, and Duncan felt a wave of pain as the g forces pushed into him. He closed his eyes, just for a few seconds, struggling to hold in the cries trying to escape from his lips. His people knew all about his wounds, but that didn't matter to him. He was their commander, and whatever it took, he would behave that way. He would set the example he wanted his spacers to follow.

He heard the distant whine, *Guardian* firing another broadside. His eyes darted toward the display, waiting for the damage assessment. Three hits…and one of them looked critical. The scanners were reporting follow up explosions, and the enemy ship's thrust dropped sharply.

"The nearer ship," he said sharply. "It's damaged. All guns concentrate on the closest ship." He could smell the kill, and he wanted it. If he could take out the one ship, *Guardian* would have a one on one battle, at least right now.

And that was a fight he knew his people could win.

*   *   *

Jovi Grachus leaned back in her seat and let out a deep sigh. She was exhausted, and her flight suit was nearly soaked through with sweat. Her hands ached from gripping the throttle as tightly as she had for so long, and her head pounded. Her people had faced wave after wave of enemy fighters, each of them fresh as they'd hit her ever more fatigued and depleted squadrons. Her people had done what they'd had to do. They'd fought and defeated each Union wing, taking on every ship the enemy could send their way.

They hadn't done so without cost. More than half her people were gone now, some dead, others nursing damaged ships or floating in escape pods. Their hope for rescue depended heavily on *Dauntless*'s survival. If the battleship was destroyed, it was far from certain any other ships would get there soon enough to conduct rescue operations.

Of course, if Dauntless *is destroyed, none of the fleet ships will even get this far. The pulsar will gut Striker's formations before they even get close.*

She opened her hands, stretching her fingers, trying to work the tightness from her muscles. Then, she gripped the controls of her ship again, and moved her hand to the starboard, bringing her fighter around, toward the last group of enemy survivors.

The Union fighters were in wholesale flight now, their morale thoroughly broken. But Grachus had come up in the cold militarism of the Alliance service, and she knew any functional enemy ships could cause damage. She wasn't bloodthirsty, but she wasn't going to risk the lives of any of her people, or her allies, by showing mercy to defeated, but still dangerous, enemies. She'd given the order to pursue and destroy the last Union formations, and her people were doing just that, with a grim determination that suggested they understood completely.

She increased her thrust to full power, pursuing the closest Union fighter. Her Palatine-class ship was slower than the Confederation Lightnings, and even than the Union fighters. It wasn't a large difference, but it was a burden in battle. The Alliance had mastered the art of war, and for all her respect for her Confederation allies, one on one, she still felt Palatian warriors were unmatched. But a nation sixty-years from slavery and despair, one that had funneled all its best and brightest into the military for that entire half century, paid a price in terms of science and technology. Most of the Alliance's systems and weapon designs had been taken from conquered worlds, and for all the science and tech its armies had pillaged, the Palatian realm was a step behind both its new ally and its new enemy.

Grachus squeezed the trigger, watching the scanner as her shot went wide. She fired again...and again. The range was long, but it was only going to get longer. The panicked Union pilot was blasting at full thrust, and every passing second pushed him a bit farther from her pursuit. She stared intently at the screen, adjusting her angle slightly, and then firing again.

Her shot was closer this time, but still a miss. She didn't have much time...a few more seconds, and her victim would elude her for good. She could see the Confed pilots pulling to the forefront of the chase, but the ship she was after was too far from them. If she missed, the enemy pilot would escape.

For an instant, she wondered if that would be so bad. Then, she imagined that pilot, now so intent on fleeing, coming back later, killing one of her people. War was war, and there was no way to soften it.

She stared at her screen, her hand clenched, ready to fire. Then, she squeezed the trigger...and an instant later, her target vanished from the screen.

One terrified pilot killed. One less enemy to threaten her comrades, her friends.

One tiny step closer to victory.

*   *   *

Sara Eaton stared at the display, trying but failing to hide her shock and horror. *Resolute* was gone...completely gone.

One instant, the battleship had been on the display, in its position in the line, and then there was a massive energy spike, one that almost exceeded her instruments' ability to measure... and the massive ship was no longer there.

Over a thousand crew. Four and a half million tons of ship. Just gone, nothing left except a cloud of hard radiation.

Eaton had known the pulsar could destroy a battleship with a single shot, but sitting on her bridge, watching it happen, it still hit her hard. The fleet was thirty thousand kilometers outside the projected range of the enemy weapon.

A significant margin of error…

She wanted to be angry, to blame the intel services or the engineers who'd analyzed the scant data on the enemy weapon, but it was nobody's fault, not really. Everyone who'd given an opinion on the pulsar's range had been sure to state that it wasn't much more than a guess. And it didn't make a difference. The fleet had to go in…and it would have gone in anyway, even if they'd known the pulsar had a longer range.

But that makes the gauntlet that much longer…that much more time for them to blast us to bits before we can even fire…

She hadn't been ready, not yet. Eaton had a persona she wore in battle, a shield she put up that pushed aside feelings of loss and even fear…but she'd found it difficult to put in place this time. She'd been in desperate fights before, even the crushing defeat at Arcturon, but she'd never stared into the face of hopelessness as intently as she did now. The pulsar wasn't just an enemy, and moving toward it wasn't only a fight. Striker had to try, she knew that, but she was also well aware it was a long shot that any of them would get close enough to attack.

"I want damage control parties on full alert, Commander. On all ships."

"Yes, Commodore." The tactical officer relayed her order, first to *Repulse*'s chief engineer, and then to the other ships of the task force.

Eaton felt strange, different than she had in her other battles, and she suspected her crews felt the same way. It was one thing to go into a fight, even outnumbered, outgunned…but now the ships of the fleet pushed forward, into deadly fire to which they couldn't respond. The crews of each ship could only move forward, executing evasive maneuvers to make their vessels more difficult targets…and wait to see if they died.

When they died.

She wondered if *Resolute*'s crew even knew what had happened, if they'd had time to be terrified, to think last thoughts of loved ones…or if they died never knowing what was happening. The pulsar was a powerful weapon, but only a direct hit could obliterate a battleship so quickly and totally at this range.

Perhaps *Resolute*'s spacers had been fortunate. They'd been spared the ordeal of struggling to keep their crippled battleship alive for a bit longer. There had been no pain, no burns, no long, slow deaths from radiation poisoning. No protracted periods of stark terror. Eaton knew any ship wounded in this fight was lost, its crew walking dead from the moment the pulsar's deadly beam shattered their vessel. The fleet would advance toward the pulsar, desperately trying to get close enough to destroy the deadly weapon. But they would almost certainly fail…and, even if they didn't, the shattered remains of the Confederation navy would face every ship the Union had been able to scrape up. Whatever ships escaped from the Bottleneck, they wouldn't be battleships grievously wounded by the pulsar, limping back on crippled engines.

The display flashed again, another shot registering, the massive energy readings showing up as a bright streak and then disappearing. This time, the pulsar missed. Eaton felt a wave of relief, but it didn't last. The enemy weapon's range was so long, it would get dozens, even hundreds of shots before the fleet was in range to fire back. Even wild evasive maneuvers were only so useful against the sophistication of the ancient targeting system. She didn't do the math, but she had a good idea of the odds against them.

She turned her head, looking toward the long-range scanners, and her thoughts wandered. *Are you still out there, Tyler?*

She knew her friend and his ship were in trouble. They were badly damaged, behind enemy lines, with a dozen battleships headed their way, and the pulsar just waiting to finish them off if the stealth generator failed again. She tried to imagine the terror of *Dauntless*'s crew, how alone they must feel.

She also knew Tyler Barron and *Dauntless* were the fleet's best hope. Maybe its only hope.

*   *   *

Villieneuve stared at the main display, watching the Confederation fleet advance. The operation had gone more or less according to plan. He'd expected his flanking force to remain hidden for longer, and he knew he owed their discovery to Van Striker's meticulous nature. But that wasn't what troubled him the most.

His mind was fixed on the Confederation battleship operating behind his lines. The Confeds clearly had some kind of stealth capability, though the fact that only one ship seemed to be so equipped suggested it was highly experimental...or perhaps a unique piece of old tech. Whatever it was, it complicated his plan. That ship was after the pulsar...that much was obvious. And it couldn't be allowed to get close enough to attack, however long the odds of it succeeding in its mission.

He'd already dispatched a force of battleships to find and destroy the Confederation ship, but it would take some time to get there. Time he might not have.

The Confed ship's fighters, far more than he'd ever seen launched by a single vessel, had trounced his own squadrons, both those from *Temeraire* and from the stations deployed to defend the pulsar. The Confed wings were badly hurt, too, and he was confident they didn't have the firepower to destroy the pulsar itself, but he didn't know about the battleship. It had taken a hit, and his best guess was the damage had been extensive. But if she had operational weapons and could get close enough to the pulsar undetected...

"Get me *Temeraire*," he snapped.

"Yes, Minister. You may transmit on your line."

"Captain Turenne, this is Minister Villieneuve. I need a status report. You must find the enemy battleship and destroy it... at all costs."

Villieneuve sat and waited. *Temeraire* was a good four light seconds from the fleet flagship. An extra eight seconds didn't sound like much between exchanges, but in practice it was annoying even when the parties weren't under enormous stress. Right now, Villieneuve was ready to punch the wall waiting for a response.

"We are pursuing the enemy, Minister. We have considerable damage, and are operating with limited thrust capacity.

The enemy seems to have reestablished their stealth capability. I have analyzed all possible locations the Confeds could reach based on their apparently degraded engine capacity, and I have cross-indexed with likely routes toward the pulsar."

Villieneuve was impressed, not just in what Turenne had said to him, but in the officer's confidence, his strength of will. He'd been ready to space *Temeraire*'s commander earlier for disobeying orders, but Turenne's willful action had created the best chance to intercept the Confed ship before it could make an attempt on the pulsar.

"You must squeeze more thrust from your engines, Captain. Do whatever you can, take any risk...just destroy that Confed ship."

The wait seemed even more interminable, but finally, Turenne's voice came through the comm speakers. "Yes, sir. I've already got the reactors on overload." A pause. "But we still have to find the enemy. I've narrowed it down to possible locations, but that's all I've been able to do. We won't be able to target the ship unless they drop their cloak...or it fails again."

"They'll have to drop it, Captain, to attack the pulsar." He didn't know that, not really, but it made sense. And even if they didn't have to cut the cloak, their first shot would give away their position. "I need you to be ready. You've got to take out that ship...and if you do, it will be Admiral Turenne."

Villieneuve generally found negative reinforcement to be more effective than rewards, but that was far from a universal rule. Turenne was clearly much more capable than the average Union officer, and the best people needed to be treated in their own way.

And if *Temeraire* found that Confed ship, and destroyed it, Gaston Villieneuve would pin those admiral's stars on Turenne's collar himself.

Chapter Thirty-Six

"We've got a message on the comm, Andi." Vig Merrick looked over at her. His voice was edgy at first, but then she recognized genuine surprise. "It's Admiral Striker."

She sighed. *Looks like we're busted.* "Put him through."

"Andi, this is Admiral Striker. You did one hell of a job sneaking into this system and working your way around the edge of the fleet without being detected…but you've got to go. Now."

Lafarge shook her head as she listened to the message. She hadn't come this far just to turn around, to leave Barron and her friends to their fates. She could see the situation in the system, and she'd watched the battleships of the fleet moving toward the pulsar.

And she knew what Barron was doing. She hadn't had scanners powerful enough to detect *Dauntless* when the stealth generator had failed, but she'd picked up enough from comm chatter to piece together what was going on. Barron was deep behind enemy lines…he'd snuck back there to destroy the pulsar. But the ancient artifact hiding his ship had failed, more than once, with nearly disastrous consequences.

She'd also watched as the ships of the fleet began taking loses, one big battleship obliterated with the first shot from the enemy superweapon, and another three severely damaged and effectively disabled. She'd taken *Pegasus* on a wide course around the edges of the action, but she'd never expected to get this far without being challenged.

"Admiral Striker, I know what's happening here, and I've come to help." She realized immediately how ridiculous that sounded. Van Striker had brought the largest fleet every assembled to the Bottleneck, to face an even more powerful weapon... and she was sitting in her tiny old free trader saying she'd come to help.

The comm was silent as her message made its way to the flagship and a response returned. She'd intended to say a lot more than she had, but she'd run into a wall. She didn't know what she intended to do here, or even any way she thought she might be able to do some good. But she wasn't leaving.

"Andi, listen to me. This is dangerous. You can't do anything here. *Pegasus* doesn't have the firepower to make a difference in this fight. Go back. Now. It's what Tyler would want, too."

She was shaking her head as she listened to his words. She knew she should go back...and that it was exactly what Tyler would want. At least that would save her crew. She loved them for interfering as they did, for coming with her, but now she wished they hadn't. It was simpler when she planned to be alone. Her sacrifice—if that was what it came to—would have been hers alone. Now, if she left, if she turned and slipped back out of the system, leaving Barron to his fate, she could at least ensure Vig's safety, and Dolph's and Lex's. It was one thing if she felt driven to get herself killed...out of duty, or insanity. Or love. But it was another to condemn her loyal shipmates to that fate.

She almost gave in to Striker. The guilt was too much. If she'd really believed she could make a difference, that her presence improved Tyler's chances by even the slimmest of margins, perhaps she could have justified staying. But she had no idea how she could even help.

Then she looked across the tight confines of *Pegasus*'s bridge, toward Merrick. He was shaking his head.

She looked at him quizzically.

"You can't go, Andi. We can't go. If you leave and Tyler is killed, you'll never forgive yourself. And we won't let that happen."

She put her hand over the microphone and looked back at her second. "Vig, if we stay we could all die. Probably *will* die. I can't lead you to that."

"Don't you think we knew what we were getting into? We knew about the danger when we ambushed you in the docking bay, same as we know now. But, we're with you. And we have to finish this. Tyler Barron saved all of us. We may not be in this as deep as you, Andi, but we pay our debts."

Lafarge sat silent, stunned. She'd always believed she thought the best of her people already, but they could still surprise her. The guilt remained, but Vig's words had restored her resolve.

"Andi, are you still on the line?" Striker's voice was insistent.

"Yes, Admiral. I'm here…and this is where I'm staying. I don't know what we'll be able to do, but we're not leaving, not until I know exactly what happens here."

"Andi, you have to go. Reverse your thrust now, and get the hell out of here."

She looked across at Merrick and forced a smile to her lips.

"I'm sorry, Admiral, your transmission is garbled. I can't hear what you're saying." She reached out and closed the line. Then, she took a deep breath.

"Well, Vig, we're in this deep now…so let's press on and see what we can do."

*   *   *

"The generator's out again, sir. I'm down by the starboard batteries, but I left Walt Billings up there, and he knows everything about that device that I do. He says it's completely dead now. No chance of restarting it, not without tearing it apart and figuring out what's wrong. No power readings at all." There was a short pause, then: "I'm sorry, sir."

Barron could hear the self-flagellation in Fritz's voice, and he suspected his engineer blamed herself for everything that was going wrong...the stealth generator failing, the weapons systems going down, her not being with the artifact when it scragged, even the dozen enemy battleships heading right for *Dauntless*. Barron had more problems than he could easily count, and, truth be told, he had no idea what to do next. But he still hated the idea that Fritz was taking so much guilt on herself.

"Fritzie, you worked miracles keeping it going this long." Barron could feel the silence and tension on *Dauntless*'s bridge. His people had faced extreme danger before, but he couldn't see any way out of this one. He suspected every officer on the bridge felt the same way. They couldn't even fight to the death, not with all the weapons down.

"What do you want me to do, sir? Should I stay with the batteries or try to get back to the generator?"

There was no point in sending her back. *Dauntless* would be dust and plasma before she even got there and, while Walt Billings wasn't Anya Fritz, he was the next best thing. If he said it was hopeless, Barron was sure that was the case, whether Fritz was there or not. Especially in the miserable few minutes they had left.

"Stay on the batteries, Fritzie. Try to get me something that shoots." He turned toward Travis. "Atara, tell the engine room we need more thrust...now. I don't care what it takes. Or what risks they have to take."

"Yes, sir." She relayed the order, with a forcefulness that surprised even Barron. Then, she turned back toward his chair. "Sir, Commander Stockton and the fighters..."

Barron's head snapped around. With the generator not drawing power anymore, Travis had upped the power on what remained of *Dauntless*'s sensor suite.

The fighter squadrons were in two separate groups, and the first thing Barron noticed was the gaps in their ranks. Fewer than half the ships he'd launched appeared to be left.

Then, he saw where they were. One group was relatively nearby, in the final stages of a dogfight with Union fighters. They were in the mop up phase, the battered survivors finishing off the last of the enemy ships. He noticed the Alliance fighters were all there, also at fewer than half the numbers they'd started with.

His eyes moved to the other group. Jake Stockton was leading that force. Barron was relieved to see his strike force commander still alive. Then he saw the rest of the ships, the shattered remnants of Blue and Scarlet Eagle squadrons...and every remaining bomber in the force. All heading toward the pulsar.

No, not the pulsar. They're going toward the power stations. Of course!

Barron suddenly felt a rush of hope. *Dauntless* might not be able to destroy the pulsar, but if Stockton and the surviving fighters could take out enough of the reactors that powered the thing, they could shut it down...long enough, at least, to save the fleet, to allow the battleships to close with the Union line and fight a straight up battle. One he was confident they could win.

He felt a little of the excitement slip away as his eyes landed on the battleships moving back toward *Dauntless*. He'd fought against long odds, but there were a dozen ships heading his way, and he didn't have an operational gun onboard.

Still...if Stockton can take out those power plants, at least it won't be in vain. The fleet will be saved.

He looked around the bridge, watching his people with a combination of sadness and pride. They truly were the best the Confederation had to offer, and if their lives were what it took to save their tens of thousands of comrades, and billions of fellow Confederation citizens...well, there were worse reasons to die.

He watched, waiting to see if the pulsar's next shot would hit, if the giant weapon would get a solid lock on *Dauntless* before Stockton's people could shut it down. If they could shut it down.

Barron knew his ship and people had almost no hope of

survival, but there was still a part of him that refused to yield to destiny. It wasn't rational, and he couldn't conceive of any plan that would get his people out of the Bottleneck alive, but the spark burned nevertheless, resolute, defiant.

Everyone on *Dauntless* might die.

But they would die fighting to the last breath.

*   *   *

The rearguard fought hard, its ships firing their weapons relentlessly, its crews ignoring pain, fatigue, casualties. But it was being pushed back. Duncan had brought his ships almost to a dead stop, but the enemy hadn't cut their velocities. The Union ships charged right through the zone where the Confederation primaries raked them before they could return fire. Then, they entered close range, and the two forces engaged in a furious firefight, laser cannons and short-range rockets firing back and forth, gutting vessels on both sides. Still, throughout the deadly fight, the Union forces held their velocity, ripping right past the Confederation ships, turning as they did to bring their guns to bear and continue the exchange as they moved away.

Duncan had sworn at least a dozen times, first to himself, quietly enough to spare his crew, and then out loud as his frustration grew. His mission was to hold back the enemy, to prevent them from hitting the main fleet in the rear, just as they engaged the primary Union line…or, if it came to that, tried to retreat through the transit point. He'd expected the enemy to stop, to line up and engage his forces in a protracted duel. But now it was clear that wasn't going to happen.

"All ships…prepare for 6g thrust, heading 300.230.280, directly after them." Duncan couldn't make the enemy stop and fight him, but he could damned sure follow them. The Union ships had a velocity advantage, one it would take his forces time to overcome. His targets would be moving farther away, at least for a while. But, if he executed things perfectly, he could accelerate his ships enough to maintain primary weapons range. The recharge time of the long-range guns would be offset by their hitting power…and by the fact that the enemy would no longer be able to return fire.

"All ships report ready, sir."

Guardian shook hard again from yet another hit. Duncan's flagship had been in the thick of the fighting. His force had taken significant damage, and lost three ships outright, though they'd given rather better than they'd gotten. "Primaries?" He shot a glance over at Sonya Eaton.

"Still online, sir."

He nodded. Based on the most recent reports, about half his ships still had their primaries operational. The big guns were fragile, subject to damage not only to themselves, but to the intricate web of power lines that fed their almost insatiable need for energy. Considering the intensity of the fight, he was lucky to have half the systems functioning.

Still, the damaged half would lessen his firepower…and his gut told him a few more ships would see the particle accelerators knocked out before the Union ships moved out of their own firing range.

"Increase that thrust level to 8g, Commander." Duncan shook his head. He'd have pushed higher if he hadn't thought half of his ships were too battered to make that speed *and* fire their weapons. He had to keep up with those enemy vessels. If they managed to hit Admiral Striker's ships as they were engaging the enemy fleet and the pulsar…

"Thrust level 8g, sir. All ships report locked and ready."

Duncan sat in his chair, silent for a few seconds, trying not to think about the pain he was about to bring on his battered body. Then he turned toward Eaton.

"Execute."

*   *   *

Grachus tightened her fingers, squeezing the firing stud slowly as her ship came around, matching the vector of her target. An instant later, the high-pitched sound of her lasers firing filled the cockpit, and the small dot on her screen disappeared.

The warrior inside her rejoiced at victory. Her latest victim had been the last enemy ship on the display. A few had escaped, blasting away deep into the system, but she knew she'd seen the last of them. They would die in their cockpits as their life support waned, alone and far from aid. It was a poor death for a warrior, to suffocate or freeze fleeing from battle, but so be it. The cowards had chosen their destiny, and she had no pity for them.

Her emotions were reserved for her own warriors, Alliance and Confederation alike. The pilots under her command had held fast, enduring wave after wave of fresh enemy fighters coming at them. Not one had broken and fled from the fight, and more than half had been knocked out, killed outright, or stranded in escape pods or crippled ships, facing an end likely little different than that awaiting the Union routers.

Save for the fact that they will die as heroes, with honor. They will be remembered, and their sacrifices will inspire their people.

Grachus had believed in that once, with all her heart. She still did, to a point. But she'd come to see war differently than she had as a young warrior, steeped in Alliance orthodoxy. Defending one's nation, family, comrades…these were noble pursuits, without question. But war was a dark undertaking, and she no longer glorified it as she once had. *If we worshipped war less, would Kat still be alive? Is any victory, any honor in battle worth the life of a friend? A sister?*

She had no uncertainty about the rightness of this fight, however. She was doing all she could to pay a debt to her allies, and she was battling a dishonest and treacherous enemy. There was honor here, even amid the death and suffering of good men and women.

She wondered, for an instant, why war was so endemic to people, one conflict seeming to lead only into the next.

She didn't have any answers…and she suspected she never would.

Chapter Thirty-Seven

"Blues, Eagles…we're going in. There are no enemy fighters, and most of the defenses are back by the pulsar. But that doesn't mean they don't have some point defense platforms here, and you all know those bombers handle like pigs. So, we're going to clear a path for them. I know you're all exhausted, that your fuel's running low, that your batteries are drained. But, we've got to do this. For *Dauntless*, for Captain Barron. For everything we hold dear." Stockton was yelling into the comm, trying to give his worn pilots all the support and encouragement he could muster.

The fighters had blasted hard to overtake the slower bombers, and now they were leading the way in. Behind them sat *Dauntless*, once again visible on the scanners, and, even farther back, the entire Union fleet. A dozen battleships were ahead of the others, advancing at full thrust, but they wouldn't get there in time, not to stop Stockton's attack. His shattered fighter squadrons and his wing of bombers had a clear path ahead of them, save for whatever guns the enemy had deployed around the reactors. And, he was going to make damned sure none of them stopped his attack craft from doing their jobs.

"Bombers, you're all at full thrust. *Dauntless* is exposed again, so that means we're out of time. You've got to get in there and dust those reactors…knock out the power to that big gun before it blasts *Dauntless*."

A wave of acknowledgements and "yessirs" flooded his comm line, and he could tell from the tones of his people, they were ready. Most of the pilots who'd launched with him were veterans, and almost all of those who survived were experienced and seasoned warriors. They knew what was at stake…and what they had to do.

Stockton pulled back on his controls again, blasting forward, feeling heat from behind him as his reactor and engines began to overload. He'd taken the usual anti-rad drugs before launching, but he was pretty sure he'd need a serious cleanse when he got back, if not more. He hadn't even looked at the radiation readings in the last hour, and he'd ordered the AI, in no uncertain terms, to stop warning him every five minutes about the toxic levels.

No weapons platforms showed on his scanner. That was good. It meant, at least, that the enemy didn't have any large fortresses with the reactors. But that didn't guarantee they hadn't tucked point defense batteries onto the various stations that housed the power plants. He knew he'd never pick those up, not without some idea of specifically where to look, and that meant his interceptors were bait first and attack craft second. They'd know where the batteries were when the guns opened up and fired at them.

He brought his ship around, closing rapidly, his eyes darting from one screen to the next, waiting for any signs of enemy fire. A few seconds later there was a bright flash on the left most of his displays. The pulsar…

He felt his stomach tighten, knowing that, in that instant, *Dauntless* could have been destroyed. But, as he looked frantically, he could see the small blue oval still on the screen. The battleship had remained, and an instant later, he confirmed that the great weapon had missed. Barely.

Even as he was focused on *Dauntless*, his alarm system went off. His close-range display was alive with activity, point defense turrets opening up all along the line of reactors.

He'd been right. The weapons were built right into the stations holding the power plants. It looked like quad turrets on each one—dangerous but not as bad as he'd feared. He angled his ship hard to bring it about, heading right toward the nearest station, moving his hand wildly, giving the enemy gunners as difficult a target as he could.

"These things are armed, just like we thought. Be as careful as you can, but we've got to go in now. *Dauntless* needs us…and we're out of time."

His scanner lit up as more turrets opened fire. Blasts of focused laser-light zipped past his ship, but his erratic approach pattern was doing its job…and as each battery opened up, it gave away its location.

His eyes narrowed, zooming in on the gun on the closest platform. He was coming in quick, and that meant he'd only get a few shots before he whipped past. The bombers had to come in behind him. The cumbersome attack craft would present a much easier target to any batteries he missed.

He fired, and then again, and he felt a grin break out on his face as he saw he'd hit. The gun was silent now, and he was already looking for his next target. He was past the first wave of platforms, but he could see his comrades following his lead, blasting away at the stations all down the line. They were battered and beyond fatigued, but they all knew what was at stake, and he watched on his scanners as they scored hit after hit against their mostly-stationary targets. Their lasers weren't powerful enough to destroy the stations, or to disable the reactors, but they were picking off the point defense installations.

They were taking losses, too. Charging right into the guns was a dangerous tactic, even with the best evasive maneuvers. But there was no hesitation, not a single question from any of his pilots. They threw themselves at the stations, ignoring the danger.

Stockton fired again, taking out a turret on the last station, before his momentum took him past the line of targets and back out of range. He began to decelerate, but he knew there was no time. Long before he was able to change course and come back around, the bombers would have completed their run.

And if they didn't succeed, *Dauntless* would be gone, blasted to dust with everyone onboard.

*   *   *

Tyler Barron watched in awe as his fighters threw themselves at the line of power stations. He wondered how those men and women had anything left. From the numbers on the scanner, he knew just how many of their brethren had been lost already. But they'd mustered the courage and stamina to hurl themselves once more into the deadliest danger.

He'd been just about certain that *Dauntless*'s remaining lifespan would be measured in seconds, but now he watched as his pilots fought mightily to give the old ship one more chance. If they could knock out enough of the power supply, even enough to delay the pulsar's next shot...

"The bombers are going in now, sir." Atara Travis watched the same scene Barron did, and he'd have bet her conclusions were identical. They were witnessing heroism, in its purest unadulterated form. It was a desperate, fragile hope those ships were giving *Dauntless*...but it was hope. And it was all Barron and his people had.

His body was tight, his shoulders hunched forward from the stress, expecting the killing shot to come at any moment. The bombers could complete their mission, but if they did it a second too late, *Dauntless* would be gone.

Still, even temporarily disabling the ancient weapon could turn the tide of the battle, allow the Confederation fleet to engage and defeat their Union rivals. Barron preferred the thought of surviving to see that victory, but he didn't let himself think that far ahead. Even if the bombing wing saved *Dauntless* from the pulsar, there was a damaged, but still dangerous, enemy battleship minutes from range...and a dozen more coming up behind, enough to finish his ship even if it survived the first encounter.

The interceptors had destroyed more of the gun emplacements than Barron had thought possible, but some still remained, and now he saw symbols disappearing from the display, bombers falling victim to the defensive fire.

He sat still, silent, barely remembering to breathe as the first torpedoes launched. The plasma weapons streaked forward, and Barron felt his hopes surge. The same emplacements that had fired at the bombers themselves redirected their focus to the incoming warheads, but they were too few to effectively interdict the wildly gyrating drones, accelerating at 25g toward their targets. Then, he saw the symbols change, the tiny dots converting to larger, fuzzier circles.

The plasma torpedoes had converted to pure energy. Nothing could stop them now, and unlike the battleships that were their usual targets, the power stations were mostly immobile. They were firing their repositioning jets, but Barron could see that was going to prove almost entirely ineffective. The lack of effective defensive fire had allowed the torpedoes to close to point blank range before triggering the reactions that formed the massive plasmas.

The plasmas were on fixed courses now, and the stations used what minimal maneuvering power they had to escape from the approaching doom. A few of them managed, barely. But more than two-thirds of the torpedoes slammed into their targets.

Barron was excited, anxious, waiting for the damage assessments. It was far from certain the small strike force had possessed enough destructive power to take out the large stations. Or, at least, enough of them to cripple the pulsar.

He watched his scanners, waiting. Seconds passed by, each seeming like an eternity—and each feeling like the one that would see the pulsar firing again, blasting *Dauntless* to a cloud of radioactive dust.

Barron was tense…hell, he was scared to death, not only of his own fate and his ship's, but of what would happen to the fleet if his people failed.

He stared, his eyes unmoving, just as he knew every officer

on the bridge was doing. Then, one of the stations disappeared from the display. The data that flowed in just after left no doubt. The torpedo hit had breached its containment, releasing the vast energies of the thermonuclear reaction.

Then, another followed. Data was pouring in, now, a fast and furious stream, and Barron could see there was massive damage to other stations. The ones that had managed to shut down their reactions in time were still there. They were gutted hulks, perhaps, but the plasma torpedoes were not powerful enough to disintegrate targets of that size. That didn't matter. Each power station that shut down was one fewer feeding energy to the Union's massive gun. Barron didn't know how many it would take to shut the pulsar down, to save his ship, but as he saw more and more of the stations destroyed outright or disabled, his hope began to grow.

He turned, looking to the side of the display, to the orange sphere that represented the pulsar. It was still there, undamaged, but it hadn't fired. He glanced at the chronometer. Enough time had passed since its last shot. At first, he tried to control his expectations. He told himself maybe the great gun was pausing to refine its targeting, to ensure that it finished *Dauntless* with the next shot. Or that the reduced power had increased the recharge time. But more seconds, elapsed…and then minutes.

Dauntless's bridge was silent, no one daring to speak, to state what they were all thinking.

The bombers had done it. They'd cut the power supply to the pulsar and saved *Dauntless*.

At least for now.

Chapter Thirty-Eight

CFS Vanguard
Formara System
"The Bottleneck"
313 AC

Striker's eyes were fixed on the display, watching *Dauntless*'s squadrons assault the power stations. The idea was a brilliant one, and Striker had decided outright, whoever had come up with it would be decorated with every medal he had the power to bestow. Destroying the pulsar was the ultimate goal, of course, but even disabling it would allow the Confederation fleet to close and engage the Union forces without being cut to ribbons, and then move on the weapon itself.

Still, for all his hope and admiration for the plan, he was far from sure it would succeed. No scanner would show that the pulsar was out of operation, no alarms would go off confirming the enemy weapon was now inoperative for lack of power. All he could do was watch, and allow his hope to increase with every passing second that didn't see *Dauntless* or another of his ships blasted to plasma. He'd already lost half a dozen of his front-line battleships outright, with as many more badly wounded. His best guess was that, including the losses from the forces fighting the enemy flanking force, more than ten thousand of his spacers had died already in the fight, with thousands more

300

no doubt wounded on their damaged vessels.

He'd expected to see the superweapon's next shot by now, but the fact that the blast was thirty seconds overdue was far from conclusive. The delay could be the result of a hundred other factors. Nevertheless, his excitement grew. He was so focused on what was happening deep in the system, he even forgot the endless pain that had wracked his body since he'd first boarded *Vanguard* at Grimaldi base. For a moment, at least.

"Admiral…we're seventy-five seconds past the projected time for the last enemy shot."

Striker nodded, and he grunted softly. It was the officer's job to make reports like that, but he couldn't imagine *anyone* not realizing he already knew *exactly* how long it had been. He doubted there was a spacer in the fleet who didn't know.

He hesitated, perhaps for another ten seconds, turning his head slowly, looking out over the rows of officers at the workstation clusters all around the fleet command center, dozens of men and women, all of them veterans of six years of bloody war. All the battles, the losses, the almost unfathomable suffering and destruction…and now he sat in his chair, realizing it had all come to this. The next few hours would decide the war, he was certain of that. And, as he watched the still silent pulsar on his screen, he dared to hope that decision would prove to be a victory.

"All task forces, maximum acceleration. Engage and destroy the Union fleet…and then on to the pulsar." He suspected his voice sounded remarkably calm, but it was all a façade. Inside, despite years of endless battle, stress, losses, pain…he felt like a cadet on his first cruise, his insides twisted into knots. All the spacers he'd lost, those back in the fleet's many hospitals, struggling to recover from horrible wounds…they were all with him now. The time had passed with agonizing slowness, as he'd held the fleet back, waiting, hoping Barron and *Dauntless* could somehow do what they'd come to do. But the wait was over.

All of the Confederation was there.

It was time. Time for the final battle.

*   *   *

"Sir, we have analyzed the enemy attack, and there *is* a danger. The power flow to the reactor has dropped…"

"Do you think I'm a fool, Admiral? That I cannot see what is happening?" Villieneuve didn't yell, he didn't raise his voice a decibel. But it would take an astonishing level of unawareness not to perceive the danger, the deadly threat implicit in every word he spoke.

"No, sir, of course. But there is nothing we can…"

"No, Admiral. There is not." Villieneuve glared at the now-terrified officer. "Did I not question you when I arrived, ask you if the pulsar was adequately protected?"

"The pulsar is very well defended, sir. No fighter attack could have seriously damaged it."

"You didn't consider the power source that allows the weapon to fire to be important?"

"We had three hundred-sixty fighters stationed there, sir." Admiral Bourbonne was retaining his composure…just.

"Which were sent in piecemeal and destroyed by a vastly smaller Confed force."

"Minister, I…"

"Silence, Bourbonne. There is no time for excuses and idle chatter. We must act at once. In all likelihood, the pulsar is inoperative now, but it is not damaged. The reactors were costly, but they are replaceable." *Though how am I going to replace them… and stave off disaster while I do? That is tomorrow's problem.* "The pulsar is not. It is unique, its value without price. It must be withdrawn at once. The fleet is to advance now and engage the enemy. We must keep them back long enough to get the pulsar out of the system."

"But, sir, without the pulsar's support, and with the detachments we have made…we will be at a grave disadvantage against the Confederation's main force." A short pause. "I will at least recall the ships sent back to deal with the enemy battleship…"

"You will do no such thing. Those ships are to escort the tugs pulling the pulsar from the system."

"But there are a dozen capital ships in that force!"

"Yes, and if they and the pulsar are the only things that get out of this system, then so be it." *Them and me, of course.* Villieneuve would find some meager satisfaction in watching Bourbonne die with the fleet, but he had no intention of joining in himself. "None of this would be necessary if you'd deployed adequate protection to the pulsar, as I commanded, Admiral." Villieneuve knew he himself was at fault as well. He could have deployed more units to the rear on his own initiative, but instead, he'd taken Bourbonne's assurances at face value. It was a grave error for a man who generally believed almost nothing of what he was told.

The truth was frightfully simple. Gaston Villieneuve was no expert in space war, and he'd never imagined the Confeds would manage to sneak some kind of infiltrator around his entire fleet. He'd planned for every contingency that seemed possible. There had been no way to anticipate what had happened, no reason to consider it a possibility…at least none that would have occurred to anyone beforehand.

None of that mattered now. The reality was clear. He had to salvage the situation somehow, and find a way to buy enough time to build a new power system for the pulsar…once he got the ancient weapon out of the Bottleneck and to, at least temporary, safety.

Bourbonne would serve well enough as a scapegoat, though Villieneuve suspected he was on very thin ice with the Presidium himself and would have a much harder time manipulating his way out of this situation. He had eyes on them all, of course, as he'd had for years, but he was way out at the Bottleneck, beyond easy reach of his various intelligence assets. If his colleagues met and decided to turn on him, it would almost certainly be too late by the time he found out.

I'll have to do something about them too. But first things first.

"The detached battleships are to get to the pulsar at maximum velocity…and the rest of the fleet will hold the enemy back however long it must to ensure the weapon's escape." A pause, then he continued ominously, "Command this operation now, Admiral, as though your very life depended on it. Hold back that Confederation fleet."

Villieneuve suspected his words, and the grimness of this tone, would get the very best Bourbonne had to offer.

Still, Villieneuve seriously doubted he would spare the fool, no matter how well he did in the hours to come. Bourbonne was expendable, and his death for the failure in the Bottleneck would only help Villieneuve's own efforts to save himself.

*   *   *

Barron stared at the display, hesitant to believe what his eyes were telling him. It had been nearly five minutes since the pulsar had fired, at least three or four times the largest interval he'd seen before. It wasn't a guarantee, certainly, and he had Travis continuing *Dauntless*'s wild evasive maneuvers, but he was beginning to believe Stockton's people had done it. That they had taken out the pulsar's power source.

He looked around the bridge, seeing, even feeling, the relief of his officers. *Dauntless*'s crew were veterans all, but that didn't make them immune to fear. They'd stared at imminent death, feeling it mere seconds away. He'd never know just how close the pulsar came to firing that last, killing shot. No more than a few seconds, he guessed.

His relief was short-lived. There might be hope that *Dauntless* would escape the pulsar's deadly fire now, but there was still an enemy battleship bearing down, and Barron's ship didn't have a single operational weapon.

"Fritzie, what's the status on those batteries?" Barron leaned over the comm, feeling the tension return in full force as he did. The Union battleship was only moments from range, and if *Dauntless* couldn't fire back, it would be a one-sided battle…and a very short one. His people would be no less dead if *Dauntless* was picked apart by enemy laser cannon than if she'd been vaporized by the pulsar.

"Captain, this is Lieutenant Billings, sir. Commander Fritz is up on the catwalk. She's trying to connect the powerline bypass, and get some juice to the starboard aft batteries."

Barron could hear a voice in the distance. He could barely make out the words. "…tell him we're restoring…now."

"Very well, Lieutenant," Barron said. "Tell Commander Frit…"

His words were interrupted by a sound in the distance…not an explosion, exactly, but something similar. Barron's gut tensed as he heard screams now, and then a shout for a medic.

"Lieutenant, what is happening?"

Nothing. No response.

"Lieutenant Billings, are you still on the line?" Barron almost jumped up from his seat, a pointless gesture, since it would take him at least fifteen minutes to get to *Dauntless*'s aft section, assuming all the lifts and cars were working. Which they weren't.

He clenched his fists, staring down at the comm unit. It was still functional. He could hear sounds in the distance, and shouts. Then, finally, Billings's voice returned.

"Captain, we've had a problem down here. Commander Fritz was trying to reroute the main power line, and something went wrong. The whole thing shorted out." He paused, and Barron's insides tensed. He could tell what was coming from the engineer's tone. "She took a heavy shock, sir…and she fell over the side of the catwalk. It's a four-meter drop, Captain. We're trying to get to her now. I don't know if she's…"

Barron sat still as Billings's voice tailed off. The engineer couldn't say what he was thinking, but it was crystal clear to Barron…and everyone else on *Dauntless*'s bridge.

Barron paused, just for a second, wondering if his longtime engineer—his friend—was dead or alive. But there wasn't time for that now. "Let the medics deal with Commander Fritz, Lieutenant. I need you to take her place. We still need those guns." He hated himself for the words coming out of his mouth, but he also knew it wouldn't matter if Anya Fritz was alive or not if *Dauntless* got blasted to atoms in ten or fifteen minutes.

"Captain, I'm almost…"

"Now, Billings. That's an order." Barron cut the line. Let Walt Billings hate him, let him see a cold, heartless monster in *Dauntless*'s captain. None of that was important. The only thing that mattered now was getting those guns back online.

And Barron knew one thing for sure. Anya Fritz would have been the first one to tell *him* that.

*   *   *

"Here they come…" Vian Tulus sat bolt upright, the very image of the Palatian Patrician going into battle. He'd fought many times, led warriors into countless desperate struggles, but now his people would fight farther from home than any force in the history of the Alliance. Until moments before, he'd been worried his fleet would do nothing save advance and be destroyed by the fire of the enemy pulsar. While there was nobility in the service to an ally, regardless of outcome, Tulus had been grim pondering the virtual certainty of being obliterated before his ship could fire a weapon.

He considered Tyler Barron his friend…more than his friend, a true brother in arms. Barron's courage and fortitude had shamed Tulus for his earlier prejudices against the Confederation's warriors, and he knew there would not even be an Alliance now, at least not one as he knew it, without Barron's skill at war. But despite his feelings, the immeasurable respect he felt for his Confed colleague, he realized only now, with the enemy pulsar apparently out of action, just how little faith he'd had that Barron and his people could succeed on their almost crazy mission.

More shame on me, Tyler…this time for having too little faith in a friend.

There was relief, of course. Even a Palatian Patrician disliked the idea of advancing directly toward certain death. But it didn't last. The pulsar may have been disabled—and that wasn't certainty, not yet—but there was still a Union fleet to face, and as Tulus stared at the display, he felt his blood begin to boil. It was Union treachery that had plunged his people into civil war, that had cost the lives of the Imperatrix and thousands upon thousands of noble Palatians. It would be years, a decade perhaps, before the Alliance could regain the strength that was lost, and now, those responsible were before him, drawn up for battle.

He knew what to do now. It was deep in his blood.

"Put me on the intership comm, Optiomagis," he said softly.

"You are connected, sir."

"Palatians of the fleet, this is Commander-Maximus Tulus. We are far from home, fighting at the side of our allies. Some may look at this as the Confederation's war, yet these vermin before us are those responsible for all the sorrows that have befallen us of late. The Gray and Red dead in the civil war are victims of Union treachery. We are indeed here to aid our friends, who rallied to us in our time of need. But this fight is more than that, far more. It is our chance to avenge our own, our time to wash away the shame of Palatian killing Palatian. The Union is our enemy, as much as the Confederation's. Fight now, all of you, and do not cease until the enemy is destroyed."

He cut the line, and turned toward the display. His ships would be in range in seconds.

He stared straight ahead, counting the seconds silently.

"Optiomagis, all ships are to open fire...now."

*   *   *

Barron stared at the display. His eyes had been fixed on the approaching enemy battleship, the one *Dauntless* was trying to evade. But now he was looking at the pulsar, and as he did, his heart sank.

There were tugs moving all around the superweapon, and massive portable engines. The mobile system the enemy had worked so hard to create, the one that had necessitated the entire desperate mission to the Bottleneck, was in motion. Stockton's attack had cut off the pulsar's power supply, rendering the weapon harmless. At least for now. But if the Union could withdraw the artifact, the danger would still be there.

They could move it, redeploy it…even succeed in copying it and building more of the terrifying guns.

He turned toward the other side of the display. The fleet was coming in range of the Union line. The battle was heating up, with Eaton's and Tulus's forces already heavily engaged, and the rest of the ships just opening fire. Barron managed a fleeting smile through his growing gloom, a silent salute to Vian Tulus, for the intensity with which his warriors were fighting the Union ships. The Alliance fleet had already destroyed two Union battleships, and they were cutting deeply into the overall formation.

Sara Eaton's flotilla was fighting no less furiously, but her ships had taken heavier damage during the earlier engagement, and many of her vessels had only partial broadsides. Still, they were moving relentlessly forward, taking everything the Union line could throw at them and giving it back in full measure.

Barron knew the fight would be a brutal one. He'd been surprised at the size of the forces the Union had managed to assemble to defend the system. Still, as he saw the allied Confederation and Alliance forces moving forward, he was confident they could prevail. They would pay a heavy price, but they would win. They would take the Bottleneck.

It's a strategic piece of real estate, no doubt, but if the pulsar escapes, the war will go on. The fleet would have to refit and resupply before it could advance…and that would take months, and give the Union time to gather together another array of reactors to put the ancient weapon back into action.

He couldn't let that thing get away. Whatever it took.

He looked over at Travis. "Any status on those batteries… or on Commander Fritz?"

"No, sir. All weapons systems remain offline. The med teams just reported they were able to reach Commander Fritz. She is critical, but still alive. They're transporting her to sickbay now, Captain."

Barron exhaled hard. He was glad to hear that Fritz had been rescued. Of course, she might still die…and she certainly would if *Dauntless* was destroyed.

"What's our maximum thrust?" A short pause. "I mean *maximum*, Atara…every hundredth of a g we can push through the engines, regardless of risk."

Travis hesitated, but only for a few seconds. "I think we can get 8g, Captain, maybe even 9. But I don't know how long we can keep it up. It could fail at any moment…possibly badly."

Barron nodded. He knew just what "badly" meant. "Can we outrun that ship on our tail?" Barron already knew the answer, but he was hoping his own quick calculation was wrong.

"Outrun to where, Captain?"

He stared right at the display, his eyes fixed on the symbol in the center, surrounded now by tiny circles and triangles representing tugs and mobile superstructures.

"To the pulsar, Atara." His voice was cold, emotionless.

"To the…" Her voice stopped suddenly, as she realized his meaning. "You want to ram the pulsar." It wasn't a question, but even Travis usual control was shaken as she uttered the words.

"Yes, that is exactly what I want to do." He didn't turn his head at all, but he could feel every pair of eyes on the bridge burning into him. "We can't let that thing escape. If we do, thousands more will die attacking it again…and if the enemy can replicate it, the Confederation is doomed." He finally turned and looked over at Travis. "We *have* to destroy it."

She nodded, slightly, a barely perceptible communication to him alone. She was with him. Completely.

"But we're not going to ram anything if that ship on our tail can blow *Dauntless* apart without us getting so much as a shot in return. Unless we can stay far enough ahead."

He was still staring over at Travis as she looked back and answered. "There's no way to be sure, sir." Her tone was heavy with doubt.

"Well, we have to try. Meanwhile, let's get all shuttles, escape pods—anything that will provide life support—ready to go. I want all non-essential personnel to begin evacuation procedures immediately. Only engine crew and damage control teams will remain until the last minute." He looked around at his people, every one of them staring at him. "All non-essential bridge personnel are to evacuate as well."

The bridge was silent.

"That means now...all of you except gunnery and engine control. Get moving." He stood up and pointed toward the lifts. He wasn't sure the elevators were working, but the emergency ladders were right next to them.

"Go," he roared, as the entire bridge crew still remained in place, staring at him. "If you waste time, you'll just get in the way of the rest of us when we follow. No one's committing suicide here. The AI will handle the final approach. Let's keep our shit together. So, get going!"

A riot of activity broke out on the bridge, all but the five officers in the positions Barron had specified to remain moving toward the exits in a moderately disordered retreat. There was no fear, no panic. In fact, Barron could still feel the hesitancy of his people to leave without all of their fellows. Without him. Even though he'd just told them he had every intention of following.

He shook his head, his thoughts repeating what he had just said. *No one is committing suicide.*

No one but you, old girl...

He looked around, but this time his gaze went past the officers moving toward the ladders...and there was moistness in his eyes. He looked at the walls, at the equipment and the armored bulkheads, at the steel and plastic and...something else...that was *Dauntless*.

She'd had been his now for seven years, and he'd served her as faithfully as she'd served him. He fought back a wave of doubts, an urge to cancel his last order, to think again, to try to find a way to get his ship out of the fire one more time. But there was no choice. *Dauntless* had made it this far, but she wouldn't see the end of the war. There wouldn't be an end of the war, at least not a tolerable one, unless she could complete this final mission.

"I'm so sorry," he whispered, almost inaudibly, fighting to hold back the tears, to spare his retreating crew—and the few officers remaining at their posts—the spectacle of their captain crying on the bridge.

"I'm so sorry…"

Chapter Thirty-Nine

"Get me more thrust, Commander." Turenne was leaning forward, his fists clenched tightly as he watched his ship on the display, closing with the Confederation vessel.

"We're at maximum now, sir." Maramont's voice was frayed. The officer had risen to the challenge, embraced serving a commander of Turenne's ability, but now, the exhaustion and fear—and the constant need to do the impossible—had worn him down.

"I said more." Turenne had also lost his professional demeanor, and he sounded like a man crazed, almost possessed. He was focused, nearly to the level of obsession. He'd been determined to catch the enemy ship, the ship *he'd* found…when no one off of *Temeraire* would believe him or would even listen to his arguments. He was frustrated, angry that his wounded ship and battered crew had to take on the enemy alone…solely because Admiral Bourbonne hadn't taken his warnings seriously. Minister Villieneuve had finally detached a huge force, but it wouldn't get there in time.

Not before that ship destroys the pulsar…

Turenne had been chasing the enemy for hours now, tracking slight variations in dust clouds for most of that time. But this was the conclusion, the moments that would decide if the Confeds were able to destroy the pulsar, or if the weapon was withdrawn to be deployed yet again.

The pulsar was inoperable now, a victim of the Confed vessel's squadrons, of their attack on the power stations. But Villieneuve had ordered the weapon's withdrawal, and even now, the tugs were connecting, preparing to move the ancient artifact before the Confed fleet could reach it. They would succeed in that mission. Admiral Striker's line was still too far away.

But one Confed ship was close enough to attack.

"Captain, engineering says if we crank the engines up any higher, they could blow at any moment."

"Give me something, anything. An extra g." *Temeraire* was going to get into range before the Confed could get to the pulsar, he was pretty sure of that. The enemy ship was already in primary range of both *Temeraire* and the ancient weapon. The fact that they hadn't fired pretty much confirmed Turenne's suspicions. The pulsar's shot had knocked out the enemy's long-range guns.

That was a break, a big one, not just because the Confed couldn't fire the primaries at Turenne's ship, but also because they'd have to get closer to attack the pulsar. And that gave Turenne time.

Temeraire was damaged too, many of its systems down or functioning at partial power. Still, he didn't think his vessel was hurt as badly as the Confed ship. A few blasts from Confederation primaries, and his battleship would have been a floating hulk, but if those fearsome weapons were inoperable, he was confident he could take his enemy.

"The engine room is increasing power slowly, sir. They're going to try to up acceleration by 1g."

"See that they do better than try, Commander." He'd been close on the enemy's heels, almost in range, but then the Confederation ship had managed to increase its own thrust. And its vector left no doubt it was heading toward the pulsar.

"Increasing thrust now, sir. One-quarter g…" Maramont sounded nervous, but Turenne ignored it. There was no time now for doubt, for fear.

If they want to fear something, it should be what Gaston Villieneuve will do to everyone on this ship if that enemy vessel somehow manages to destroy the pulsar…

*   *   *

Dauntless shook hard.

"Damage report," Barron snapped into the comm.

"Hit amidships, sir…some hull damage and minor system failures." The voice was not immediately familiar. With Fritz wounded and Billings and half the engineering team working on the damaged batteries, general control management had fallen several layers in rank. *Lieutenant Hoolihan*, Barron remembered after a few seconds.

"Stay on it, Lieutenant. Report anything further at once."

"Yes, sir." The junior lieutenant had only been on *Dauntless* for two years. The battles out in the Alliance had been his first, and the nervousness in his voice showed, especially compared to Fritz's iron composure.

He turned toward Travis. "Status on evacuation?"

"Three hundred six personnel launched, Captain. Another two hundred sixteen pending." *Dauntless's* people were leaving her, sent away by Barron's order. He stood by his decision. He had to stop that pulsar from escaping, whatever it took. But the wound he'd opened in himself widened as he watched his ship's crew streaming away, abandoning her. Their futures were uncertain at best, stranded deep behind enemy lines in a series of escape pods and small craft. But they had some chance, at least. The battleship that had served them so well, that had fought enemies from the Rim to the Badlands, had none. Barron had condemned his beloved ship, and as he sat on the bridge, sweating the attack from his Union pursuer, the wound he'd opened in himself cut deeper with each moment's realization at the finality of the sentence he'd pronounced on his beloved and loyal vessel.

He knew it was foolish to personify *Dauntless* as he did, but he couldn't stop himself, and he ached with sorrow for what lay ahead for her.

"Do what you can in terms of evasive maneuvers, Atara." He spoke softly, aware as he did that there was very little she could do that she wasn't doing already. Any wild gyrations in thrust would wreak havoc on the evacuation operation…as well as adding time until *Dauntless* could reach the pulsar. There was a zero-sum game at work. He might make each enemy shot a bit more difficult, but adding minutes increased the number of volleys the enemy would get before *Dauntless* got to her target.

"Yes, Captain." He could tell from the sound of Travis's words, she didn't think the ship would make it to the pulsar.

What made it worse, though, wasn't his first officer's doubt. It was his own.

He didn't think *Dauntless* could make it either. He'd come to believe his vessel was as special as her reputation had made her, that she was unstoppable, that she could get through anything. But the pulsar's hit had severely damaged her, and the systems that were still online were functioning by the grace of God… and Anya Fritz's wizardry.

And now, he'd lost Fritz too. He'd ordered his engineer evacuated from sickbay as soon as possible, and given a place on one of the largest shuttles. If anyone had done her part in *Dauntless*'s victories, it was Anya Fritz. She deserved the best chance to escape this last mission, whether success or failure awaited, and Barron intended to make sure she got it.

If she survives her injuries…

Fritz was badly hurt. He knew that much, but nothing more. Sickbay had been full of wounded, all of whom were now being evacuated. It had been chaos, at a level that prevented the medical staff from taking time to issue reports on patients. For all he knew, his engineer was already dead, or she might die in her medpod as her shuttle blasted away from *Dauntless*.

The thought of losing Fritz was painful, but Barron's mind was focused on the what he had to do now. For seven years, he had brought his ship back from one desperate mission after another. But not this time. *Dauntless* was doomed…the only question that remained was whether the great vessel would die in victory…or in defeat.

*   *   *

"Dammit!" Stockton had relished the excitement of his bombers blasting the pulsar's reactors to scrap…for all of perhaps two minutes. Now, he watched as the Union battleship, the one he'd spared by pulling away Federov's bombers for their run at the enemy artifact, closed on an already badly damaged *Dauntless*.

Stockton had hoped, at first, that *Dauntless* could fight off its pursuer, but then the awful truth dawned on him. The ship's weapons were down. And Captain Barron wasn't making an attack run at the pulsar. He was going to ram the enemy weapon.

But Dauntless *will never make it there, not with that ship on its tail.*

His eyes dropped to the display, staring at the hopeless mess his strike force had fallen into. His ships were scattered around, all on different vectors, blasting off at high velocities. It would take a miracle to get them all turned around…and back to *Dauntless* in time to attack that enemy ship, to finish the job his assault squadrons had begun.

It was a long shot, of even getting there, and once there, launching an attack that could take out the Union battleship. He had nothing but a handful of interceptors, not much to destroy a ship of the line. But, there was no choice. That ship was going to destroy *Dauntless*, far short of the pulsar. Unless he got it first.

His scanners were also picking up smaller contacts. Lifeboats. Barron was already evacuating the crew. But when *Dauntless* was gone, those shuttles would be at the mercy of the Union battleship. He *had* to stop that ship. Somehow.

He angled his controls, bringing his ship around, ignoring the screeching sounds as he pushed his engines once again past their rated capacity. "All squadrons," he said into the comm, the urgency of the situation clear in his tone, "we've got to get back and attack that enemy battleship. We damaged it already, but now we've got to finish the job." He knew what had to be going through the minds of his pilots. Their ships were battered, abused...and the bomber squadrons didn't have so much as a single torpedo.

There was a moment of silence. Then, the responses began. "Commander, there's no way we can get there. It will take twenty minutes for me just to reverse course."

"We're too far...we'll never make it in time."

"My engines are down to thirty percent."

Stockton shook his head as each answer came in. He wanted to argue, but he knew they were only telling him the hard truth. His ships, most of them at least, were too far away, their positioning and vectors impossible to reverse in time. He kept his hand on his own throttle, bringing his ship around, even though he knew he, as well, was too distant and poorly positioned.

He'd never get there, not in time.

He felt a wave of despair, even as he continued to push his ship to its limits, a pointless risk, since he knew he was too far away.

"We can get there, Commander."

The voice took him by surprise, and for an instant it was unfamiliar. Then, there was recognition.

Jovi Grachus.

He normally felt anger when the Alliance pilot crossed his path, but now there was nothing but confusion. He still blamed her for his friend's death, but he'd watched her take terrible risks to save his own pilots as well as Alliance ones.

He'd seen Grachus and her pilots fight alongside his Confederation squadrons, and he couldn't deny she'd done a brilliant job. The enemy had more fighters positioned around the pulsar than he'd expected, and that could have been a complete disaster. But Grachus somehow kept her people in the fight, battling endlessly, ignoring damage, fatigue, dwindling fuel...even as one fresh wing after another came at them. The dogfight had been nothing short of a miracle, one capped off by Grachus's own almost unbelievable total of personal kills. Sixteen.

Stockton had never seen anything like it, and he had to admit to himself, he was far from sure he could have done what she just had. He had a good idea the personal risks she'd taken to do it.

"What's your fuel status, Commander?" Stockton already knew. As strike force commander, his AI received regular updates from the ships under his command. The dogfight had gone on almost endlessly, and sustained combat burned fuel rapidly.

"Enough to make it there, sir." That wasn't a lie, not exactly, though Stockton knew Grachus hadn't told him everything.

"Maybe, Commander. Enough to blast there at full thrust… but not enough to slow down for a proper attack. And certainly not enough to come back around. Your ships will sail past the enemy, and then you'll head out into the outer system with no way to come back around…and very little hope of rescue."

Stockton looked down at his controls, as he waited for his signal to reach Grachus and for her response to come back. He was trying to recalculate, to come up with another answer, *any* other answer. But he kept getting the same result. A small group from her force, mostly her own Alliance pilots, could get back to the enemy ship. But they couldn't decelerate, either to attack or to keep themselves from blasting into the dark reaches of the outer system.

"There's no choice, Commander. It's the only way to save *Dauntless*. By my count, eight of my Alliance ships are in position to make the run. They've all volunteered to go, and we've already engaged thrust." A pause. Her last words hit Stockton hard, and now he realized he could hear the difficulty in her speech as she struggled with the g forces to push her words out. "I know we've had our…differences…Commander, but my people are going in, no matter what. Please…" He could hear a vulnerability in her normally strong voice, almost a pleading. "…don't make this an act of mutiny. Give us your blessing, sir. Perhaps I can find some redemption in saving Commander Jamison's ship."

Stockton had felt nothing but rage and resentment against Grachus, for as long as he'd known her name. But now he could hear a voice, Kyle Jamison's, telling him to let go of his anger. Grachus had fought like a demon. She had saved countless Confederation pilots...and now she was taking an even greater risk, to rescue *Dauntless*, to give Tyler Barron the chance to finish evacuating the ship, and to take out the pulsar once and for all.

"Go, Commander," he said softly. "My best wishes are with you and those who serve you." He knew the whole thing was a desperate effort. But he also knew they had to try.

There was an even smaller chance any rescue operation could reach her or her pilots before their dwindling life support was exhausted. Stockton had acquired some familiarity with Alliance culture, and he knew just how hateful that kind of death would be to a Palatian warrior, to sit in a cockpit and wait for cold and lack of air to take her.

He knew one more thing, a ray of knowledge that shattered his prejudice, his rage. He'd been talking to a true hero. His pain-fueled hate had been misplaced. War was war, when Grachus had killed Jamison, just as it was now, when she was putting her life on the line for the slightest chance to save *Dauntless*. He'd wasted too much time hating a true ally, a friend. He would make his peace with Jovi Grachus. He swore it to himself.

Assuming he got the chance.

He stared at the silent comm for an instant, and then he blasted his thrust again. He couldn't get there in time for the attack run, but he was going to try anyway.

Chapter Forty

AFS Vexillum
Alliance Flagship
Intarus System
Alliance Year 64 (313 AC)

"All reserves forward...now." Tarkus Vennius sat where he had many times before, in the command chair of an Alliance flagship, commanding his warriors in battle. He'd gone into his fights with unbridled enthusiasm as a young man, and with varying degrees of fatigue and disillusionment as an older one, but his record of victory stood proudly in the annals of the Alliance. Now, however, he faced his greatest challenge.

"Yes, Your Supremacy." An instant later. "All ships are underway."

The battle wasn't the largest he'd fought, nor were the Krillians an enemy that should have threatened the Alliance with defeat and destruction. But, the civil war had dramatically weakened the fleet, and with the diversion of so many ships to Tulus's expeditionary force, the Palatian realms lay open to invasion.

Vennius had never faced such a disadvantage in battle, save for the struggles against Calavius and the Red Alliance forces. Never since his people had thrown off their chains had an external foe so challenged the Palatians. Vennius was tired, and the Imperator's duties weighed heavily on him. He longed for retirement, for quiet years on his estates. But he was a Palatian Patrician to the core, and duty came first to him, above all things.

Vexillium shook hard as the flagship took another hit. Vennius was an old school commander, and he led from the front. He could hear the distant high-pitched sounds, as his ship returned fire. The Krillian marksmanship was no match for that of his spacers, though his ships were crewed mostly by second-line forces and retirees returned to the colors. His people were superior in every way to their enemies...every way but one. They were badly outnumbered.

Yet again, Vennius cursed the Alliance's weakness in intelligence gathering. He felt the same distaste the rest of his people did for such a career, but he also knew an agency as effective as Confederation Intelligence—not to mention the awesome Sector Nine—would have alerted him to Calavius's scheming, allowing him to avert the tragedy of the civil war. It would also have warned him the Krillians had nearly twice the hulls they'd been expected to possess. He would have sent the expeditionary force regardless, but he might have held back a few frontline battleships, assets that would be invaluable to him now.

Vennius stared at the main display, watching his ships move forward into battle. Questions about whether the Alliance needed more spies, or if he should have sent fewer ships to aid the Confederation, were moot now. A warrior dealt with reality, not might have beens. The way was clear enough on that, and Vennius had lived his entire life in accordance with its mandates. All that mattered was winning the fight his people were in now.

Vexillium was jerking back and forth, evasive maneuvers making the flagship as difficult a target as possible for the Krillian ships facing it. Vennius was proud of his collection of retirees and second-line spacers. They were rising to the cause, fighting with all the courage and skill he'd have expected from the very best warriors. But it wasn't going to be enough.

The Krillians were simply too strong, their advantage in hulls too great. Vennius had analyzed the battle, extrapolated the loss rates forward. His Alliance forces would give out more damage than they would take, no question, but they would still come up short.

His eyes were fixed, coldly on the screen, moving from one symbol to the next. Vennius knew his people would lose a straight up fight, but he had another idea, a way to salvage the victory, and to save Palatia.

Vexillium was in the forefront of the Alliance line, right where a Palatian flagship should be. But Krillus was a different animal, and Vennius knew his adversary's advantage in numbers did not make him a true warrior, certainly not in the Palatian model.

Vennius was looking for Krillus, for the enemy counterpart to his own *Vexillium*. His forces couldn't prevail in a normal fight, he was convinced of that, but there were other ways to win a battle.

He knew the current situation was his responsibility, as Imperator, and as the man who'd allowed Calavius to plunge the Alliance into civil war. It had been his command that sent the cream of the fleet to fight against the Union, and it had been his pride that assumed none of Palatia's neighbors would dare to move against the Alliance. Tarkus Vennius had accepted his responsibilities all his life, and he wasn't about to shirk them now.

Krillus was a dictator, an absolute ruler with unquestioned power. His regime murdered any officers who showed independent initiative, any who were perceived as a threat to him in any way. Every decision went through him, and his officers were terrified of his wrath. Therein lay the route to victory. Through Krillus himself.

Vennius's eyes focused on a single icon, a small oval on his screen. It was tucked behind two other ships, back a good bit from the front line. As he looked at it, he *knew*. That was Krillus's flagship.

"Commander…set a course toward contact 11A. Maximum thrust."

"Yes, Your Supremacy."

Vennius wished he could fight Krillus one on one, that the two of them could land on some planet in the system and battle

each other in single combat, sparing the thousands of their warriors who would die in the fight now underway. But that wasn't
possible. Not against a gutless coward like the Krillian.

Still, there was another way. Vennius's forces likely couldn't
defeat the enemy fleet gun for gun...but he could lop the head
off the beast. He was going to take *Vexillium* right through the
enemy line, directly toward Krillus's flagship.

And he was going to destroy it. He was going to kill his
enemy...whatever it took.

*   *   *

"What is that ship doing?" Krillus sat in his elaborate raised
chair, staring at the display.

His officers were clustered around him, sycophants, mostly,
though there was some skill in their ranks.

"It is advancing, Great and Terrible Krillus. The entire Alliance force is closing on us rapidly."

Krillus had watched as his fleet exchanged fire with the
enemy. He was angry that the Palatians scored a hit ratio far
in advance of that his own forces had managed, but all in all,
things were going well. But that ship troubled him. It was the
largest vessel in the Palatian fleet, and it outmassed his heaviest
ships by a considerable margin.

That is the flagship.

He continued watching as the ship moved forward, firing the
ships in range, but only as it passed. It didn't decelerate, didn't
slow to engage. It just moved relentlessly forward.

That is the Alliance commander.

Krillus had wondered who was leading the Alliance fleet.
Commander-Maximus Tulus was in command of the expeditionary force, his intelligence assets had confirmed that. So,
there was either a lower-level Palatian on that ship, or...

Tarkus Vennius.

Krillus had never met Vennius, but he knew much about the
Palatian leader. Enough to fear the man.

His mind raced, and he began to feel unsettled. He'd seen

the AI analysis, and he knew his forces were likely to win the battle, but something was…wrong.

Was Vennius leading his people into the fight? Was he setting the example for his warriors?

Krillus stared at the screen, and slowly, he began shaking his head. No, that wasn't it. He could see the enemy ship's velocity increasing, and its vector was becoming clear. Vennius wasn't leading a charge, he wasn't setting an example.

He's coming for me…

Krillus's mouth went dry, and he felt as though a cold hand gripped his spine. He was cocky, arrogant, a man who felt fully entitled to the power and position he'd inherited…but now all that drained away. Tarkus Vennius was a famous warrior, a man who had been leading fleets since before Krillus was born.

It was one thing to terrorize his officers and his people, to wield the power his secret police gave him over those who lived under his rule. But now the shadow of this Palatian hero cast over him darkly, and he felt lost. Terrified.

"Pull us back," he said, a robotic tone to his voice.

"Sir?"

"Back I said. Pull the flagship back. The fleet will continue the battle, but we will fall back."

"Yes, Great and Terrible Krillus." There was hesitancy in the officer's voice. "Sir…"

"Do it! That madman is coming for us. He is coming for me! Now pull us back, before it is too late!" Krillus had completely lost his composure. The thought of the legendary Tarkus Vennius coming for him was more than he could handle.

"Yes, Great and Terrible Krillus." The officer repeated the orders into the comm, and a few seconds later, the ship lurched hard, its engines blasting at full, decelerating, killing its momentum toward the Alliance fleet.

Krillus stared at the display, at the rows of symbols marking his ships, and the Alliance forces they were battling. But he really saw only two. His flagship's…and that of Vennius's vessel, driving right through the battlelines. There wasn't a doubt in his mind now.

Vennius was coming for him.

*   *   *

The blade slipped right between the man's ribs, and a quick jerk to the side finished the job. Marieles had her arm wrapped around her victim's body, her hand clasped over his mouth to muffle his scream. Krillus and his people had underestimated her. They'd come to see her as just another of his concubines, even as an ambassador, but they'd neglected to fully understand that she was a Sector Nine assassin. Krillus had told her to remain in his quarters during the battle, but he'd made the mistake of leaving only a single guard to watch her. It had been almost ridiculously easy.

She grabbed the sentry's keycard. She'd deduced that Krillus's personal guards had access to every area of the ship, and the small bit of plastic would get her where she was going. To the shuttle bay.

She had no idea if Imperator Vennius had blinked, if he had recalled any of the forces deployed to aid the Confeds, but there was little else to do now. The battle in progress now would decide the Alliance-Krillian conflict. If Krillus and his forces prevailed, they would have a chance to bring down the entire Alliance, a victory of almost astonishing proportions. But she would only face the victorious monarch's anger as none of the help she had promised arrived. And, if the Palatians won, she shuddered to think of the vengeance they would unleash on the Krillians, and most of all on their leader. She didn't imagine a Union representative would be treated much better in the aftermath of the civil war Sector Nine had instigated.

No, whatever happened next, it was time to leave.

She slipped out into the corridor, listening carefully as she moved toward the bay. She had tucked the knife under her belt, and she carried the dead guard's pistol as she stepped silently toward the lifts, grabbing onto a set of handholds as the ship shook hard. Another hit.

She knew enough about the Alliance to understand their

response in ways Krillus never could. The Palatians valued honor above survival. They would sacrifice themselves, in great numbers if need be, to defeat the invaders, to exact their revenge on those who'd dared to invade their space. And, despite the fact that Krillus's forces outnumbered his enemies significantly, she'd have wagered on the Palatians.

She turned and looked up and down the deserted hallway. The crew were all at battlestations, and she was willing to bet the way to the hold was open. She might have to take down a sentry or two, but she didn't doubt she'd manage to escape...and get the hell away from the conflict she'd instigated.

*   *   *

Vennius looked across the bridge, through the clouds of acrid smoke, at his crew. *Vexillium* had been pounded as more and more Krillian vessels closed on the Alliance flagship. Vennius had gotten somewhat of a jump, but then the enemy realized what he was doing.

Krillus realized.

The Krillian leader had reacted just as Vennius had known he would, ordering more and more of his ships to converge on the Alliance vessel threatening him. Vennius was disgusted at a monarch who would issue orders solely on the basis of self-preservation...orders that threw his battle line into turmoil, even as the Alliance ships pressed on, taking advantage of that disorder. Vennius's move, his bold advance through the enemy line had accomplished much already, helping to turn the tide. But the Imperator had come for more. He'd come to settle this fight with a grim finality.

Vennius was ready to see it through, ready to advance into the maelstrom, to grab Krillus and jump into the pit of hell with his enemy. Death in battle was honorable, more so if such sacrifice saved the homeworld from danger. He was ready enough to die, to join Kat, and more friends and comrades than he could easily count. His life had been well-lived, but naught lay ahead of him but the prison of the Imperator's palace, a position he'd never wanted but now could not escape, save into the arms of death.

The Alliance would be better off with a younger man in the office, one without Vennius's fatigue. It was one last duty to perform, and his only regret was that his people on *Vexillium* would make the sacrifice with him. But they were Palatian warriors as he, and many of them were old too, retirees called back to fight one last battle. Any who died here would be long remembered and honored. There were far worse fates a Palatian might face.

Vexillium shuddered yet again, lights flickering and sparks flying across the bridge. Vennius's ship had exchanged fire with the battleships moving on its flanks, but now he'd ordered the batteries to go silent, to hold back whatever energy remained. There was only one target he thought of, one ship he vowed to destroy before he marched off to join his lost comrades.

"Krillian flagship dead ahead, sir. Coming into range now."

Vennius nodded, and he sat for just a few seconds, steeling himself for what he suspected would be his final battle. He flipped on the comm unit. "Palatian warriors, crew of *Vexillium*, I can ask no more of you than that you stand with me today, that you follow me again into the vortex. Our enemy is on that ship ahead of us, he who would have gone on to Palatia and bombarded our sacred homeland. Now, we advance, and damned the cost. Now, we show this petty dictator what Alliance warriors truly are." A short pause, then: "All guns…fire."

*   *   *

Globus sat on *Patentia*'s bridge, staring in awe and horror at the scene unfolding. *Vexillium* was pushing forward, relentless, unstoppable, despite the attacks coming in at her from all angles. Globus had been nervous when Vennius had ordered him to transfer to *Patentia*, but he'd told himself the caution was warranted, that splitting the top commanders was militarily correct. Now, he knew Vennius had been planning this all along, that he'd intended from the beginning to take his ship right into the maw of the beast, toward Krillus's vessel itself.

"I want more thrust…all ships, full power, forward." Globus had long considered Vennius to be a brilliant tactician, a warrior almost without peer, and he was seeing that in action now. The Imperator's boldness, his willingness to risk all, to face almost certain death to destroy Krillus, was cause enough for admiration. But Vennius's stratagem ran far deeper. He knew Krillus was no Palatian, that he was merely the latest scion of a line whose nobility had long been played out. He had unnerved his enemy, and caused him to send out frantic orders to his ships, commanding them to come to his own aid, to intercept the Palatian battleship that every second moved closer to his own person.

All along the line, the now-disordered Krillian ships fell to the guns of the crisply organized Palatian fleet. The Alliance vessels surged ahead, pouring into the gaps in the enemy formation, and wreaking even more havoc on their foes. Within moments, a battle that had looked like a certain defeat had swung around completely, and victory was there for the taking. But as Globus watched that lone symbol moving deeper and deeper into the heart of the enemy force, the glowing white icon that represented *Vexillium*, he knew the terrible cost Vennius was like to pay for pulling victory from the jaws of defeat.

"All ships in sector three, move toward *Vexillium*. Close and engage the ships attacking." Even as he spoke the words, he knew it was too late. The Alliance ships were too far away to intervene in time, and they were still locked in battle with the Krillians. Vennius and *Vexillium* had plunged forward alone, and that was how they would face this final battle.

Globus watched, despising the helplessness he felt. *Vexillium* had closed to range, and now the Imperator's ship was firing on the Krillian command vessel. Enemy ships closed from all around, blasting relentlessly, even as *Vexillium* gyrated wildly with evasive maneuvers. Most of the incoming shots missed, but some hit, and as they did, *Vexillium* slowed, and one by one, her guns fell silent.

The Krillian flagship shuddered as well, as Vennius's gunners planted hit after hit into her hull. Streams of air and fluid blasted out from both ships' shattered hulls, flash freezing the instant they hit space. Internal explosions wracked the two vessels, great plumes of smoke driving their way through the huge gashes in the hulls.

But *Vexillium* had half a dozen adversaries, and its target only one. The superior gunnery of the Palatian crew stood out, as did the greater mass and power of Vennius's ship. But the odds were just too great, the number of attacking ships too overwhelming.

Vexillium's fire waned, and finally stopped altogether. The great ship was dead in space, moving forward on its last vector and velocity. Helpless.

Krillus's ship was crippled as well, nearly a wreck, but Vennius's attack had fallen short. Just short.

The next few seconds seemed to stretch out into an eternity for Globus. There was nothing he could do, no help he could send. All he could do was sit and watch as *Vexillium* was blasted to scrap. Finally, the great ship split nearly in two, its immense steel spine snapped in half, and the last of its power readings gone.

Globus looked at the screen, a somber expression on his face. His mind flooded with feelings—sadness, respect...anger. He knew one thing for certain as he watched the readings come in. Tarkus Vennius, a man he'd considered his mentor since his days as a cadet, was dead.

Globus sat for a few seconds, stunned. But then he rallied himself. Vennius had sent him to *Patentia* for a reason, and he would not fail his fallen leader. He couldn't bring back Vennius, nor any of the heroes aboard *Vexillium*, but he could make sure they hadn't died in vain. He could finish the job Vennius had set out to do. He could kill Krillus...and send the enemy fleet streaming back across the border a broken wreck.

He flipped on the comm unit, his finger moving the dial to the fleetwide channel. "All ships, this is Commander Globus. The Imperator has fallen. He has died a hero, and his sacrifice has saved the fleet...and the homeworld. But mere victory is not enough of a testament to Tarkus Vennius, not by any measure. The Imperator was attacking the enemy flagship…he was seeking the life of Krillus, our true enemy, he who ordered his forces to invade the Alliance. Move forward, every ship. Krillus does not escape, whatever it takes. Destroy this enemy, now. Finish this vengeance. Do it for our leader, a man who will live in our hearts forever. Do it for Tarkus Vennius!"

Chapter Forty-One

"Fighters launched, sir."

"Very well. All batteries, prepare to open fire." Turenne glanced across the bridge toward Maramont's station. His number two was showing some signs of stress, of course, but overall, he was pleased with the officer's performance. It wasn't possible to overstate the importance of the current mission. Turenne and his people bore no responsibility for the fact that the pulsar was in danger—indeed, they were the only ones who'd shown enough initiative to be in a position to save the weapon. But that didn't matter in the Union, and Turenne suspected his officers were as aware of that as he was. If the pulsar was lost, everyone remotely involved would be scapegoated, and fairness and justice would play no role in their fates.

"All batteries ready, sir."

Turenne watched his ragged band of fighters moving toward the enemy ship. His wings had been savaged by the Confed squadrons that had engaged *Temeraire*. He'd worked his people as well as he'd been able, but whatever vessel that was over there, they had the cream of the Confed fighter corps with them, that

331

much was clear. Turenne had never seen fighters handled so well, and for a few minutes, he'd been sure his ship was doomed. Then, after the first attack wave hit, the rest of the bombers had broken off. He hadn't understood what was going on, not until he saw the enemy squadrons go after the pulsar's power systems.

The enemy bombers had taken the ancient weapon out of the fight, but they'd had to spare his ship to do it. Now, he would finish that enemy battleship. He would save the pulsar.

He watched as the distance counted down on his display. He was well within the range of the enemy's primary batteries, and the lack of any fire confirmed his guess that they were inoperative. And that meant he had a real chance to take the enemy ship down. *Temeraire* was damaged as well, but his gut told him his ship was in better shape than its adversary.

"Sir, we've got enemy fighters approaching."

Turenne snapped his head around, his eyes moving over the display, focusing on the small cluster of enemy ships inbound.

He shook his head, almost in disbelief. Those ships had to be nearly out of fuel. And they were coming in at almost half a percent of lightspeed. They'd only have the briefest instant to attack his ship...and none of them were bombers.

His eyes moved to the equally small cluster, his own fighters. Should he redirect them, send them to intercept the incoming enemy force?

Temeraire was vulnerable. The two plasma torpedoes that had hit her had left massive rends in her hull. Even interceptors could cause critical damage if they managed to target those weak spots. But that seemed almost impossible at such speeds...and he didn't see how the attacking ships could possibly have the fuel to slow down.

"Our fighters are to continue their attack run, Commander." Maramont hadn't suggested altering the plan, but Turenne knew every officer on the bridge had been thinking about it. But there was no point in recalling his battered squadrons. The enemy was coming in too fast. His ships would have only the slightest instant to intercept them. They might score a hit or two, but they'd never stop the attack. He would just have to take the chance, to rely on the odds.

And the odds said, no pilots could hit such pinpoint spots at that velocity.

His eyes moved back to the range data. It was time.

"All batteries…open fire."

*   *   *

Dauntless shook hard. Another hit.

Barron sat quietly, his eyes focused on the display. His ship was moving toward the pulsar, right on the course he'd set. But the enemy battleship was closing, and his mind confirmed what his gut had already told him. *Dauntless* would never endure the pounding, not long enough to reach its target.

Billings and his engineering team were still trying to get the rear batteries operational, but as Barron saw the time slip by, he knew there was no point. A few laser cannons wouldn't be enough to destroy the pulsar or to defeat the enemy vessel coming up from behind. It was too little, too late, and not something for which he could justify risking the lives of his people.

"Atara, Billings and his teams are to evacuate. The gunners, too." Eighty percent of *Dauntless*'s crew had already abandoned ship, and now Barron intended to get the rest of them off.

"Yes, sir." He could hear the understanding in her voice, her realization that he'd given up on any hope of regaining the weapons. The plan was simple now. Hope that *Dauntless* could endure the enemy attack long enough to close with the pulsar. He suspected his first officer didn't have any more faith in that than he did…but there simply was nothing else to do.

"And, Atara…I want you to go, too." They were the last of the bridge crew remaining onboard.

"Tyler…" Travis turned and looked over at him, a pleading look in her face.

"Go, Atara. Please." A pause. "I'll be right behind you. I just want to get us in closer, under one hundred thousand kilometers…and then I'll follow. The AI can take her the rest of the way." He looked at his number two—his best friend—silently for a moment. "Do this for me, Atara. I have to be the last one off. I just have to."

Travis had a stricken look on her face, as though the idea of leaving the bridge, abandoning ship with Barron still at his post, was the most horrifying prospect imaginable. But after a brief hesitation, she just nodded, and walked over toward his chair. She reached out, and put her hand on his face. "One hundred thousand kilometers...no closer. Promise me?"

"I promise, Atara. Now, go. I want you out there with the lifeboats. Take command, find the safest place you can for our people." *As though there's anyplace safe in this system...*

She hesitated, looking as though she'd have preferred to follow virtually any order other than the one Barron had given her. But, finally, she just nodded, and then she turned and walked toward the ladder...and disappeared below the deck.

Barron turned and took a deep breath. He looked around the bridge, feeling a moistness in his eyes. "It's just you and me now, old girl."

He took a deep breath. "You and me."

*   *   *

"We're only getting one shot at this, so make it your best." Jovi Grachus was leaning forward in her cockpit, her body as tense as it had ever been. She'd watched the Union ship attacking *Dauntless*, and she knew Barron's ship had very little chance of enduring the assault long enough to complete the mission. Her people *had* to disable that vessel. It was the only way.

She glanced quickly at her fuel gauge. She had enough to power her positioning jets to aim her shot—she hoped—but she didn't have much more. Decelerating was an impossible dream, and her course would take her into the outer system after her attack, and then into deep space.

She pushed the thought from her mind. That was a problem, of course, a huge one. But it was next in line, behind stopping the Union battleship.

"I know this is a difficult attack, but you are the best pilots

I've ever commanded, the deadliest aces, I'd wager, that exist anywhere. It has been my privilege to lead you, and my great honor. Now, let's finish this battle. Confeds, you're making this run to save *Dauntless*. I know what that means to all of you. And, Palatians, you are here to fight alongside our allies, the men and women who came to our aid when we needed them." *And the less all of you think about what happens next, the better…*

Grachus tapped her throttle, slowly feeding power into the positioning thrusters. She knew she'd pass by the Union ship in less than a second. There would be no time for second-guessing, no time for careful aiming. Her guts, her instincts…they would determine success or failure here, as they would for her comrades.

"That ship's got two gaping wounds, and we've got to hit right there. A few shots at the hull won't get it done. Use your targeting computers…but trust your intuition as well, your feelings. Good luck to you all."

She shut the comm line. She didn't want any distractions. She was in command, but there was nothing more she could do for her people now. They were all on their own, reliant on their own talents and skills.

She figured they'd need two solid hits, maybe three, to disable the battleship…though that was mostly wild guesswork. She didn't even think about the odds of scoring a single hit, much less multiple ones. It was what they had to do, so somehow, they would see it done. She vacillated between agreeing with that thought and questioning it.

She had eight Alliance fighters and four Confed birds, all of her people who'd managed to adjust their vectors in time to join the attack run. The rest of her people were coming, but they were too far back, and they wouldn't make it in time.

She fixed her eyes on the display, nudging her controls, adjusting her targeting data. There were two spots, the locations where *Dauntless*'s bombers had struck. Grachus didn't know much about the architecture of Union ships, but her focus went to the location closest to the ship's aft. The gash in the hull was a little larger…and it was close to the engines. Her fighters didn't have much hope of destroying the enemy vessel outright, but there was a good chance the reactors were near the engines. If they could cut the flow of power to the ship's weapons, even for a few minutes, just maybe they could buy Commander Barron the time he needed.

She tapped her throttle, lightly. For all practical purposes, she was out of fuel, but her ship was still responding, and she needed those last fragments of engine power. Most of her people would go in ahead of her, the result of their positions and vectors when the frantic attack had begun. She felt like she should be in the lead, but there was nothing she could do about that except watch…and learn what she could from her comrades' attacks.

She watched as the first two ships went in, both of them targeting the same spot she'd chosen. The lead ship was a Confed, one of the birds from *Dauntless*'s Yellow squadron, and the second was one of her Alliance comrades. They were coming in, one right after the other.

She sat, still, focused, watching as the first shot impacted the hull…perhaps one hundred meters too far to the aft. Any hit at all at these velocities was impressive marksmanship, but she shook her head as the laser blast hit the battleship's armored hull. It caused damage, of course, but nothing that would make a difference.

Then she saw the second ship go in. Another hit…and another impact, perhaps two hundred meters from the hull gash. Her people were doing an extraordinary job of hitting the enemy ship at the breakneck velocities at which they were passing by, but not good enough.

Another three ships went by, two of their shots just missing the battleship, while the third impacted against the starboard armor. Then, the next fighter went by…and it's shot was right on target, the laser blast going right into the large hole on the ship's hull.

Grachus felt excitement as she saw a great geyser of energy flowing back out of the hull breach, secondary explosions ripping through the enemy vessel. For an instant, she hoped to see some effect, a stoppage of thrust or silence from the ship's batteries. But the vessel was blasting as hard as it had been toward *Dauntless*, firing its ragged broadside as it did.

Damn.

Still, that pilot, one of her Confeds, had proven—to her and the rest of those stacked up, coming in on their own attacks—that it could be done.

She watched again as the ship in front of her went in, and planted yet another hit in almost exactly the same spot. Another series of inner explosions tore through the ship, flames ripping out of the hull breeches in huge blasts of escaping air, before they were extinguished by the frigid vacuum.

Grachus felt another burst of excitement, but there was no time to think about damage assessments. Her own fighter was on its way past. It was time.

She took a deep breath, tried to relax her hand, to allow her instincts to take over. She opened her mind, allowed herself to feel her enemy's presence, to let the warrior spirit inside her pull the trigger. Her ship zoomed up toward the enemy ship, and as it did, she tapped her throttle, slightly to the port. She felt her fingers tightening, heard the sound of the laser cannon firing echoing inside her cockpit.

Then, she was past the target, her ship blasting away at just over one-half percent of lightspeed. She was several thousand kilometers past the Union vessel by the time she was able to review her scanner readings.

A direct hit. She'd planted the laser blast deep inside the enemy ship, right where her two comrades had hit. The readings were off the scale, massive plumes of radiation and heat escaping from the stricken vessel, pouring out into space.

She flipped the rear scanners on at full power, getting whatever readings she could from the last watts of power her exhausted ship had to offer. The enemy vessel had been hit hard. But there was no way to be sure its weapons were out, not without watching, checking to see if it fired again.

Grachus knew she would have to take success on faith. A few seconds later, the scanners died as the flow of power was exhausted, most of her screens going to black. Her thrusters were silent, the laser cannons dry. She was out of fuel. Completely out, with no way to decelerate or change course.

She still had passive scanners, at short range at least, and she could tell all her ships had passed by. And, one by one, they too, were running out of fuel.

She looked out into deep space, the far reaches of the system into which she and her pilots were plunging, and she sighed softly, hoping it had been worth it.

Hoping they had saved *Dauntless*.

Chapter Forty-Two

Barron sat on *Dauntless*'s bridge, alone, staring at the display in stunned surprise. The Union battleship was still there, but now it was spewing radiation from internal explosions, and its guns were silent.

Jovi Grachus. Once again, the Palatian pilot had come through. Barron remembered weeks earlier, when she'd pled with him to allow her to bring her squadron aboard. He'd almost refused her request, concerned about integrating Alliance and Confederation pilots, worried about Stockton's reaction...and, just perhaps, burdened by some residual resentment for the damage she'd done to his forces when she'd served the Red Alliance. Now, she had saved the mission.

"Evacuation status?" Barron leaned over, speaking into the comm unit that was now tied into the ship's AI.

"All personnel have been evacuated, Commodore." The AI had never been reprogrammed with the informal demotions the crew had given themselves for the mission. "You are the only remaining life form aboard."

He turned and looked at the display. The pulsar was there,

larger now, and the small symbol representing *Dauntless* was moving closer with every passing second. Stockton's attack had disabled the weapon, giving the fleet a chance to win victory in the Bottleneck…and now, it was *Dauntless*'s job—her final job— to see the menacing artifact destroyed once and for all, to push this nightmare of a war closer to final victory.

"Time until impact with pulsar?"

"Projected impact in eighteen minutes, twenty seconds, Commodore."

Barron found it oddly unnerving that the AI showed no emotion. Not that there was any reason to expect a computer to have some sort of breakdown, but *he* would be leaving the ship in a few minutes…the AI would remain…and be destroyed in the fiery collision that obliterated both *Dauntless* and the pulsar.

Barron knew he personified his ship, and he also knew it was irrational…but still, the pain cut deeply at him. He felt the urge to fire up the engines, to veer off and keep his ship alive. He shook his head. That wasn't possible. Too many lives depended on destroying that weapon. Besides, if *Dauntless* was still here when the dozen enemy battleships arrived—in less than thirty minutes, he reminded himself—she would be destroyed anyway. This way, she would at least be sacrificed in victory. She would save thousands, even millions. And her name would always be remembered.

Barron looked at the display. The enemy battleship had definitely been disabled…but the fighters it had launched were still coming in. He didn't anticipate the Union pilots would be anything like Grachus's warriors, but *Dauntless* was wounded just as the enemy battleship had been, and her starboard side was torn open, with gaping holes in her armor. Normally, he wouldn't be too concerned about a few disordered fighters, but he felt the tension in his gut as he stared at the small yellow dots.

And at the cluster of tiny white circles behind. Stockton, and a handful of his people, blasting toward *Dauntless* with what he suspected was something well beyond their full rated power.

Grachus had faced the entire fighter force defending the pulsar, and routed it utterly, and then she returned and saved *Daunt-*

less from the Union battleship. Stockton had led the assault on the pulsar's power plants, disabling the deadly weapon. Now, he was leading a handful of his people back, to intercept the incoming Union fighters.

Barron had never been comfortable when the bulk of praise for *Dauntless*'s victories was heaped on his shoulders. Jake Stockton, Anya Fritz, Atara Travis—and heroes who were gone, Kyle Jamison, Tillis Krill, so many who'd been lost—had all played their part in the fierce struggles his ship had come through. *And now, Jovi Grachus,* he thought, realizing in full measure just how much she had contributed to the battle. For a passing moment—all he had for idle thought now—he considered the improbability of such a group of talented and capable people coming together, and he wondered if they hadn't created each other to an extent, if each of them hadn't driven their comrades to greater levels of success and heroism.

Whatever answers might exist, Barron knew one thing for sure. He was honored to have led them, to have served these years with such men and women.

*   *   *

"Let's go! I know you're low on fuel. I know you're exhausted. But we've got to take down those ships. We've got to keep them off *Dauntless.*"

Stockton pulled back on the throttle, nudging up his ship's acceleration. He didn't know what was keeping his reactor and his engine together, not after the hell he'd put them through. He remembered reading reports, failure rates assigned to various levels of engine overpowering. Now, he suspected that had all been garbage, nonsense published to discourage the kind of reckless behavior he so often displayed in battle.

Without which, the pulsar would even now be blasting the fleet to dust...

Stockton wasn't one who liked being told what to do. He could obey orders—usually, at least—but he wasn't about to listen to prechewed warnings written by engineers who'd never been in a battle, much less in the cockpit of a fighter.

His eyes were focused on one of the enemy ships. His lasers were pretty well drained, and he didn't figure he had more than a dozen shots left. That meant aiming was vital…no pot shots hoping for a lucky hit.

He moved up, staring at his prey, his view shifting every few seconds to keep track of his comrades, of the handful of fighters he'd managed to get back to defend *Dauntless*. He almost fired, but he stopped himself. He didn't have the lock yet…and he didn't have the shot to waste.

He tapped his throttle, swung his ship around slightly, and then he squeezed the firing stud. Once. A second time. A third.

He scored the hit, and his prey disappeared from his scanner. But the attack had cost him close to thirty percent of his stored energy. He'd have to cut his engines to restore his batteries and, by the time he did that, the Union fighters would have completed their attack runs.

He swung his ship around, hard to starboard, angling toward another of the enemy ships. His people were cutting a huge swath through the battered attack force, but even as he fired twice more, taking out his second target, he knew at least a few ships were going to get through.

Then he saw three fighters, at the edge of the formation. None of his people were going to reach them in time.

He blasted his thrust at full, gritting his teeth as his ship swung around, bringing the targets onto his forward scanners. They were far out, difficult shots with laser cannons, but he had no choice. He'd never close, not before the ships were able to complete their runs on *Dauntless*.

He fired, a reckless shot that went far wide of his intended target. Then again, this time much closer. His eyes dropped to his readout. He had four shots left, maybe five.

He pressed the stud again, his shot zipping just to the port of the target. Then again, a glancing hit. The enemy fighter was still there, but it was rolling wildly to the side. The pilot might survive, but he wouldn't be attacking *Dauntless*.

That left two. Stockton drove his ship forward, squeezing

everything he could get from the engines. The range dropped slowly. Another two minutes, and he'd be in close range. But he didn't have two minutes.

The enemy ships were closing fast, and they'd be firing any second. Whatever he was going to do, it had to be now. He fired, then again. Both misses.

He shot twice more, both shots close, but neither hitting. Then he stared straight ahead, his hands moving across the controls, adjusting the target lock. He had one of the enemy ships dead to rights, he was sure of it. He squeezed the trigger…and nothing.

Damn!

His batteries were drained. He'd done all he could…but at least two birds were going to get through to *Dauntless*.

*   *   *

Barron watched as Stockton's pilots tore into the attacking Union fighters. One after another of the interceptors went down, until finally, the survivors broke and ran.

Save for two.

Stockton himself had chased those birds, pursuing them with an intensity Barron could almost feel from the bridge. But then the ace's guns went silent. Barron didn't have an active line to Stockton, but he guessed the pilot's lasers were out of power.

"Two fighters," he said softly, half to himself, and half to *Dauntless*. Two interceptors weren't normally a major threat to a battleship, but *Dauntless* had the same weakness that had brought down the Union vessel. Worse, even. The pulsar's hit had left a jagged gash over seven hundred meters long down the hull. It was a big target, and any shot hitting the exposed innards of the ship would be massively more destructive than one impacting on the armor.

Barron leaned back in his chair. His ship had already lost its weaponry, and he didn't need anything more now than enough power for course adjustments. The pulsar was mostly immobile, but it did have its own positioning jets…and the enemy was racing to get tugs hooked up to the artifact. As long as one of *Dauntless*'s reactors stayed online, with at least some engine capacity, the battleship would be able to complete its mission.

And the escape pod…

Virtually every shuttle and pod on the ship had been launched, evacuating the giant ship's crew and wounded. There was a single pod remaining, just in the corridor outside the bridge…the one the crew had specifically left for their captain.

Barron looked around the bridge, one last time. He'd already plotted the approach orders into the AI. The ship's main computer would adjust the thrust and vector as needed to match any enemy efforts to move the pulsar from *Dauntless*'s path.

It was time for him to leave.

He got up from his seat, pausing for an instant to look around the bridge. He was still worried about the attacking fighters, but there was nothing he could do about that, and no reason he could think of to stay longer.

He took two steps across the bridge, and then *Dauntless* lurched wildly. One of the fighters had scored a hit, a bad one, he knew immediately. He stumbled to the ground, but then the grav compensators gave out, plunging the bridge into zero gravity.

Barron pulled himself up, and made his way carefully back to his chair. He'd been scared for a moment that the hit had knocked out the engines, but the readouts showed twenty percent power. Not great, but enough.

He took a deep breath, steadying himself, holding onto the armrests of his chair. He was about to go, but then he decided to confirm one last time that the engines were still functional. "Activate thrust, 1g pulse, forward for two seconds." It wouldn't be enough to upset the approach course, just a quick burst to ensure the systems were still online.

But there was no response.

"AI, this is Commodore Barron. Give me a 1g engine pulse for two seconds."

Nothing.

Barron pulled himself down into his chair, his fingers moving feverishly over the workstation. He pulled up the AI's diagnostic display, and the second he looked at the screen, he felt his hope slip away. Dead on all readouts. Whatever else that last hit had done, it had taken out *Dauntless*'s main AI.

The reality closed in on Barron as he sat there, staring at the display, at the growing icon representing the pulsar. *Dauntless* could still complete the mission, but she would need manual control over the engines.

Barron had to stay, at least until the last instant. Then, hopefully, he could make a run for it.

It would be close. Very close.

Chapter Forty-Three

"What is he doing?" Andi was staring at the small display on *Pegasus*'s bridge, watching as the battleship moved closer and closer toward the pulsar. She'd been waiting for the battleship to open fire—it was well within range—but there had been nothing. No shots at all.

"We're picking up a number of small craft, Andi."

"Fighters?" She'd watched as *Dauntless*'s squadrons hit the Union battleship, and again as they'd taken out most of the attacking enemy fighters. But those ships had moved out of the area now, carried off by their high velocities.

"No, not fighters." A pause. "My guess...shuttles. And escape pods. It sure looks like they abandoned ship, Andi."

She shook her head. Something wasn't right about what she was watching. She reached down to her comm unit and sent a signal toward the battleship. *Pegasus* was close now, and the transmission time was minimal. But there was no response.

"*Dauntless*, this is *Pegasus*. Do you read?" She resent the message.

Still nothing.

346

"Maybe they all evacuated, Andi. I'm picking up a *lot* of small craft and escape pods. It sure looks like enough to be the whole crew."

"Maybe." She knew Vig was making sense, but she had a strange feeling something was wrong. She turned toward her number two. "Send out a wide-angle signal to those lifeboats, Vig. See if you can raise Tyler. Or Atara."

"On it." He leaned over his workstation, his hands moving over the controls. "This is *Pegasus*, looking for Commodore Barron or Captain Travis...do you read?"

She listened as Vig repeated the same words a second time... then a third.

"*Pegasus*..."

Andi heard the voice, and she recognized it even before the speaker could identify herself.

"...this is Atara. Are you there, Andi? What are you doing here?"

"Atara...I'm so glad to hear your voice. Did you evacuate *Dauntless*?" A pause. "Is Tyler..."

"Andi, Tyler's still aboard *Dauntless*. The weapons are down. He's..."

Travis's words vanished from Lafarge's mind as a single thought formed and, for a few seconds, blocked out everything else. *He's going to ram the pulsar.*

"He can't..."

"He has an escape pod near the bridge, Andi...but he should have launched it by now."

"We have to get him off of there." Andi felt her insides tighten. She felt like she was going to retch.

"We can't, Andi. The shuttles and escape pods don't have enough thrust to get to *Dauntless*...not on time. We've been trying to reach Tyler, but that last hit must have knocked out the comm."

Lafarge stared at the screen, at the small oval representing *Dauntless*. She knew what she had to do...she just didn't know if she had time.

"Well, *Pegasus* has enough thrust...and we're heading right toward *Dauntless* already." She gritted her teeth and looked across the small bridge toward Vig. "We're going in, Atara. We're going to get Tyler out of there."

*   *   *

Argentum's bridge was a scene of silent efficiency. Tulus and his warriors were doing what they'd been born to do, or at least raised to do, and before them, their enemies fell, one after another. Tulus had seen Tyler Barron's ships in action at Palatia, and the sense of calm superiority he'd always had as a Palatian had been sorely shaken. Barron's people conducted themselves with courage and honor, even as they advanced into Palatia's defenses, a web of fortresses previously thought to be impregnable.

Tulus was here now, repaying that debt...and coming to the aid of friends. But there was pride on the line too, and he couldn't allow his forces to perform with any less zeal and ability than Barron's had done in Alliance space.

He watched as the Union ships began to fall back. This enemy lacked the warrior spirit he'd seen in Barron's crews, and he stared at them with disgust. The Union was dangerous, no doubt, but its threat came not from the warrior spirit or martial skill. Their strength came from numbers, and from their dangerous ability to work in the shadows, to undermine from within. It was a repugnant way to make war, at least to Tulus's Alliance sensibilities, and he was determined to make the enemy pay, not only for attacking the Confederation, but for all the harm their deceits and machinations had done to his own nation.

"All ships, continue to advance. Keep them in close range, and maintain full fire."

He could see what the Union forces were doing. They wanted to flee...he could *feel* that. But they were mostly holding, fighting hard to hang on long enough for the pulsar to withdraw. And, as much as it galled him to acknowledge it, they were going to succeed. Tulus's force had penetrated the deepest into the enemy line—save perhaps for Sara Eaton's battered ships, which, despite the heavy damage many had sustained, were driving forward with a vigor that matched that of his own people.

"All ships matching enemy acceleration levels, Commander. Maintaining fire."

Tulus looked to the long-range display, to the symbols moving around the pulsar. The tugs were almost hitched up. In a few minutes, the enemy would begin moving their ancient weapon. Tulus had no doubt the fight in the Bottleneck would be a victory, but as long as the pulsar survived, the fate of the Confederation—and the Alliance—would remain in limbo.

He began to turn back toward the close-range screen, but something caught his eye. It was a symbol, a small oval, and the instant he saw it, Tulus knew what it was.

Dauntless.

She was heading toward the pulsar. Directly toward it.

"My God," he whispered softly, as realization dawned. Tyler Barron was going to ram the pulsar.

Tulus shook his head, his eyes fixed on what he was watching. He wondered if Barron would manage to escape—or if he already had, if *Dauntless* was moving under its computer's control.

And he had one other thought, one he'd had before, but now could no longer deny.

He couldn't explain it, but he was sure Palatian blood somehow flowed in Tyler Barron's veins.

*   *   *

"Commander Grachus, this is Jake Stockton. Are you reading my signal?" Stockton was blasting his ship hard, burning through far too much of his scant fuel. But he had to maintain contact. Grachus and her survivors were careening toward the outer system, and Stockton had to stay with them if there was any hope of rescue.

"Commander Stockton, this is Jovi Grachus." Her voice was soft, somber. Stockton could tell immediately she'd given up any hope of rescue.

"Listen carefully, Commander. I'm going to maintain a line on your people. The fleet is advancing, and when the first ships get here we can get some retrieval boats out to your people." A short pause. "Do any of your fighters have *any* fuel left?"

"A few, Commander. I'm out entirely. So are several others."

Stockton paused for a few seconds. Then he said, "Any of your ships with remaining fuel need to decelerate at once. There's nothing else they can do." He knew those pilots had a better chance of rescue than Grachus herself, or any of the others who had burned through all their fuel in the fight.

In Grachus's case, she had exhausted her power fighting like no pilot Stockton had ever seen. The number of kills she'd amassed, the speed with which she'd gotten her squadrons where they had to be...it had been nothing short of astonishing. Stockton's anger, the searing hatred he'd had for her had changed, morphing into a grudging respect. It had been less than a year since she'd been in his sights, since he'd come half a second from killing her...and now he wanted—he *needed*—to save her.

But he didn't know if he could. Her ship was already deep in the system, and there was no help to be had, not until the fleet arrived.

He'd calculated half a dozen times, and he'd come up with the same result in each instance. Grachus and her comrades would run out of life support long before the fleet got there.

But Stockton refused to give up. It wasn't his way.

*   *   *

Jovi Grachus shivered. She'd turned her heat levels down to the absolute minimum. It was normal protocol for the situation, an attempt to extend her life support, to increase the amount of time she could survive without rescue.

It was pointless, too, she realized. First, because it did nothing to increase her oxygen supply, which, if anything, was in worse shape than the heat. And second, because she knew, in her head and her gut, that she was just too far out, that no rescue could make it to her in time.

She felt a strange satisfaction that Commander Stockton seemed to have gotten past his anger toward her. He hadn't forgiven her, at least not in so many words, but then she hadn't forgiven herself either. She'd been a fool to join the Red Alliance, and her efforts had helped to keep that terrible conflict going. Hundreds were dead because of her, perhaps thousands. She didn't want to die, and it saddened her to think she'd never see her children again…but she was ready.

Ready to atone.

Ready to follow Kat.

She thought of her friend, of the years they'd spent together, growing up on the Rigellus estate, and of the loyalty Katrine had always shown her. She owed her entire career to Kat, her position as anything but a common footsoldier. Kat had given her the chance to shine, and she liked to think, save for the unfortunate Red Alliance episode, that she'd made good use of the opportunity her friend had made possible.

Even now, she could look at the battle in the Bottleneck with some level of pride. Her squadrons—Alliance and Confed—had held off a huge enemy fighter force, and then they'd managed to disable the enemy battleship moving against *Dauntless*. She didn't know if Tyler Barron would succeed in destroying the pulsar, but she was sure she'd done her part. And there was satisfaction in that, some level of redemption for her actions of the previous year.

She didn't know why it mattered as much as it did to her that Stockton accepted her. The two were very much alike, she suspected. They should have been friends, comrades…but they'd been born to different worlds. She remembered Tyler Barron's words to her about Kat, about the feelings he'd had when he'd finally spoken to her, right before she destroyed *Invictus*, killing herself and all hands. He'd spoken of a strange familiarity, a feeling that this enemy he'd just fought should have been something different. Should have been a friend.

But war didn't conform itself to feelings or wishes, and they'd all been born on their own paths. Kat's fate had been to fall to Tyler Barron and *Dauntless*. And Grachus's had been to survive long enough to reach this point, to serve alongside the Confeds, to help solidify the growing friendship between the two nations.

She'd fought well. That, at least, was a solace. She was scared, sad at the prospect of death, of never seeing her children again. But she knew they'd be well cared for, that their futures were assured. None less than Tarkus Vennius had promised her that.

She had followed Kat most of their lives…and now she was ready to follow her in death. She had done her duty, she had redeemed her family name.

The way is the way…

*   *   *

Barron stared at the shattered panel, cold realization setting in. His first thought when he'd seen the damaged controls for the escape pod had been to activate the overrides, to force open the hatch and control the launch sequence from the pod itself.

Then he saw the real extent of the damage.

His people had left him the pod nearest to the bridge, the one that would be easiest to get to…but luck, which had saved his people more than once, had swung against him this time. Along with the damage done to *Dauntless* by the last two fighter attacks, the escape pod had been wrecked.

Barron guessed it had been hit by a chunk of debris flying off from some other part of the ship. But none of that mattered. The pod was beyond repair, that was clear, and it meant Barron was stuck where he was. His plan of guiding the ship in manually, of staying this post and escaping at the last minute, was gone.

For an instant, he considered blasting the engines, trying to change course to avert the impending collision. But he couldn't do that. Too many people would die if the pulsar was allowed to escape…far too great a price to pay for the life of one man.

He walked back onto the bridge, to his chair. He wanted to live, he wanted to see his people again…and he wanted a chance to talk to Andi, to tell her he was sorry he'd been so cold to her the last time he saw her.

That, he had already done, at least in a way. The message he'd left for her at Grimaldi explained everything. He'd just had to get her away, to know she was safe somewhere. And when the pulsar was destroyed, she truly *would* be safe. There was peace for him in that realization.

He sat back in his chair, and let out a deep breath. His grandfather had died in the last war with the Confederation... and, now, he would die in this one. He couldn't be too angry about it. He'd escaped his share of close calls, and he'd always known that, sooner or later, fate would come for him.

He stared at the screen on his workstation, reaching out to the makeshift nav controls he'd set up. He adjusted *Dauntless*'s vector, slightly, keeping the massive ship on a direct line toward the pulsar. The enemy tugs were moving feverishly, but they were going to be too late.

He fought to hold back the flood of emotions that wanted to consume him. The comm was down. There was no way to call for help...or even to say goodbye.

He sighed softly, staring at the main display. Eleven minutes. Eleven minutes to impact. Eleven minutes left to live...

Chapter Forty-Four

Presidium Square
Liberte City
Planet Montmirail, Ghassara IV,
Union Year 217 (313 AC)

"See to it at once." Ricard Lille gestured for his operative to go, to complete his mission with all possible haste. Lille generally liked to work alone, but that wasn't always possible, especially on missions of significant scope. And nothing he'd ever done had matched what he was about to attempt. Trusting anyone, even his few loyal retainers, with even partial knowledge of what he was going to do was dangerous…but he just couldn't pull it off alone.

He stood along the side of the street, the shade from the massive presidium building shielding him from the midday heat of Liberte City's high summer. Everywhere he'd traveled in the Union, the signs of economic collapse and despair had been evident…save here. Liberte City was the Union's capital, the home of its highest government functionaries, and it would remain pleasant and well supplied, Lille knew, no matter how many millions of its citizens starved.

Ricard Lille was a cynical man, one who believed almost nothing he saw or was told. In his estimation, most people lived in a perpetual state of self-delusion, greedily accepting the lies

354

they were told because the truth was too uncomfortable, too depressing. The Union was supposed to be a worker's paradise. Its core founding documents spoke extensively of the rights of workers and the demand for equality.

Lille shook his head. The political power brokers of the Union lived as staggeringly plush a lifestyle of any of the nobles who'd been massacred in the revolution almost two centuries earlier, and the plight of the common man had only worsened since then. Organizations like Sector Nine had become adept at spying on the population and removing troublesome elements, and for almost two hundred years, every movement designed to win some level of freedom had been stillborn, extinguished as often as not by Sector Nine kill squads, wiping out the founders before they could spread the word.

Lille wasn't a dreamer, and he certainly didn't care about the workers. As far as he was concerned, people who let themselves be herded as sheep deserved no better than they got. He didn't believe in the Union…he didn't believe in anything. But the current government had always suited his needs. He lacked the self-destructive lust for power that drove members of the Presidium, and those in the lower strata of the Union's ruling structure, to constantly scheme and struggle. He liked to live well, but as long as his comforts were attended to, he had only one other vice.

He loved to kill.

He'd never understood his natural affinity for murder, nor the intense pleasure it gave him, but he'd long ago acknowledged it to be true. For years, he had worked with Gaston Villieneuve, eliminating the Sector Nine chief's worst…problems. He'd been happy in that relationship, and he lived his life of privilege and quiet debauchery between assignments.

But success inevitably bred expansion. As he became more and more successful, Villieneuve had begun to tap him for more assignments, missions outside his core competency of killing. Lille fancied himself among the very best at his curious trade, but he was no spy. Still, Villieneuve had become more and more desperate as the war went on, and he'd come to Lille for aid, to take on missions such as his disastrous foray to the Alliance.

Lille had reluctantly accepted the assignments—and he still felt, if he'd had a bit less bad luck he might have prevailed—and the resulting failures had begun to poison his relationship with Villieneuve.

He'd considered killing his mentor. He had no animosity toward Villieneuve, but his most recent failure at Barroux was almost certain to bring the spymaster's wrath down upon him. Striking first had been the only option that came to his mind.

At least before he'd decided to kill the Presidium.

The thought was still a strange one, a task so herculean in nature, so utterly outrageous, it was hard to wrap his head around it. The supreme council that ruled the Union had seen its share of assassinations, singly, and usually with the cooperation or consent of a good number of the other members. But for an outsider to kill not, one, but all of them, was unprecedented.

It would be a masterpiece for a man who loved killing over all things.

And it would leave Villieneuve in unquestioned control of the government…and deeply in Lille's debt. Certainly enough to wash away his recent failures.

Lille had pondered ways to accomplish the mission. The biggest issue was killing them all within a brief window. Word would spread quickly if Presidium members started dying, and the others would retreat to their inner domains, surrounded and protected by their most loyal retainers. No, there could be no warning…to any of them.

He had to kill them all at the same time.

*   *   *

"The plot is far more extensive than we thought, sir. Sector Nine seems to have some level of control over a number of Senators, and the peace movement is gaining strength." Shane Darvin leaned in toward Holsten as he spoke, his words barely a whisper.

"The Senate is full of fools and imbeciles." The disgust in

Holsten's voice was obvious. He was a committed advocate of republican government, but sometimes the combination of stupid, uninformed voters and corrupt career politicians shook his beliefs to their core. "Half of them are reprobate idiots, and the others are worse. They are hardcore criminals."

"Could it really be that easy for Sector Nine to gain control over the Senate? Just money?"

"Money isn't *just money* when you're a pleasure-loving fool who's squandered all he inherited, and now faces ridicule and humiliation back home...and perhaps a scandal salacious enough to actually deter the voters from rubberstamping your next reelection. Nothing is more unthinkable to these creatures than losing their seats, facing a life without the perquisites of power."

Holsten frowned. He'd been born with more than enough wealth and name to secure his own Senate seat, but the idea had always made him retch. He despised politicians, and he'd pursued the path he had out of what he liked to think of as pure patriotism. The Confederation's government was flawed—deeply flawed—but compared to horrors like the Union, it was a virtual paradise. And that was worth preserving, whatever the cost.

"We should be able to contain this plot, Shane...at least as long as the Union terms are so onerous. That treaty would cripple the Iron Belt worlds. The Oligarchs would never tolerate that, and they control the Senators from their planets." He paused, looking over at his agent. "What we need to worry about is how to stop this if the Union becomes less greedy, if they offer reasonable terms. The Confederation is tired of fighting, and I'm afraid the Senate would jump on a chance to end hostilities in any tolerable way...and leave us with yet another war to fight.

*   *   *

"We are gathered here to discuss the activities of Gaston Villieneuve. Minister Villieneuve has apparently engaged in a protracted disinformation campaign designed to mislead this body. I am prepared to submit evidence of this treasonous activity, and a when this presentation is complete, I will ask for a vote to expel Gaston Villieneuve from the Presidium and remove him at once as the head of Sector Nine. Further, I shall propose the issuance an immediate warrant for Minister Villieneuve's execution." Quentin Lebecque stood at the head of the table, looking out over his comrades as he spoke.

The men and women gathered around the table stared back, some with looks of genuine surprise, others seeming as though they'd harbored at least some suspicions.

"I would like to begin by introducing Ricard Lille, one of Sector Nine's most senior operatives and, until recently, a close compatriot of Gaston Villieneuve. Mr. Lille had seen firsthand the level of Minister Villieneuve's corruption, and he is here to enlighten us."

Lille walked over to the head of the table. "Thank you, Your Excellency," he said, his tone ringing with feigned respect. He stared out at the table, feeling almost patriotic as he watched his intended victims. However it had gotten there, the Union was in real trouble, and the truth was plain to see. Villieneuve was by far the most competent member of the Presidium, and whatever chance existed to preserve the Union, it rested with his continued, even enhanced, control. Lille didn't have the slightest hope that the group of fools gathered around the table could address the myriad problems closing from all sides.

He stood at the head of the table and described all the things Villieneuve had done, the missions, the frauds, the diversion of resources. He portrayed his friend not in any fictional terms but in the context of his actual deeds. He didn't have to lie. Villieneuve was guilty as hell. He'd gone to great lengths to draw power into his own hands, and he'd violated a seemingly endless list of laws and rules to do it.

The truth was more useful now than a pack of lies. Not only would his descriptions match whatever shreds of real intel anyone in the room possessed, but his delivery would be all the more effective for its truthfulness.

He felt odd speaking out, seemingly turning against his old mentor. He would have been suspicious of anyone in his shoes, but he knew how the Presidium members thought. To them, it was entirely normal for a subordinate to sabotage his superior, clearing the way for his own advancement. He suspected every other individual in the room was sure he expected Villieneuve's seats—both on the Presidium and as the head of Sector Nine—as his reward, and that served his purpose well.

He wasn't there to testify against Villieneuve, nor to conspire to attain offices he didn't want. But his testimony had been the easiest way to gain access to the Presidium's Inner Sanctum, the meeting area where only members of the council and the very occasional invited guests were ever allowed. There were no guards, no retainers, no one but the ruling members of the Union's top body...and him.

There were no weapons allowed, either. That was to be expected. But weapons took many forms, and as a man who considered himself the foremost assassin of his day, Ricard Lille possessed many tools to use in the killing of his victims.

The deed was actually done already, though that wouldn't be apparent for several hours. The virus was a bio-engineered marvel, custom-designed by Sector Nine as an assassination tool. Lille had seized it for his own use—and taken the precaution of terminating its creator to maintain secrecy. He'd kept it in reserve, until a worthy mission presented itself.

The virus had an incubation period of three to four hours, after which, the victim—or victims—would die quick, and somewhat painful, deaths. Lille was infected, too, of ocurse... there was no way to smuggle the virus into the Inner Sanctum, save in his own body. But the contagion rate was one hundred percent, and that made his own body the murder weapon.

And, unlike the Presidium members, Lille had the only know antidote waiting for him. He would give himself a shot and endure several hours of what promised to be considerable gastro-intestinal distress...while the others present, every member of the Presidium save Gaston Villieneuve, would die in panicked agony, blood pouring from every bodily orifice.

It was of such images that masterpieces were created.

Chapter Forty-Five

Free Trader Pegasus
Formara System
"The Bottleneck"
313 AC

"We're cutting this awfully close, Andi…" Vig was at the controls as Andi stood on the other side of the bridge, zipping up her survival suit.

"I know." It was all she could think to say. She hated the danger she was putting her people in, but she couldn't leave now. She didn't know why Barron hadn't evacuated yet. Maybe he was hurt…or…

It didn't matter what. She wasn't going to stand on *Pegasus*'s bridge and watch him die.

"You know *Dauntless*'s layout as well as I do, Vig. Get me as close as you can to the bridge. That's where he's most likely to be."

"I'll do the best I can, Andi." It was clear Merrick wasn't happy about her going aboard *Dauntless* with no idea of the conditions there. But she was also sure he knew better than to try to argue with her. At least about this. "Hurry. We don't have much time."

She walked toward the hatch, ducking into the corridor beyond. "I'll be quick." She was tense, not just because of the danger, but because she wasn't sure what she'd find. From what Travis had said, Barron should have evac'd by now. That meant something was wrong.

She turned and stuck her head back through the hatch, looking at Merrick. "Vig, listen to me. If I'm not back in…" She looked at the chronometer on her wrist. "…eight minutes, you get the hell out of here. Do you understand?"

Merrick returned her gaze, but he didn't reply.

"You won't help me by getting Dolph and yourself killed. Eight minutes…and not a second longer." She turned and moved down the corridor, far from confident he would obey her orders.

She turned toward the hatch, waiting for the green light to come on, signifying the connection was solid. Every second passed by slowly, almost torturously, and then it popped lit up.

She opened the hatch and stepped inside, walking down the umbilical until she got to a chunk of black, scarred metal. *Dauntless*'s hull.

Breaking into a battleship was generally not an easy thing to do, but among the other bits of obscure knowledge she'd picked up over the past few years was *Dauntless*'s access code. She punched it in the battered keypad next to the hatch and, after a few tense seconds, she heard the sound of it popping open.

Please, Tyler…you've got to be okay…

She found herself overwhelmed with the fear that she'd step onto the bridge and see Barron lying next to his chair, dead. She paused for an instant, struggling to regroup herself. *You have to do this…you have to hold it together…*

Then, she let out a deep breath and crawled through the hatch and into *Dauntless*.

*   *   *

Barron stared at the display, looking at the pulsar. Looking at his own death.

He had minutes left, and all around the fringes of his mind, images danced. His crew, Admiral Striker, his grandfather… Andi. His life had been one full of war, a destiny to which he'd been born, but it had also been a good one, filled with some extraordinary people.

He was helping to save them all…that, perhaps more than anything, made his fate seem almost palatable. He was scared of course. Anyone facing approaching death who said he wasn't scared was a liar. But he'd made a peace of sorts with it. If he had to die, destroying that deadly weapon, saving more lives than he could easily count—was a pretty good reason.

He imagined Atara and his people in their escape pods and shuttles, watching, frantically wondering why he hadn't followed them. He'd almost panicked for a moment, thinking Atara or some of the others might try to come back for him—which would only get them killed too—but then he realized there was no way for the light ships to reverse their momentum in time. He was sorry he didn't have any comm, that he couldn't say goodbye, but he was glad to know they all had at least a chance.

He spun around. He'd heard a sound, a strange one, and he looked in the direction it had seemed to come from. *Are you hearing things?*

He shook his head, about to dismiss it, when he heard it again.

"You've got to hold together, old girl…just a few minutes more." He knew *Dauntless* was critically wounded, that there was damage all throughout his beloved ship that he didn't even know about. The reactors were straining to keep the ship accelerating toward its target, and even the main structural supports were weakened, perhaps to the point of failure. With his crew gone, there were no engineers working on repairs. The loss of the AI meant there wasn't even any substantial status monitoring of the various systems on the massive ship. For the most part, he was blind to *Dauntless*'s deteriorating condition.

He leapt up from the chair and turned again. He was definitely hearing something. It was a clanging sound, almost like a hatch slamming open. But that wasn't possible. Unless he was losing hull integrity near the bridge…

That would be a problem for him, one that could rob him of his last few moments of life...but, far worse, the air blasting through any breach might throw *Dauntless* off its carefully-plotted course.

He turned and took a step in the direction of the sound, and then he stopped dead...stunned, silent.

There was a figure standing just inside the bridge, wearing a survival suit and looking at him.

His first thought was one of the crew had failed to evacuate. But then, he realized the suit wasn't military issue. It was civilian in design, a bit out of date. The kind of thing rogue adventurers might use.

For an instant, he thought of Andi, but then he forced it out of his mind. She was lightyears away, safe...he had seen to that. Hadn't he?

The visitor took a step forward...and then ran across the bridge toward him. He was about to move to defend himself when the helmet popped open, and a riot of familiar dark hair spilled out. Then, the visitor reached his position, and threw her arms around him.

"You're alive...I knew you were alive!"

Barron was stunned. It wasn't possible. Yet, there she was.

"How?" It was all he could manage to say.

"You're not as clever as you think you are." She let go and took half a step from him, turning and glancing back the way she had come. "But I think we can discuss that later, don't you? Right now, let's get the hell out of here."

Barron was still in shock, but he just nodded, and then he followed her toward the corridor, and back to the hatch she'd used to board. She crouched down and climbed back into the umbilical, but Barron hesitated.

"Come on, Tyler...we're almost out of time."

He heard her words, and he knew she was right. But he couldn't move his legs, couldn't force himself to leave. He turned and looked back toward the bridge, his eyes moist, scenes of his first day as *Dauntless*'s commander dancing in front of him.

He had ached for his own command since his earliest days in the Academy…earlier even, on those few occasions when his grandfather had discussed his wars. He'd built it up in his mind, something no reality could match, and yet, when it had finally happened, it had exceeded his every expectation.

Dauntless was part of him…and he knew he'd never totally get over her loss. It took everything he had to leave his ship now, to abandon her to her final mission, and to total destruction.

"Tyler, I know this is hard for you, but we've got to go."

He could feel Andi's hand on his arm. Part of him still felt the urge to stay, to send her away and face the end at *Dauntless*'s helm. But she would never leave without him, he knew that. And he couldn't endanger her.

He took one last, teary-eyed look, and then he turned and followed Andi into the umbilical…and into *Pegasus*.

*   *   *

"Vig, we're secure. Get us the hell out of here." Lafarge was tugging at her survival gear, pulling off as much as she could easily remove. She turned toward Barron. "Hang on…we don't have time to strap in." She reached out and grabbed onto the netting hanging from the wall, wrapping her arm around the material and getting a good grip.

Barron followed suit. He didn't have the countdown clock… that was still on *Dauntless*, but he knew there wasn't much time. His ship was heading toward the pulsar at close to .003c, and the kinetic energy the collision would unleash would be enough to vaporize the pulsar…and anything else close by.

The ship shook hard, a loud clanking sound echoing through the halls as it disconnected from *Dauntless*. His ship was truly gone now, and he knew he'd never set foot on her again.

He reached out to the small screen in the corridor, flipping it on. He didn't know his way around *Pegasus* like Andi did, but he was no stranger to the ship.

He could see her watching him, and he knew she was wondering if she should let him watch. He thought she might interfere, but she remained silent. He knew they had much to talk about, not the least of which, how she'd managed to follow him to the Bottleneck…but he couldn't. Not now.

His eyes focused on the tiny screen, even as he worked the controls, centering on two large symbols…*Dauntless* and the pulsar.

He could see there was less than a minute left, even as *Pegasus* fired her engines, and he was hit with a solid 3g of force. A third symbol appeared, smaller than the other two and slowly moving away. Andi's ship wouldn't be that far from the impact…but hopefully, it would be far enough.

He stared through watery eyes, watching as the blue oval, the manifestation *Pegasus*'s computer used to represent *Dauntless*, moved steadily toward its target. The vector was dead on. The enemy tugs were almost in position, but not quite. Barron had gotten his ship there in time, before the enemy could withdraw the deadly artifact.

He felt excitement—and despair, too. Part of him, an emotional, undisciplined part, had been hoping *Dauntless* would miss its target, that somehow she would survive the battle in the Bottleneck. But *Dauntless* could only live at the cost of the enemy saving the pulsar…and that was just too great a price to pay.

Barron watched, silently, as his ship moved forward, steadily, relentlessly, unstoppably. He imagined the terror of the pulsar's crew, of the panic on the tugs and support ships, watching as utter destruction approached their superweapon. The pulsar was the Union's chance to win the war, and now Barron watched his victory unfold, a triumph that would help end the war, despite the cost that ripped at his guts.

His eyes were still fixed, his head unmoving, his mouth closed, utterly silent, as the two symbols came together…and both disappeared, replaced by energy readouts that went off the scale. Barron watched, staring at the scanning data as it poured in, reading the numbers and analyzing them, even though he already knew what they meant. The pulsar had been completely destroyed.

And *Dauntless*, too. His ship was gone, nothing left of her but pure energy…and a spirit he knew would never die.

Chapter Forty-Six

CFS Vanguard
Formara System
"The Bottleneck"
313 AC

"It's hard to be sure, sir. So much energy has been released, it's interfering with our scans. But nothing material could have survived there."

Van Striker listened to his officer's words, even as he stared at the display himself. It was true. Against all odds, Barron had succeeded in his mission. *Dauntless* had rammed the pulsar, and even without a direct confirmation, Striker knew the enemy artifact was gone.

He felt a flood of emotions. Relief, of course, and excitement over how the pulsar's loss changed the military situation. His fleet would need to refit before it could advance beyond the Bottleneck, but given six months and a large convoy of supplies, he would be ready to move forward. After three bloody, mostly inconclusive wars, he could finally cripple the Union, even destroy it. It would cost, of course, but a true victory would relieve future generations of the blood tax that had haunted their parents and grandparents.

Then, the worry set in…worry for Tyler Barron and his people. He'd had enough reports to be sure many had evacuated, but they were still floating around in vulnerable escape craft in the middle of a war zone. And he had no way of knowing if everyone had gotten off *Dauntless*. Tyler Barron had saved the Confederation fleet, he'd accomplished an almost impossible mission…and the thought of him dying aboard his ship was too much to bear.

Striker stared straight ahead for another moment. But then, his resolve took charge. He was worried about Barron and his people, scared about what he might find when his ships got deeper into the system. But there was no time for that now. He knew what he had to do, and he was determined to see it done. Barron's people—alive or dead—had given the fleet this opportunity.

And Van Striker wasn't about to see it squandered.

"All ships," he said, his voice cold, hard. "Advance at full acceleration. It's time to finish this."

*   *   *

Barron stood in the corridor, letting his grip on the netting relax as Pegasus's thrust cut out. The free trader was perhaps ten thousand kilometers from where it had been, and it was moving farther every second. It wasn't a great distance in terms of space travel, but it had been enough to clear the ship from the cataclysm of *Dauntless* ramming the pulsar.

Barron was devastated about his ship, and the idea that *Dauntless* no longer existed, that she wasn't somewhere, waiting for him to return, cut at him deeply. But there was more…there was pride, too. His battleship had not died in vain. She had won her final victory, and she had covered her memory, her history, in more glory than any ship in the fleet's history.

The reality of the war was slow to set in as well. The loss of the pulsar almost certainly doomed the Union to defeat. The wars that had recurred so many times…perhaps they were finally over. The combined Confederation-Alliance fleet could advance all the way to Montmirail. They could impose a new government, one less malignant than the one that had ruled the

Union for two centuries. Barron had no children, but he dared to hope that if he did one day, they could grow up as the first generation in nearly a hundred years not to face war.

All these thoughts swirled around in his head, but they were secondary for the moment, in the background. Right now, he looked at Andi, standing next to him, returning his gaze silently, and she was all he could think about. He had no idea how she'd managed to follow him, to be right in the thick of things at the vital moment. He'd always respected her abilities, but now he was dumbstruck. He owed her his life, he knew that much. He thought about ways to thank her, to tell her how extraordinary she was...or to scold her for taking such a chance when he'd tried so hard to keep her safe. He thought of a million things to say, the words whipping in and out of his thoughts at a dizzying pace. But in the end, he didn't say anything. Not a word.

He just turned and looked at her for a few seconds...then he reached out and pulled her toward him and kissed her.

*   *   *

It was too much.

Villieneuve stared at the small screen in the shuttle's main cabin. He'd watched in stunned horror as a Confederation battleship moved steadily toward the disabled pulsar. The weapon had been moments from being connected to the series of tugs that would have removed it from the system, withdrawn it to a place of relative safety. Now, it was gone, obliterated so completely, there weren't even pieces of it left to research or try to repair.

The implications were hitting him like a rapid series of hammer blows. The Battle of the Bottleneck was as good as over, and all along the line his ships were breaking and running for it, fleeing from the approaching Confed and Alliance vessels. All that remained of the fight was to see what of his forces would escape and how many more ships he would lose.

The pulsar was gone, the great weapon that had been the lynchpin of his plans for victory lost and irreplaceable.

The war was lost, too. That, he knew with unquestioned certainty. He'd already sent a directive to his agents on Megara to alter the plan before the Senate. He'd been planning for a favorable negotiated peace, one that would cripple the Confederation's economy and provide an influx of currency to restore the Union's, but that was no longer possible. All he could hope for was an outright ceasefire, though even that seemed unlikely.

He wondered if it even mattered. The Union was on the verge of total collapse, its starving and persecuted people finally pushed too far. But Villieneuve wondered if he'd even survive long enough to try to deal with those problems. When his colleagues in the Presidium discovered all he'd done, the secrets he'd kept from them, the economic ruin that was coming to pass…he had no doubt they would turn on him. For all he knew, they had already condemned him. He might get back to Montmirail to find a detachment of Foudre Rouge there to arrest him, or more likely, kill him on sight.

Villieneuve shook his head. He'd actually been one of those urging caution about launching a new war against the Confederation, but he'd been overruled and, when war became inevitable, he had committed to seeing it won, whatever that took. His efforts had been plagued by bad luck, but nothing had led to his defeat more than Tyler Barron and his cursed battleship. Barron had destroyed the great supply base that had supported the initial Union invasion, and he'd prevented Villieneuve's people from capturing the ancient planetkiller. He'd led forces to the Alliance, not only wrecking Ricard Lille's plan to bring the Alliance into the war against the Confederation, but turning that power into a Confed ally to fight the Union.

Villieneuve wasn't an emotional man. He tried to focus on his goals, to do what had to be done without allowing feelings to interfere. But he hated Tyler Barron with a raging passion. He truly didn't know if he could survive the challenges he faced now, but if he did, and if he came out of it with his power intact, he promised himself one thing.

He would see Tyler Barron suffer, whatever it took.

But first, he had to figure out how to navigate the storm

unfolding all around him, and, truth be told, he had no idea how he was going to do that.

Chapter Forty-Seven

Jake Stockton looked out over the large open space of Vanguard's launch bay. The great ship's fighters had been stowed in the hangers below the flight deck, as had Stockton's own bird, and those of *Dauntless*'s other surviving pilots. His worst fears, that all his ditched pilots would die, had proven to be overly pessimistic. The abrupt rout and panicked retreat of the Union forces had allowed the main fleet to advance quickly enough to mount rescue operations, coming to the aid of many of his pilots, and to the rest of *Dauntless*'s crew.

They hadn't been in time to save everyone, however.

He stared at the rows of metal rectangles, eight of them. The coffins of the pilots who had been too far to reach in time, who had died of cold and suffocation, trapped in their depleted fighters.

Jovi Grachus and seven of the warriors she had led against the enemy battleship.

Stockton stepped down the bank of stairs, his feet clanging on the metal of the flight deck as he walked toward the eight metal canisters, laid out in two rows of four. Fighter crews didn't

373

often see their bodies brought back from battle, but these ships had finally been recovered and taken to *Vanguard*, along with their fallen pilots.

Stockton had been among those rescued alive. He'd burned the last of his fuel chasing after Grachus and her people, maintaining contact with them, assuring them they would be rescued. His words had been positive thoughts at first, and blatant lies later, and he suspected Grachus, at least, had known the truth from the beginning.

He walked across the deck, uncomfortable in his seldom-worn dress uniform. He was astonished at the twists life tended to take, and the last thing he'd ever expected was to step up in front of *Dauntless*'s surviving pilots and give a heartfelt eulogy for a woman he'd wanted dead until just days before.

Jovi Grachus had been his enemy for most of the time he'd known of her existence, first overtly so, as the commander of the Red Alliance's fighter corps, and later as the pilot who'd killed his best friend. But now, he found that he truly mourned her loss.

He hadn't forgiven her for killing Kyle Jamison, not exactly… but she'd also saved *Dauntless* from the Union battleship that had been closing on it, and in the end, she'd given her life, and those of her compatriots to see it done. Without Grachus, and her sacrifice, Commodore Barron would be dead, and Commander Travis, Dirk Timmons…and Stara.

And the Union would have withdrawn the pulsar, allowing the war to drag on endlessly, killing untold thousands more.

Grachus had been his nemesis, but now he mourned her as a friend…worse, he regretted the fact that they'd never had the chance to be friends, or even real comrades. Circumstance—and Union deceit—had caused her to be his enemy at first, but it had been his own rage and stubbornness that had protracted the animosity. Now, he would never have the chance to speak with her as an ally. As a friend.

He stepped up to the makeshift platform. The ceremony had been hastily-assembled, and *Vanguard*, like most of the fleet, was still nursing considerable battle damage. He paused for a moment, looking out at the assemblage. Every pilot still alive from *Dauntless*'s contingent was there, as was Commodore Barron and many of *Dauntless*'s other officers. And, to Stockton's surprise, Admiral Striker sat silently in the front row.

He hadn't expected the fleet commander to attend the memorial for a handful of fighter pilots, but then he realized that he'd underestimated Striker. The admiral understood just what these few pilots had contributed, and just how many lives their sacrifices had likely saved.

He took a breath, still uncertain exactly what he was going to say. It seemed wrong that he should be the one delivering the eulogy, but his closest companions had been united in their agreement that it was right, and that no one could stand in his place. He'd thought about refusing, about trying to get out of it…but then he decided he owed Grachus more than that. There was little enough he could do for her now, save for this.

"Thank you all for coming here this afternoon. We are joined together to remember a group of comrades, of heroes…"

*   *   *

"What is it? I came as soon as I got your message." Tyler Barron knew something was terribly wrong the instant he stepped into the room. He'd seen Vian Tulus sitting in a cell, facing execution without the slightest display of emotion, and he'd stood at the Palatian's side in battle, watching him calmly commanding his forces. But he'd never seen the man as pale as he was now, nor with such a stricken look on his face.

"It is the Imperator. Tarkus Vennius." A pause, then: He is dead."

The words hit Barron like a sledgehammer. He had fought alongside Vennius, and he'd come to call the Alliance leader his friend. "How?" It was all he could force out.

"The Krillians took advantage of the fact that the expeditionary force was so far from Alliance space. With the losses in the civil war, the Imperator was hard-pressed to repel their assault." He turned and looked up at Barron. "He sacrificed himself and his flagship, driving toward Krillus's vessel. His heroism saved the battle, and the Krillian forces were crushed."

Barron didn't know what to say. He was nearly overcome by mourning for those lost in the battle, but this news shocked him. He wondered what could have made a fringe power like the Krillians take on the feared Alliance…and in his gut he knew the answer. He doubted he would ever be sure, but there wasn't a question in his mind the Union was behind it. If there was a saving grace for all the loss and the struggle endured in the battle, it was the fact that the fleet would now move forward, it would topple the Union's oppressive government and end this protracted struggle once and for all. But standing there, his mind full of thoughts of Tarkus Vennius, it was cold comfort.

"I have to go back to Palatia." Tulus's words had an almost numb sound to them. "I will leave the bulk of the fleet, but I must return at once." He paused, and he stared at Barron with a stunned look on his face. "I received a communique from Commander Globus. Imperator Vennius left a missive urging the high command to appoint me…as his successor."

Barron just nodded. "Vennius was a great man…and he made a wise choice. You will be a strong leader to your people, Vian Tulus…and a man I will always be proud to call an ally And a friend."

*   *   *

"This is not possible!" Van Striker was a man of composure, one who acted coolly, rationally, even in the heat of battle. But he was unhinged now, and he threw the tablet he'd been holding across the room, shattering it against the wall.

"I understand your anger, Van…and I promise you, I did everything possible to prevent this. But there were too many Senators ready to end the war any way possible. The economy is pushed to the limit, and the government's debt is at catastrophic levels. In the end, it just wasn't possible to get them to vote against a ready peace. The treaty forbids war between the two powers. It calls for lasting peace."

"And you believe that?" Striker's tone dripped with caustic bitterness.

"No, of course not. But I'm telling you, there was no way to get enough Senators to oppose a treaty that meant immediate peace, not when it came at no cost. I understand the concerns in the long term, but the Union's fleet is broken. They won't be a threat to us for a long time."

"It is words like those that have given us four wars, Gary. You know that as well as I do."

"They *are* in considerable disarray. Many of their systems are in open revolt. They may collapse on their own…and even if they don't, they face a long road to any kind of recovery."

"And people will use words like that to justify slashing military budgets, mothballing half the fleet. Your doves in the Senate, having abandoned our chance to conclude this endless conflict decisively, once and for all, will then proceed to weaken us, to set up the next cycle."

"That may be, Van, but there is nothing we can do about it. The Confederation is a republic. I have stepped over the line repeatedly, violated more laws than even you know to pull us through this war. But we can't defy the Senate on this…and there was no way to get them to vote against the treaty, not when eighty percent of Confederation citizens support an immediate end to the war."

Striker shook his head slowly. "So, we just let them off? They attack us, kill hundreds of thousands of our people, and we just let it go? Back off and let them rebuild?"

"We don't have a choice. Not unless you want to be the admiral who destroyed Confederation democracy. Do you want to lead your forces to Megara, compel the Senate to yield to you under the guns of the fleet?"

Striker frowned. "No, of course not. But…"

"There is no but, Van. We don't have to like it, but we do have to accept it. No doubt, you're right about budget cuts and force reductions…but you are one of the great heroes of the war. Your voice will carry great power. Make your arguments against weakening the fleet. You may not win every battle in that war, but I'll wager you can do some good."

"That is work for a politician," Striker said, not even trying to hide the distaste in his voice.

"It is work for an admiral who wants to see his navy strong enough to deter future wars. An officer who wants to do what he can for his spacers...and for those to come."

Striker was silent for a moment. Then he said, "This is a mistake, Gary. One that will cost lives down the road."

"That may be, my friend. But it will save lives now, and as much as you want to crush the Union, you know what that would entail. How many more of your people would die, now and in the next year or two of sustained fighting?" A pause. "They have suffered enough, my friend. Perhaps they deserve the peace now...even with the risks it pushes into the future."

Striker didn't look convinced, but he didn't say anything else for a long while. The two men, friends and comrades, stood silently, each deep in his own thoughts.

$$*\qquad\qquad *\qquad\qquad *$$

"They can't do this. Not after all those who died to bring us to the cusp of victory." Tyler Barron was sitting on the small couch in his quarters, shaking his head as he spoke. Admiral Striker had told him of the peace treaty the day before, but he was still raw from it.

"I understand, Tyler, but at least this way no one else has to die. I'm no military tactician, but you know very well the invasion of the Union would be a nightmare, even with their fleet so battered, one that would go one for what...years?" Andi Lafarge was sitting next to Barron, and her hand was moving gently across his back.

Her touch was calming him, at least a bit, something nothing else had been able to do in the last twenty-four hours. He turned toward her and managed a tiny smile. "I still don't know how you managed to get all the way to the Bottleneck, and slip around the Union fleet. I owe you my life, you know."

"Yes," she said, returning the smile. "I know."

Barron looked at her intently. He'd transferred to Vanguard for the journey back to Grimaldi, but *Pegasus* had arrived first… and Barron remembered the message he'd left for Lafarge. He'd only intended for her to read it if he didn't make it back. It had been an extended missive, full of far more emotion than he was comfortable divulging. He'd deleted it as soon as *Vanguard* docked, but he hadn't been sure if she'd seen it or not. He still wasn't sure. She hadn't let on in any way he could detect, but one thing he knew about Andi Lafarge was the staggering effectiveness of her poker face.

"Thank you," he said softly. "Thank you for coming for me."

She slid closer to him and smiled broadly. "Any time…you know I'll always be there when you need me."

"Yes," he said softly, reaching out and taking her hand in his. "I do know that. And, I'll always be there when you need me."

The exchange wasn't poetic, nor full of mad recitations of love and devotion…but it was one that suited them both perfectly. Their lives would pull them apart again, Barron had no doubt about that. But now he was just as sure they would always be connected, that the two of them had a bond that could be stretched, but never be shattered.

And that made him smile again.

Epilogue

Villieneuve stood on the side of the street, staring at the still-smoking ruins of the Presidium complex. The great compound, once the pinnacle of Union government and power, was now almost completely gone, nothing but a few blackened girders still rising more than a couple meters above the ground. It was an astonishing sight to any who lived in the Union, who understood the iron control that body had maintained over the nation. But far more amazing, strange even to him, was that this great monument to political power had been destroyed by his own operatives...on his express order.

Unlike the angry, uncontrolled mobs that had been behind most of the fires and vandalism in Liberte City over the past weeks, the arsonists here had been Sector Nine agents, and the destruction of such an overwhelming symbol of the old regime was a key part of Villieneuve's plan not only to survive and retain his power, but to enhance it.

The streets were filled with shouting crowds, as they had been day and night. He watched the throngs, workers, mostly from the factories that ringed the city, noting their mannerisms, the brutish and unsophisticated way they conducted themselves. He was doing his best to understand them, even to act like he was one of them, the new man of the people. He was dressed as a common worker, coarse denim pants and a heavy canvas shirt, both in dull shades of gray. It was a touch of well-placed symbolism, one that seemed to be working, as he walked among the crowds, shaking hands with many of those near him. He imagined it would look terribly good on the evening broadcasts, which, of course, was the whole point. No one watching later would have any idea the whole thing was entirely fake.

The suit he'd shed hours before—and would change back into the instant he was behind closed doors—had cost more than a year's wages for those screaming his name in the streets. The workers in his immediate vicinity, the ones he was greeting so warmly, had been hand-picked…and cleared by his security. The rawer masses that formed the real crowd were nearby, but his own location was cordoned off, and Foudre Rouge snipers covered the area from every rooftop. The feeling of liberty, of freedom after centuries of repression, was entirely manufactured, as was the image of a man of the old government who'd risen up, disowned the corrupt ways of his fellows…and taken personal risks to bring them all down and turn the government back to the people. To even Villieneuve's astonishment, it was working.

He'd expected to return to an execution squad sent by the Presidium, but instead, Ricard Lille had been waiting with news so unexpected, it had taken Villieneuve a considerable time to process it. Lille was an amazing assassin, but this time he'd outdone himself. The entire Presidium, save Villieneuve himself, dead. Every rival, every minister with enough power to move against him, gone.

Lille had failed on Barroux, though that hardly seemed relevant considering his extraordinary accomplishment on Montmirail, and Villieneuve had absolved his friend for his mistakes during the war. He would need his top assassin in the coming months and years. The two had made their peace, based, as most of their relations were, on an odd combination of utility and friendship.

Despite Lille's incredible assassination, Villieneuve's prospects for preserving his power had still seemed to be a long shot. The Union was collapsing economically, the people were rioting in the streets on a hundred worlds, entire systems were seceding and declaring independence. But signs of hope began to materialize almost immediately.

He'd considered it a miracle when word arrived that the Confederation Senate had accepted the peace proposal he'd ordered his operatives to push after the destruction of the pulsar. Even he had underestimated the tendency of the Confederation's people and politicians to seek the easiest route back to normalcy.

The peace, at least, eliminated the prospect of invasion. One less problem he had to face…and a change of circumstances that freed up what remained of the fleet for his own internal pacification operations. There was grumbling and near-mutiny in the fleet, but that was far more controllable than the unrest on the Union's many worlds, especially with the coming of peace. With the prospect of having to fight the deadly Confederation fleet gone, it hadn't taken more than a few promotions and some pay increases to bring things back to order.

Nevertheless, for the first few weeks, the situation had been tenuous, to say the least.

The idea on how to proceed had come to him in those dark hours, a thought he'd almost dismissed outright. The people couldn't be so gullible as to accept him, the last member of the Presidium, as the leader of a new revolution. Could they?

He'd kept the deaths of the Presidium members secret for the first few days, but then, he used the bodies of his former colleagues to launch his campaign. He'd had them dragged into the streets, and claimed credit for their deaths, for the liberation the Presidium's fall promised to the people. He'd put bullets in their heads before he had them cast to the mobs—the image of corrupt, tyrannical leaders being shot made for better propaganda than bio-engineered viruses delivered by a Sector Nine assassin.

Then, he'd taken to the streets, the information nets, anywhere he could reach eyes and ears…and he railed against the Union's government, screamed that he had tried to reform it from within, spoke in soaring tones of a true workers' paradise, the dream that had been the Union before it had been hijacked by the corrupt and power mad. And to his stunned surprise, people believed him. The blood of his former comrades painted his road forward.

He'd continued with a purge of epic proportions, the members of the old government with the highest public profiles eliminated in huge numbers, dragged into the streets and killed by the mobs, murdered in their beds, shoved up against walls and shot. And with every execution, every member of the old regime scapegoated, Gaston Villieneuve's popularity soared.

The mobs cheered his speeches, shouted his name. He

abandoned his old titles, telling all to call him, only Citizen Villieneuve. He rallied the workers, the crowds, while in the shadows his trained killers rooted out the last holdouts of the old power structure...and any among the mob who spoke against him.

He had no official title, but Sector Nine was still fully-operational and firmly in his grasp...though he knew he'd have to rename the infamous service. He had no official mandate, yet he controlled what was left of the Union with a level of concentrated and absolute power that had been impossible in the days of the Presidium.

He controlled the Foudre Rouge, too, though he knew he had to rename them as well. The clone soldiers were too tied to the old government, the fear they'd struck into the civilian populace too memorable. Perhaps he would cast them, too, as victims of the old government, freed by his rebellion.

He had much work to do, to consolidate power, and to restore the Union to its former size and power. Fewer than half the former systems remained now, and the first order of business would be bringing the others back into the fold, by the kind of persuasion that had worked so well on Montmirail, if possible...and by more direct means, if not.

The economy had to be completely rebuilt, and new institutions created. It was a monumental task, one that seemed almost impossible. But, he would see it done. He would create the new Union in his image...and he would rule it, absolutely and forever.

And when he had restored the Union to its former power, when he had secured his iron grip...he would take his revenge.

On Tyler Barron and his damnable crew.

And on the Confederation.

*   *   *

"You look well-rested." Van Striker smiled as Tyler Barron walked across the room. Barron saluted, and then the two shook hands warmly.

"I am. It's amazing what a few months without war can do." Barron was glad the Confederation was at peace, that the killing had stopped...but he was still nagged by the feeling his countrymen would come to deeply regret their failure to finish the Union once and for all.

Barron turned toward the third man in the room. "It's good to see you, too, Mr. Holsten." He extended his arm, a repeat of his greeting to Striker.

"Gary, please." Holsten reached out and clasped Barron's hand. "I am glad to see you as well." A slight pause. "And, let me take the chance to congratulate you for your success in the Bottleneck. I wish I could have been here to see the victory."

Barron just nodded. He knew Holsten had done his best to influence the Senate. No one knew as well as the head of Confederation Intelligence the potential problems that had been kicked down the road.

Striker turned toward the observation portal and gestured toward the pristine new battleship docked just outside. "What do you think of her?"

"She's a beauty, sir. *Repulse*-class, no? But there's something else there too."

"You have a good eye for ships, Ty. She is something new, a late-war mod to the *Repulse*-class. She's got everything *Vanguard*'s got plus...a few extras. Five million, eight hundred thousand tons, the biggest ship the Confederation's ever launched. That anyone has ever launched, except for the old empire, of course."

"She's impressive, sir." A pause. "I'm surprised she got past the force cutbacks." His comment was less than literal. He realized a brand-new ship would likely be spared any fleet downsizing. The mothballing efforts would start at the bottom, with the oldest vessels.

"She's yours." Striker looked over at Barron.

"Mine?"

"Your flagship."

"Flagship? For what?"

"I have an assignment for you." Striker paused. "It will be dangerous...and it might be long. Very long."

Barron was confused. "What kind of assignment? There's no trouble at the border…"

"No, nothing like that." He hesitated again. "You know how close we came to disaster at the hands of ancient technology. You saved us from the first by destroying the planet-killer…and the second by taking out the pulsar. But both situations were close calls…and either one could have ended in disaster."

"No argument from me, sir. The stealth generator was ancient tech, too, don't forget."

"Which only makes this mission all the more vital."

"What do you want me to do, sir?"

Barron had posed the question to Striker, but it was Holsten who responded. "We want you to lead an armada…deep into the Badlands. Beyond the distance any known expedition has reached previously."

"The Badlands?"

"It's no secret the Union has always had the jump on us. Sector Nine has worked our own ports ceaselessly, buying contraband and clues to artifact locations right under our noses. I've tried to combat it, but my hands have always been tied by the international treaty provisions…restrictions the Union has widely ignored."

"I'm well aware of that." His tone had come out harsher than he'd intended. As with most military officers, he resented political games that usually ended up costing the lives of his comrades. Then: "I'm sorry…I know you've always done all you could."

"But we've always been behind. We've always been reacting. Until now. That's why Van and I want you to take this mission."

"What, exactly, is the mission?"

"We want you to lead your fleet deep into the heart of the old empire…and we want you to explore, to find any old tech artifacts that are still out there. Your people would be going where no one has been for centuries."

"I understand the idea, sir, but is it really that urgent? The Union looks like it might collapse entirely. I'm not naïve about the likelihood of what type of government might…"

"Gaston Villieneuve has murdered the entire Presidium, and he has seized absolute control. He is the unchallenged ruler of at least half of what had been the Union…and we don't expect it will take him long to consolidate control over the rest." A pause. "And, no one understands the potential value of old tech like Villieneuve."

Barron stared back, stunned. Villieneuve was evil, but he was no fool. A Union under his control would become dangerous again…quickly. And Barron knew the Sector Nine chief would be looking for more old tech as soon as he possibly could be. If he was in power now, it was possible he already had efforts underway.

"I'll do it, sir." He knew there was no choice. "What kind of force will I be commanding?"

"A powerful one, Ty. A second purpose of the mission is to divert as much fleet power as possible away from the budget cutters. It's hard to get the Senate to worry about a war that might not happen for ten or twenty years, or at all, but the pulsar shook the hell out of them. They're afraid of old tech, and they'll likely approve anything we suggest for an expedition to go hunting for it."

Barron nodded. "My personnel?"

"Yours to choose. I assume you'll want all your old people from *Dauntless*. Possibly Sara Eaton as your deputy fleet commander."

"Yes, definitely." A pause. "How many ships are we talking about?"

"At least eight battleships. Twelve if I can swing it. Plus escorts and support vessels. This will be the biggest exploration mission we've ever launched." Striker looked at Holsten, and then back toward Barron. "We're calling it the White Fleet. Gary came up with the idea."

"It's PR, really. A way to help sell it to the Senate."

"The White Fleet?" Barron's tone had a touch of doubt, but in truth, he thought it was a good name. Hopeful, at least, which befit an expedition with a mission to explore rather than fight.

He turned and looked out at the ship docked alongside the

station. "And that's the flagship. What's she called?"

Striker and Holsten exchanged glances. "She's not christened yet, Ty," Holsten finally said. "I think the initial plan had been to call her *Indomitable*...but we're going to scrap that idea."

Barron looked back, a questioning expression on his face.

"We thought you might do the christening, Tyler." Holsten reached out and put his hand on Barron's shoulder. "And, as far as we're concerned, there's only name that could ever work."

Barron turned, even as Holsten finished what he was saying. He was staring at the newest, largest, highest-tech ship in the navy, but his eyes were seeing another vessel, old and battered.

Holsten's words continued: "We thought we'd call her *Dauntless*."

Blood on the Stars Continues With

The White Fleet

Spring 2018

Also By Jay Allan

Marines (Crimson Worlds I)
The Cost of Victory (Crimson Worlds II)
A Little Rebellion (Crimson Worlds III)
The First Imperium (Crimson Worlds IV)
The Line Must Hold (Crimson Worlds V)
To Hell's Heart (Crimson Worlds VI)
The Shadow Legions(Crimson Worlds VII)
Even Legends Die (Crimson Worlds VIII)
The Fall (Crimson Worlds IX)
War Stories (Crimson World Prequels)
MERCS (Successors I)
The Prisoner of Eldaron (Successors II)
Into the Darkness (Refugees I)
Shadows of the Gods (Refugees II)
Revenge of the Ancients (Refugees III)
Winds of Vengeance (Refugees IV)
Shadow of Empire (Far Stars I)
Enemy in the Dark (Far Stars II)
Funeral Games (Far Stars III)
Blackhawk (Far Stars Legends I)
The Dragon's Banner
Gehenna Dawn (Portal Wars I)
The Ten Thousand (Portal Wars II)
Homefront (Portal Wars III)
Red Team Alpha (CW Adventures I)
Duel in the Dark (Blood on the Stars I)
Call to Arms (Blood on the Stars II)
Ruins of Empire (Blood on the Stars III)
Echoes of Glory (Blood on the Stars IV)
Cauldron of Fire (Blood on the Stars V)
Flames of Rebellion (Flames of Rebellion I)

www.jayallanbooks.com